Acclaim for Robert Whitlow

"With strong writing and solid characters, Whitlow weaves a good tale of a woman straddling two worlds, dream and real. Good pacing and an intricate plot, woven through with spiritual themes and laced with tension, make this an amazing read."

— *Romantic Times* 4-1/2 star review of *The Living Room*

". . . an intensely good read . . . Any woman facing the demands of work and family will relate to Amy's life. The excitement and vivid spirituality Whitlow generates, however, are what will keep readers turning the pages."

— *Booklist* on *The Living Room*

"Readers will find plenty to love about this suspenseful novel as they watch its appealing main character juggle personal, professional, and spiritual crisis with a combination of vulnerability and strength."

— *CBA Retailers + Resources* on *The Living Room*

"Gripping and powerful, *The Living Room* deftly weaves a stirring account of mystery and faith through one woman's struggle with family, work, and dreams, both literal and figurative. Crisp writing, engaging characters, and a deeply spiritual message, this is Robert Whitlow in top form."

— Billy Coffey, author of *When Mockingbirds Sing*

"With deft sleight of hand, wonderful characterization, and carefully layered plots, Robert Whitlow has crafted a gripping story about the mysteries of God's power to shelter the people he loves."

— Erin Healy, author of *Afloat*, regarding *The Living Room*

"As someone who is deeply involved in the pro-life fight, I found *The Choice* to be a very relevant overview of what we fight for in this movement. It shows the struggles of abortion and the courageous act of adoption in a way that I haven't read before in any other book. I had a hard time putting this book down."

— Abby Brannam-Johnson,
former Planned
Parenthood Director
and author of *Unplanned*

"Whitlow captures the struggle of many women trapped in the battle over abortion in a truly sympathetic and affecting way."

— *Booklist* review of *The Choice*

"This inspirational story about a mother's sacrifice has special appeal for pro-life advocates and fans of the legal novel."

— *CBA Retailers + Resources* review of *The Choice*

"Christy Award–winning Whitlow is a lawyer who knows his profession, as his newest legal thriller shows."

— *Publishers Weekly* review of *Water's Edge*

"A great mystery that will keep you interested until the end."

— *Romantic Times* review of *Water's Edge*

"Fans of Whitlow's series will enjoy the mix of suspense and romance as Tami has to choose between her love interests."

— *Library Journal* review of *Greater Love*

The Confession

ROBERT WHITLOW

THOMAS NELSON
Since 1798

NASHVILLE MEXICO CITY RIO DE JANEIRO

Published in Nashville, Tennessee, by Thomas Nelson. Thomas Nelson is a registered trademark of HarperCollins Christian Publishing, Inc.

Thomas Nelson, Inc., titles may be purchased in bulk for educational, business, fund-raising, or sales promotional use. For information, please e-mail SpecialMarkets@ThomasNelson.com.

Publisher's Note: This novel is a work of fiction. Names, characters, places, and incidents are either products of the author's imagination or used fictitiously. All characters are fictional, and any similarity to people living or dead is purely coincidental.

Library of Congress Cataloging-in-Publication Data

Whitlow, Robert, 1954-
The confession / Robert Whitlow.
pages cm
ISBN 978-1-4016-8886-8 (paperback)
1. Public prosecutors--Fiction. 2. Cold cases (Criminal investigation)--Fiction. 3. Guilt--Fiction. 4. Georgia--Fiction. I. Title.
PS3573.H49837C66 2014
813'.54--dc23

2014006235

Printed in the United States of America

14 15 16 17 18 19 RRD 6 5 4 3 2 1

Confession is a bridge everyone must cross. This book is dedicated to the guides of grace who help us in the journey.

If we confess our sins, he is faithful and just and will forgive us our sins and purify us from all unrighteousness.

—1 John 1:9

Prologue

Calico was the name his friends gave him when he showed up in fourth grade wearing a multicolored shirt his aunt sent him for Christmas. The name stuck long after the shirt was cut up for cleaning rags. Holt Douglas ran his fingers through his wavy brown hair as he watched Calico's eyes shift unnaturally in his head.

"Where's Leanne?" Calico asked.

"On the back deck." Holt paused. "You're not going to do anything stupid, are you?"

Calico leaned in. Holt could smell the alcohol on his best friend's breath.

"She invited me, didn't she?" Calico asked. "And you slipped in on my coattails."

"Yeah, but—"

"By the time we graduate next month, Leanne and I will be together again." Calico pressed his index finger against his thumb, then took out his wallet and flashed a thick stack of cash. "How much do you want to bet?"

Holt's wallet contained a wrinkled five-dollar bill. He pushed Calico's hand away.

"Nothing, and you're totally wasted. Stay away from that green stuff in the punch bowl. I don't know what Leanne put in it. I drank one glass and started feeling weird. Since then I've been sticking to beer."

Calico placed his hand against the wall. "The room is spinning like crazy, and I can't get it to stop. What time is it?"

Holt checked his watch. "It's a little past midnight."

Calico shook his head as if trying to dispel the fog from his brain. "Dude, your parents are out of town, but I have to make it home and up to my room without getting busted. Our family is going out of town in the morning. Here . . ."

Calico dug in his pocket and took out the keys to the new convertible he'd received two months before. He handed the keys to Holt.

"I have no chance of finding reverse. You're going to have to get us home."

"I've never driven a stick shift before," Holt protested.

"It's like that race car game we play at the arcade. You can do it."

Calico's face turned pale. He spun around and stumbled into the bathroom, leaving the door open. A couple of seconds later Holt heard him retching. Holt slipped the car keys into his pocket. When Calico emerged, his face was wetter than after basketball practice.

"I tried to take a bath in the sink," he said. "It didn't work. Holt, I feel worse than lousy. This party is over for me; we need to get out of here."

"Sure."

Holt was feeling light-headed himself and knew another beer would push him over the edge. He turned toward the door and took a couple of steps. Calico reached out and grabbed his shoulder.

"No, I've got to see Leanne first."

Before Holt could stop him, Calico lurched toward the rear of the house. On the broad deck, two massive speakers were blasting music. A group of twenty-five teenagers milled around laughing and yelling. The green punch bowl was almost empty. Someone grabbed Calico and pulled him toward a group of guys. Leanne came over and put her arm around Holt's neck. Holt glanced over his shoulder and saw that Calico had his back to them.

"Take me for a walk down to the lake," the tall brunette said. "I need to get away from this craziness for a minute and want to show you my dad's new ski boat."

A walk with Leanne would likely involve more than a look at a boat.

"What about Calico?"

"He's dreaming if he thinks we're getting back together." Leanne squeezed Holt's muscular bicep. "And he doesn't have these."

Out of the corner of his eye, Holt saw Calico lean over the wooden railing. He was about to earn a new, less cute nickname.

"Calico's in bad shape," Holt said.

"And whose fault is that?"

Calico raised his head and stumbled over to them. He burped and raised his hand to his mouth.

"Are you okay?" Leanne asked. "You look kinda green."

"It's the green stuff in there." Calico managed a crooked smile as he pointed to the punch bowl. "The dye is coming through my skin."

"That's Hawaiian punch," Leanne said.

"It's punched him out," Holt said. "He's done."

"He could pass out on the couch in the den," Leanne said.

"No." Calico raised a shaky hand. "And I gotta get Holt home before he gets in trouble on his curfew. Thanks for the invite. I'll give you a call tomorrow after I come back to earth."

Leanne grabbed Holt's arm and pulled him down to her level so she could whisper in his ear. "You stay and let him go. I'll take you home after everybody is gone."

A two-sport athlete, Holt was in great physical shape, but his knees suddenly felt weak. It took all his loyalty to Calico forged over a decade of friendship to shake his head.

"No. We came together."

"Your loss," Leanne said as she let go of his arm.

—

"What was Leanne saying to you?" Calico asked as they walked up the long driveway.

"Nothing," Holt snapped. "Why couldn't you stay away from that punch bowl?"

"It happens. Hey, who took care of you when you were almost unconscious the night of the beer bash at Tony's house?"

"I learned my lesson."

"And this is mine."

Holt grunted. They reached the back of a shiny white convertible. Calico held out his hand.

"Dude, I'm doing way better. I made it up the driveway without crashing on my face. Give me the keys."

"Are you sure?"

"Yeah."

Holt hesitated, then handed over the key ring. Once in the car, he watched as Calico unsuccessfully tried to insert the key into the ignition switch. After the third attempt, Holt reached over and grabbed the keys.

"That's it. I'm taking over. If you can't start the engine, you can't drive. You'll get both of us killed."

Calico mumbled something unintelligible as they passed each other near the rear bumper.

"Put the top down," Calico said as soon as they were back in the vehicle. "I need tons of fresh air or I'm going to throw up again."

Holt released the latch that secured the ragtop. "Where's the button for the roof motor?" he asked.

"There." Calico pointed at the console.

Holt found the button and pressed it. The roof slowly lifted up and peeled back into an opening behind the rear seat.

"That's way better," Calico said as he closed his eyes and rested his head against the seat.

A diagram beside the shifter showed Holt where the stick needed to be if he wanted to put the car in reverse. Calico opened his eyes and stared upward.

"Can you see any stars?"

Holt glanced up. They were far enough from the house that the night sky had unfurled above them. "Yeah."

"Holt, I'm not going to medical school."

"Good idea. They don't want drunks operating on people."

"I'm serious."

In spite of his silly nickname, Calico was a straight-A student and had a full scholarship to Vanderbilt in the fall. For two years he'd had his whole life mapped out—chemistry major, medical school, and so on.

"Why not?"

"I haven't told my parents," Calico continued, gazing up at the sky. "I'm going to major in English and go to law school. Do you remember my uncle Frank who came to visit last month?"

Holt had met the stocky man in his fifties with a prominent jaw, bushy gray eyebrows, and piercing dark eyes.

"Yeah."

"He's been a federal prosecutor for years. Listening to his stories sounded way better than having sick kids cough in my face. My father doesn't think so, but you don't have to be a doctor to make your life count for something. The money government lawyers make isn't that great, but it's all I've been thinking about since he left." Calico paused. "Along with Leanne."

"You're drunk."

Calico closed his eyes. "Yeah, but not the smart part of me."

Holt pushed in the clutch and started the engine. Taking a deep breath, he tried to force the shifter in the proper direction. The gears grated and ground in protest. Holt had operated a riding lawn mower with a clutch, but it was much more forgiving than the high-powered car.

"Gun it," Calico said, his eyes still shut. "Oh, and keep mashing in the clutch or we'll run into Mark's truck."

Holt pressed down on the gas pedal until the engine roared. The shifter grudgingly slid into place. Holt slowly let out the clutch as he pressed down on the accelerator. The car lurched backward, and he quickly applied the brake to avoid hitting a car parked behind them. The engine died. Calico turned his head toward Holt.

"Dude, maybe we should spend the night out here. I can call my dad from Leanne's house and tell him we had car trouble or something."

Holt thought about Leanne's tempting offer. Calico would crash on the couch, and they could deal with the consequences of the green punch bowl in the morning. Then an unnatural sound came out of Calico's mouth, and his friend leaned over the side of the car and got sick again.

"No, I want to go home," Calico said, wiping his mouth with the back of his hand. "If I call my old man, he'll drive out here to see what's wrong with the car. One look at me, and I won't be leaving the house after dark for a month."

Calico's father was a former army surgeon, and his mom couldn't handle the truth without freaking out. Holt started the engine again and forced the shifter into first gear. He turned the steering wheel and slowly pulled away from the curb. He barely cleared the bumper of Mark's truck, then gave the car more gas. It shot forward. Holt pressed in the clutch and shifted into second gear. By the time they reached the highway that ran in front of the lakeside development, he'd made it to fourth gear. He slowed as he approached a stop sign and pressed in the clutch. They came to a smooth halt.

"You've got it," Calico said, leaning back and closing his eyes again. "When we get to my house, don't turn into the driveway. Leave the car parked on the street. I'll move it into the garage in the morning. It's a tight fit, and I don't want you putting a big scratch down the side of my father's new Mercedes."

"Okay, let's get you home," Holt said more to himself than Calico.

He waited until there weren't any cars coming from either direction and pulled onto the highway. This time he shifted much better through the gears. The wind whistled past his face as he accelerated to highway speed. He checked the speedometer to make sure he wasn't going too fast. They rounded a looping curve and came to a long, straight stretch of road. No headlights approached. Holt glanced in the rearview mirror and didn't see a car behind them. They had the road to themselves. Holt stepped on the gas, and the engine growled as the car sped up. The convertible was a lot smoother than the car Holt normally had to drive, a cheap import passed down from his older sister.

Suddenly, out the corner of his eye, he saw movement. Calico had his hand over his mouth. Holt flipped on the car's high beams. There was a sharply descending ditch on the right-hand side of the road, and he couldn't see a good place to pull over so Calico could throw up. Calico leaned his head toward the side of the car. Holt took his eyes off the road to make sure Calico wasn't getting sick on the beige floorboard carpet. The car swerved slightly, and the right front tire slipped off the roadway and dropped down onto the soft shoulder.

The next few seconds were an insane swirl of twisting chaos. Then everything went black.

—

Holt woke up to a voice.

"He's over here!"

Holt groaned. He raised his hand and touched the side of his head near his right ear. It felt sticky and wet. He was lying in a bed of pine straw. A tree branch was poking him in the lower back. He struggled to sit up. Sharp pains shot through his chest. A light shone in his eyes, accompanied by the voice he'd heard.

"Stay down! Don't try to move!"

—

The high-speed ride to the hospital was a blurry haze of sirens and flashing lights. An oxygen mask over Holt's face kept him from talking. Two male EMTs rolled him through a set of large sliding-glass doors into a triage room. A few moments later a middle-aged nurse slipped the oxygen mask from his face. She stuck a thermometer in the corner of his mouth.

"Where's Calico?" he mumbled, trying not to dislodge the thermometer. "Ken Morgan."

"He hasn't arrived yet," the nurse said as she took the thermometer from his mouth and recorded the reading. "Are you having any trouble breathing?"

Holt took a deep breath and winced in pain. "My chest hurts."

"You may have broken some ribs. You're going to radiology as soon as I'm finished here. Your parents have been notified and are driving in from someplace in the mountains."

"My grandparents have a cabin at Big Canoe." Holt raised his hand to the place near his ear. "My head—"

"There's a gash, but the bleeding has almost stopped. The doctor will decide if you need stitches."

The nurse put a blood pressure cuff on his arm, inflated it, and listened through a stethoscope. Even though he was lying down, Holt felt dizzy.

"Your blood pressure is normal," she said as she slipped it from his arm. "Have you been drinking?"

Holt hesitated.

"You may as well admit it," the nurse said as she turned his left arm so she could see his veins. "Because the blood I'm about to draw from your arm won't lie."

"Uh, yes, ma'am. I've had a couple of beers."

The nurse grunted. "I've heard that line more times than I can count, sometimes by people who couldn't remember their name or age."

"I'm Holt Douglas. And I'm eighteen."

"Were you wearing a seat belt?" she asked.

Holt couldn't remember. He usually strapped himself in, but in the stress of figuring out how to drive Calico's car, he couldn't remember.

"I don't know," he said, then paused. "I guess not because I was thrown from the car."

"Do you think you'll make that mistake again?"

"No, ma'am."

When the X-ray technician brought Holt back to the triage room, a broad-shouldered Georgia state patrolman was standing beside a cabinet where bandages were stored. Holt swallowed hard. The officer had two wallets in his right hand. Holt recognized them. The thin one was his; the much thicker one belonged to Calico.

"I'm Officer Merriwether with the Georgia State Patrol. I need to ask you a few questions."

"Yes, sir." Holt swallowed, then blurted out, "How badly was Ken hurt? Nobody has told me anything about him since I got here."

Ignoring Holt's question, the officer took out a driver's license and looked at it.

"Are you Holton Thomas Douglas?"

"Yes, sir."

"Who else was in the car with you?"

"Ken Morgan. Please, how is he?"

The officer's face was grim. "Both of you were ejected from the vehicle. Mr. Morgan suffered severe head trauma. He died at the scene."

"He's dead?" Holt asked in disbelief.

Holt's last memory of Calico was his friend in the passenger seat of the car, his hand to his mouth, suffering from alcohol-induced nausea.

"The vehicle is registered to Jacklin Morgan," the officer continued.

"That's his dad, but his folks gave it to Ken as an early graduation present." Holt stopped.

The realization that Ken "Calico" Morgan would never graduate from high school, go to college, or hang out with Holt during breaks and summer vacation caused tears to suddenly rush into Holt's eyes. Tiny rivulets streamed down his cheeks. The patrolman waited until Holt dried his eyes.

"Had the two of you been drinking?" the officer asked in a slightly softer tone of voice.

Holt sniffled and nodded his head.

"How much?"

Holt cleared his throat, but his voice broke as he spoke. "I had a glass of spiked punch, and three beers."

"How about Mr. Morgan?"

"I'm not sure, mostly spiked punch."

"Who was driving?"

Holt paused. The patrolman's badge glistened in the bright lights of the hospital room. Silver handcuffs hung from a thick black belt. On his hip was a service revolver with a brown handgrip.

Calico's life was over. Holt's didn't have to be.

"Ken," Holt said, trying to keep his voice steady. "It was his car."

The officer checked his notepad. "That's what Ms. Leanne Tompkins told us. She also indicated Mr. Morgan appeared highly intoxicated when he left her parents' house on Lake Allatoona. Is that true?"

"Yes, sir," Holt said as he winced from a sudden pain in his side. "He was drunk."

1

Ten Years Later

Patricia "Trish" Carmichael checked her face in the mirror before entering the courtroom. The regulation khaki shirt and dark brown pants of her deputy sheriff's uniform were unbelievably dull, but she did what she could with the part of her appearance under her control—from the neck up. She brushed her long blond hair, applied a touch more lipstick than she normally wore during the day, and followed that with an extra layer of slightly iridescent shadow above her blue eyes. Coworkers who saw her wearing a dress when she was off duty frequently did a double take.

Trish's primary job was tracking down deadbeat fathers who failed or refused to pay child support. Malcolm Callaway was more than a deadbeat dad. He was a deadbeat dad who beat his wife. Trish had worked closely with Holt Douglas, the handsome young assistant district attorney, in preparing the case for trial. Holt rocked back in his chair as she entered the courtroom. Tall as a model, Trish walked down the center aisle.

"How's it going?" she asked, flashing a smile.

"The jury is deliberating," Holt responded. "If we don't get a verdict tonight, the judge is going to bring them back early tomorrow, which will mean postponement of your other cases for two weeks."

Trish glanced at the closed door of the jury room. "I wanted to hear the closing arguments."

"You didn't miss much. Clare Dixon did a decent job, especially considering what she had to work with. But I can't imagine a jury with more women than men letting Malcolm walk. Of the four counts, the only one that worries me is count three. That's the one in which Amanda started the fight by trying to hit him with a baseball bat. She missed with the bat; he didn't miss with his fist."

"It was your closing argument I wanted to hear," Trish said, then immediately felt her face flush. "I mean, I got to watch you a couple of months ago in the case against the woman charged with stealing from all those old people in the nursing home. You did a great job."

"I had a confession in that case," Holt said and shrugged. "That always makes it easier. This one reminds me of the opening line from a novel I read in college: 'All happy families are alike; each unhappy family is unhappy in its own way.'"

"*Anna Karenina* by Tolstoy," Trish responded immediately.

"Yeah," Holt said in surprise.

"It was a question on *Jeopardy* last night. My mother and I watch it after I get home from work. There was a category on the show about famous lines from Russian literature."

Trish, who had been an honor student at Paxton High School, went on to attend the local community college and earned a two-year degree in criminal justice before joining the sheriff's department. She'd heard of Tolstoy, but her taste in reading ran more to Christian romance than classic literature.

Clare Dixon returned to the courtroom. Without acknowledging Trish's presence, the petite defense lawyer with short dark hair dropped a photograph of Amanda's bruised face on the table in front of Holt.

"You can keep this," she said. "He'll do it."

"Take the plea deal?" Holt asked, raising his eyebrows.

"Yeah, what he heard in court today has been eating away at him while he's been cooped up in the back for the past few hours. He's afraid of the jury."

"Are you sure?"

"I asked him three times, but I guess we won't know for sure until Judge Lomax puts the questions to him."

"Okay. Let's do it. Do you want to notify the judge?"

"Sure."

Clare left. Holt shook his head.

"I didn't know this could happen," Trish said. "I thought once the case went to the jury, all deals were off the table."

"Not necessarily. I could have withdrawn the offer, but Ralph told me not to. He's all about statistics. In his book, a plea is as good as a conviction."

Judge Clarence Lomax, the first African American superior court judge in the history of the Coosawattee Judicial Circuit, reentered the courtroom. Trish stepped back and sat in the front row.

"Bring in the defendant," the judge said to the bailiff.

When Malcolm Callaway returned, the cocky demeanor Trish had seen in the defendant when the day began was gone. He'd been a cruel dictator of the quarter acre of scraggly land on which his mobile home sat, but the merciless legal blows Holt landed throughout the day had taken their toll. Malcolm now looked like a cur dog that had been kept on a short chain for a month. He joined the lawyers in front of Judge Lomax, who spoke directly to him.

"Ms. Dixon tells me you want to change your plea to guilty. Is that correct?"

Malcolm shuffled his feet and stared down at the floor.

"Mr. Callaway, if you don't want to change your plea, then I'll send you back to the holding cell while we continue to wait for the jury to deliberate."

"Nah, I'm a-goin' to take their deal."

"What is the plea agreement?" the judge asked Holt.

"If the defendant pleads guilty to count one of the indictment, the state will ask the court to impose a sentence of five years to serve, followed by five on probation. The remaining charges will be dropped."

"Have you discussed this with Ms. Dixon?" the judge asked Malcolm.

"Yeah. And she promised me if'n I get convicted, I might spend a lot longer locked up."

"If you plead guilty, you will lose your right for the jury to decide the case," the judge said.

"That's what the lawyer told me."

"Other than the plea agreement outlined by Mr. Douglas, have you been promised anything else to change your plea?"

"Not that I know 'bout."

The judge picked up the indictment. "Are you in fact guilty of count one, which alleges that on or about January 25 of this year you struck Amanda Callaway on and about the face and chest with your fists and put her in apprehension of further serious bodily injury by throwing a cement block at her head?"

"She took a swing at me first with a bat."

"I heard your testimony to the jury," the judge said.

Malcolm didn't respond. Trish saw the defendant clenching his fists. The judge continued.

"Mr. Callaway, if you do not believe you are guilty of count one, I will not accept your change in plea."

"Okay, okay. I'll say it happened thataway."

"Have you been coerced or pressured into entering this guilty plea?"

"What do you mean?"

"Is someone making you plead guilty, or is it your own decision?"

"I'm the one who will have to do the time."

The judge repeated the question.

"Nah, the lawyer told me it was up to me."

"Do you realize I do not have to accept the state's recommendation as to sentence?"

"Huh?"

Even though she'd witnessed the entry of guilty pleas many times, Trish always tensed during this part of the litany.

"I don't have to go along with the five years to serve followed by five years on probation—" Judge Lomax explained.

"Then I ain't gonna do it!" Malcolm interrupted and looked at Clare as if she'd been the one who tried to hit him with a baseball bat.

The judge continued smoothly. "However, having heard the evidence, I will accept the state's recommendation for sentence upon a change in plea to guilty without the necessity of a presentence investigation."

Malcolm responded with a puzzled look.

"The judge is going to approve the plea agreement," Clare said.

"Is that so?" Malcolm asked the judge.

"Yes."

"Okay. I guess I'll do it."

Malcolm's shoulders slumped as the judge completed the rest of the formalities related to accepting a guilty plea.

"I hereby sentence you to serve five years in the Georgia penitentiary, followed by five years on probation." The judge then turned to the bailiff. "Please take the defendant into custody and notify the sheriff's office to send a patrol car to pick him up."

The bailiff led Malcolm out of the courtroom.

"Mr. Douglas, where is the complainant?" the judge asked Holt.

"With her family in the break room."

"Notify them, and we'll bring in the jury."

"Your Honor, I can get the family." Trish spoke up from her position behind the railing.

"That would be appreciated, Deputy Carmichael," the judge replied.

—

The Ashley County courthouse was built in the 1920s when farming was the sputtering economic engine for the local area. The ravages caused by Sherman's scorched-earth march to the sea during the Civil War were still unhealed when the Great Depression piled on another layer of devastation. Nevertheless, the two-story redbrick building had a measure of charm that came from surviving for almost a hundred years.

The broad wooden steps creaked beneath Trish's feet as she went downstairs to the basement. The break room was a windowless space with stark white walls. There were two vending machines and a single drink machine against one wall. A microwave and coffeemaker sat on a small table beneath a sign that warned "For Official Use Only." Amanda and five members of her family were seated around a rectangular table with a plastic laminated top. They had the room to themselves. Trish remained in the doorway. Her time with Amanda's family had increased her sympathy for the battered wife.

"Judge Lomax wants you to come upstairs," she said.

"Has the jury done made up their minds?" Amanda asked, clasping her hands together in front of her.

"No. Your husband decided to plead guilty."

"What?" Amanda's father asked.

"Mr. Douglas and the judge will explain everything to you," Trish said.

"Is Malcolm gonna get sent off to jail?" Amanda continued anxiously.

Trish hesitated.

"No!" Amanda wailed. "If he ain't locked up forever, he's gonna kill me as soon as he gets out! He told me so hisself!"

Amanda's father stood up angrily. "My youngun didn't go through all this to have that sorry—"

"Stop it, Elmer," Amanda's mother interrupted.

"Is he a-goin' to jail?" her father insisted.

Trish hesitated. "Yes, but I can't say anything else about it."

Without waiting for another verbal salvo, she turned and rapidly climbed the stairs two steps at a time. Holt needed to be warned about the storm following in her wake.

2

Trish reentered the courtroom as the jury was filing into the jury box. She rushed up to Holt, who was standing behind the prosecution table.

"Amanda and her family are really upset," she said, slightly out of breath.

"Why?"

"Because Malcolm isn't going to get locked up for life."

"What did you tell them? They should have heard about the sentence from me or the judge."

"I know. No, I didn't. I mean, all I said was—"

The back door of the courtroom flew open, and Amanda's family stormed in. Holt left Trish and met them halfway down the aisle. Trish slipped down the bench until she was close to the jury box. The jurors had puzzled looks on their faces and were whispering to one another. Holt remained in the aisle. One of Amanda's brothers was talking to him and gesturing angrily.

"Mr. Douglas!" the judge called out. "I'm ready to proceed."

"Yes, Your Honor."

Holt made one more comment to the family and then put his index finger to his lips. The sign might work with kindergartners, but Trish doubted its effect on Amanda's kinfolk.

"Where's Malcolm at?" one of Amanda's brothers asked in a loud voice.

"Sir, please sit down," Judge Lomax said.

"Wait, this here is about my daughter!" Amanda's father jumped to his feet. "And I ain't gonna let anything happen—"

Judge Lomax banged the gavel on the bench. "If you say anything else without my permission, I'll have you ejected from the courtroom!"

The men muttered as they sat down on the wooden benches. Amanda looked to be on the verge of tears. After a final stern glance in the direction of the family, Judge Lomax addressed the jury.

"Ladies and gentlemen, the defendant has entered a guilty plea, which relieves you of any further need to deliberate the case. The clerk's office is closed, so the checks for your service will be mailed to the address you provided—"

A middle-aged man wearing a dark suit and sitting in the front row of the jury box raised his hand. The judge paused.

"Your Honor, we reached a verdict in the case. We were just waiting for the bailiff to bring us back into the courtroom to let you know."

Trish glanced at Holt, who licked his lips. Clare Dixon, the defense lawyer, stared wide-eyed at the jury.

"What was it?" shouted a man from Amanda's group. Trish recognized the voice as coming from one of the brothers. "That sorry Malcolm—"

"Bailiff, escort that man from the courtroom!" the judge boomed.

The bailiff started toward the group but then stopped. He obviously didn't know who'd violated the judge's instructions.

"He's the one wearing a blue shirt," Trish spoke up.

Amanda's family glared at her. Trish knew the bailiff, a retired deputy, was incapable of forcibly removing Amanda's brother from the room if the younger man wanted to resist. She placed her hand on the gun strapped to her waist and moved in the direction of the group. There weren't any bullets in the weapon, but no one knew it. The bailiff didn't carry a sidearm.

"Come on," the bailiff said, sucking in his stomach. "You'll have to wait outside."

The brother slouched from his place, and the bailiff led him from the courtroom. Trish removed her hand from the gun.

"Because the defendant entered a plea, there's no need for the jury to publish its verdict," the judge continued. "Thank you for your service. Court is adjourned."

Judge Lomax struck his gavel and exited through a door next to the witness stand. The jury started to leave the box. Holt stepped over to them. Trish kept her eye on Amanda's family, who pressed forward against the railing.

"What were you going to do?" Amanda's father called out in the direction of the jury.

"Just a minute," Holt said, holding up his hand, "and I'll talk to you."

Holt spoke briefly with the juror in the dark suit before directing the rest of the panel to leave via a doorway opposite the one used by the judge. Clare Dixon was putting her papers into a large briefcase on wheels. Holt came over to her and whispered in her ear, and she left through the same door. Trish appreciated Holt's desire to protect the jurors and Clare from a tense confrontation with Amanda's irate relatives. He walked over to the family. Trish edged closer so she could listen.

"The jury found Malcolm not guilty of all the charges. If he had not entered a guilty plea, he would have walked out of the courtroom a free man."

The faces of everyone in Amanda's family registered total shock.

"How could they do that?" her father asked angrily. "After all he did to my Amanda? Didn't they listen to what she told 'em?"

"I didn't have time to get the details, but the foreman said they thought there was so much fussing and fighting going on it wasn't right for Malcolm to be prosecuted and not Amanda too."

"You ain't gonna arrest her, are you?" Amanda's mother asked in a shaky voice.

"No, no," Holt replied. "In my opinion, the jury was wrong and got off track, but that's a risk we take when we bring a case to court."

"What's gonna happen to Malcolm?" Amanda asked.

"He pleaded guilty to count one of the indictment and will spend five years in prison followed by five years on probation. He's been in jail for four months waiting for the case to come to trial, so he'll get credit for time served. There's the possibility he may get out sooner for good behavior, but the parole board in Atlanta is making more and more criminals guilty of violent crimes serve their full time."

"What am I supposed to do when he's cut loose?" Amanda asked.

"You're gonna get a divorce and move back home," Amanda's father said. "And this time you're gonna go through with it!"

The remaining brother muttered in agreement.

"I need to talk to Amanda," Holt said to the group. "Alone."

"Why?" her father demanded.

"Just wait for me outside, Pa," Amanda said. "I'll be there in a minute."

"Don't try to talk to any jurors if you see one of them in the parking lot," Holt said to the departing family.

Trish turned to leave, too.

"Officer Carmichael, would you stay, please?" Holt asked.

Trish realized Holt didn't want to be alone in the courtroom with Amanda. "Yes, sir."

As soon as her family was gone, Holt turned to Amanda. "Have a seat," he said.

Amanda sat on the bench with Trish beside her. Holt positioned his chair so he faced them.

"Do you want to go back to Dahlonega with your family?" he asked.

"No, a big reason me and Malcolm moved down here was to get away from all the mess up there. But we brought our own mess with us." Amanda sniffled. "But I ain't got no choice. I don't have a place to live. We're getting kicked out of the trailer at the end of the month, and finding work with two younguns to take care of is impossible."

"Katelyn is in first grade, right? And Buddy can go to pre-K in the fall."

"Yeah."

Holt put his hands together in front of him and leaned forward. "That means you're going to have to find a job that fits with the school schedule."

"They have a program that lets kids stay till five o'clock, but it costs money that I ain't got unless I can get me a decent job."

"Would you be willing to work at the chicken plant? You have to stand up all day, and it's cold and wet, but they have a day shift that doesn't begin until after you drop the kids off at school, and you could leave in time to get them by four o'clock."

"I tried to get on there, but they told me they weren't hiring any new hands."

"They're always hiring. I know one of the managers at the plant and could talk to him for you. The problem is you'd have to pay for day care for the kids while school is out for the summer."

"I met a woman at Food Lion who keeps kids at her house and doesn't charge as much as most places," Amanda said. "She gave me her card."

"What's her name?" Trish asked.

Amanda dug in a beat-up purse until she found a battered card. "Betty Lou Franklin," she said. "She lives on Baxter Street."

"I know her," Trish said, glancing at Holt. "She's legit. If I talk to her, I think she'll work with Amanda until she gets her first paycheck. My church may be able to help, too. I'll check as soon as I get back to the office."

Amanda's eyes filled with tears.

"Do you think it would be a good idea for you to find another place to live?" Holt continued. "That trailer is filled with bad memories for you and the kids."

"Yeah, but I don't know where to look."

"There are subsidized apartments not far from the chicken plant," Holt said. "With Malcolm in jail and two kids to take care of, you may qualify. If you do, it'll be a lot cheaper than what you're paying for the trailer."

By this point tears were streaming down Amanda's face. Trish handed her a box of tissues.

"I'm ashamed of what I done." Amanda sniffled, blowing her nose. "Hearing it today, I felt like my insides was being ripped out. That juror man was right. I've been wrong, too."

"Think about what I suggested and let me know," Holt said in a gentle voice. "I'll be in my office tomorrow. The phone number is on my card."

Amanda wiped her nose. "My pa is gonna want me to pack up the kids and go home with them tonight."

"But it's up to you to decide what's best for you and your children," Holt said.

"My ma knows why I left home." Amanda nodded. "Sometimes she can talk sense into my pa. I think she'll side with me."

"Either way, let me know if I can help. Okay?"

"Thank you, Mr. Douglas. If'n you hadn't talked to me, I never would have stood up to Malcolm. Maybe jail will be good for him." Amanda glanced at the back door of the courtroom. "I'd better git and catch up to my folks."

Amanda left, and Holt began packing up his file. Trish watched as he neatly placed the folders in the oversize briefcase. Her admiration for the lanky lawyer had just gone up several notches.

Some people in the sheriff's department didn't like the young lawyer from north Atlanta and wanted Ralph Granger, the district attorney, to fire Holt and give his job to Sheriff Blackstone's nephew, who was graduating from law school in a few weeks. Trish wished those who criticized Holt could have witnessed his practical concern for Amanda Callaway.

"Do you think Amanda will divorce Malcolm?" Trish asked as they walked up the aisle toward the main door of the courtroom.

"Probably, unless she forgets the past three years and starts fantasizing that he's somebody he's not."

"People change."

Holt glanced sideways at her with a skeptical look on his face as he held the door open for her.

They walked down the broad steps in front of the courthouse. The early May evening was cool enough to be comfortable. The sun was about to descend below the line of pine trees to the west of the courthouse annex. There was no sign of Amanda or her family. Holt checked his watch.

"Will you make it home in time to watch *Jeopardy*?"

"I'm not sure. This is the night I pick up Chinese food."

"My girlfriend likes Chinese," Holt said. "We usually go to Wong Foo Palace. It's the only place in town that has decent sushi."

"Wong Foo is okay. But my mother likes the spring rolls from Mister Chang's."

At the bottom of the steps, Holt turned toward the courthouse annex. "See you in the morning," he said.

"Okay. I'll have the files in order."

"You always do." Holt smiled.

Trish watched Holt walk away and sighed. It was nice that he treated her as a colleague, not an underling. But she couldn't help wishing for more.

3

Holt walked across the parking lot to his office located in the courthouse annex. Sitting at his desk, he buried his face in his hands. He'd come way too close to losing the Callaway case. The cause of justice could be an elusive mistress, and if Malcolm hadn't lost his nerve, she would have slipped out of the courtroom. Holt could only hope that Malcolm's time behind bars would give Amanda Callaway a chance to create a new life.

Holt knew about second chances. He'd been living one ever since Calico's death. He opened the middle drawer of his desk and took out a picture of himself and Calico taken several months before the fatal wreck. In the photo the friends were standing beneath the basketball goal at the high school. Calico was a scrappy guard, Holt a power forward.

"You would have been better at this than I am," Holt said. "But hang with me. I'm going to make a difference."

Holt returned the photo to its place and sent a short e-mail to Ralph Granger telling him about the Callaway trial. Ralph would be happy with the result so long as the local paper didn't run an article that the jury actually found the defendant not guilty. Holt wasn't worried. There hadn't been any reporters in the courtroom, and Clare Dixon wouldn't publicize the fact that her client pleaded guilty minutes before the jury was about to set him free.

Behind Holt's desk was a long credenza. Ralph's preferred method of assigning cases was to bring a file into Holt's office and put it on the credenza without telling Holt about it. The unorthodox way of delegation kept Holt on his toes.

The pile looked suspiciously larger, and Holt picked up a fresh folder. Inside was a police report about a burglary at a residence in a run-down part of town. Poor people usually stole from other poor people, and the house involved was a dilapidated, single-story wooden structure with a small porch in the front and a yard that was more weeds than grass. A second photo showed a door that had been knocked out of the frame, most likely by a hard kick from a boot. The inventory of items taken included a ten-year-old computer, a box of costume jewelry, a skinny gold necklace, and a child's bicycle. Beneath the police report was the single most important piece of information in an investigative file, and the one Holt wanted to see more than anything else—a confession.

Shortly after Holt had come to work at the district attorney's office, he'd noticed that an overwhelming number of the individuals charged with crimes confessed, either before the police began formal questioning or soon thereafter. Miranda warnings did little to stem the tide of incriminating statements. People seemed more willing to try to explain why they'd done something wrong, or blame it on someone else, than to refuse to talk about it at all. If criminals simply kept their mouths shut, the conviction rate for the district attorney's office would drop precipitously. With a confession in hand, Holt's main job was calculating an appropriate punishment.

Moving the new case to a different stack, Holt noticed a slightly discolored folder that was different in shape from the ones typically used by the office. The Callaway case had sapped his energy and drained his reserve tank, but he decided to see what else Ralph had dumped on him.

Files in the DA's office were labeled "*State of Georgia v.* [the defendant's name]." On this folder's tab he saw a single name—"Meredith, R. T." Inside was a death certificate, a crude diagram of a room with the location of a body outlined on the floor, and a two-page report written by Harold "Butch" Clovis, a local detective, who concluded that Rexford Theodore Meredith died from a self-inflicted gunshot wound to the upper chest.

Rex Meredith, the county's largest landowner and one of its richest citizens, had killed himself a couple of years before Holt came to town, but everyone who lived in Paxton knew Meredith's name, and his legacy continued to cause ripples in the community. Every few months or so there would be a brief article in the newspaper about his estate. It might be the renovation of a commercial building he'd owned, a gift from the charitable trust administered by his stepdaughter, or the announcement of an upcoming auction of several hundred acres of farmland.

Holt yawned. He could find out tomorrow why Ralph wanted him to look at the old file. Now all he wanted to do was go home and collapse. He had one last stop to make on the way, though. Holt loosened his tie and turned out the lights as he left the building.

He drove two blocks south of the courthouse and turned onto Broadmore Street. Two houses from the corner was a Victorian residence that had been turned into the All About You Salon and Spa. Angelina Peabody had confounded the small-town doubters who said a place that offered facial massages, high-fashion hair care, and expensive manicures and pedicures could not make it in a town like Paxton. The robin's-egg-blue building was bursting with light from every window. Two days a week it was open until 8:00 p.m., another innovation that had proved to be an astute business move. Women who couldn't get away from jobs or families during the day flocked in during the extended hours to be pampered. Holt drove past the crowded parking area in front of the building and parked on the street. He climbed the broad wooden steps to the porch and went inside.

"Hey, Holt," said Brittany, the receptionist who served as traffic cop, scheduling clients for different services and directing them where to go when they arrived. "Patsy had a cancellation for a manicure and pedicure, so you can go right in. She'll be thrilled to see you."

"Right," Holt replied.

"Don't turn up your lawyer nose," Brittany scolded. "We had two men come in earlier today. It's only a matter of time before all the attorneys in town are letting us take care of them."

"Who were the men? Were they lawyers?"

"You know I can't tell. That's confidential client information."

"I could cross-examine you and find out in less than five minutes, but I'm way over my quota of questions for the day. Where's the boss?"

"Taking a break in the kitchen. She just finished a two-and-a-half-hour cut and color for a woman whose hair looked like it had previously been styled in a food processor."

Located at the rear of the house, the kitchen served as both a break room and an overflow space for supplies. Holt passed an industrial-size clothes washer that was furiously spinning a large load of towels. The door to the kitchen was closed, and he cracked it open. Seated at a round glass table was Angelina. Her eyes were closed as she rubbed her temples.

"I'm here for my haircut and shave," Holt said.

"No, you're not," Angelina replied, not opening her eyes. "You're here because you knew I'd want to see you before I tackle one last, impossible makeover."

Holt stepped closer and kissed her lightly on the lips. "Open your eyes, sleeping beauty."

Angelina opened her brown eyes and shook her long dark hair. Women paid a lot of money for hair that mimicked what Angelina had naturally.

"What a day," she said, squeezing Holt's hand.

"Brittany told me about your client with food-processor hair."

"That's being generous. But I think she was happy when she left. If only people in this town understood about tipping. How are you?"

"I've been in court all day."

"That's right." Angelina sat up straighter. "What happened?"

Holt briefly told her about the case.

"Wow, that was lucky. I bet Clare is steamed about her client pleading guilty. I think she's on the books for a color treatment toward the end of the week, but of course I won't say anything about it."

"Clare Dixon dyes her hair? How old is she? Twenty-seven?"

Angelina smiled. "Don't worry your curly brown head about it. To survive in this world, women need all the help they can get."

"Yeah, the place is packed."

"And I'd better get back to it. My last appointment is getting her hair washed as we speak."

Angelina stood and gave him another kiss. She was so short that she had to stand on her toes, and he had to lean down to make it work. The kitchen door opened. They quickly parted.

"Oops," said Brittany. "I should have known you two would be smooching back here."

"And everywhere else I get the chance," Angelina said, giving Holt a pat on the cheek.

"Mrs. Boisin is ready for you," Brittany said. "It's her first visit, and—"

"I know. I'll be right there."

"Will Friday evening still work for you?" Holt asked.

Angelina pointed at Brittany. "Unless she's booked an appointment for me after four o'clock."

"No, ma'am," Brittany said and saluted. "I know your social life comes first."

—

Leaving the salon, Holt turned down Magnolia Avenue, a broad, tree-lined street where the finest older homes in the area were located. He slowed to a stop when he reached the Meredith mansion, the crown jewel of the neighborhood. The rambling wooden structure was meticulously maintained, even though no one had lived there since the owner's death.

An elderly caretaker whose name Holt couldn't remember lived in a cottage nestled behind the residence and kept everything tidy, as if expecting Rex Meredith to return any moment from an overnight trip out of town. The century-old house had a broad wraparound porch. Latticework on the corners of the porch supported flowering vines. Brick pavers led to the house and around to the backyard, which was enclosed behind a white fence. The shrubs in front of the house were neatly trimmed, the grass lush and green. A massive magnolia tree with shiny green leaves and saucer-sized white blossoms dominated the front yard.

While Holt watched, lights suddenly came on in two rooms on the main floor of the house and one on the upper floor. Startled, Holt tried to see if anyone was moving around inside, then realized the lights were probably on a timer linked to the security system. If a burglar tried to kick down the door at the Meredith mansion, multiple patrol cars from the sheriff's department would arrive on the scene within seconds.

Holt eased his car forward. His house was about a mile from the Meredith mansion, but it was in another economic hemisphere.

4

The salary of an assistant district attorney in Ashley County wasn't enough to convince a bank to open the vault and loan money to buy a fancy house. So when he moved to Paxton, Holt rented a forty-year-old redbrick, ranch-style home on a street much narrower than Magnolia Avenue. The most common trees on Holt's street were pin oaks and pine trees. The neighborhood was a melting pot of blacks and whites. Fifty years of integration had broken down the divide between the races. Holt's neighbors to the north were a white family of four. The father worked as a produce manager for a grocery store chain, and the mother was employed as a part-time aide at an elementary school. To the south lived a retired black couple who'd saved their money and bought a house in town closer to family and doctors.

Holt pulled into his driveway. The house was in the middle of a large lot, with a backyard surrounded by a sturdy chain-link fence. A fenced yard meant Holt would have room for a dog, and owning a dog was one of Holt's top priorities in life. Within two months after moving into the house, he bought a Jack Russell terrier.

As soon as he opened the car door, Holt could hear Henry barking.

Between sharp yelps, the small white-and-brown animal jumped up as if trying to scale the fence. Holt had no doubt that if Henry ever figured out how to wedge his feet into the spaces between the links, he would clamber over the top and leap to the ground below. Not far from the gate was a flat-roofed doghouse where Henry rested in the shade on hot summer days.

"I know. I'm late," Holt said as he walked over to the gate.

Beside the gate latch was a yellow sign that read "Beware of the Dog." Beneath the printed letters, Holt had added in permanent black marker, "We're Not Kidding." The sign wasn't an idle threat. Three people could attest that Henry considered biting humans a legitimate canine activity. The meter reader for the local natural gas company was a two-time victim, and Holt now called in the numbers from the meter once a month. A teenage boy taking an unauthorized shortcut to a friend's house hopped the fence one Saturday morning and ended up with Henry swinging from the bottom cuff of his blue jeans. The final victim was more serious. One evening, Holt returned from jogging and saw a man trying to hit Henry with a tree limb. When the man took his eyes off Henry, the dog latched onto the man's hand. With a yell, the man dropped the branch and ran away into the gathering darkness. The intruder looked familiar, and Holt suspected he was the older brother of a man Holt had successfully prosecuted on a drug charge. In Holt's mind, Henry was a better deterrent to intruders than an alarm system or loaded gun.

Originally bred as foxhunters, Jack Russell terriers needed an outlet for their energy and drive. Since foxes were rare in Holt's backyard, Henry shifted his genetic focus to the nimble gray squirrels that craved the nuts from the large oak trees. There were easier, safer pickings for the squirrels from the oaks in the neighbors' yards, but that didn't deter them from trying to invade Henry's domain. Especially in the fall, it wasn't unusual for Holt to return home and find a gray squirrel carcass triumphantly placed on the small wooden deck at the rear of the house.

Holt opened the gate and watched Henry race around several times in a circle before slowing down and coming close enough to be scratched behind his ears. Inside the house, Henry went directly to the old-fashioned kitchen with its out-of-date appliances and began lapping water from a metal dish. Holt poured a cup of dry food into another metal bowl, and the dog began to contentedly munch his food.

Holt was hungry, too. He'd drunk a cup of black coffee for breakfast and nibbled on peanut butter crackers while working through the lunch break during the trial but eaten nothing since. He took a frozen dinner from the refrigerator and popped it into the microwave.

While his supper cooked, Holt went to the bedroom and changed into blue jeans and a short-sleeved shirt. His bedroom contained a king-size bed on a metal frame, a large wooden chest of drawers he'd bought at a secondhand shop, and a small nightstand. Holt's mother had unsuccessfully offered to take him furniture shopping.

His closet, on the other hand, was filled with tailored suits and custom-made shirts. Two rows of shiny shoes lined the floor of the closet, and there was an extensive selection of silk ties on three racks. Holt knew appearance was a big part of any first impression, whether for a jury or for a judge. "Dress for success" and "Clothes make the man" were clichés he didn't doubt. However, he drew the line at getting a manicure at Angelina's salon.

Holt used a small second bedroom as a home office. In addition to the volumes on his e-reader, Holt had two bookcases. He liked biographies about famous trial lawyers and owned books about Clarence Darrow, Melvin Belli, F. Lee Bailey, Gerry Spence, and Earl Rogers, the California lawyer who inspired the *Perry Mason* TV series. When reading about attorneys, Holt would jot down anecdotal nuggets to use in the courtroom. An effective metaphor has a long shelf life.

The microwave beep sounded. Holt went into the living room and turned on the TV. Surfing through a few channels, he saw Alex Trebek's face. It was time for the double-point round on *Jeopardy*.

Holt stopped to watch while he ate.

—

Trish placed a dish of freshly cut-up strawberries topped with whipped cream in front of her mother, whose wheelchair was placed at the end of the kitchen table so she could see the TV. It was a competitive night on *Jeopardy*, and all three contestants had a chance to win.

"There's nothing better than Chinese food and strawberries," Trish said with a smile.

"Keith called just before you got home," Marge Carmichael said.

"Did he say what he wanted?"

"No, but if he's going to propose, I think he'd do it in person."

"Mama!"

"I thought you believed he was the one God had for you."

"I did after we spent so much time together during the Christmas holidays, but Keith doesn't seem to be getting the message."

Marge ate a strawberry. "Waiting is hard," she said, "but the woman usually knows these things before the man. That's the way it was with your father and me. It took him six months to realize he ought to ask me out, and another year to propose. You and Keith have been seeing each other a lot less than that."

"Yeah," Trish sighed. "We talked for a while at the singles' Sunday school cookout last weekend, but he spent most of the evening pitching horseshoes with his buddies."

"He took home the blueberry cobbler you made for him."

"And gave me a long hug when he thanked me," Trish said, then paused. "I don't know. Keith is kind of boring. I mean, even though he's two years older than I am, we've known each other since middle school. Maybe that's not what I want."

"Boring? What is that supposed—"

"Do you remember the Russian literature category last night?" Trish interrupted as Alex Trebek announced the topics on a fresh board.

"Uh, I know there were questions about famous sisters."

"Holt Douglas, the assistant DA, quoted a line from one of Tolstoy's novels this afternoon in court, and I knew which one it was."

While they ate the strawberry dessert, Trish told her mother about the Callaway case, of course leaving out any mention of her budding romantic interest in Holt Douglas. Keith Pierce wasn't the first male Trish had marked as God's man for matrimony, and she didn't want to make her mother's head spin by adding a new name to the list so soon.

"The Louisiana Purchase," Marge blurted out when Trish stopped to eat a final bite.

"What?" Trish asked.

"That's the answer," Marge replied. "The question was, what major nineteenth-century US land acquisition was thought by many at the time to be unconstitutional?"

"Are you listening to me?"

"Yes, but you know questions about US history are my favorite." Marge shook her head. "And the goings-on in a courtroom make me nervous. I'm sorry."

"That's okay," Trish said, checking her watch. "Hey, I promised Sue Ann we would hang out together after she puts the baby to bed. Mark is at a baseball game in Atlanta with some friends from work and won't be home until late."

"I wonder where their seats are."

"Probably in the outfield," Trish replied. "He and Sue Ann don't have extra money for expensive tickets."

"The Braves are playing the Phillies tonight. I'll be on the lookout for Mark. They always show a close-up of the bleachers when someone hits a home run."

Trish quickly rinsed the plates and started the dishwasher. Her mother would take out the clean dishes and put them away as soon as they cooled. They'd used some of the insurance money from the accident to modify the house and make it handicapped-accessible. Of course, there were many things money couldn't fix or replace.

Getting in her father's old red pickup, Trish backed out of the driveway. She drove the truck enough to keep the battery charged and used it every Saturday for a trash run to the local dump. Trish and Marge's house was less than two miles from the Paxton city limits, but it was in a rural area. There was no urban sprawl beyond the town limits. Cow pastures and soybean fields came right up to the city boundary.

Trish flicked on the truck's bright lights. There were two houses on the half mile of road between their house and the main highway to town. A neighbor's German shepherd raced out to the road and barked fiercely as he chased the truck to the edge of his owner's property. If Trish stopped the truck and got out, the dog would come over and lick her fingers.

Sue Ann Jackson, Trish's best friend from high school, lived in a ten-unit apartment complex on the edge of town. Her apartment was on the second floor, a significant obstacle now that Sue Ann had to haul groceries and coax Candace up the steps. Trish opened the unlocked door and entered.

"It's me!"

"I'm in the baby's room!" Sue Ann replied. "But don't come in here without a gas mask on!"

Trish ignored the warning and walked through a living room cluttered with toddler toys. Candace, a hefty two-and-a-half-year-old, no longer qualified as a baby. The child's room was at the end of a short hallway.

"Whew," Trish said when she reached the nursery. "You weren't kidding."

"I wouldn't lie to you about something like that," Sue Ann said, her back to Trish. "I'm going to have to give Candy another bath. I put the diaper in a plastic bag by the changing table. Would you mind taking it out to the Dumpster?"

Trish saw a partially closed plastic bag from one of the local grocery stores. Holding her breath, she gingerly picked it up and carried it out of the house. Even outside, the stench from the bag was potent. Trish tied it shut and threw it into the large metal container behind the building. She quickly walked away and sucked in a few gulps of pure air on her way back to the apartment. Candace was getting lathered up in the bathtub when she returned.

When she saw Trish, Candace called out, "Tish!"

"Hey, sweetie," Trish said.

"Please hand me her shampoo," Sue Ann said. "It's somewhere up on that cabinet. Mark bathed her before he left and sometimes he puts it out of reach. It's in a pink bottle."

Trish retrieved the shampoo. Mother and daughter had wavy brown hair and brown eyes. Sue Ann's baby pictures were virtually indistinguishable from Candace's, a fact that made Mark jokingly question whether any of his genes contributed to the child's creation. Trish leaned against the sink while Sue Ann finished vigorously washing and rinsing her daughter.

"Aunt Tish, she's all yours," Sue Ann said, pushing a stray strand of hair out of her eyes. "I'll spray deodorizer in her room."

Trish rubbed Candace dry with a soft towel. The child's sturdy legs held rock-solid against the pressure of the towel. Trish finished and picked her up.

"I walk," Candace protested.

"I carry," Trish replied.

Taking the little girl into the bedroom, which now smelled more fruity than foul, Trish transferred her to her mother, who expertly slipped on a clean diaper and fresh pair of pajamas.

"She was asleep when she had the stinky diaper," Sue Ann said.

"It's a good thing you checked on her."

"Yeah, but I'm never going to let her eat as many beans as she wants for dinner again. Mark thought it was funny."

Sue Ann laid Candace in a bed with side rails. Trish knelt down beside the bed.

"I like your new big-girl bed," Trish said.

Candace smiled and batted her eyelids.

"We had to do it," Sue Ann said. "She was climbing out of the crib."

Sue Ann leaned over and kissed Candace on the forehead. "Good night. I love you."

"Play, Tish?" Candace asked.

"Not tonight," Trish replied. "It's time for you to go to sleep."

Candace grabbed a small stuffed horse that Trish had given her as a baby gift, rolled onto her side, and inserted her right thumb into her mouth. Sue Ann turned off the overhead light. A night-light flickered on.

"Will she stay in the bed?" Trish asked softly as Sue Ann carefully closed the door.

"So far, which I consider a miracle on the same order as the Israelites crossing the Red Sea on dry ground."

"What about her thumb? I thought you were going to give a pacifier another try."

"I did. For the fourteen millionth time. She spits it out like it was covered in hot sauce. She's a natural girl. I can only pray the thumb won't mean braces later on."

The two women went into the living room. Sue Ann collapsed into the recliner where Mark usually sat. Trish sat on a plush sofa and crossed her legs.

"I want adult conversation," Sue Ann said, rubbing her forehead with her hand. "And I want it now."

"Okay," Trish said slowly. "I was in the main courtroom this afternoon with Holt Douglas."

Sue Ann sat up straighter in the chair. "And?" she asked.

"We talked."

"Did you tell him how good you are at chess? That will impress him."

"No, it didn't come up."

Trish stopped.

"Keep going," Sue Ann demanded. "Don't make me drag it out of you. I want every tiny detail."

5

Holt and Jim Montgomery met at the coffeepot in the back corner of the DA's office. Jim, the other assistant DA, was a career prosecutor who liked to wear wrinkled khakis and occasionally neglected to shave before coming to work. He kept an electric razor in the bottom drawer of his desk and a dark suit on a hook in the corner of his office in case he had to unexpectedly be in court.

"What happened in the Callaway case?" Jim asked.

"The defendant accepted a plea bargain while the jury was deliberating," Holt replied as he stirred a single packet of sugar into his coffee. "The judge finished accepting the plea a few minutes before the jury came back with a not-guilty verdict."

"You're kidding." Jim raised his eyebrows. "Did you have any idea you were in trouble?"

"No, and I would have plowed ahead oblivious to the cliff at my feet. Trying to guess what a jury is going to do is like playing the lottery."

"I stay away from the lotto. I don't want to exchange one addiction for another. It sounds to me like your higher power kept you out of the fire."

Jim went to three or four AA meetings a week, and his conversation was frequently sprinkled with the group's lingo. He had successfully sponsored several recovering alcoholics and carried a seven-year chip in his pocket.

"I don't know about that," Holt replied. "But it would be nice if someone could teach me how to read people better."

"The trick is spotting the mavericks who sneak onto the jury panel and persuade others to buy into the half-baked theories defense lawyers throw up against the wall."

"That's what happened yesterday. The foreman believed both Amanda and Malcolm should have been on trial."

Ralph Granger, district attorney of the Coosawattee Judicial Circuit for the past twenty-two years, joined them at the coffeepot in time to hear Holt's last comment.

"Which is another variation on the 'Try anyone in the courtroom but my client' defense," Ralph said in a gravelly voice. "Vernon Mitchell did that better than anyone else. He'd make the arresting officer look guiltier than the defendant. If he'd had the Callaway girl in the crosshairs, it would have been hard for him to miss."

"Why didn't you say something to me when I briefed you on the case last week?" Holt asked.

"Because you were going up against that mousy Clare Dixon and superconfident about your chances. If you recall, I still strongly urged you to pursue a plea deal."

"Yeah," Holt admitted. "I remembered that when I brought it up to Clare while the jury was deliberating."

Ralph poured himself a cup of black coffee. "What do you fellows have on your docket this morning?" he asked.

"I'm meeting with Detective Kimborough in Sanford County about the Casper case," Jim replied. "And I'd better get on the road."

Jim snapped a lid onto his coffee cup and left. Sanford County lay across the Coosawattee River from Ashley County.

"I'm handling Judge Lomax's calendar call," Holt said. "Nothing major. Mostly arraignments, contempt citations, bond forfeitures, traffic tickets, and a few guilty pleas."

"What about the Lambert DUI case that was on the trial calendar?"

"It was continued to the next term because a defense witness wasn't available."

"That's one of Dirk Rangel's standard tricks," Ralph growled.

"But it was the first time he'd used it in this case. And Rangel had a statement from the man's doctor stating the witness wasn't fit to be in attendance at the trial."

"What was it? A stent in the guy's heart?"

"Yes. How did you know? Has Rangel used that before?"

"Belinda told me when I called her yesterday from Triplett County."

One of the irritating things Ralph Granger did was frequently test the credibility of the people who worked in his office. He would ask a question he already knew the answer to in order to find out what the person would say. It was a good habit for a prosecutor in the courtroom, but it didn't help office morale. An innocent slipup could result in an unpleasant visit to Ralph's office for further cross-examination. Once again, the tactic had caught Holt off guard.

"I was ready to go to trial in the Lambert case, Ralph," Holt said defensively. "I'm not going to lie to you about it."

"Who said you lied?"

"I don't know. You tell me."

Ralph narrowed his eyes. Holt saw a storm coming that he didn't want to weather.

"Okay, okay," he quickly added. "But it would be nice to know you trust me to do my job."

"And it's my job to make sure you do."

"Yes, sir."

Arguing with Ralph was like punching a tar baby. It would only get stickier and more annoying. Holt turned away.

"I'm not finished," Ralph said. "Did you review the files I put on your credenza?"

Holt tried to take the emotional edge off his voice as he answered. "Yes, I looked over the new burglary case and read the confession from the eighteen-year-old. It looks solid against all three defendants."

"It is. There's also a work-in-progress folder about a cruelty to children matter that's still at the investigative stage. I want you to get involved early so it doesn't get messed up. The man and woman under suspicion are bad news."

"Sure, and I saw the old file about Rexford Meredith's death. What do you want me to do with it? It was ruled a suicide."

"That's not for you to see," Ralph answered quickly. "Bring it to my office ASAP."

"Okay."

As steamy as his coffee, Holt went into his office and, in an act of minor rebellion, left the Meredith information lying on his credenza. A few moments later, Belinda Nichols came in with a big stack of files in her hands. The chief administrative assistant had been working in the DA's office longer than Ralph and knew more about the flow of cases through the office than the lawyers. She was also a good source of information about prospective witnesses and jurors. She plopped the files onto the corner of Holt's desk.

"This is what you need for this morning," she said, straightening the stack with a pudgy hand adorned with multiple rings. "Nothing major. They're in the same order as the calendar on the bench in front of the judge."

"Thanks." Holt glanced over his shoulder at the door. "Ralph told me he called you yesterday about the Lambert DUI case."

Belinda rolled her eyes that were too made-up for a woman who would be sixty on her next birthday. Her hair was dyed an auburn color. "Did he give you a hard time?"

"A little. I hate it when he goes behind my back."

"He's paid to be suspicious. Oh, there's a memo on my desk from Trish Carmichael about the child-support contempt files. Her summaries are good enough to read to the judge without changing a word."

"She's sharp."

"And athletic," Belinda said brightly. "Did you know she played basketball in high school? Her senior year the team made it to the state quarterfinals."

Holt, who was glancing through the first case on the docket, didn't look up. "No, but I'm not surprised," he said. "She's tall."

"And on the homecoming court three years straight."

"Good for her, but the case summaries are more relevant for me."

Belinda left. Making sure he kept the files in proper order, Holt carefully loaded two catalog cases. Electronic records had come to the federal courts, but Ashley County still lived in a world filled with paper. Holt checked his watch. He needed to leave immediately if he wanted to be early enough to unpack everything in the courtroom. He met Belinda in the doorway on his way out of his office.

"Here are Trish's summaries," Belinda said as she handed him three sheets of paper.

"Thanks. If Dirk Rangel calls about any of his cases, I won't be able to get back to him until this afternoon. He's anxious because the plea deal in the McDonald case expires today."

"What are you going to do if Dirk calls your bluff and turns down the offer?"

Holt smiled wryly. "Get humble and offer him a better deal. As long as Dirk doesn't know we can't take the case to trial, I'm going to keep working him. His client is guilty. I just can't prove it."

—

Holt walked briskly across the parking lot to the courthouse where he joined a throng of people flowing into the building. In a few minutes the courtroom would be filled with friends and family members of the men and women brought over from the jail or required to appear in court to answer pending charges. Judge Lomax was in charge, but it would be up to Holt to smoothly orchestrate the proceedings. He'd been nervous the first few times he handled calendar calls on his own, but he was beginning to feel more comfortable on the courtroom stage.

—

Trish had come in an hour before her scheduled shift to spend extra time preparing the memo for Holt. She'd been in court enough to develop an ear for what lawyers wanted to say and what the judge needed to hear. After proofreading the memo for the third time, she'd sent it as an e-mail attachment to Belinda, who was the only person besides Sue Ann who knew about her interest in Holt. Belinda didn't have to be asked twice to take on the challenge of matchmaker.

Trish drove the three blocks from the sheriff's department to the courthouse. She shared use of an unmarked law enforcement vehicle with four other people in the office. As a female deputy, Trish always drew stares and sideways looks from the people streaming into the courthouse.

"Trish!" a male voice called out from behind her as she neared the entrance to the courtroom.

Turning around, it took Trish a few seconds to connect the chiseled face and dark hair with a name. It was Donnie Crowder, a star football player who'd earned a scholarship to a small school in Tennessee. He'd been on the same team with Keith.

"Hey, Donnie," she said. "I didn't realize you were back in town."

"Hopefully only for a few minutes." Donnie flashed the smile that had given Trish and her friends chill bumps. "You look great in that uniform."

"Yeah, right," Trish said, blushing. "What are you doing here this morning?"

Donnie held up a yellow piece of paper. "Speeding ticket when I was driving in to visit my mom a couple of months ago. I live in Nashville and thought about paying the fine through the mail, but the points were going to send my car insurance premium through the roof, so I turned the court date into another excuse to see my family. Do you think I can get the charge knocked down?"

"Uh, I don't know. Holt Douglas is the assistant DA running the docket this morning. You'll have to talk to him."

"Could you do it for me? I'm not even sure what to ask."

Trish knew she would say yes even if she didn't really want to. Turning down Donnie Crowder wasn't an option girls usually chose. He'd never asked Trish out, but she would have accepted, if only for bragging rights of one date.

"I'll mention it to him if I get a chance. How fast were you going?"

Donnie handed her his copy of the ticket. "It's somewhere on here, but it's hard to read."

Trish tried to decipher the officer's handwriting, but it was a deputy whose penmanship was deplorable.

"Is that a nine or a seven?" she asked, holding out the ticket.

"I'm sure it's a seven," Donnie replied. "There's no way I was going ninety-five in a fifty-five-mile zone. If it's dropped to less than fifteen over the speed limit, I can avoid the slam on my insurance."

Trish looked up. "I thought you didn't know what you needed to do."

"I know that much but not how to make it happen."

Donnie was wearing an expensive-looking suit. Trish didn't know what the former high school heartthrob did for a living, but he looked like he could afford a lawyer. Then she remembered something else about Donnie. He was notoriously cheap. His idea of spending a lot on a date meant ordering two toppings instead of one on a medium pizza.

"Let me hang on to the ticket," she said. "I'll check with Mr. Douglas."

"Thanks," Donnie replied. "And see if it can be taken care of first thing. I really don't want to hang around all morning."

"Okay, but no promises."

"You can do it," Donnie replied, trotting out his smile again. "You were always a winner."

As she entered the courtroom, Trish knew she would no longer have any trouble turning down Donnie Crowder, even if he asked her out for pizza with as many toppings as she wanted.

The court reporter was setting up her equipment next to the witness stand. The judge hadn't appeared. Holt was sitting at the table used by the prosecutors with his back to her and entering information into his laptop. A bevy of defense lawyers were huddled on the opposite side of the courtroom. Seven or eight prisoners had been brought over from the jail and were sitting in chairs that lined a wall near the defense lawyers. Trish recognized three men who were in court trying to get out of jail on previous contempt orders for nonpayment of child support. Her job was to keep them locked up until they presented a bona fide plan for payment. She tapped Holt on the shoulder.

"Yes," he said curtly as he turned around. "Oh, good morning. Thanks for the summary you sent over. It was well done. Anything else I need to know?"

"Not on my cases." Trish cleared her throat. "But I ran into an old high school friend who's here on a traffic citation. He lives in Nashville and wondered if you could take his case out of order and knock down the charge. His name is Donald Crowder."

Holt picked up his calendar. "It will be a couple of hours before we reach the traffic matters. What's his name again?"

"Crowder."

Holt pulled a file from the lower third of one of the two stacks on the table and opened it. "Ninety-five miles per hour in a fifty-five-mile zone. What does he want to do?"

Trish swallowed. "Reduce it to less than fifteen over. I didn't know it was that much—"

"How good a friend is he?" Holt asked, glancing at the door where Judge Lomax would enter the courtroom.

"Just an acquaintance. We never dated."

Trish inwardly kicked herself for mentioning the totally irrelevant tidbit of social trivia. Holt didn't seem to notice as he continued to study the file.

"Tell him I'll talk to him at ten thirty when the judge takes a break," Holt said as he continued to flip through the file. "Your friend has two speeding tickets in Tennessee within the past year and needs to slow down before he kills himself or someone else." Holt paused. "At least there's no indication of alcohol involved."

"Thanks," Trish said as she retreated. "And I'm ready to testify in my cases if you need me."

Judge Lomax entered the courtroom and everyone rose to their feet. As the crowd sat down, Trish looked over her shoulder and saw Donnie, who smiled again.

She didn't.

6

It was 12:30 p.m. by the time the courtroom cleared, and Holt handed Judge Lomax an order revoking bond for a defendant who hadn't appeared in court.

"I'm sorry we cut into your lunchtime," Holt said as the judge returned the signed order to him. "I know this is your day for the Coosawattee Club."

"As long as I'm counted present I won't get into trouble," the judge replied, standing up and stretching. "It's not your fault that the wheels of justice were gritty this morning. You did a good job keeping things on track."

"Thank you."

"You should think about joining Coosawattee," the judge continued. "I'd be glad to sponsor you."

Holt hesitated. Since coming to town he'd kept a low profile. Ralph Granger was a member of the Citizens Club and had been trying to get Holt to join for over a year. The local bar association was split equally between the two groups.

"I appreciate the invitation," Holt answered slowly.

"That's an offer, not an order," the judge said with a smile. "I know Ralph has been hitting you up for Citizens. Both organizations are about service and networking."

"Yes, sir."

"I won't bring it up again, but let me know if you're interested."

The judge left the courtroom. Holt turned off his laptop and returned the now-jumbled files to the two catalog cases.

Commitment to groups hadn't been a high priority for Holt since high school. He attended rush week in college but turned down pledge offers from three fraternities. He'd lost his taste for hard partying and limited himself to an occasional beer or glass of wine. When he did drink, he never drove. And he always buckled his seat belt.

—

Returning to the office, Holt saw the Meredith file on his credenza and read it again. The death of such a prominent citizen hadn't generated much paperwork. The absence of information, particularly interviews with family members or business associates, made no sense. Holt jotted down on a legal pad some of the steps that should have been taken. It didn't take long to list almost twenty. Then he read the list, tore out the sheet of paper, wadded it up, and threw it in the trash can. Ralph Granger wouldn't allow him to waste his time on a theoretical case. Holt stepped down the hallway to Ralph's office to return the file, but the DA's door was shut. Since office protocol forbade knocking except in an extreme emergency, Holt returned the file to his desk before leaving for lunch.

Stopping by a local restaurant with a great salad bar, Holt fixed one for himself and another to take to Angelina. He added smoked turkey for protein.

"Hey, Holton," Brittany said when he came through the door. "What's for lunch? Angelina is starving and in the mood for sushi."

"She's always in the mood for sushi. However, I believe the discovery of fire to cook meat was one of mankind's most important advances. Why go back to eating raw fish?"

"Who said it was a man who discovered fire? Maybe it was a woman sitting in a cave waiting for her husband to return from hunting a mastodon."

"I wouldn't doubt it. Mastodon sushi sounds gross."

Brittany laughed. "I'll let Angelina know you're here. She's finishing up a color and should be free in a few minutes. Go on back to the kitchen."

Holt moved past Brittany.

"And lock the door this time," she called after him. "I had nightmares after seeing you two kissing. Isn't there a law against forcing me to witness workplace displays of affection?"

Holt didn't answer but smiled for the first time that day. The calendar call had been devoid of humor.

He didn't wait for Angelina. Her appointment with the client could stretch out longer than anticipated, and she wouldn't mind if he went ahead. Sometimes he ate at the salon even when Angelina wasn't available. The quiet kitchen gave him a midday respite from the pressure and constant interruptions of work. The district attorney's office was like a fire department in that the tyranny of the urgent often trumped the important. Holt had a big bite of food in his mouth when Angelina came through the door and kissed him on a bulging cheek.

"Thanks," she said.

"You're welcome," he managed with his mouth slightly open.

Angelina set a bottle of water on the table beside her plate. "No onions?" she asked.

"Right," Holt said as he swallowed the bite. "Do you think a stout whiff of onion on my breath might convince a guilty man to confess?"

Angelina smiled. "You're persuasive with or without onions. But we can't talk about that right now. I need to get some fuel in my tank if I'm going to make it through the afternoon."

During the next few minutes, there was more eating than talking. Angelina wasn't afraid of silence. She'd told him that other men found her willingness to be quiet intimidating. Holt found it refreshing.

"Can we get together for dinner tonight?" Holt asked. "I bet you'd like something raw and Japanese."

"Sorry, I can't," Angelina said and shook her head. "I'm volunteering at the nursing home on Cambridge Avenue. One of the other stylists and I are giving free cuts and perms to some of the residents."

"Wow," Holt replied.

"Don't be impressed with me. It was Jessica's idea. Her grandmother lives there. It will be good PR. A reporter from the newspaper is going to be there."

Angelina chugged the rest of her water and gave Holt a quick kiss before heading out of the kitchen.

"Having lunch with you here in the kitchen makes me feel like we're an old married couple," she said with a smile.

Holt, who was chewing a last bite, raised his eyebrows.

"Not that I'm hinting," she quickly added. "And you don't know if I'd say yes."

—

As he drove back to the office, Holt thought about his mother's not-so-subtle hints that he propose to Angelina before she got tired of waiting on him to act and moved on to someone else. He'd pointed out that Angelina wasn't an unfulfilled woman spending ninety-five percent of her time thinking about marriage. She was a successful businesswoman who'd carved out a nice niche in life. Her decision to let Holt enter her world was made from a position of strength, not need. At least that's what he'd argued before her comment in the salon kitchen.

Holt parked next to an unmarked government car. Inside, Trish Carmichael was talking to Belinda. The deputy sheriff stood when he entered.

"Could I talk to you for a minute?" she asked him.

"Is it about your high school classmate who treated Highway 127 like his personal drag strip?" Holt replied.

"Yes." Trish hung her head.

They went into Holt's office, and Trish sat down. Holt left the door open.

"I'm so sorry and wanted to tell you in person. He tricked me into helping him." Trish paused. "No, I agreed to do it without thinking things through, and then he was totally out of line in the way he presented the situation to you. I didn't promise him anything, only that I'd see if you would talk to him before—"

"Relax," Holt said, holding up his hand to stop the flow of words. "That wasn't the first time someone has tried to manipulate me and used a law enforcement connection to do it. I knew the guy wasn't telling you the truth. He doesn't know it because he was too cheap to hire a lawyer, but with his prior record, cutting the ticket down to fifteen miles over the speed limit will still trigger a huge insurance premium increase. My hope is that this will convince him to slow down. If it doesn't, sooner or later he's going to get jacked up by a judge either here or in Tennessee."

"You're not mad at me?"

"No. I moved on with the calendar and didn't give it a second thought. Judge Lomax had more important matters to consider."

"Thanks," Trish said with obvious relief. "I've been worrying about it ever since I left the courthouse. I called Belinda, and she suggested I apologize to you in person."

"Your unnecessary apology is accepted."

Trish managed a smile. Holt glanced down at his credenza and saw the folder about Rexford Meredith's death. Wanting to help the female deputy move on to another subject, he asked her a question.

"Do you remember when Rex Meredith died?"

"Of course. For weeks it was all anyone talked about."

"What kind of talk?"

"Oh, everything from how much he was worth to who was going to get it. One of his ex-wives tried to swoop in, but she lost in court pretty quickly to Mr. and Mrs. Stevens."

Holt held up the skinny folder. "What about the cause of death? Our file isn't much more than a two-page report from the investigating detectives concluding Meredith died of a self-inflicted gunshot wound to the chest. Do you think there was anything else going on?"

Trish hesitated. "Well, there were rumors about a cover-up of some sort to keep the family from being embarrassed."

"Embarrassed?"

"I'm not sure. Maybe by the suicide or what they found inside the house. A lot of people have secrets. I was in a criminal justice class at the community college, and my professor criticized the way it was handled. I can't remember the details, but he thought it wasn't very professional."

"What was the professor's name?"

"Simpson, but he had a heart attack a couple of years ago and died."

"Then he wouldn't make it on the list," Holt muttered.

"You're reopening the investigation into Mr. Meredith's death?" Trish's eyes opened wider.

"No, no," Holt corrected himself. "Just curious. I believe the owner of my house bought it from Rex Meredith."

"I wouldn't be surprised. Mr. Meredith owned a bunch of rental houses in your neighborhood."

"You know where I live?"

"Yeah. Over on Montgomery Street. Brick ranch-style house with a fenced-in backyard."

"Have you been stalking me?" Holt asked.

Holt watched Trish's face turn red and immediately regretted his words. "I was joking," he added quickly.

"I knew that," Trish replied unconvincingly. "I worked on a case last year involving a man who lived a few doors down from your house. The deputy who went with me to make the arrest showed me where you live."

"That makes sense."

"We never found the defendant. I think someone tipped him off and he left town. He's still on the run."

"Let me know if he surfaces. I want to keep the neighborhood safe."

Trish stood up. Holt's embarrassment about his awkward stalking comment increased, not diminished. He racked his brain for a different topic to end their conversation as he escorted Trish to the front door.

"I appreciate all your help in court," he said. "You have great administrative skills."

"Thanks, that's what every woman loves to hear."

Holt watched Trish walk toward an unmarked police car. She moved with an easy grace. He could definitely imagine her playing basketball.

He spent the next few hours organizing his courtroom notes for Kathy Arnold, the secretary he shared with Jim, then deposited the files on the corner of the secretary's desk. The dark-haired clerical worker was a harried single mom in her late thirties.

"Any fires in there?" she asked when she saw the files. "Don't forget I have to leave thirty minutes early today to take my daughter to the orthodontist."

"No, it's routine. Most of it can wait until tomorrow."

Holt glanced over his shoulder at the door to Ralph Granger's office. It was still shut. "What's Ralph up to?" he asked.

"Meeting with the finance committee for his election campaign."

"That's not until next year."

"I heard him talking to Belinda earlier. He wants to raise a lot of money now and hopes it will discourage anyone else from running against him."

Holt nodded. It wasn't a bad strategy. "Who's on the committee?"

Kathy rattled off the names of four men, including the owner of the town's largest automobile dealership.

"Of course, Greg Stevens is the key," she concluded, lowering her voice. "His wife inherited all the Meredith money from her stepfather. Stevens can stroke a check that would scare off anyone."

"I met him last year at the United Way fund-raiser. I wonder—" Holt started, then stopped.

"What?" Kathy asked.

"Nothing," Holt replied. "Will you let me know when Ralph finishes?"

"Sure."

Back in his office, Holt held the Meredith folder in his hand. He couldn't get over the look in Ralph's eyes when he'd ordered Holt to return the file. To deviate from the DA's specific instructions would be clearly insubordinate. Holt hesitated. Ralph Granger was undeniably paranoid, but sometimes paranoia had a basis in fact. What was Ralph afraid of? And why did he have the Meredith file in the first place?

Rich people did commit suicide, but the skimpy information in Holt's hand spoke of a cover-up, not justice. Holt's job, his duty as a district attorney, and, more importantly, the promise he'd made to Calico's memory, was to do the right thing, no matter what. He removed the sheets from the file and took them to the copier. Kathy was feeding a stack of documents into the machine.

"I'll be here for a few minutes," she said when she saw him. "I can make your copies and bring them to you."

"No, I'll come back later."

Holt waited until Kathy passed by the door of his office on her way back to her desk, then returned to the copy machine. Glancing over his shoulder, he entered the file number for the Meredith investigation into the meter that recorded all copies. He paused with his finger over the Print button, but instead of pushing Print, he canceled the Meredith file number and entered the general number used for miscellaneous copies. There could be no record of his defiance.

He watched as the sheets of paper spit out the other side of the machine.

7

Trish left her cubicle in the administrative area of the sheriff's department and retreated to her car in the parking lot beside the jail. She needed a break from the embarrassing events of the day. First, Holt accused her of stalking him, and then he complimented her administrative skills. It was enough to send a woman into clinical depression.

Turning on the car's air-conditioning, she logged on to a speed chess website on her phone. Players had a maximum of thirty seconds to make a move, and games rarely lasted more than ten minutes.

Trish had started playing chess as a little girl because it was something her father liked to do. When she was eight, she won for the first time, and he printed out a certificate, naming her "The Unbeatable Wonder," which she used as her screen name. The framed certificate now hung on the wall in her bedroom. By the time she was ten they were splitting games fifty-fifty. Two years later, her father almost never won and considered a draw a victory.

There was something about the pieces and the way they moved that made sense to her. Chess books introduced her to basic strategy;

however, Trish possessed the innate ability to see the whole board, anticipate an opponent's likely moves, and plan multiple avenues of attack. Her favorite piece was the queen because of its versatility, but Trish had also developed a knack for utilizing her two knight pieces that gave her opponents fits. The unique movement pattern of the knights made them deceptive defenders and cunning warriors. Trish wished her skill on the chessboard transferred better to the challenges of everyday life.

Her adversary of the day was well known to her. "Pawn King" was a good player, and they often played to a quick draw. Today he uncharacteristically beat her in five minutes when she made an obvious blunder that allowed him to dominate her back row.

"What's wrong?" Pawn King typed in the message box beside the game.

"Stupid move," Trish replied. "But thanks for playing."

"You seem distracted. Are you at work?"

"And have to get back to it."

Trish closed the program. She didn't use the chess site as a place for social networking and knew nothing about the people behind their screen names. It was anonymous, bloodless combat without actual consequences. She returned to work.

Cases flowed to Trish's desk from different places—the county Department of Family and Children's Services, the local juvenile court, and Belinda at the district attorney's office. A key trigger to Trish's involvement occurred when children started receiving government benefits that wouldn't be necessary if a parent, usually the father, were paying adequate child support. Her job was to locate the delinquent parent and try to persuade him or her to voluntarily fulfill their financial obligations to their children.

It wasn't always as black and white as the pieces on a chessboard. Discretion played a role when there were reasons such as poor health or inability to work that explained why support wasn't being paid. The toughest part of the job was trying not to let her heart rule her head, in either righteous anger or misplaced mercy. Trish didn't consider herself intimidating, but when she called and identified herself as "Deputy Carmichael," some people quickly gave her respect. Others cursed and hung up the phone.

She clicked open the attachment to an e-mail from a DFACS worker. This time a mother was in the legal crosshairs. The woman had lost custody of her little girl in a juvenile court proceeding and was ordered to pay child support while the child lived with a foster family. After two payments the woman stopped depositing money with the court clerk. She'd not returned phone calls from the case worker and hadn't made an effort to exercise the limited visitation with her daughter granted by the judge.

The mother wasn't working when she'd gone to court, and Trish guessed she'd borrowed the initial two payments of child support from family members. Trish opened a new screen on her computer so she could take notes, said a quick prayer, and dialed the last known contact number.

—

Ralph Granger brought the members of his campaign finance committee to Holt's office. When the group appeared in his doorway, Holt slid the Meredith file away from the edge of his desk and stood up.

"Some of you may know Holt Douglas," Ralph said. "He's been with us for, what is it, Holt? Eighteen months?"

"A little over two years, sir."

"And he's doing a great job," Ralph said. "He was a top student at Emory Law School and turned down a job at King and Spalding to come here."

"I interviewed with them on campus but didn't get a call back," Holt corrected. "My offer was from a firm in Buckhead."

"Which would have paid you a lot more than you're making serving the people of this judicial district," Ralph responded smoothly. "Having someone of Holt's caliber on board is a selling point for the campaign. Retention of skilled prosecutors is a challenge for non-urban areas, and with Holt and Jim, I've been able to do that."

Holt winced. Jim Montgomery had settled comfortably into the role of a second-string career prosecutor with no ambition beyond a state pension. Holt's future plans included the goal of landing a job as a federal prosecutor like Calico's uncle. He'd not made any long-term promises to the DA.

"Ralph, you did a good job training Skip Patrick," said Pat Kirby, owner of Kirby's Auto Sales. "He's doing a super job as our company lawyer. He knows how to write an opinion letter even I can understand."

All the men except Ralph laughed. The DA didn't say anything. Holt knew Ralph considered Skip a traitor for leaving after only a few years of public service. Kirby turned to Holt.

"I saw you and Skip eating at the Crosswalk Café last week."

"We're still friends," Holt said, glancing at Ralph. "It's great that you're pleased with his work. He helped me a lot when I first came to Paxton."

Greg Stevens stepped forward. The balding, middle-aged man who managed Meredith Enterprises had the demeanor of a bookish accountant. Holt shook Stevens's hand, which was surprisingly soft and slightly greasy. The thought crossed Holt's mind that Stevens used lotion.

"We met last year at the community fund-raiser," Stevens said. "I think you bid on the bamboo fly-fishing rod I donated."

Holt was impressed that Stevens could recall the early bidding on the classic piece of fishing equipment. The auction tag on the rod indicated it had originally been purchased by Mr. Meredith for three thousand dollars.

"I didn't get the rod, but at least I drove the price up a few hundred dollars before dropping out."

"It was one of several that Mr. Meredith owned. If you'd ever like to borrow one and take it on a fishing trip, let me know. No one uses them now."

"Thanks, but I'd be afraid I might damage it."

"They're insured," Stevens replied with a wave of his hand.

"It would be fun to see what it felt like," Holt admitted, "but I don't have any trips planned right now."

Stevens reached into his jacket pocket and handed Holt his card. "Call me when you do."

"I won't keep you gentlemen any longer," Ralph said. "Thanks again for agreeing to help. I couldn't do my job without folks like you behind me."

A few minutes later, Holt glanced up from his desk and saw Ralph walking down the hallway. He grabbed the Meredith folder and caught up with the DA near Belinda's desk.

"Here's the Meredith information," he said.

Ralph jerked the file from Holt's hand. "I thought I told you to get that back to me immediately."

"Sorry. I hope it didn't create a problem with Mr. Stevens."

"Why would it?"

Holt had fallen into a trap of his own making. "Uh, I'm sure it's still a sensitive subject."

"The family has moved on from the tragedy."

"Sure," Holt said, nodding. "How was the meeting with the campaign finance committee?"

"Very good." Ralph's face brightened. "We're going to wait until a couple of months before qualifying opens and announce the formation of a reelection committee. Word will leak out that I have as much money in the bank as I spent for the entire campaign when Lynnwood Nolte ran against me three years ago. Have you heard the rumors that he wants another crack at my job?"

"Yes."

"Who mentioned it?"

"Someone we both know who doesn't want to be quoted on the record."

"Skip." Ralph grunted.

Holt allowed silence to serve as confirmation.

When he left the DA's office after two and a half years, Bernard "Skip" Patrick went to work for the largest firm in town. Vernon Spratt III, the firm's senior partner, had served eight terms as a legislator in the General Assembly in Atlanta and wielded a lot of political clout in Ashley County. He viewed Ralph as an outsider because the DA was from Triplett County and therefore shouldn't be in charge of anything that had to do with the most populous county in the judicial circuit. When he first encountered such microscopic regionalism, Holt was amused. Now he accepted it as reality for those who'd grown up in the area.

"What about Sheriff Blackstone?" Holt asked. "Will he back you?"

"That's being negotiated," Ralph answered cryptically. "Getting Craig Stevens on my side for this round was a coup. Rex Meredith never supported me, but he couldn't get anyone from Ashley County who knew their way around a courtroom to run against me. If Nolte had been around back then . . ." Ralph stopped as he considered the catastrophic possibility.

"If you want to keep Stevens on your side, you'd better call him Greg, not Craig," Holt said.

Ralph slapped his hands together. "I went to high school with a boy named Craig Stevens, and I'm always having to catch myself when I'm around Greg. I hope I didn't slip up during our meeting."

Muttering, Ralph continued down the hall to his office. Even if Ralph had a big war chest, Holt knew Lynnwood Nolte was a legitimate threat. Nolte had been practicing law in Paxton for ten years and had an engaging personality. He devoted only a small percentage of his law practice to criminal cases—the vast majority of people charged with crimes who could afford to hire a good attorney retained Dirk Rangel. But Nolte was a natural politician, and lawyers could be elected district attorney based on popularity. A public stumble or embarrassing mistake by any member of the district attorney's office could turn the tide of an election in a flash.

At 5:45 p.m. Holt left the office. After pulling into his driveway, he went inside the house and let Henry in from the backyard. Holt loved daylight saving time. The extra hour of sunlight in the evenings allowed him more time to be outside when he got home from work. While Henry ate his supper, Holt changed into gym shorts, T-shirt, and basketball shoes. When Henry saw what Holt was wearing, the dog abandoned his food bowl and dashed toward the front door, jumping up toward the doorknob.

Holt played basketball at an outdoor court set up in the parking lot of the Paxton Apostolic Church, located four blocks from his house. Basketball goals at each end of the court were strung with metal nets. A bright orange line divided the court, and the lanes beneath the baskets and free throw lines were marked with lime-green paint. Holt popped open the trunk of his car and took out a leather basketball. Henry danced around at his feet until Holt rolled the ball onto the court.

"Go!" Holt commanded.

The dog took off after the ball and corralled it with his nose and front legs. Pushing it in front of him, he guided it back to Holt.

"Good boy," Holt said.

Holt dribbled the ball across the court, and Henry took up his usual position beneath one of the baskets. The dog's eyes didn't leave the ball as Holt stepped to the free throw line for some warm-up shots. The first five shots went through perfectly, but on the sixth try the ball bounced off the side of the rim and toward the edge of the court.

"Go!" Holt called out, and Henry shot after the errant ball. He rolled it back to Holt's feet, and Holt scratched the top of the dog's head as a reward.

Holt continued shooting free throws, not stopping until he'd made a hundred shots. His longest unbroken streak of the evening was thirteen. After completing the free throws, he stretched his muscles for a few minutes and then went through some of the drills that had been part of his life when he played basketball in high school. Routines he'd found tedious as a teenager were now welcomed as aerobic exercise. It was a fast-paced workout designed to elevate his heart rate as quickly as possible and keep it in the training zone. Henry barked encouragement and retrieved balls when they bounced toward the edge of the court. After a series of fast drives from one end of the court to the other, each time ending in a layup, Holt paused with his hands on his knees to catch his breath. The back door to the church opened, and a slightly stoop-shouldered black man came out of the brown-brick building.

Bishop Alexander Pennington made his way toward the basketball court.

8

Holt didn't know Bishop Pennington's exact age, but the gray-haired preacher had been an influential figure in the community since he was a young minister during the racial tensions of the late 1960s. Maligned then as a troublemaker by those chained to the status quo, the bishop had been an agent for progress whose moral integrity and persuasive oratory influenced both blacks and whites.

Holt bounced the ball to him. The minister caught it in one of his large hands and in a single motion rolled it toward the opposite end of the court.

"Go!" he yelled to Henry in a sonorous bass voice.

Henry chased down the ball and returned it to Holt.

"Your voice is way better than mine," Holt said, picking up the ball, "but he plays on my team."

Bishop Pennington smiled. He walked over to the free throw line, and Holt handed him the ball.

"God casts his gifts with a broad hand," the minister said. "I've got my voice. You've got your jump shot."

Bishop Pennington eyed the basket for a few seconds and carefully took a shot. It went in, touching nothing but net. Holt handed the ball to him so he could shoot again, but he shook his head.

"No. One for one is a good day on the basketball court for me. And I didn't come down to interrupt your workout."

"I'm finished except for a few cool-down exercises."

The bishop went to the edge of the court and slowly lowered himself to the ground. Henry trotted over and he scratched the top of the dog's head. The minister was one of the few people in the small circle of Henry's human friends. When Holt traveled out of town, Bishop Pennington took care of the dog.

"I'm glad to see you," Holt said as he stretched to one side. "I have a case I wanted to ask you about. Do you know Samuel Byers?"

"Yes," the bishop replied. "I know Sammy and his daddy and his uncles and both his brothers. I heard he was in trouble. What are the charges against him?"

"It's a felony theft case, one count. I'm wondering whether he deserves a second chance through the first offender program or needs jail time to be taught a lesson."

Bishop Pennington occasionally gave Holt useful background information, and he valued the minister's insight into people and his perspectives on justice.

"Was he with someone else when this happened?" the bishop asked.

"Darryl Taylor."

"Darryl's been getting into trouble for years."

"Right, but the most I can hang on him is a coconspirator charge. Byers did the crime."

"Darryl likely put Sammy up to it, which isn't an excuse, but spending time in jail around more people like Darryl isn't going to point Sammy in the right direction. If he's on probation, Sammy's family will rally around him. He struggled in school and is more of a follower than a leader. Put him with the right crowd, and he'll be okay."

Holt nodded. "That helps."

"I'd like to come to court when he's sentenced so I can speak a word or two while his heart is tender. I know one of Sammy's uncles real well. It might be good if he's there, too."

"I'll be sure to let you know when it comes up."

Holt stretched a different set of muscles. Bishop Pennington looked up at the trees along the edge of the church property where some small yellow birds were flitting from branch to branch.

"What kind of birds are those?" Holt asked.

"American goldfinch. They've been eating seed from a finch sock I hung up outside my office window in the church a couple of weeks ago. I hope they're calling their friends over for a picnic."

Holt finished stretching and retrieved the bottle of water from his car. Before drinking any himself, he poured a small amount into his hand for Henry.

"May I give him some?" the bishop asked when Henry finished.

Holt poured water into the cracked palm of the black man. Henry quickly lapped it up. Holt took a deep drink himself and offered the bottle to the bishop, who shook his head.

"Thanks, but you and Henry need it more than I do."

Holt listened again to the call of the birds and thought about the bishop's insight into Samuel Byers's situation.

"I wish you could put what you know about life and people in a bottle so I could drink it."

The minister looked up from his seat on the ground. "Are you serious?" he asked. "Knowledge comes wrapped in responsibility."

Holt glanced down into the bishop's eyes. The wisdom of the old man's soul was way over Holt's head.

"Uh, maybe not," Holt said and took another drink of water. He held out his hand and helped the bishop to his feet.

"That saved me a few aching moments."

It was the bishop's turn to stretch his arms and bend over slightly. Holt screwed the cap onto the water bottle and picked up his basketball. Henry trotted around his feet in a tight circle, not sure if they were going to play some more or leave for home.

"Hey, how well did you know Rex Meredith?" Holt asked as he cradled the ball beneath his arm.

The bishop stopped and stared at him for a moment. "That's the second big question you've asked me in the past few minutes. Unless you want to make me late for supper, you'd better whittle it down to a smaller size or save that discussion for another day."

"We can save it. I don't want you to go hungry."

—

Trish plodded through the front door and collapsed in her father's old recliner.

"The food's in the oven," Marge said from her wheelchair in the kitchen. "It'll be ready in less than five minutes."

"I'm not sure I want to go to church," Trish said. "I've had a rough day. Why don't I drop you off and come back later to pick you up?"

Ever since she was a little girl, Trish had loved the variety offered at the weekly covered-dish suppers held at the country church she and her mother still attended. As a teenager, she'd taken pride in preparing a dish that people outside her family could enjoy. But now, because of her work schedule, it fell to Marge to do the cooking. Her specialties were casseroles made with vegetables grown in the small garden they planted each spring. Much of the harvest was frozen in plastic bags to use until the next crop came in. Marge's broccoli and yellow squash casseroles were world-class quality.

"No, you need something to take your mind off whatever happened at work," Marge said. "And you've enjoyed Brother Carpenter's series on the tabernacle."

Marge was right. Trish had found the messages about the symbolism contained in the tent of worship and Old Testament sacrifices much more fascinating than she would have expected.

"I was stuck in the wilderness today," Trish sighed. "Do you remember Donnie Crowder? He showed up in court this morning and convinced me to help him with a speeding ticket."

Halfway through her story, the timer beeped in the kitchen. Trish took a squash casserole out of the oven. The dish was topped with bubbling cheese. Bits of chopped onion peeked through.

"This looks great," she said to her mother.

"And I'm not going to let you have any if you stay here. You'll have to eat leftovers when I come home."

"There won't be any leftovers."

"It's your choice," Marge said.

"Okay, I'll go," Trish sighed.

—

"Do you think Keith will be there?" Marge asked later as Trish opened the door of the customized van they used to transport Marge and her wheelchair.

"I don't know."

"Did you call him back?"

"Not yet."

Trish knew she should have returned Keith's call, but her mind had been on Holt Douglas. However, she now wondered if her budding interest in the young prosecutor should be nipped like the first blossoms on a tomato plant.

Trish waited while her mother rolled her wheelchair onto the electric lift before she pressed the button that caused it to rise to the level of the van's floor. Trish was strong enough to pick up her more petite mother, but keeping Marge in the wheelchair worked the best when going to church. Trish carefully placed the casserole dish at her mother's feet.

It was a ten-minute drive to the church that was founded in 1865 when a group of local farming families started holding religious services beneath a brush arbor. Now the congregation met in a narrow wooden sanctuary painted white and topped by a steeple with a bell that a deacon rang before the eleven o'clock service on Sunday mornings. Covered-dish suppers took place in an adjacent fellowship hall. The church had experienced a growth spurt under Brother Carpenter's leadership, and the deacons had recently rented two trailers formerly used by the local school system to provide more space for Sunday school classes. Stretching most of the way up a hillside to the north of the sanctuary was the church cemetery. After 150 years, even a small church could populate a large cemetery.

Trish's father was buried in the northeast corner. She no longer glanced toward the grave every time she drove onto the property, but this evening, as she lowered her mother's wheelchair to the ground, she noticed Marge's eyes wander up the gently sloping hill.

"The daffodils on the grave were gorgeous, weren't they?" Trish said. "There were twice as many as we had last year. Now that they're gone, do you want me to put together an artificial arrangement?"

"That would be nice, but I'd like to help select the flowers."

"We'll do it this weekend. I don't have to work on Saturday."

Marge's arms were strong enough to propel the wheelchair across the parking lot. Carrying the hot casserole with oven mitts, Trish walked beside her. Inside the fellowship hall, Trish placed the dish in the section reserved for vegetables, between a ceramic bowl of creamed corn and pot of green beans seasoned with tiny bits of smoked sausage. The meat selections on a long table included fried chicken, baked chicken, chicken casserole, barbecued pork, and a sliced ham. Trish recognized the platter beneath the ham as belonging to Keith's mother. People were milling about the room. Keith wasn't there. His mother, a jovial, rotund woman, came over and gave her a hug.

"Keith may get here later," Mrs. Bonita Pierce said. "He's on the road coming back from Montgomery."

Trish genuinely liked Keith's mother and believed the jolly, easygoing woman with kind brown eyes would make a great mother-in-law. Bonita encouraged Trish's and Keith's interest in each other with unabashed zeal. Initially, Trish had valued her as an ally. Now she saw Bonita as someone who might be hurt and disappointed. Trish sighed. Terminating a romantic relationship with someone whose family attended the church could turn out to be a big mess.

Trish joined her mother, who'd parked her wheelchair in a corner of the room. More and more people arrived and filled the fellowship hall with noise. Someone let out a loud whistle, and conversation died down. Brother Carpenter, a microphone in his hand, took his place behind a slender wooden podium.

"Before I pray the blessing for the meal, I want to let everyone know we're in for a treat tonight. After we finish eating, we'll be joined by two special guests who will make an important announcement about the future of the church."

"Is it the two witnesses in the book of Revelation?" called out a man to the right of the preacher. "I'd like to know who those fellows are."

"No, Bill. And if you remember, one of their jobs was calling down fire from heaven that destroyed everyone who was in rebellion against the Lord. We don't want them visiting here until we all get a chance to repent."

"I'm hungry!" another male voice spoke up.

"Which is why I'm going to pray," the preacher replied and then bowed his head.

People quickly lined up at the long row of tables covered with food.

The rest of the room was set up for seating. Trish and Marge held back. Marge didn't like the special attention she received because of her paralysis, even though Trish tried to reassure her that people deferred to her because they loved her, not out of pity. Brother Carpenter came over to them.

"Get in line, Marge," he commanded. "Nobody here likes you holding back."

"I've tried to tell her that," Trish said. "But she won't—"

"All right," Marge said grumpily as she propelled herself forward. "I'm not going to fight both of you."

Trish looked over her mother's head at Brother Carpenter and mouthed a silent thank-you. The two women went down the line together. Over half the squash casserole was gone by the time they reached it. Trish scooped out a generous portion for herself.

"I'll pass on it so someone else can have some," her mother said.

"Not me," Trish said. "Charity has its limits when it comes to one of your casseroles."

"Amen," said a deep voice behind them that belonged to Marvin Frick, one of the church deacons. "I'd rather ask for forgiveness than miss out on your squash."

When their plates were full, they returned to a table at the back corner of the room. Trish was hungry. She'd skipped lunch so she could wait for Holt and apologize.

"Where's Keith?" one of her mother's friends asked.

"His mama said he's coming in tonight from Montgomery," Trish said.

"That Keith Pierce is a hard worker," another woman said. "It'll be a lucky girl who catches him."

Trish didn't respond. The back door of the fellowship hall opened, and Brother Carpenter jumped up from his seat. Trish turned so she could see who had come into the room.

It was Greg and Valerie Stevens.

9

Except for Brother Carpenter, who always wore a coat and tie, the weekly supper crowd at Trish's church dressed casually. Greg Stevens was wearing a blue suit, white shirt, and yellow tie. His wife, a petite woman in her mid-forties with dark hair and brown eyes, had on a simple blue dress that nevertheless looked expensive. As she passed close by, Trish could see a gold necklace around her neck with something very large and shiny hanging from it. Marge leaned over to Trish and whispered the question that was echoing throughout the room.

"What are they doing here?"

No one sitting within earshot offered an opinion. Brother Carpenter ushered the couple to the front of the room, where there were two empty chairs waiting for them. Everything seemed to have been planned in advance. The preacher picked up a handheld microphone.

"Good evening, everyone. I'd like us to give a warm welcome to Mr. and Mrs. Greg Stevens."

The preacher stepped back and started clapping. Puzzled, Trish put her hands together a few times. There was spotty applause around the room, more so from the area where most of the deacons sat with their wives. Brother Carpenter cleared his throat.

"At our annual leaders' retreat last year, the board of deacons adopted a new church vision statement. Several of the action points from that meeting have already been implemented. We've added two new Sunday school classes, the missions committee identified a couple who are now receiving monthly support for an outreach to orphans in Sri Lanka, the padding in the sanctuary pews has been replaced, and"—Brother Carpenter paused and glanced at Mr. and Mrs. Stevens—"we're expanding our ministry to abused and battered women."

The outreach to women in trouble was unusual for a rural congregation and thrilled Trish, who'd referred several women, most recently Amanda Callaway, to the church for short-term help.

Brother Carpenter continued, "The greatest challenge we face as we move forward as a congregation serving this community is inadequate space. Carol, my new administrative assistant, has an office the size of a closet, and the midweek meeting has outgrown this building. Church growth experts agree that these types of problems can stop a church in its tracks." Brother Carpenter raised his voice to preaching volume before saying, "But we're not going to let that happen, are we?"

A smattering of "Amens" came in response to the minister's challenge. Trish suspected where the meeting was going but not exactly how it was going to get there. Brother Carpenter reached down and picked up a large piece of foam board and placed it on a flimsy easel that Marvin Frick opened behind him. It was an artist's rendering of a building.

"The deacons have been working with a local architectural firm on the design of a new multipurpose structure to be built where we now sit. This building will be torn down and replaced by a facility that will serve people in this part of Ashley County for the foreseeable future. All of this would still be a dream in our hearts if not for the offer of help from Mr. and Mrs. Stevens. They learned of our need from Luther Fletchall, and a generous door of God's opportunity opened."

Fletchall, a deacon, did maintenance work on residential rental property owned by Meredith Enterprises.

"At this time, I'd like to introduce a man who needs no introduction to most of you. Please welcome Mr. Greg Stevens."

This time the applause was more enthusiastic and spread across the room. Brother Carpenter handed the microphone to Mr. Stevens.

"Thank you, Reverend Carpenter," Greg Stevens said. "It's an honor for my wife and me to be with you this evening."

Trish watched the preacher's expression. No one called him "Reverend Carpenter," and he often told the congregation the only reverends he knew wore black robes and served fancy churches in big cities. Apparently Mr. Stevens hadn't gotten the memo on ministerial titles. Tonight, the toothy smile on Brother Carpenter's face remained fixed.

"As many of you know, the Meredith family has been committed to the growth and prosperity of Ashley County for generations. My wife's stepfather, Rexford Meredith, carried on this tradition and spent his whole life seeking to make this a better place for all to live."

Mr. Meredith had a reputation as a hard, stingy man, and Trish doubted Stevens's claim would receive majority agreement in the room.

"After meeting with Reverend Carpenter and other leaders of the church, Valerie and I believe this congregation deserves our help." Mr. Stevens pointed to the artist's rendering. "The estimated cost of the multipurpose building is $1,500,000. My wife and I are willing to commit $500,000 toward the project, so long as the remaining balance is raised by gifts and pledges over three years from the members of the congregation and other supporters in the community. We look forward to partnering together in this worthwhile cause. Thank you very much."

Stevens sat down. Trish's mouth had dropped open, and she quickly closed it. The cost of the building might not seem like an astronomical amount to some churches. Her church wasn't one of them. She didn't question Mr. and Mrs. Stevens's ability to write a huge check without putting a dent in their lifestyle. The mystery was where the money to trigger the matching gift would come from within the congregation. When the offering plates came by on Sunday morning, there was more cash than checks in them. There wasn't a doctor, lawyer, or accountant on the church roll. The only semiprofessional member was an independent insurance agent who had a tiny office in a strip center on the edge of Paxton.

Trish and the other women at their table returned to their meals, but there was now only one topic of conversation in the room.

"Old Mr. Meredith would spin in his grave if he knew they were giving away some of his money to a country church," said the woman who'd mentioned that Keith was a hard worker and prize matrimonial prospect.

"Hush, Frieda," said another woman. "You know what the Bible says: 'The wealth of the sinner is laid up for the just.' We should be thankful."

When Mr. and Mrs. Stevens got up to leave, all eyes in the room followed them as Brother Carpenter escorted them to the door. After they were gone, Trish took a deep breath and exhaled. She wasn't sure exactly why.

The Bible teaching for the evening focused on the table of shewbread in the tabernacle. Trish took a few notes but had trouble concentrating on the message. After the service ended, the conversation immediately returned to Greg and Valerie Stevens and their gift. Normally, Trish and her mother lingered on covered-dish nights so

Marge, who spent most of the week housebound, could enjoy the social interaction with her friends.

"Let's go," Trish said to Marge.

"Why? You're not going to sleep when we get home. You'll be up on your computer for hours."

"Not tonight. I'm really tired."

It was dusk as they crossed the parking lot to the van. A vehicle with its headlights on approached. It was Keith's car. The square-jawed former high school linebacker had inherited his mother's kind brown eyes and his father's reddish-brown hair. He pulled up to them and rolled down his window.

"Sorry I didn't get back in time for supper," Keith said. "The traffic was terrible when I hit Atlanta, but I wanted to at least say hello before I head to the house."

"You missed a big meeting," Marge said. "Greg and Valerie Stevens came. They're going to—"

"Yeah, I know all about it," Keith cut in. "The half-million-dollar challenge. How did it go?"

"I think everyone is in shock," Marge said.

"And I'm wondering how the congregation is going to come up with the matching part, much less an extra five hundred thousand," Trish added. "It sounds like the new building will get a lot of good use, but what if Brother Carpenter gets a chance to go to a bigger church? A lot of the new folks are here because of him. If he leaves, will they stay?"

"I guess the deacons can try to borrow some of the money from a bank," Marge said.

Keith shook his head. "That's against one of Mr. Stevens's stipulations. Didn't they mention that in the meeting?"

"No," Trish replied. "How did you know about all this in advance?"

"Brother Carpenter took me to lunch last week and told me. He's trying to get a feel for what the congregation can give. He knows I've had a few good years because my business is growing like crazy."

Trish's eyes widened. Keith had been driving the same car since he returned home after graduating from college, and he didn't have any of the trappings of increasing wealth. She had no idea how much he made in a year.

"I've paid off all my student loans and saved every penny I can set aside," he continued. "For the future."

"We'll all have to dig deep to help the church," Marge said.

"Yeah," Keith said, then looked at Trish. "Hey, I'm in town for the next four days. Can we get together? I've missed you."

"Uh, Friday night is open. I work the early shift and get off at three in the afternoon."

"Great. I'll pick you up at six? Have you been to the new steak house?"

"No, but I've heard it's good."

"Let's check it out."

"Sure, I'd like that."

Keith drove off. Trish opened the door of the van and lowered the wheelchair lift. Neither woman spoke as they left the parking lot.

"How much money do we have left from the settlement for the wreck?" Marge asked after several minutes passed.

Trish tightened her grip on the steering wheel. "Mama, you know you shouldn't touch that. It's all you've got for the future, and I'm planning on you living for a long, long time. If I ever get married and move out of the house, you'll need to be even more careful with your money than we are now."

"Maybe I'm supposed to trust the Lord for my future."

"This van has over one hundred thousand miles on it. It's going to need to be replaced with another one that can accommodate the lift. And Dr. Ross said there could be all kinds of health issues that may come up as you get older that you wouldn't have had to face if—" Trish stopped.

"I was normal? That's how I'm trying to think for the first time in four years. If your daddy were alive, he'd give first and worry about the consequences later. That's the way he looked at things our entire marriage."

Trish didn't respond. There was no denying that her father unselfishly cared about people. She ran into men and women all the time who shared stories of his anonymous giving and private acts of kindness. And unlike Greg and Valerie Stevens, he'd written checks that had an impact on those families' lifestyles. Her parents had remained in the same house when it would have been financially possible to move to a bigger one. Trish felt torn between wanting to protect her mother and being generous like her father.

"There's $387,542, give or take a few dollars," she said as they neared home. "That's how much is in the bank as of the statement we received last week. And don't forget, you already wrote the church a big check when the case settled."

"You heard what Brother Carpenter said about helping more women in trouble."

"Yes, and I'd like more details about the plan."

Trish helped her mother roll the wheelchair up the ramp to the front of the house. As she unlocked the door, Trish heard the phone ringing. She hurried inside to answer it.

"Hello."

"Trish?"

"Yes."

"This is Brother Carpenter. I didn't get a chance to speak to your mother before you left this evening. Is she available?"

Trish glanced toward the front door as her mother slowly navigated her way into the house. "Not right now. Can I give her a message?"

"Of course. I'd like to set up a time to sit down and chat with her about the exciting opportunities at church. Part of that could be an enduring legacy that honors your father."

"Okay, I'll let her know." Trish pressed her lips together tightly as she hung up the phone.

"Who was it?" her mother asked.

"Brother Carpenter. He wants to talk to you about giving to the building project. They probably want to stick a plaque on the wall and put Daddy's name on it underneath Greg and Valerie Stevens's names. Who knows? If he gives enough money, they might put Keith's name on it, too."

10

On Holt's desk was a copy of the local newspaper opened to the article about Angelina's visit to the nursing home. The upbeat text was supplemented by photos of before-and-after pictures of residents whose hair had been cut and styled. Holt smiled as he read the article. Angelina knew how to turn on the charm, and he was sure she'd been a hit with the older ladies. He dialed the phone number for the salon. Brittany answered. Holt disguised his voice.

"This is Dexter Strickland. I understand from the article in the newspaper that you specialize in haircuts for older women. I'd like to schedule an appointment for my ninety-year-old mother. She's a sweet lady, even though she drools a lot and forgets to—"

"Holt, this isn't working," Brittany interrupted him. "Angelina told me your mother drives a red SUV and looks ten years younger than her age."

Holt dropped the facade. "How did you know it was me?"

"Duh. The caller ID popped up from the district attorney's office. Who else could it be? You're the one showing signs of early senility, and I bet you drooled all the time when you were a baby."

"I'm sure I did. Is Angelina available?"

"No, she's in the middle of a color for a woman who came in early this morning. I think the customer is going out of town or something."

"Okay. Tell the boss the article was great, and I'm proud of her."

"She had a blast. I think they're going to do it again around Christmastime and take the entire salon. They'll make those ladies so hot every bachelor in town over the age of seventy will be hanging around the building like stray dogs. Hey, I gotta go. Two lines are ringing."

After Holt hung up the phone, he pulled the Samuel Byers case from the file cabinet and sent an e-mail to the defendant's lawyer, proposing closely supervised probation with harsh penalties if Byers slipped up again. Within seconds Holt received a reply from the attorney that he would discuss the offer with his client.

There were several new files on Holt's credenza, and he spent the rest of the morning organizing them and making phone calls to determine the holes he needed to fill. He'd learned how to sift through the police jargon that made the cases sound more airtight than they were. Shortly before noon he received a text message from Skip Patrick inviting him to lunch.

—

There were more eating options in Paxton than a visitor might have guessed. Holt walked to Hamilton Street, the main thoroughfare that ran in front of the courthouse, and turned right. Two blocks later, he ducked into a side alley that was so narrow only a single car could pass at a time. A hundred feet down the alley was a low-slung building with red paint peeling off the wooden exterior. A faded sign identified the place as Jake's Smokehouse. Puffs of aromatic wood smoke drifted over the top of the building and drew in customers like late summer bugs to a front porch light. Holt opened a screen door and went inside. At 12:05 p.m., the restaurant was already packed with a lunchtime crowd. Skip raised his hand. He was sitting at a table for two on the right-hand side of the room. Holt made his way over to him and slid into a chair across from the shorter, heavier lawyer whose dark hair was beginning to thin on top.

"I ordered our drinks," Skip said. "It's so busy we'll be lucky if HC brings them in the next five minutes."

Holly Carol Smith, or HC to everyone who knew her, was Jake's wife and served as hostess and dining room supervisor. There were plenty of men in Ashley County who went by some combination of initials, but it was unusual for a woman to shorten her name to two letters of the alphabet. Most of the servers and cooks at the smokehouse were family members. If one of Jake's relatives was laid off or needed a place to work in between jobs, they knew where to go. HC placed glasses of tea on the table in front of them. Her wiry body was as full of energy as a coiled spring.

"If you want to tell me what you're eating, I'll put it in for you, and one of the girls can deliver it," she said. "You can see we're slammed."

"Brisket plate with mac and cheese and baked beans," Skip responded immediately.

"And you'll have burnt ends with skillet-fried yellow squash and slaw," HC said to Holt without waiting for him to speak.

"Yes, ma'am. Thanks for taking care of me."

"You're still on my good side," HC replied as she turned and headed toward the kitchen.

"I wish Jake had gotten a speeding ticket while I was working at the DA's office," Skip said.

"It wasn't just a speeding ticket. His driver's license had expired, the car hadn't been inspected in three years, he had no proof of insurance, two taillights were out, and he had an illegal muffler."

Skip laughed.

"And I took care of it over a bowl of banana pudding," Holt said. "He didn't even have to come to court."

"Did you pay for the pudding?"

"You bet I did. Otherwise it would have been an ethical violation."

Holt squeezed a thick slice of lemon into the tea to cut its intense sweetness and took a sip.

"How's politics at the DA's office?" Skip asked.

"Heating up," Holt replied.

"Mr. Spratt found out about the meeting Ralph had with Greg Stevens," Skip said. "It really set him off. He thought for sure Stevens would back Nolte this time around."

"No comment," Holt replied.

"Come on," Skip said. "It's me. Who else was at the meeting?"

"Somebody who really likes cars."

"Pat Kirby?"

Holt took another sip of tea.

"Mr. Spratt can't get mad at him," Skip said. "The firm does a ton of work for him."

"And Kirby sang your praises," Holt said.

"In front of Ralph?"

"Yes."

Skip grinned. "I bet he loved that."

One of the regular waitresses brought their food. Burnt ends, the heavily smoked bits of charred meat cut from the edge of a thick piece of brisket, weren't listed as a regular menu item and were reserved for special customers. Once gone, there wouldn't be any more until the following day.

"Give me one," Skip said, eyeing Holt's plate.

There were six chunks of blackened meat on the plate, each amounting to no more than two or three bites. Holt hesitated.

"I have some gift cards at the office for the new steak house," Skip said. "We did the legal work for the owners, and they want to build a customer base. I'll give you one so you can take Angelina out for dinner."

Holt stuck his fork into the smallest burnt end.

"No." Skip reached across the table with his fork and stabbed a much larger one. "That makes it a fair trade."

For the next few minutes they focused on food. Holt's first bite of the burnt ends yielded a nice crunch followed by the pungent smokiness of the moist meat within.

"Something that tastes this good can't be good for you," he said as he finished off a morsel and eyed the two remaining pieces on his plate.

"If you're not going to finish them—" Skip said.

"Don't misinterpret what I mean. My comment is like the non-questions you used to ask witnesses. You know, the ones that had such an obvious answer it made the members of the jury roll their eyes."

"I don't know what you're talking about."

"*State v. Grover*. You were cross-examining a country guy named Lickety—"

"Don't bring that up. I'm enjoying my lunch," Skip cut in. "Tell me something else complimentary Mr. Kirby said about me."

"Uh, he can understand your well-crafted opinion letters."

"Who else was there besides Stevens and Kirby?"

"Larry Morris and Ben Porterhouse."

"Big financial hitters," Skip replied.

Holt sipped his tea. "Speaking of big financial hitters, what do you remember about the investigation into the death of Stevens's father-in-law?" Holt asked.

"Rex Meredith?"

"Yeah."

"Not much. Ralph handled that directly. I don't think the case was open for more than a month or so. He huddled up a few times with the detectives who worked the investigation, then issued a press release confirming it was a suicide. One evening when I was alone at the office, I peeked at the photos of the scene. It was ugly."

"There were pictures?"

"At least ten or twelve. Why?"

"Ralph left the file in my office the other day. All it contained was the death certificate, a diagram of the scene, and a two-page report by one of the detectives. It seemed kind of skimpy for such a high-profile situation."

"Who was the detective?"

"Butch Clovis."

"That sounds right. But he wasn't the only one who worked the case. There was another officer involved who left the sheriff's department before you came to town." Skip paused. "What was his name?"

Holt ignored his food while he waited.

"McHenry or McReynolds. Something like that. He quit after a few months. I'm not sure where he went."

"But he was a detective?"

"Yeah, and he wasn't a young guy. He'd worked in law enforcement before. Belinda can tell you. She remembers stuff like that. Why are you interested? Are you treating it like a cold case?"

"Not really. I was just curious, especially when I've seen thicker files in trespassing cases."

"Well, the photos may have been shredded when no charges were filed. The family wouldn't want pictures like that getting posted on the Internet."

Their waitress returned. "Room for peach cobbler or banana pudding?" she asked.

"Not here," Skip said.

"Me either," Holt added.

"And give me the check," Skip said. "My friend here only makes what the taxpayers give him."

"The taxpayer who owns this place already told me to comp his meal," the waitress replied as she motioned to HC, who was running the cash register. "You're the only one who has to pay."

Holt smiled at Skip and shrugged. "Cops and firemen get free meals," Holt said. "Why not a lowly assistant DA?"

"Hey, I'm happy for you," Skip said. "When our firm runner goes to the courthouse tomorrow, I'll have her drop off the gift card for the steak house. Make sure Angelina knows it came from me. If the two of you ever break up, I want to be first in line outside her door."

—

"I can tell where you ate lunch," Belinda said, wrinkling up her nose. "You smell smoky enough to dip in barbecue sauce and put between two pieces of white bread."

"If I had to try a case this afternoon, would that help or hurt me with a jury?" Holt asked.

"Probably help. There aren't many vegans in Ashley County."

Holt glanced toward the door to Ralph's office. It was closed. "Where's Ralph?"

"Triplett County. He's telling the home folks they aren't going to have to pony up as much money for his reelection campaign as they did last time and reassuring them that he hasn't sold out to the Ashley County crowd."

"Sounds like a tightrope walk. That's a suspicious crowd over there." Holt paused. "Do you remember a detective who worked for the sheriff's department a few years ago named McHenry or McReynolds? Skip was trying to remember his name at lunch."

"McDermott. He's probably thinking of Tony McDermott."

"Skip said he quit. Do you know why?"

"No. He was only a few years from retirement, and I thought he was going to ride it out here and then move to a place he had in the mountains. He'd worked for years in Atlanta and came here thinking it would be less stressful. He told me one time he'd seen too many of his buddies shot or killed right before they quit and didn't want to become a statistic. He was recently divorced; his wife married another police officer."

"Where did he go from here?"

"I'm not sure, but his vacation house was on Lake Burton. He carried a picture of it in his wallet. It wasn't much to look at, but he'd built it himself and was real proud of it."

Belinda picked up a sheet of paper from her desk and handed it to Holt. "Samuel Byers's lawyer dropped this off while you were at lunch. His client wants to accept the plea. If you like, I can squeeze it onto the arraignment calendar set for tomorrow."

"Yeah, Thursday's fine."

Holt went into his office and called Bishop Pennington. The preacher wasn't available, so Holt left him a message about the sentencing the next day. Swiveling in his chair so he was facing his computer screen, he opened a search engine whose use was limited to law enforcement personnel.

He typed in the name "Tony McDermott."

11

What are you up to?" Ralph Granger asked as he stuck his head into Holt's office.

Holt quickly closed the window on his computer. "Nothing important. Do you need me?"

"Yeah, I just got back from Triplett County. There's a case over there I'm going to pass off to you. The defendant is my second cousin. Jules is a lot younger than I am, and even though we don't know each other very well, I shouldn't be involved in the prosecution of his case."

"What's the charge?"

"Growing marijuana next to his tomato plants. Folks on that side of the family don't think the government has the right to tell them what to do on their property. Years ago Jules's grandpa and great-uncle were moonshiners."

"How much pot did they seize?"

"Fifteen pounds."

Holt raised his eyebrows. The criminal statutes were more lenient for amounts under ten pounds. Once that threshold was crossed, it became a more serious felony.

"Any evidence of intent to distribute?" he asked.

"I don't know. I shut down the conversation with the detective when I found out who was involved. Jules was probably smoking as much as he could with his buddies and getting his wife to make brownies with the rest."

Holt held out his hand for the file. "I hope she wasn't selling the brownies."

"I don't know. The detective said Jules was pretty scared when they hauled him off to jail."

"Maybe I can convince him to say he's sorry and promise to plant watermelons next year."

"Sounds good to me," Ralph said with a look Holt interpreted as a silent request for leniency.

After Ralph left, Holt read the investigative report. It seemed people bought fresh produce from Jules's garden on Saturday mornings. While waiting to make a purchase, a deputy sheriff looked over the fence and saw a row of enormous marijuana plants at the rear of the property. Behind that row was another. Initially, Jules claimed the marijuana was a form of bamboo that had sprouted on its own, but shortly after he arrived at the jail he confessed and signed a statement. His signature looked like the work of a fourth grader. Holt made a note of the arraignment date.

"I'm going to handle a case for Ralph in Triplett County on the twenty-sixth," he said, standing in front of Belinda's desk. "How big is the calendar? Maybe I can cover all of it."

Belinda hit a few buttons and checked the screen on her computer. "Only six cases. Both the economy and crime are down over there."

"But the soil is rich enough to grow prizewinning marijuana plants."

—

Trish, Sue Ann, and Candace left the discount store. Trish was pushing Candace in a shopping cart filled with diapers, jumbo jars of applesauce, soft drinks for Mark, and a cute Sunday outfit Trish insisted on buying for the little girl. Sue Ann was an expert at pinching pennies, and everything except the outfit was on sale.

"I'm just concerned about Mama's savings and whether the church can keep growing," Trish said. "Later, she told me I needed to be more respectful of Brother Carpenter, even if I was only talking to her. Paxton isn't like places in other parts of the country where people don't go to church at all. How many people do you know who never go to church?"

They reached the car, and Sue Ann popped open the trunk.

"Several of the guys who work with Mark spend Sunday mornings getting ready to watch football. And I don't think Kay and her husband are in a church. They go rock climbing on Sunday or run in marathons."

Kay, a former high school classmate, was deep into personal fitness. She was ridiculously skinny except for muscular calves.

"Where does Holt Douglas go?" Sue Ann asked as she hoisted Candace out of the shopping cart.

"Belinda says he doesn't." Trish paused. "I'd like to reach out to him about it, but it's hard to see him at my church, whether we have a new building or not."

Trish pushed the shopping cart to a corral. She'd been upset since the supper at the church and was having trouble shaking it. She returned to the car, got in, buckled her seat belt, and let out a big sigh.

"It all made me think a bunch about my daddy," Trish said to Sue Ann.

Sue Ann turned sideways in her seat and put her hand on Trish's shoulder. "How?"

"You know how bighearted he was. And when I listened to myself talking to Mama, I know he wouldn't have approved."

Trish paused as a tear escaped and rolled down her cheek. Sue

Ann squeezed Trish's shoulder, then released it and handed her a tissue. Trish blew her nose.

"It was another one of those grief moments," Sue Ann said softly. "You can't keep them from happening. And you really don't want to."

Trish nodded. "Even though it hurt, it made me feel close to him again."

"Tish!" exclaimed Candace from her car seat behind her.

"I'm here, baby." Trish turned sideways and gave the little girl a teary-eyed smile.

Trish held out her index finger, and Candace grabbed it in a tight fist before letting go. Candace put her chubby hand to her mouth and blew Trish a kiss.

"You and Candy are so awesome. You can read me like a book, and she always cheers me up. You're too big, but I need to bottle her up and keep her in my purse."

Sue Ann put the key into the ignition. "Along with diapers, wipes, and hand sanitizer."

Working second shift at the sheriff's department was part of Trish's normal schedule. People in danger of criminal prosecution didn't always make themselves available during regular business hours, and evening was the only time she had a shot at tracking down some of the hard-to-locate defendants who were part of her caseload. When she finished her prep work, it was too early to eat the salad she'd brought from home. Most of the clerical staff at the sheriff's department were gone for the day, so Trish, who had been sitting at her desk for a couple of hours, got up to stretch.

"Hey, Lynn," she said to a woman stationed near Sheriff Blackstone's office. "Expecting a busy night?"

"Part of it depends on you," the middle-aged woman replied. "Are you going to arrest anyone?"

"Hopefully. Nick Watkins and I are going to try to catch a guy who's been dodging us for months. I got a phone call from his ex-wife that he's going to be in town tonight to pick up a car from a guy on Highland Drive. We need to pick him up instead."

"Be careful. That's a rough area."

"Nick is a big boy. I'll let him go first."

Lynn smiled. "Two of you could hide behind Nick."

Trish rested her hand on a filing cabinet. There was a label on the front with an "M" written on it. She thought about Holt Douglas's question.

"Were you working here when Rex Meredith died?" she asked.

"Yes, but back then I was a part-time receptionist at the jail."

"Where's the investigative file for the case?"

"In the storage room if it's not been taken off-site. Why?"

"Someone from the DA's office was asking me questions about it the other day, and I didn't know the answers."

"Do you want me to look for it?" Lynn volunteered. "I don't have anything to do right now."

"Sure, if it's not too much trouble."

Lynn got up from her desk, and Trish returned to her computer. While away from her desk, she'd received an e-mail from the ex-wife of the man they wanted to arrest, confirming that he'd arrived in town and would pick up the car at 8:00 p.m.

"Here it is," Lynn said as she deposited a file on the corner of Trish's desk. "It doesn't look like there's much there since it was a suicide."

"Thanks."

Trish waited until Lynn was out of the room and then dialed the number that rang directly into Holt's office. The young DA answered.

"Hey, Holt. This is Trish Carmichael. I'm glad I caught you."

Trish felt her face flush. "Do you remember asking me the other day about Rex Meredith's death?"

"Sure."

"I have our file in case you want to look at it."

"Yes, I do. When can I see the file?"

Trish looked at the clock on her computer. "I'm leaving at seven with one of the deputies to make an arrest. I can take a break in a few minutes if you want to come and—"

"I'm on my way," Holt interrupted. "I'll phone your desk when I get there so you can buzz me in."

"Okay."

Trish rushed into the women's restroom and checked her hair and makeup. As she brushed her hair, she reminded herself of the Bible verse that said a woman's inner beauty is more important than her outward appearance. The phone on her desk was buzzing when she returned from the restroom. She grabbed it.

"Hello," she said, slightly breathless. "I'll be right out."

"What?" a male voice asked. "Is this Deputy Carmichael?"

"Yes, who is this?"

"Nick Watkins. Any chance we could leave now? I'm back early from a call."

"No!" Trish responded more emphatically than she intended before taking a deep breath. "It has to be timed exactly. If we're early, the defendant may not be on the scene, and he won't stop if he sees a patrol car."

"Okay, no problem. I'll take a supper break."

"I think you should."

Trish rolled her eyes at her suggestion. Nick could miss a week of meals and barely affect his waistline.

"See you at seven," she added. "Thanks for checking in."

After she hung up, a flashing light on her phone indicated she'd missed a call. She didn't bother to listen to it but walked straight to the lobby area. Holt was standing outside and peering through the door. There was a switch beneath the receptionist's desk that triggered the electric lock on the front doors. Trish waved and pressed the switch that released the locking mechanism. Holt came inside the building.

"Sorry," she said. "I had a call from the deputy who's taking me out later. Not on a date. He's assisting with the arrest."

"Okay." Holt gave her a slightly puzzled look.

Trish knew her face was red. She quickly turned away and led the way to her cubicle.

Holt positioned a chair so it was close to the corner of Trish's desk. She handed him the folder. Sitting this close to the handsome assistant DA made her feel tingly.

"Does anyone know you have this?" he asked before he opened it.

"Lynn Braswell pulled it for me."

"Did you tell her I wanted to see it?"

"No."

"Good. Let's keep my interest in this between us, okay?"

"You're in the DA's office. You have a right to look into things. That's your job."

"Yes, but I'd still like to keep this confidential."

"Yeah, sure."

"Great."

Trish glanced past Holt. "Lynn is in the next room," she said. "If she comes in—"

"Are any of the detectives here?"

"No. Detective Atwood is the only one working this shift. He's in the field interviewing witnesses until later tonight."

"Let's go to one of the interview rooms."

Her heart pounding a bit faster, Trish followed Holt to one of the windowless rooms where detectives conducted interrogations. Holt flipped on the light and closed the door with a heavy thud. There was a single table in the middle of the room surrounded by four chairs. Holt sat down and opened the file. Trish sat across from him and watched his face. Holt had curly brown hair that probably didn't respond to combing. He rubbed his jaw as he flipped over a sheet of paper with a large right hand that could definitely palm a basketball.

"McDermott was involved in the investigation, but there isn't a report from him in here," Holt said. "No photos, either."

"Photos?"

"Of the crime scene. I mean, of the corpse and the room where Meredith died. It says here he was in the study of the house on Magnolia Avenue."

"I remember that from the newspaper articles," Trish commented.

"Take a look at this." Holt slid a piece of paper across the table to Trish. "It's a transcript of the 911 call that came in on the evening of Meredith's death."

Trish read out loud:

"911. Is this police, fire, or medical?"

"Medical. My father-in-law has been shot, and we need an ambulance at 217 Magnolia."

"Who is this?"

"Greg Stevens."

"I'll dispatch an ambulance immediately. Is the door to the house open?"

"I don't know, but I'll make sure it is."

"Medical personnel will be there shortly. Unless you have medical training, please don't try to do anything yourself."

"I won't, but I think he's dead."

Trish looked up. Holt was staring at her with the brown eyes that she knew could bore a hole through a witness.

"What jumps out at you from that?" he asked.

Trish glanced down at the sheet again. "Mr. Stevens doesn't seem very upset?" she offered.

"Exactly. We can't tell that without actually listening to the call, though. Look at the first line. He says, 'My father-in-law has been shot.'" Holt leaned forward. "He doesn't say Rex Meredith shot himself."

Trish's mouth went dry. "You think Greg Stevens may have killed Mr. Meredith?"

"I have no idea, but I would have asked him questions based on the 911 call." Holt tapped the folder with his index finger. "And there's no indication here or in the records at the DA's office that he was ever interrogated. That makes no sense to me."

"If Mr. Stevens . . . ," Trish started, then stopped.

"I'd like to make a copy of the file," Holt said.

"I'll do it for you," Trish responded immediately as she stood up. "That way Lynn won't get nosy."

12

Holt left the sheriff's office with a copy of the file in his hand and a commitment from Trish Carmichael to keep her mouth shut. In addition to the transcript of the 911 call, he had a toxicology report confirming that Rex Meredith was legally drunk with a blood alcohol level of .20 at the time of his death. A level that high could cause depression, dizziness, blurred vision, and difficulty talking, walking, and standing. As a depressant, alcohol may have nudged him closer to the brink of self-destructive action. However, the dead man's blood alcohol level didn't prove anything.

The sheriff's file also contained several newspaper articles, none of which mentioned the results of the toxicology test. Instead, the newspaper reporters focused on Rexford Meredith's business, financial accomplishments, and the tragedy of his sudden passing. There was a simple quote from Valerie: "My stepfather will be missed and mourned by all who knew him."

Back at the DA's office, Holt spread everything he'd accumulated on top of his desk. Objectively, he didn't have enough to move forward with a criminal investigation. The 911 call could also be interpreted as referring to a self-inflicted wound. The gun that fired the fatal shot was found in Meredith's hand. Extensive gunpowder burns on Meredith's clothing proved the gun was held very close to his chest when fired. All those factors supported Butch Clovis's conclusion that the cause of death was suicide. Holt leaned back in his chair and glanced out the window.

There were enough legitimate cases on his credenza and in the file cabinets to keep him busy. There was a shredder beside his trash can. He could destroy the sheets of paper on his desk in less than a minute, go home, feed Henry, and forget about Rex Meredith and Greg Stevens. But Holt knew he couldn't let the matter go. Not yet. He returned everything to the bottom drawer of his desk.

—

Thursday morning, Holt and Belinda stood in the main courtroom behind the table reserved for the prosecution. Several cases had been added to the morning's calendar at the last minute due to Judge Lomax's taking an unexpected vacation the following week. The courtroom was filled with people. On the second row, Holt saw Bishop Pennington and another gray-haired black man. Holt leaned over the railing.

"Business is booming," he said. "I'm sorry, but there may be a wait before we reach the case you're here for."

"I'll just have to move my pickup basketball game to later in the day," the bishop replied.

"Can I play?"

"Only if you bring Henry to be the ball dog."

Judge Lomax entered the courtroom. "Mr. Douglas, call the first case on the calendar."

Having Belinda with him was a big help. While Holt argued a motion or orchestrated the entry of a guilty plea, she got everything and everyone set up for the next few cases on the docket. She whispered to the defense lawyers where they stood in the day's order of business so they could keep their clients informed. For unrepresented defendants, she called them forward and made a quick determination of whether they qualified for a court-appointed lawyer or would have to hire their own legal representation.

When Samuel Byers's case was called, Bishop Pennington and the man with him joined the defendant and his lawyer in front of the judge.

"Good morning, Bishop," Judge Lomax said.

"Good morning, Judge." The minister put his hand on the shoulder of the man he'd brought to court. "This is Zachary Byers, Sammy's uncle."

The judge nodded to the other man and turned to Holt. "Proceed."

Holt outlined the terms of the plea agreement, then the judge asked the defendant the required questions. Byers hung his head the entire time. If his body language indicated the level of his remorse, the young man was sorry for what he'd done. There were no slipups, and the judge accepted the deal. As they turned away, Bishop Pennington and Zachary Byers put their arms around Sammy's shoulders. The gesture made the courtroom seem like a church, and the railing an altar.

Belinda tapped Holt on the arm to get his attention and handed him a file. It was one of the major items on the calendar and had been added at the last minute.

"*State v. Morton*," Holt said. "Hearing on defendant's motion to suppress evidence."

Dirk Rangel stepped forward with his client, a college-age white male wearing a nice suit.

"Ready for the defendant," Rangel said.

"Before we hear any testimony, give me a short summary, gentlemen," the judge said.

"There was probable cause for the initial stop of the vehicle due to malfunctioning equipment," Holt replied. "When Detective Clovis approached the car, he saw a clear plastic bag containing a quantity of methamphetamines in plain view on the rear floorboard. The defendant was placed under arrest and taken to the jail."

The defense lawyer stood and shifted his shoulders. Rangel had cultivated a flair for the dramatic regardless of the situation. He gestured grandly with his right hand.

"Judge Lomax, the evidence will show that my client's car was stopped by Detective Clovis without probable cause in violation of the Fourth Amendment. Thus, any alleged contraband in the vehicle was illegally seized and cannot serve as the basis for a criminal offense. There is extensive judicial authority, beginning with *Mapp v. Ohio*—"

"That's enough," the judge interrupted Rangel. "I'm familiar with the case law. I'm here today to determine the facts. Mr. Douglas, proceed for the state."

"The state calls Detective Harold Clovis."

From the middle of the courtroom a broad-shouldered man with a thick neck and closely cut brown hair walked down the aisle and through the gate in the bar. Even though it was the defendant who was trying to exclude evidence, the prosecution had the burden of proving there hadn't been a violation of the Fourth Amendment's prohibition against unlawful searches and seizures. Holt planned on meeting that burden of proof through the testimony of the arresting detective.

Clovis could no longer catch a fleet-footed fugitive, but once he wrestled a suspect to the ground, the chase was over. No one escaped from the grasp of his powerful hands. Holt administered the oath, and Clovis sat down.

"Please state your name and occupation."

"Harold Clovis, senior detective, Ashley County Sheriff's Department."

"Detective Clovis, were you on duty the evening of April 23 of this year?"

"Yes, I was patrolling in an unmarked car on the west side of town when I observed a 2012 Hyundai Sonata with a malfunctioning right-rear brake light. I turned on my blue light and pulled the car over in front of Morrison's Quick Stop."

Clovis could testify on autopilot, but Holt knew there needed to be the give-and-take of question and answer.

"Is it customary for a detective to make a traffic stop?" he asked.

"All of the officers at the sheriff's department are charged with keeping the streets of Paxton safe."

"Who was driving the car you pulled over?"

Clovis pointed to the young man sitting by Dirk Rangel. "Paul Morton. I asked to see his driver's license along with proof of insurance for the vehicle. I'd called in the license plate information at the time of the stop, which confirmed that the car was titled in Mr. Morton's name."

"What did you do at that point?"

"I told Mr. Morton his right-rear brake light wasn't working, and that I could give him a ticket for malfunctioning equipment. He told me that—"

"Objection to anything my client said," Rangel interrupted. "There is no indication that he'd been given his Miranda rights and waived the right to have counsel present."

"Sustained," the judge said.

"What did you do next?" Holt asked.

Clovis looked at Rangel as he spoke. "I turned on my flashlight and shined it in the rear of the vehicle. I saw a clear plastic bag lying in plain view on the floorboard behind the driver's seat."

"What did you do at that point?"

"I opened the back door of the car and took out the bag. Upon closer inspection I determined it contained a quantity of clear and slightly yellow rock-like crystals consistent with the appearance of crystal methamphetamine. I asked Mr. Morton to step from the car and placed him under arrest. I read him his Miranda rights and transported him to the jail."

"Did he make a voluntary statement at that time?"

"Objection," Rangel said.

"Overruled," the judge replied.

"Mr. Morton stated that he didn't know the plastic bag was in his car and claimed he'd loaned the vehicle to an out-of-town friend who'd driven it for several days. He then refused to give me the name of his friend."

"What did you determine about the substance in the plastic bag?"

"A sample was sent to the state crime lab, and I received a report that—"

"Objection on hearsay, Your Honor," Rangel said. "The individual who performed the chemical analysis would be the only competent witness to testify on this point."

"Mr. Rangel, you filed a motion to suppress," the judge said testily. "Do you want to turn this into a bench trial on the merits?"

"No, sir, but we reserve our rights to dispute the identity of anything taken from the vehicle."

"Noted. The witness will answer."

"The bag contained crystal methamphetamine."

"That's all from this witness," Holt said.

Holt returned to the counsel table. Belinda leaned over to him. "What is Rangel going to argue when this case gets in front of a jury?" she whispered. "That his client was hauling cotton candy for a birthday party?"

Rangel stood and approached the detective. Holt knew the two men had sparred many times before.

"Detective Clovis, what happened to my client's car when you took him to jail?"

"It was towed to the secure lot beside the jail."

"Is that the lot surrounded by a ten-foot fence topped with razor wire?"

"Yes."

"While my client was your guest at the jail, did he have access to his car?"

"Not until he posted bail."

"Would anyone else have access to the car?"

"Not without permission from the sheriff's office."

"That's why it's called a 'secure lot,' correct?"

"Yes."

Rangel looked up at the judge. "Your Honor, that's all from Detective Clovis," he said.

"The state rests," Holt said to the judge.

"Mr. Rangel, do you have any evidence to present?" the judge asked.

"Yes, Your Honor. The defense calls Dale Brown to come forward and be sworn in."

Holt turned sideways in his chair and watched as a man dressed in dark blue mechanic's overalls stained with grease walked down the aisle. The man glanced around nervously as he came through the railing and approached the witness stand. Rangel administered the oath.

"Mr. Brown, tell the court who you are and what you do."

Brown turned in his chair so he was looking up at Judge Lomax. "I'm Dale Brown. My brothers and I own a garage on Westover Street."

"Mr. Brown, do you know my client, Mr. Paul Morton?"

"Yes, sir. We've done work on his car."

"Was his car in your shop in April of this year?"

"Yes, sir. He brought it in for an oil change and a twenty-three-point inspection."

"As part of a twenty-three-point inspection, did you determine if the brake lights were functioning properly?"

The witness pulled a wrinkled sheet of yellow paper from the front pocket of his uniform. "Yes. I got a copy of the work order here with me. It says we changed a bulb in one of the rear brake lights and checked the others."

"What was the condition of the brake lights when the car left your shop?"

"They was working."

"Do you have an extra copy of the work order for the judge?"

The witness dug in another pocket of his overalls and pulled out a white sheet of paper.

"Yes, I made a copy like you asked me to do."

Rangel took it from the witness and walked over to Holt, who made sure it was for the right car and handed it back to him. Rangel raised the paper in the air like a banner.

"Your Honor, we tender Defense Exhibit 1."

"No objection," Holt replied.

"Admitted."

Rangel placed the exhibit on the bench in front of the judge.

"Mr. Brown, when was the next time you saw Mr. Morton's car?"

"Over at the jail."

"Why did you see it at the jail?"

"You called me and asked me to check it out."

"How did you obtain access to the secure lot surrounded by a ten-foot fence topped with concertina wire?"

Belinda leaned over to Holt and whispered, "I thought it was razor wire."

"Not now," Holt replied. "I think I know where this is going, and I don't like it."

Brown shifted in the chair. "We do work on county vehicles, so

I went by to see Sheriff Blackstone and asked if he'd let me check out Mr. Morton's car. He took me to the lot hisself."

"Was Sheriff Blackstone with you at all times while you were in the secure lot?"

"Yes, he told me he couldn't let me go out there by myself."

"Tell the judge what you and Sheriff Blackstone did."

"He had the keys to the car. I asked him to get in and start it up and then press on the brakes to see if the lights was working."

"And did the sheriff do as you requested?"

"Yeah. The lights came right on."

"Both sides?"

"Yes. Then I got in the car and pressed the brakes while the sheriff stood behind the car and watched."

"What did he see?"

Holt was on his feet. "Objection, Your Honor. That would be hearsay."

Rangel stretched up to his full height. "Judge, I served a subpoena on Sheriff Blackstone prior to coming to court this morning but agreed that he could attend to his official duties and be on standby. He's ready to fully corroborate the testimony of Mr. Brown on the matter before the court."

The judge looked down at the witness. "Did you check the wiring of the lights?" the judge asked.

"Yes, sir. I popped open the trunk and there weren't nothing wrong with the wiring and the bulbs was screwed in tight."

"As a mechanic, is there any explanation why the brake lights worked for you but may not have come on a few days earlier while Mr. Morton was driving the vehicle?" the judge asked.

"No, sir. They either worked or they didn't."

Judge Lomax looked at Holt and then Rangel. "Based on the testimony of this witness, I'm going to grant the motion to suppress. Please prepare an order and provide a copy to Mr. Douglas."

Holt turned around and looked for Butch Clovis. The detective was no longer in the courtroom.

"Your Honor, may I be heard?" he asked.

"Other than the testimony of Detective Clovis, do you have any other evidence on this issue?" the judge asked.

"No, sir; however, I respectfully urge the court to give greater weight to the testimony of a detective with over twenty years of experience than the opinion of Mr. Brown."

"In this case, I find Mr. Brown's testimony about the condition of the car credible," the judge replied. "Therefore, I'm granting the motion."

"Thank you, Your Honor," Rangel said.

Holt returned to the counsel table and leaned down to Belinda. "Call the sheriff's department as soon as we're finished. I want a meeting with Clovis before I leave this afternoon," he said.

"You'd better check with Ralph first," Belinda said. "If anyone is going to get chewed out, he'll want the first bite."

"Mr. Douglas," Judge Lomax said. "Let's get going. Please call the next case."

13

Trish didn't get home from work until 2:30 a.m. She and Nick Watkins had arrived too late at the house on Highland Drive to catch the suspect, who'd already picked up the car. They ended up tracking the man from one end of Ashley County to the other before finally cornering him at an abandoned house at the end of a long gravel road.

Marge was watching a preacher on TV as Trish walked through the living room to the kitchen that morning.

"I didn't hear you come in last night," she said.

"I tried to be quiet," Trish said, smoothing down her disheveled hair. "It was after midnight when we made the arrest."

"Were you in any danger?"

Trish remembered the churning feeling in the pit of her stomach as she and Nick approached the darkened house in the middle of the woods. They were so far out in the country it would have taken a backup car at least thirty minutes to reach them. Nick shined a flashlight through a curtainless window, and a few seconds later the front door opened, leaving Trish face-to-face with the suspect, who glared at her with coal-dark eyes and lurched forward. She froze. Fortunately, Nick grabbed the man before he had a chance to hit her.

"No," she said, fudging the truth. "The deputy who went with me on the call took good care of me. Were you up late?"

"Yes, the Braves baseball game went into extra innings, and I stuck with it to the end hoping I'd see you come through the door."

"I wish you wouldn't do that."

"I can't help being a mother no matter how old you are. At least it was a good game. The Braves won, which makes three in a row."

Trish poured a big glass of orange juice. She rarely drank coffee and relied on juice to jump-start her day.

"Brother Carpenter came by to see me after supper," Marge continued. "We had a good talk."

Trish set her glass on the counter and stepped from the kitchen into the living room. "What happened?"

"He told me the deacons had me on the list of people most likely to help with the building fund. He left a nice brochure."

"Did he ask you to sign a pledge card?"

"Yes, but I told him I needed to discuss that with you since you'll get whatever I have left when I'm gone."

"Mama! You make it sound like I'm waiting around here like a vulture for you to die!"

"I don't think it came across like that. Anyway, the brochure and pledge card are on the nightstand beside my bed. You can look it over later. He told me Mr. and Mrs. Stevens paid for the architectural drawings they had the other night at church."

"That's something else that bothers me," Trish said. "How clean is their money? Everyone knows what a stingy man Mr. Meredith was. He would place a big order for farm equipment with Daddy and then find something bogus to complain about after it was shipped to Paxton. He'd pressure Mr. Henderson into reducing the price because it would cost more to send the stuff back than to agree to an extra discount."

"Yes, but that shouldn't keep the church from accepting a gift from Mr. and Mrs. Stevens."

Trish thought about her conversation with Holt and the 911 call. "What do we really know about Greg Stevens? He could be worse than Mr. Meredith."

—

It was Trish's final day on the second shift for several weeks. Three young unmarried male deputies were loitering in the break room when she arrived for work and put her supper in the refrigerator.

"Hey, I heard you were out late last night with Nick," one of them said.

"Yeah," another one chimed in. "What does it take to get on the list to chauffer you around town after dark?"

"Sign me up," the third deputy added.

"Calm down, boys," Trish replied as she turned away from the refrigerator. "Working with me is hazardous duty. Nick is a big guy and has gotten a lot stronger carrying around those twins of his. Would I feel any safer working with any of you?"

The three men exchanged glances. "Yes," they all replied within seconds of one another.

Trish touched the gun resting against her hip. "With Nick I didn't have to get this out of the holster"—she paused—"and point it at him. Right now, I'm not sure I can say the same thing about any of you."

"Hey, we're professionals," the first deputy protested. "Or at least I am."

The other two men pushed the first deputy.

"What are you talking about?" one of them said to him. "I scored higher on my tests last month than you did."

The three deputies began to argue among themselves.

Trish quietly left the room. As one of three female deputies who worked for the sheriff's department, she'd had to get used to playful banter, some of which occasionally made her feel uncomfortable. However, nothing had happened that warranted a complaint to the county human resources director. Coming up with a lighthearted response and getting away from the situation had been the best strategy.

Logging on to her computer, she finished a report about the recovery of a large amount of child support from a man who sold cattle for cash and tried to pretend he didn't have any income. It had been a satisfying victory. To catch the defendant, Trish had put on a cowboy hat and boots and gone undercover to a cattle auction in a neighboring county, where she kept track of what the man received from the sale of his livestock. She then subpoenaed the records from the auction house to expose the man's under-the-table income.

Late in the afternoon, the phone on the edge of her desk buzzed, and the dispatcher told her Holt Douglas was on the line. Trish sat up straighter in her chair.

"Congratulations," he said. "I saw on the jail report that you caught the guy you were looking for last night."

"Yeah, it was a long night. We'll see if the inside of a cell changes his mind about supporting his kids."

"Judge Lomax is out of town next week, so the defendant will have a chance to count the bars until the judge returns."

While Holt talked, Trish racked her brain trying to figure out what was going on. Holt never called to make small talk about her cases, which were tiny footnotes on the court calendar.

"You do an excellent job. Not many officers would put their heart and soul into what is often a thankless job."

"I appreciate you saying that."

There was an awkward pause.

"Have you thought any more about the Meredith matter?" Holt asked.

"A little."

"Let me tell you what happened in court today with Butch Clovis."

Trish listened to the story about the brake light that was or wasn't broken without making a connection to Rex Meredith's death.

"What's the scuttlebutt around the sheriff's office about Clovis?" Holt asked when he finished.

"Uh, he and Sheriff Blackstone are close friends. They go hunting a few times every year." Trish lowered her voice. "And everyone knows Detective Clovis is lazy. He has two or three more years before he can take early retirement, and he isn't trying to impress anyone. All the hard cases are assigned to Detectives Atwood and Burns."

"Ralph Granger wouldn't let me confront him about his testimony in court, which made me wonder why he'd want to protect Clovis. Then I remembered that Clovis signed the investigative report in the Meredith file."

The same churning feeling that hit Trish in the stomach when she and Nick approached the abandoned house in the woods suddenly returned.

"Are you working second shift?" Holt asked.

"Yes."

"Could we get together for a sandwich during your supper break? Maybe at the sub shop on Eastway Drive."

"I brought a salad from home," Trish replied, then realized she didn't want to turn down a chance for one-on-one time with Holt. "But I'd rather go out. How about seven? That's when I usually eat on second shift."

"Great. I'll see you then."

The call ended. Trish stared at her computer screen. She'd not asked the most important question. Why did Holt want to involve her? Her experience lay in the area of deadbeat dads, not cold-case murder investigations.

—

Holt parked in front of the salon. He didn't have to meet with Trish Carmichael for another thirty minutes. Brittany greeted him with a wave of her hand and a yawn when he came through the door.

"You're working late," he said. "Does the boss realize you might get into overtime pay?"

"No, and if you tell her, I'll do something horrible to you."

"I've been threatened by a lot scarier people than you."

"I hadn't thought about that," Brittany said, wide-eyed. "I mean, you're trying to lock up big-time criminals."

"Yeah, we have a lot of those in Paxton, along with international jewelry thieves and drug kingpins."

"Don't laugh. A woman came in today for a manicure and pedicure and told me there's a gang at one of the high schools. The members all get the same tattoo on their left forearm."

Holt was aware of the problem, and the issue had been a topic of discussion with Ralph and Jim.

"Where's Angelina?"

"Upstairs in the office. Do you want me to let her know you're here?"

"No, I'll surprise her."

The second floor of the house contained several former bedrooms now used by hairstylists and the salon's massage therapist. Angelina's tiny office was adjacent to the largest room. When the house was a private residence, the small space had been an infant nursery. Angelina was sitting with her back to the door. Holt tapped on the doorframe, and she swung around, causing her hair to swirl. Her face lit up with a smile.

"Oh, I was expecting Larissa, a new stylist who's struggling. I don't know how she got a cosmetology certificate; she doesn't know how to do anything except simple cuts. She has a great attitude, and I'm thinking about using her to cut men's hair like yours and give shampoos for some of the other girls."

"What's wrong with my hair?" Holt touched the top of his head.

"Baby, you have foolproof hair. No matter where it's cut, there are other sprigs to take the place of those that leave. I tried her out on Skip this afternoon, and he seemed pleased."

"Skip's hair is getting thin on top."

"I know. Have you suggested he go to the doctor and get a prescription? There are products that work if a man takes them early enough."

"That's not been a topic of conversation, but I'll keep it in mind the next time he irritates me."

Angelina glanced at her watch. "Have you eaten supper tonight?" she asked.

"No, I'm going to grab something at the new sandwich shop on Eastway Drive."

"If you can wait five minutes, I'll come with you. Except for a banana and cup of yogurt, I haven't had a bite to eat all day."

"Uh, I'd like to, but I'm meeting someone."

"Is it a tall blonde?" Angelina raised her eyebrows.

Holt managed a nervous laugh at Angelina's random accuracy. "It's a deputy sheriff who is helping me with an investigation. The officer is working the second shift, so this is the best time to connect."

"If you'd rather spend time with a 250-pound guy who chews tobacco than with me, I totally understand."

Holt quickly changed the subject. "But the main reason I stopped by was to see if I can take you out to dinner at the new steak house on Friday night."

"And use the gift card Skip gave you?"

"Now I'm definitely going to give him a hard time about going bald."

"He said he'd take me if you didn't," Angelina said, then paused. "Tell me, what do you think about Skip and Brittany? She has tons of personality and is interesting enough to keep a guy from getting bored. I know she's younger than he is, but you're older than me and that seems to be working out."

"By six months."

"I'm serious. If you get a chance, would you bring it up with Skip? We could even go on a double date with them to see a movie to break the ice."

A mental image of Skip and Brittany sitting awkwardly in the rear seat of the car while the four of them drove to a movie theater made Holt chuckle.

"What's so funny? Do you think Skip is too good for Brittany just because he's a lawyer?" Angelina flipped her hair to the side. "She's a sharp girl, even though she dropped out of college a semester short of graduating. Her mother got sick, and Brittany came home to help out with her little brothers and sister."

"It's not that," Holt quickly backpedaled. "Brittany is probably smarter than Skip and twice as witty. It's the thought of us going on a double date with them that seemed funny. It's so high school. But I'll look for a chance to mention it."

"Thanks."

Angelina opened a small safe beneath the desk and put a thick envelope inside.

"Good day at the cash register?" Holt asked.

"And month. Revenue is up thirty percent from this time last year."

"Wow, that's great." Holt nodded. "The people who told you a high-end place like this wouldn't make it in Paxton were wrong."

"Yeah. Women who were driving an hour one way to south Atlanta can get to this salon in less than five minutes. I picked up a couple of rich clients today. You probably know them: Valerie Stevens and Lauren Kirby."

"I saw Greg Stevens earlier in the week. He's on the finance committee for Ralph's reelection along with Pat Kirby, Lauren's husband. What's Valerie like?"

"Very quiet. I'm not sure if it's because she's shy or just a private person. After she told me what she wanted me to do with her hair, she didn't say much, and I gave up trying to have a conversation with her. Lauren Kirby was the chatterbox. They came in together, and I think they're best friends even though their personalities are totally different. You know how opposites attract."

"Just like us."

"What do you mean by that?"

"Oh, that you're gorgeous and have all the qualities a man could hope for in a woman, and I don't know what you could possibly see in me."

Angelina rolled her eyes. "That was nice till you went overboard," she said. "But I'll let you tell me some of my stellar qualities over dinner tomorrow night."

"I'll be by a little before seven thirty."

Holt leaned over and gave her a peck on the lips.

"Not so fast," Angelina said as she stood up and threw her arms around his neck.

The next kiss, followed by another, made Holt consider standing up Trish Carmichael at the sandwich shop.

"That's one thing we do well together," Angelina said when they parted.

"Yeah," Holt managed.

Angelina patted him on the shoulder. "You'd better get going. I don't want you to be late for the meeting with your deputy buddy."

Holt walked down the stairs much slower than he'd climbed them.

14

Holt wondered if Trish was going to stand him up. It was fifteen minutes past the time for their meeting. The surge in business for supper at the sandwich shop had tapered off. The only other people in the restaurant were a family of three with a restless little boy and an older couple. Holt watched the couple step to the counter and order. They bought a footlong sandwich to split between them. It was a cheap way to eat, but Holt couldn't imagine sharing a sandwich with Angelina. They had different, strongly held preferences that ran from the type of bread and meat to the amount of mayonnaise. The front door opened, and Trish rushed in.

"Sorry I'm late," she said. "A woman I've been trying to contact for over two months showed up at the sheriff's office, and I had to take advantage of the chance to talk to her."

"No problem. Are you hungry?"

"Yes, it's been a long day."

The menu items were listed on the wall behind the meats and condiments. Trish stared at it for a moment.

"I'd like a smoked turkey with provolone on whole wheat, toasted," she said.

"What size?" the young woman behind the counter asked.

"Eight inch, please."

"What else are you going to get on it?" Holt asked Trish.

"Uh, light mayo, tomato, a few pickles, lettuce, and the seasoning mix they sprinkle on top."

"That's exactly what I was going to order," Holt said. "Do you want to split a big one?"

"Sure."

"Make it a jumbo," Holt said to the worker. "And cut it in two."

Holt paid for the food. They sat at a table as far from the family with the rambunctious child as they could get.

"Thanks for agreeing to meet with me," Holt said as he unwrapped his half of the sandwich before he noticed that Trish had bowed her head and closed her eyes for a moment. "Excuse me, I didn't realize you were praying."

"That's okay. It's something my father always did, even when we went out to eat at a restaurant."

Holt took a bite of the sandwich. "What does he do for a living?"

"He's in heaven," Trish replied.

It took Holt a split second to interpret Trish's words. "Oh, I didn't know," he said.

Trish paused for a moment. "It happened before you came to town. My parents were driving home from a visit with a friend who was in the hospital, and they were hit by a drunk driver. My father was killed, and my mother suffered a spinal cord injury. She's a paraplegic. A teenage kid was driving the other car. He'd been at a party where high school students were drinking and crossed the center line enough to sideswipe my parents' car and force it off the road. It hit a tree."

While Trish talked, Holt's appetite vanished. "Was the boy injured?"

"Nothing more than a few bruises. Even though he was a minor, his case was transferred to superior court, and he pleaded guilty to one count of first-degree vehicular homicide, DUI, reckless driving, and everything else Mr. Granger could come up with. He's in his early twenties now but won't be getting out of prison for another five years or so."

Holt tried to keep his voice steady. "Have you had any contact with him?"

"No, but my mother has. You saw me praying, but my mother is the real saint in our family. The day the boy was sentenced, my mother asked the judge for permission to talk to him one-on-one. I don't know exactly what she said, but I know she forgave him. You could see him crying from the other side of the courtroom. I'm sure he felt bad as soon as he sobered up, but that doesn't excuse what he did. I was crying, too, but for us, not him."

Holt could feel himself becoming emotional. Trish didn't seem to notice.

"My mother sends him cards and cookies from time to time," she continued. "She even wants me to take her to the Jackson County Correctional Institute to see him, but I'm not ready for that." Trish stopped and looked across the table. "Holt, you've barely touched your sandwich. Were you serious about liking the same sub as me?"

"Yeah, absolutely. I'm just really sorry about what happened to your family."

"Thanks. I know you can relate to this better than most people."

"Why?" Holt asked, startled.

"Because you see DUI cases with injuries in court all the time."

"Oh." Holt nodded.

"For a long time seeing my mother in a wheelchair was like a daily slap in the face that kept the wound fresh. And missing my father will never go away." Trish paused. "I know this may be more than you want to hear, but our faith has kept both my mother and me from collapsing into a puddle of sorrow."

"I respect that," Holt said thoughtfully. "DUI cases are always tough for me."

"Why is that?"

"Something bad can happen in a split second for a teenager when alcohol is involved. Most of the underage defendants caught drinking and driving are like the boy who killed your father. They're sorry for what they did. Fortunately, only a few of the resulting accidents end in death."

"One is too many," Trish said flatly.

"Of course," Holt replied quickly.

"Yeah, it's hard for someone who hasn't experienced it to understand."

And in that instant Holt was transported in his mind's eye back to the hospital room and the moment when Officer Merriwether told him Calico was dead. The emotions he'd felt that night were fresher than the bread of his sandwich. A tear fiercely fought its way to the corner of his right eye. He wiped it away with his napkin.

"What's wrong?" Trish asked.

"I was thinking about someone I lost because of drinking and driving when I was in high school. He was a friend, not a family member, but I've pushed it down so deep that I rarely think about it. Listening to you made it pop up. We were—" Holt stopped as another tear appeared.

"If you ever need someone to talk to about it," Trish said as she reached across the table and lightly touched his arm for a second, "I'd try to be a good listener."

"No." Holt shook his head. "I can't talk about this with anyone."

A thick pall hung over the table as they finished eating. Once toasted and warm, Holt's sandwich was now cold. While he nibbled his food, Holt thought about Calico's funeral, the sight of his friend's mother sobbing at the graveside, the monosyllabic responses he gave to questions from classmates, and the relief he felt when he left his high school for the last time.

"Do you still want to talk to me about Mr. Meredith?" Trish asked after several moments of silence passed.

"Uh, yeah." Holt shook his head to clear his mind. "My friend's death coming up caught me off guard. It still hurts."

"I had an emotional moment about my dad this week. I'm not trying to be pushy, but it really can be good to talk with someone about how you feel."

Trish waited.

"I don't know about that," Holt replied. "But the reason I wanted to get together had to do with Rex Meredith."

"Go ahead."

"First, our conversation needs to be totally off the record. I don't want either one of us to get into trouble."

"Trouble?" Trish gave Holt a concerned look. "It's one thing to let you copy a file, but I don't want to do anything that might get me fired."

"And I wouldn't ask you to do anything wrong. But I can't reopen the case through normal channels. To me, it looks like a rush job. They shut down the investigation before it got started."

"Who?"

"Ralph Granger, Butch Clovis, and I'm not sure who else. And there's no statute of limitations on murder."

Trish felt goose bumps come up on her arms. "I'm a deputy, not a detective."

"True, but you wear a uniform, and I don't. There are people who will respect your badge more than they do my title. Also, I'd like to have someone inside the sheriff's department who can let me know if anyone finds out what I'm doing."

"I'm not in any of the meetings with the detectives."

"But what goes on behind closed doors one day becomes a topic of general conversation around the office by the next day. Don't you sit near Sheriff Blackstone's secretary?"

"Yes."

"And hear what she's saying?"

"I try not to pay attention. I have work to do myself."

"All I'm asking you to do is keep your eyes and ears open. There's one thing I'd like to know as soon as possible."

"What?"

"The connection, if any, between Butch Clovis and Greg Stevens."

"Mr. and Mrs. Stevens came to my church the other night. They're going to make a $500,000 gift to our building fund. It would be horrible if he got control of all that money by—" Trish stopped.

"So you'll help me?"

Holt waited while Trish fidgeted for a few moments.

"Yes, but I'm trusting you not to let me do anything that's wrong or that will get me in trouble."

"I promise."

They left the sandwich stop together. Trish got into an unmarked car and drove away. Holt's vehicle was parked around the corner.

The conversation with Trish Carmichael was the first time in years that he'd mentioned Calico's death. Angelina knew nothing about it. His parents believed the story he told at the time of the accident.

Holt didn't agree with Trish about letting things out. He'd seen what happened in court to defendants who did exactly that. He'd buried his lie with Calico, and that was where it needed to stay. The best thing Holt could do was honor his friend's memory. Unlocking his car, he resolved never to discuss Calico's death again. With anyone.

Trish couldn't get the look on Holt's face out of her mind. Whatever lay in his past remained tender to the slightest touch. He must have been very close to his friend. Trish had seen Holt's confidence in the courtroom and his compassion for downtrodden people like Amanda Callaway. But there was more to him than that.

Her empathy and focus on Holt had kept her own emotions in check. But as she drove back to the sheriff's office, she shed a few tears. She stayed in her car until she regained her composure. Sitting at her desk, she picked up the phone and called Belinda at home.

"It's Trish Carmichael. Do you have a minute?"

"Yes, any excuse to take a break from cleaning the bathtub is welcome. What's up?"

"I'm still at work and just got back from supper with Holt Douglas at the sub shop on Eastway Drive."

"He asked you out on a date while you were working your shift?"

"Not exactly." Trish remembered her promise of confidentiality. "It was business related. But something personal came up in the conversation. Do you know where he went to high school?"

"In the Atlanta area. Did he say you reminded him of one of his old girlfriends? I'm sure he had them lined up in front of his locker."

"No, it was something else." Trish paused. "I don't think I should mention it."

"That's not fair. You can't pump me for information and not reciprocate."

"Please—"

"Okay, okay. I'm sure it's in his personnel file at the office. I'll check tomorrow and shoot you an e-mail."

"Would you mind calling me?"

"Right. Ralph Granger and Sheriff Blackstone don't need to know what we're up to."

In more ways than one, Trish thought as she hung up the phone.

15

Even though she didn't get home until after eleven, Trish had to report to the sheriff's department the following morning at 7:00 a.m. for first shift. Fortunately, the quick changeover without a day off happened only four times a year. She was on her second large glass of orange juice when Butch Clovis walked past her desk.

"Detective Clovis!" she called out.

The detective stopped and turned toward her. "What is it, Carmichael?"

"Good morning."

"I don't know about that yet. What's on your mind?"

The detective stared down at Trish, making her feel that his question was unnecessary because he could already read her thoughts.

"Uh, do you know Greg Stevens?"

"Of course I do."

"Do you think he might be interested in making a contribution to the fund-raiser for at-risk kids that the Department of Family and Children's Services is sponsoring next month? I volunteered to be the contact person for them at the sheriff's office."

Clovis's face softened. "Mr. Stevens gets hit up for money all the time, but I'm sure he'd do something. Do you want me to ask him for you?"

"That would be great. I'll e-mail the information to you."

"No problem. I see him almost every week."

"Wow, that would be awesome. Thanks."

After Clovis moved on, Trish immediately sent him an e-mail with details about the fund-raiser, but her mind was churning about the detective's close relationship with Greg and Valerie Stevens. Trish felt a rush of adrenaline.

Shortly before noon, Belinda called her.

"I have the name of his high school," she said.

Trish wrote down the information. "Got it."

"He was an honor graduate," Belinda continued, "which I think means he was in the top ten percent of his class. Does he know you were co-valedictorian of your class?"

"No, we've not shared copies of our transcripts, but you can't compare Paxton High with a big school in north Atlanta. There were four of us with the same GPA, and the teachers picked Josh Burdick, not me, to deliver the valedictorian address. I bet Holt's graduating class was three times the size of mine."

"You would have done well anyplace you went." Belinda lowered her voice. "Are you going to give me a hint why you wanted to know about his high school? You could have found out what I've told you in the database at the sheriff's office."

"We're not supposed to use that for personal use."

"And you're one of the few honest people who always obey the rules. You're also good at dodging questions."

"I really can't say right now—"

"Just don't make me find out you're dating him from someone else. You're way more his type than the girl who runs the salon. I deserve firsthand knowledge."

"Absolutely. Thanks."

Trish waited until her lunch break, then drove home to log on to her personal computer. Her mother was napping in a recliner in the living room when Trish barged through the door.

"Sorry," Trish said. "Go back to sleep. I'll be in my room on the computer."

"Aren't you working today?" Marge asked, rubbing her eyes.

"Yes, I have to go back in half an hour."

Time flew as Trish tried to uncover details about Holt's high school years. While the search engine scanned the Web for information, she grabbed bites of a chicken-salad sandwich she'd taken to work from home and brought back with her. A breakthrough came when she identified the neighborhood paper that covered sports for Holt's school. He played lacrosse, a sport barely heard of in Ashley County, and was a member of the basketball team. Trish focused on his basketball career. From the box scores for the games, she noted that he logged a respectable number of minutes as a forward and led the team in steals. Trish smiled. Now Holt put people in jail for stealing.

—

Trish grabbed a late-afternoon nap when she got home from work. Waking up an hour later, she saw that she'd missed a call from Keith, but he hadn't left a message. Rubbing her eyes to knock out the sleepiness, she went into the kitchen. Her mother was cutting up a tomato.

"Agnes brought by a few tomatoes they grew in their greenhouse," Marge said. "She doesn't think they have as much flavor as the ones from a regular garden, but I've been craving a fresh tomato sandwich."

"I'll have one, too." Trish yawned.

"Aren't you going out to dinner with Keith?"

"I'm supposed to, but he's out of town and may not be able to make it back." Trish took a loaf of bread from the cupboard. There was a saltshaker and a jar of mayonnaise already on the table.

"And a tomato sandwich won't ruin my appetite," she said.

The wreck hadn't diminished Marge's hand dexterity. The tomato slices she cut with a sharp paring knife were clean and uniform. She assembled a sandwich for Trish and herself. Trish sat down at the table and took a bite.

"This is good," she said.

"Yes." Marge nodded as she chewed.

Trish was hungry. She quickly ate the sandwich and then made another.

"This is better than some steaks I've eaten," she said as she bit into the juicy slices of tomato. "It doesn't need much salt."

She took a huge bite to finish the second sandwich. As soon as she did, her cell phone buzzed. It was Keith.

"Hello," she said as chunky pieces of bread and tomato clung to her teeth.

"Trish?" he asked.

"Yes, it's me." Trish tried to chew and roll her tongue around the inside of her mouth to clean it.

"Are you okay? You sound stopped up."

"Fine. Where are you?"

"On my way home, but could we go later, say, seven thirty?"

Trish dislodged the last of the food from her teeth and took a quick sip of water. "That would be great," she said. "It will take me awhile to get ready."

"See you then."

Trish ended the call, and Marge burst out laughing.

"What's so funny?" Trish asked.

"You were wrestling with that last bite like it was an alligator trying to crawl down your throat."

Trish grinned. "If Keith could have seen me, do you think he'd still want to take me out to a nice restaurant?"

Friday afternoon was often a slow time at the district attorney's office. None of the attorneys were scheduled to be in trial the following week, and by two o'clock Ralph had left for the golf course and Jim was on his way to fish at a local pond filled with largemouth bass. Holt stayed to catch up on his work. The door to his office was open, and he heard a knock on the frame. It was Belinda.

"If you don't object, I'm going to let the staff go home a half hour early," she said.

"Fine with me, but send Ralph a text message to confirm it. He checks his phone the whole time he's playing golf."

Belinda coughed into the back of her hand. "How's Patricia Carmichael doing with the deadbeat-dad docket?" she asked.

"She's very well organized and thorough in her investigations."

"What do you think about luring her over here to work? She'd make a great assistant to you and could run investigations for the rest of us on the side."

Holt leaned back slightly in his chair. "Ralph and Sheriff Blackstone don't get along now. If we steal one of the sheriff's best deputies, it will get worse."

"I may check with Ralph and interview her anyway. I wanted your opinion first because you work closely with her."

Holt refocused on the document he was reading, then looked up. "I like her. A lot."

After he left the office, Holt still had time to work out before picking up Angelina for supper. He put Henry on a leash and jogged to the church. Three teenage boys were shooting baskets when he arrived. They started to leave when Holt approached.

"Hey, hold on a minute!" he called out. "Do you want to play some two on two?"

"Only if I get to guard you," the tallest boy replied with a sly grin.

The boys were half a step quicker than Holt, but he was able to score with controlled moves close to the basket. After muscling in several shots in a row, he backed off and started passing to his teammate, a slender boy who looked younger than the other two. Everyone was huffing and puffing when Bishop Pennington came out to watch. They stopped for a water break.

"Thanks for letting us play," the tallest boy said to the bishop. "They're redoing the surface of the outdoor courts at the rec center."

"Come anytime you like," the bishop replied. "The only time the courts are reserved is during practices for the church team."

"You have a church team?" Holt's teammate asked.

"Yes. It competes in a spring league. The season ended a few weeks ago."

"How old do you have to be to play?"

"Sixteen."

"I'll be sixteen in January," the boy said.

"And he has a very nice shot from fifteen feet," Holt added.

"You don't have to be a member of the church to be on the team," the bishop said, "but your parents would need to give permission."

"I'll ask my mom about it."

"What's her name?"

"Alameda Johnson."

"Okay." The bishop nodded. "And you are?"

"Jamal."

The boys finished their water.

"I'm outta here," the tallest boy said to Holt. "Next time I'm not going to give you that much space under the basket."

"Only if you can stop me." Holt patted him on the back.

The boys sauntered off.

"I don't know Jamal's mom," the bishop said as soon as the young men were out of earshot, "but I remember his father. He was a good athlete who ended up in prison. It would be great to keep his boy from making a bad mistake at an early age."

"Yeah, I'd rather see Jamal on a basketball court than in a court of law."

Holt took another swig of water and rolled the basketball across the court so Henry could chase it down.

"What were you like at Jamal's age?" the bishop asked.

"I made my share of mistakes," Holt said. "At least the statute of limitations has run out on everything I did wrong when I was a teenager."

"There's no statute of limitations on sin."

Holt, who was raising the water bottle to his lips, stopped and lowered it. His claim about the statute of limitations didn't apply to Calico's death. Lying to the state patrol officer kept alive the possibility that Holt could be prosecuted for vehicular homicide if the truth ever came out. It was another huge reason to keep his mouth shut.

"God forgives and forgets," the bishop continued, "but not until we do our part, which is to confess and repent."

"I thought you were supposed to preach good news," Holt grunted.

"It is good for those who believe and act on it."

Holt picked up the basketball and bounced it a few times. He took a shot and missed. The ball rolled away from them, and Henry took off after it. When the dog returned with the ball, Holt scooped it up and took another shot. He missed again.

"Jamal would have made that shot," he said.

"You would, too, if your mind was on basketball," the bishop said. "Whatever you do, don't put your trust in the statute of limitations."

—

Trish stood in front of the mirror. She usually wore her long blond hair in a ponytail at work, but tonight she let it fall past her shoulders. She brushed it vigorously a few more times in an effort to impart a bit more sheen to the dull gold. There was a knock on the bathroom door.

"Keith just pulled in the driveway," her mother said. "Do you want me to let him in?"

"No, I'll be there in a sec," Trish replied.

She adjusted the dark blue dress she'd chosen for the dinner date. The discipline of salads and sit-ups kept her trim. She left the bathroom and arrived at the front door as Keith rang the chime.

Keith was wearing an open-collared shirt and a sport jacket. He'd taken time to make his dark hair look nice, and Trish caught a whiff of cologne.

"You look fantastic," he said when he saw her.

"Thanks."

Marge was sitting in the living room.

"Hey, Mrs. Carmichael," Keith said.

"It's time you started calling me Marge. Once one of Trish's friends gets a real job, I make them drop the 'Mrs. Carmichael.'"

"I'll work on that," Keith replied with a grin before he turned to Trish. "Thanks for agreeing to go out later than we planned."

"I had a little snack to tide me over."

"Are you ready?"

"Yes."

"Good night, Mrs., uh, Marge," Keith said.

"I won't be late," Trish said.

"Stay out as long as you like. You've been such a good girl this week that you don't have a curfew."

Trish and Keith both stared at Marge for a moment, then realized she was joking. All three of them laughed.

A slight breeze was stirring the air as they walked down the narrow sidewalk that led from the front of the house to the driveway. Keith held the door open for Trish. He'd emptied his car of all the paraphernalia he carried in his job.

"Do you want me to drive?" Trish stopped. "I bet you're tired of spending so much time behind the wheel during the week."

"No, riding with you is nothing like being by myself late at night on a back road in Alabama."

It was a twenty-minute drive to the restaurant. They passed through Paxton toward Interstate 20, the main route from Atlanta to Augusta. The owners of the restaurant wanted to attract customers traveling on the highway as well as local residents.

"Tell me about your week," Keith said. "Except for the confidential parts, of course."

The first thing that came to Trish's mind was the tingly feeling she had when Holt scooted his chair close to her desk. That was immediately followed by their dinner at the sub shop and the tears Holt wiped from his eyes. Finally, she revisited their time together in the interrogation room poring over the Rex Meredith file.

"Uh, I ran all over the county the other night trying to arrest one of the men I've been tracking for months," she managed.

"Did you find him?"

"Yes, in an abandoned house at the end of a dirt road that must have been a half mile from the highway."

"That sounds dangerous."

"I was nervous," Trish admitted. "But Nick Watkins was with me."

Keith smiled. "We used to call him Nicky, but I doubt he'd go for that these days."

Keith began to reminisce about Nick and their days together on the football team. Trish listened and tried not to think about Holt. But it was hard to keep her mind from going where her heart wanted to take her. When they arrived at the restaurant, the parking lot was packed.

"I hope that's a sign that the food is good," Keith said.

"Or everyone had the same idea we did and wanted to check it out."

Trish was wearing high heels that forced her to shorten her lengthy stride. Keith held out his hand as they crossed the parking lot, and she took it. No tingling feeling ran up her arm.

"Did you call ahead for reservations?" she asked.

"No."

The restaurant was a wooden structure. Inside there were several dining rooms located off a central area that featured an extensive salad bar. Exposed beams cut across the ceiling. Keith approached the hostess, a young woman in a black dress.

"Two for dinner," he said.

"It'll be about ten minutes," she said. "Would you like to wait in the bar?"

Keith glanced at Trish, who nodded her head.

The bar was small and dark. Trish didn't drink. The role alcohol had played in the wreck that killed her father and paralyzed her mother tainted even an occasional glass of wine. She wasn't sure about Keith. Being a salesman on the road, she suspected he might occasionally go to a bar, especially with clients.

"You can have something," she said.

"No, I'm driving," Keith replied immediately.

His response made Trish feel warmer toward him, and she began talking more freely. Once she lightly touched him on the arm while telling him about a movie she and her mother recently enjoyed. The hostess called Keith's name, and another young woman led them to a table for two against the wall in the farthest room on the left. As soon as they were seated, Trish looked up.

And found herself staring into the eyes of Holt Douglas.

16

Holt and his girlfriend were sitting at the next table along the wall. Angelina Peabody had her back to Keith. Trish had never met Angelina, but she knew more and more women were going to her salon. Holt smiled at Trish and raised his wineglass in greeting. Trish felt herself blush. The assistant district attorney pushed his chair away from the table and stepped over to them. As he did, Angelina turned sideways in her chair. She was wearing a black dress that made her look like she'd stepped off the pages of a fashion magazine. She was stunningly beautiful. Her hair didn't look like it needed any extra swipes of a brush to make it glisten.

"Hey, Holt," Trish managed.

"Hello." Holt smiled. "It's nice to see you in something other than a deputy sheriff's uniform."

Trish felt herself blush again. She hoped the dim light in the restaurant hid her embarrassment. Angelina got up and came over. Trish was surprised how short she was.

"Keith," Trish managed, "this is Holt Douglas. He's one of the district attorneys I work with."

Keith stood and the two men shook hands. Seeing them together brought out their contrasts. Holt was taller and leaner with more chiseled features. Keith was stockier but handsome in his own way.

"And this is Angelina Peabody," Holt said.

Angelina smiled and extended her hand to Trish. Angelina's nails were also flawless. Her hands were tiny compared to Trish's.

"You have gorgeous hair," Angelina said.

"You're kidding," Trish replied.

"Don't argue with her," Holt said. "It's her business to know about that. She owns the All About You Salon and Spa."

"I know. Everybody is talking about your place," Trish said. "It's the biggest thing to hit Paxton in a long time."

Angelina laughed. It wasn't an unpleasant sound.

"You should check out the salon," Angelina said. "If you have to put up with Holt on a regular basis, you deserve a discount."

"Oh, he's great," Trish said. "I mean as a lawyer."

As soon as the words were out of her mouth, Trish wanted to crawl under the table.

"You're the one who makes me look good," Holt replied, not seeming to notice. He turned to Keith. "Trish is superorganized. She prepares such excellent summaries of her cases that I can read them verbatim to the judge. It makes my job a lot easier."

"I'm not surprised," Keith said. "But don't play chess with her. She'll blow you off the table before you realize what hit you."

"I'll remember that." Holt put his hand on Angelina's shoulder. "Enjoy your dinner. I recommend the rib eye, medium-rare with red wine sauce."

After a waiter took their drink orders, Trish and Keith went to the salad bar. Trish's emotions were in turmoil as she absentmindedly fixed her salad. She was having trouble getting the image of Holt's hand on Angelina's shoulder out of her mind. When they returned to their table with the salads, Holt and Angelina were gone.

"That was quite a compliment the lawyer gave you," Keith said as they sat down. "Maybe you should consider going to law school."

"Are you serious?" Trish asked.

"Everyone knows how smart you are. All you lack is confidence."

The way Keith spoke about her lack of confidence didn't sound like a put-down. Trish had secretly considered the possibility of law school but hadn't mentioned it to Marge or Sue Ann.

They sat in silence as they ate their salads.

After taking a drink of tea, Keith asked, "Are you familiar with the piece of property for sale on Cockburn Road? It's not far from the Eakins place."

Trish nodded. The property was about two miles from where she and her mother lived. A faded real-estate sign out front described a five-acre tract.

"Yes. It's a soybean field with a little creek running along the side."

"That's right. I'm thinking about buying it and building a house there."

"What about the creek? Doesn't that make it a floodplain?"

"The land rises toward the rear of the property, and I don't think the water would be a problem if that's where the house is located." Keith became more animated. "I mean, it wouldn't be smart to put in a basement. I talked to Mr. Eakins and asked him the same thing. He's lived next door for forty years and has never seen the creek flood the little hill I have in mind. And I thought having flowing water on a piece of property would be nice. I've been looking at house plans, and a couple of weeks ago I installed a program on my computer that lets me play around with designs. It's cool how the program automatically adds the things I would forget. Would you like to see some of the concepts I've come up with?"

"I guess so," Trish responded slowly. "I mean, I can give you an opinion, but you're going to have to decide what you want in a house."

"What you think is very, very important to me."

Trish was chewing a bite of salad and suddenly had trouble swallowing it. She took a quick sip of water to help the food go down. The waiter brought their food.

"This looks good," Trish said as she eyed her steak, a petite fillet.

Keith had taken Holt's advice and ordered a rib eye. The waiter placed a steaming dish of creamed spinach in the center of the table.

"You could grow an awesome garden on the property," Keith said. "It's all bottomland, and the creek runs year-round in case there's a drought. It's been in soybeans for years. They put nitrogen back into the soil."

Trish was chewing a bite of steak while Keith talked.

"Try your steak," she said. "Mine is delicious."

The steak got Keith's mind off the property beside the creek. Like Holt, he'd gotten the red wine–reduction sauce. Trish dipped a piece of her meat into the sauce. It had deep, rich flavors.

"Wow," she said. "Holt was right. This is very good."

"He seems like a nice guy," Keith said. "How well do you know him?"

Trish suddenly wished Keith would change the subject back to creekfront property and soybeans.

"Uh, he's from Atlanta and came here two years ago. Some people say he's the best trial lawyer in the DA's office."

"And Angelina is his girlfriend?"

"Yes." Trish licked her lips.

"Is there any chance he and his girlfriend would come to church if you invited him?"

"I have no idea," Trish replied with surprise.

The possibility of sitting in a pew with Keith, Holt, and Angelina on a Sunday morning sounded like something from a low-budget reality TV show.

"Our church isn't very sophisticated," Keith continued, "but Brother Carpenter is a good speaker. I think he could relate to a lawyer."

Trish wasn't so sure. "Maybe. Did Brother Carpenter get in touch with you to talk more about the building program? He came by the house and talked with my mom when I wasn't there."

"Not yet. We're supposed to meet for lunch again next week. I'm only going to be on the road Monday and Tuesday. The rest of the week, I'm working from my home office." Keith smiled. "Which is the same bedroom I've had since I was eleven years old. What's your shift this week? Maybe we could get together so I can show you my house plans."

"I'm on first all week."

"Great. Late in the afternoon would be perfect for me. How about Wednesday?"

"That would probably work. I'll let you know."

With a satisfied look on his face, Keith focused his attention once again on the steak on his plate. Trish took small bites and chewed thoughtfully.

—

Saturday morning, Holt woke up early and took Henry out for a morning run. The dog's short legs were built for quick bursts of speed rather than a long jog, so Holt followed a course that looped back around to the house after about a mile. Henry was breathing rapidly when Holt took him off his leash and released him into the yard. Henry pattered over to the deck and buried his face in his water dish. For the next few minutes the neighborhood squirrels wouldn't have to fear for their lives.

Holt continued his run at a faster pace. This early in the day the air was cool and the humidity low. He ran down Magnolia Avenue.

As he passed Rex Meredith's mansion, he saw a man on his knees working in a colorful flower bed. It was the caretaker whose name Holt couldn't remember. Holt slowed and walked up the brick pathway that led to the long porch.

"Good morning," he said to the man who still had his back to him.

The man spun around and held a garden trowel out in front of his chest like a knife. He was wearing a dirty denim cap and soiled overalls. Wisps of white hair stuck out from beneath the cap.

"Sorry," Holt said and held his hands up in the air. "I didn't mean to startle you, Mr. . . ." Holt waited for the man to fill in the blank, but instead the caretaker glanced down at the trowel and flicked off a piece of dirt. "I was out for a run and stopped to see the flowers."

"Be that what," the man said. "It be that."

"Pardon?" Holt asked.

The man motioned with the trowel for Holt to move on. There was no misinterpreting the message. Holt backed up a few steps and jogged to the main sidewalk. He continued into town, where he circled the courthouse and retraced his steps. When he reached the Meredith place, the caretaker wasn't in sight. Holt tried to get a better view of the small house where the man lived, but except for a corner of the building, it was hidden behind the main dwelling.

Holt's route took him past the Paxton Apostolic Church. He saw Bishop Pennington leaving through the side door near his office. The bishop motioned for Holt to come closer.

"I'm going to keep my distance," Holt said, stopping a few feet from the minister. "I got steamed up the last mile."

"I've never quite figured out the reason for jogging," the minister replied. "I guess I worked so hard when I was a youngster that I looked forward to a rest, not a workout."

"I'd probably feel the same way if I had to break a sweat for a living."

The bishop rubbed his hand across his gray hair. "I visited Jamal and his mother the other day. She promised to bring him to church tomorrow. I think she was just waiting for someone to show up and ask her. It wouldn't have happened if you hadn't been playing ball with those boys."

"You could have come out and talked to them."

"Maybe, but I suspect they'd have taken off when they saw me. Even though I'm old and slow, people still believe they need to run from me."

Since their conversation about the absence of a statute of limitations for sins, Holt could identify with that feeling.

"I just had a guy run me off. Do you know the man who takes care of Rex Meredith's house on Magnolia Avenue? I tried to say something to him, and all I got was a hostile attitude and nonsense."

"Oh, Sonny has a speech problem. What do they call it when a child sees the letters jumbled up in a sentence?"

"Dyslexia."

"Right. That's the way it is for Sonny when he talks. He understands you well enough, but he has a lot of trouble making himself understood. Did he have a writing pad with him?"

"No, he was digging in the flower beds."

"When he goes to the store, he'll write down what he wants. He can do that well enough to make clear what he needs. But he's not much for socializing with anyone. Sonny is happier being left alone."

"How do you know him?"

"We're about the same age. He played with us when we were little because the white kids made fun of the way he talked."

"And the black children didn't?"

"Not when my older brother was around." The bishop smiled. "When we were growing up, nobody messed with Jessie. He told everyone to treat Sonny nice and made it stick."

Holt glanced past the bishop to the front of the church. The bishop wiped his forehead with a clean white handkerchief.

"Was Sonny at the house the night Rex Meredith died?"

"Unless he was off running an errand, Sonny was usually on the property. But I don't recall if he was inside the house when they found Mr. Meredith's body or not. I sat next to him at the funeral. He didn't say anything, of course, but the tears rolled off his cheeks. Mr. Meredith was a hard man, but I think he had a soft spot in his heart for Sonny."

"How did you get along with him?"

"Members of my family were sharecroppers on Meredith land for generations." The minister shrugged. "I'm not sure he ever saw me as anything except a sharecropper's son."

"What about enemies? I'm sure there were people who didn't like him."

"Yeah, plenty of people he took advantage of in business. But you could start with his ex-wives. He got married before they had those prenup things. His first wife ran off with someone else and disappeared. His second wife raised a huge stink when he put her out of the house. They had a big fight over money. The newspaper didn't write about it, but that didn't keep people from talking. It's hard for me to know what was true; however, there isn't much doubt in my mind that Mr. Meredith was a mean drunk."

"How mean?"

"Mean enough to hit a woman. I'm not sure about his first wife, but the second one had pictures of the bruises he left on her. I heard he had to give her a big cash settlement before she would turn him loose."

"Did you see any of those pictures?"

"No."

"And there weren't any criminal charges?"

"I doubt it, but you should be able to find out if she ever filed a complaint against him. Her name was Rose. She was from Moultrie and had a high opinion of herself. I heard she hit him, too. Isn't that something? People can have everything the world thinks is important and be as miserable as two wet cats tied up in a burlap sack."

"No children?"

"None of his own. Carrie, the third wife, brought Valerie along with her when she came to town. Carrie was real quiet and kind of shy. She opened a dress shop and rented a space from Mr. Meredith."

"How old was Valerie when her mother and Meredith got married?"

"I guess she was twelve or so. Carrie died a year or so before Mr. Meredith; some kind of blood clot in her brain burst."

A car pulled into the church parking lot. Bishop Pennington turned away from Holt as the vehicle stopped, and five people piled out.

"Bishop!" a large woman called out. "We were on our way to Savannah, and I told Bobby we had to get off the highway and see if you were here."

"I'll check with you later," Holt said as the minister stepped forward to greet his visitors.

"Do that," the bishop said and spread his arms wide toward the people getting out of the car.

Holt jogged the last few blocks to his house. Revived, Henry greeted him by jumping up and down at the backyard gate.

17

Trish and Keith attended the young adult Sunday school class, the rural church's version of speed dating and Internet matchmaking. In the unwritten protocol of the class, a couple slightly interested in each other positioned themselves so they could make occasional eye contact and smile at one another.

The next step involved sitting close enough to be acutely aware of the other's presence but without the danger of direct physical contact. Beyond that came sharing a common Bible, which gave an excuse for a man and a woman to put their heads together as they leaned in to read a verse. Finally, there would be casual, yet intense, physical contact when hands touched while turning the pages of the Holy Book or occasional pressure against a leg when the man or the woman shifted in their seats.

This morning Keith moved directly to the final step. He positioned himself next to Trish and leaned against her several times. Not wanting to hurt his feelings, Trish didn't shrink away.

Later in the sanctuary, Trish whispered to her mother, "Keith wants to take us by the property on Cockburn Road after church. Do you want me to tell him that you don't feel like it and would rather go home?"

"I'd like to see it. I could stay in the car while you walk around on it."

"In these shoes?" Trish looked down at her feet and realized she'd worn flats that would be fine for walking on level ground that hadn't seen a rain shower for weeks.

"Yes," her mother said. "He'll want to show you the spot he has in mind for the house."

"This is way too domestic. I'm not ready to pick out curtains for a kitchen."

"Most women would welcome a man who's thinking about something other than a new deer rifle."

Brother Carpenter bounded up the steps to the platform, and the meeting began. Several times during the service, Trish cut her eyes in Keith's direction. He was sitting with his family two rows in front of her. By the end of the sermon, she'd concluded that letting Keith Pierce show her five acres of soybeans wouldn't be a terrible way to spend a Sunday afternoon.

—

They walked down the narrow rows between bushy green plants to the creek. Even without a recent rain, there was plenty of water in the slow-moving stream. Tadpoles dived for cover when Trish knelt close to the edge of the water.

"There'll be a chorus of frogs singing here every night during the summer," she said.

"Maybe they can teach me to carry a tune," Keith replied.

Trish had heard Keith sing in church. He had two notes—high and low.

"It's the melody in your heart that counts," she said.

The ground rose steadily from the edge of the creek. It didn't seem likely that the water from the small stream, even if it jumped the banks, would ever come as far as the place Keith had picked out for his house. To do so, it would have to cross two hundred yards of ground and come up at least fifteen to twenty feet. As they walked, Keith's plans for the property poured from his lips. It was a vivid vision of a rich, rural life.

—

The following morning, Trish arrived at the sheriff's department a few minutes early. Sitting at her desk, she took out her phone and scrolled again through the pictures she'd taken of the land on Cockburn Road. In one Keith stood with his back to her and his arm raised as he pointed toward the creek. It was a classic pioneer pose.

"Carmichael!" A gruff voice interrupted her so abruptly that she almost dropped her phone.

It was Detective Clovis.

"Yes, sir."

"Do you have an open file on a man named Vincent Calhoun?"

"The name sounds familiar," Trish said as she turned in her chair and clicked open the file on her computer that contained her active cases. "I have a Mitchell Calhoun."

"It's the same guy. Mitchell is his middle name. Close the case and give the paper file to me."

While the detective talked, Trish read the summary she'd entered into her computer. The man was more than twelve thousand dollars in arrears for child support payments for two children.

"That's a collectible case," she said. "He has a job."

"I'm familiar with his employment status," Clovis replied. "I'm telling you to shut it down and take if off your docket. Do I need to bring in Sheriff Blackstone to back me up?"

"Uh, no, sir. I'll do it this morning."

"On my desk before noon."

Clovis walked off. Trish looked around the edge of her cubicle at the detective's broad back as he reached the end of the hallway and turned toward his office. Trish opened a second window that provided more details about Calhoun. One item a few rows from the top immediately caught her attention. Calhoun worked for Greg Stevens.

Trish pressed the Print Screen button. She'd put everything on Clovis's desk by noon and close the file, but she'd also make a copy of the file for herself.

And Holt Douglas.

—

Belinda stuck her head into Holt's office. "Good news," she said. "Ralph gave me the okay to contact Trish Carmichael about a job."

Surprised, Holt said, "I didn't expect that."

"Natasha told him she's pregnant and won't be back when she goes out on maternity leave."

Natasha worked under Belinda and provided support to all three of the attorneys.

"Do you think Trish can handle her job?" Holt asked. "Natasha is a certified paralegal."

"Which is more important? On-the-job training and real-world experience or sitting in a classroom pretending?"

"If you look in the mirror, you'll see the answer to that question."

Belinda chuckled. "Very smooth. So, I'm going to reach out to Trish and—"

"Could you wait a few weeks?" Holt interrupted. "Natasha's not going to be leaving immediately, is she?"

"No, it will be months. But why wait?"

Holt couldn't tell Belinda the real reason—that he wanted to see if Trish would be able to feed him valuable inside information from the sheriff's department about Rex Meredith's death.

"Uh, I need to decide what I think about Trish. On a personal level."

A grin creased Belinda's face. "Gotcha. Would you like to be the one to mention the job possibility to her when the time is right?"

"Sure."

The grin on Belinda's face grew to a broad smile. "You're in charge of Trish's future," she said. "Just keep me in the loop."

—

After Belinda left, Holt opened the bottom drawer of his desk and took out the data he'd collected about Rex Meredith's death. So far it all fell into the circumstantial suspicion category, which was just a cut above a half-baked conspiracy theory. He needed an opinion from someone with the opportunity and training to evaluate evidence that would point to a different cause of Meredith's death than suicide.

Having been interrupted by Ralph before he could complete his earlier search for information on Tony McDermott, Holt once again logged on to the secure database site. He entered his personal ID. Since there was no open file on Rex Meredith, Holt grabbed a file from his credenza and entered the number for a larceny case involving a stolen pickup truck. No one in the DA's office ever cross-referenced use of the database and file numbers used to gain access.

The requested results for McDermott popped up in seconds, including an address, date of birth, marital status, names of children,

Social Security number, work history, and two phone numbers. Anthony Blake McDermott lived near Lake Burton in Rabun County, a mountainous area nestled in the northeast corner of the state. The area around the lake contained houses that cost millions of dollars and one-room cabins built from scrap lumber. Holt checked the tax records for McDermott's address. The former detective lived in a two-bedroom cabin built in the early 1980s. The next to last entry for employment was the Ashley County Sheriff's Department. After that, McDermott worked as a private security officer for a resort in the Lake Burton area. Holt pressed the Print button. There was a printer in the hallway directly outside his office. Opening the door of his office, Holt found his way blocked by Ralph Granger, who stood in front of the printer.

"Hey, Ralph," Holt said, wondering about the unlikelihood of his boss's second ill-timed appearance. "I need to grab something off the printer."

Ralph turned his head. "Me too. This is the week to clean the deadwood off your docket. What are you working on?"

Ralph lifted the sheets from the printer tray.

"An older case," Holt replied, resisting the impulse to snatch the papers from Ralph's hand. Ralph turned the pages over. Holt's stomach knotted up.

"Tony McDermott?" Ralph said. "I'm sure the sheriff's office would give you his contact information."

Holt tried to keep his voice nonchalant. "I didn't want to bother anyone. It was easier to punch his name into the system."

"What's the old case?" Ralph asked. "McDermott wasn't here for long."

In a split second Holt considered all his options, from an outright lie, to the total truth, to a hybrid couched in ambiguity. Stalling for time, he glanced around as if seeing who was within earshot.

"I need to talk to you about it in private," he said.

"Okay, let me pass these documents along to Belinda, and I'll be back in a minute."

His heart pounding, Holt returned to his office. He put the information about Tony McDermott in the Meredith folder and returned everything to the bottom drawer. He stared across his desk at his office door and tried to figure out what to do. A minute passed. Then another. Ralph didn't appear. Holt fidgeted. Getting up from his desk, he cracked open his door and looked down the hallway toward Ralph's office. There was no sign of the DA. Holt walked around the corner to Belinda's workstation.

"Have you seen Ralph?"

"You just missed him. He got a call from the county commissioner's office a few minutes ago and left for a budget meeting. We've been working on figures for the next fiscal year. It was a good thing I had them ready this morning because he thought it wasn't coming up until the end of the week."

"Okay," Holt said with relief.

Belinda leaned closer and lowered her voice. "Ralph included a line item so he could give you a raise from discretionary county funds. More money will help you plan for the future."

Holt's base salary was paid by the state of Georgia, but a local government could supplement an assistant DA's salary if it chose to do so.

"He really wants to keep you," Belinda continued. "And he knows you could make a lot more if you jumped over to private practice. He never went to bat like this for Skip."

"Skip was ready to try something else. I'm not, at least for a while."

"But Ralph doesn't know that. And you know how paranoid he can be."

"Yes, I do."

Holt returned to his office. Shortly before noon, Skip called.

"How was your steak?" he asked.

"Very good. That place is going to do well."

"I got a nice thank-you note from Angelina. Yours must be delayed in the mail."

"Or buried under the checks piled up on your desk from your monthly billings. Do you want to do lunch? It's a slow week for us over here."

"Absolutely. That's why I called."

"No barbecue," Holt replied. "I want something light."

"Let's join the ladies at Camille's."

"See you there in fifteen minutes."

After the call ended, Kathy brought a packet into his office.

"The courier from the sheriff's department dropped this off for you," she said.

Holt sliced open the envelope with a sterling silver letter opener, a present from his mother when he passed the bar exam. He quickly read Trish's notes and supporting documentation about Greg Stevens, Butch Clovis, and Vincent Calhoun. Holt wasn't naive about powerful people influencing the administration of justice, but that didn't make him like it.

He'd found an ally in Trish Carmichael. And she needed to stay employed exactly where she was.

18

Camille's was a pastry shop that featured a soup du jour and fancy salad options on the lunch menu. The tables and chairs were delicately shaped wrought iron, painted in pastel colors. Skip was sitting at an aqua table when Holt arrived. There weren't any other men in sight.

"I like the peach table," Holt said as he walked up.

"Sorry, but I'm in a blue mood," Skip replied.

"Why?"

"I asked the woman at the counter if the soup of the day was chili, and she looked at me as if I had two heads."

"What is the soup?"

Skip turned in his chair and squinted at a chalkboard behind the counter. "Uh, butternut squash bisque. She said they make it with organic squash. Can you imagine a farmer bragging to his buddies that he sold a pickup truck load of squash to this place?"

"Yes, if he made money doing it."

They both ordered a salad. Holt took a bite and nodded his head. "You have to admit the stuff here is fresh," he said.

"Sure. Otherwise, I wouldn't have agreed to meet you here. Give me details about your dinner at the steak house. I'm meeting with the owners later this afternoon and want to give them an unbiased review."

Holt told him about the meal and concluded by saying, "By any standard, it was five-star."

"Wow. The owners may want to use you in a commercial for the local cable channel."

"I don't know about—"

"I'm kidding. If they were going to shoot a commercial, they'd want to feature Angelina. Her legs are better than yours."

"Along with everything else." Holt stabbed a bite of salad with his fork. "What do you think about Brittany, the receptionist at the salon?"

"I don't really know her."

Holt told as much of Brittany's story as he could remember.

"I had no idea she was in her mid-twenties," Skip said. "I would have guessed she was just out of high school."

"Would you be interested in asking her out? Maybe the four of us could go back to the steak house."

"Is this your idea or is Angelina behind it?"

"You know the answer to that question, Counselor."

"Right." Skip nodded. "And is Angelina acting as Brittany's agent?"

"Can you think of any other possibility?"

"No, but I want to know when I'm being manipulated by a couple of women. It's not necessarily a negative feeling." Skip grinned. "Actually, I kind of like it. Can I think it over and get back to you?"

Holt checked his watch. "I'll give you five minutes, but I already know your answer."

"Don't presume to know what a witness is thinking. That kind of arrogance will get you into trouble."

Holt took a final bite of salad. "Oh, I found out the name of the second detective who worked the investigation following Rex Meredith's death. It was Anthony McDermott. He went by Tony."

"Yeah, that's the guy. Why are you interested in Meredith's death? There's nothing there."

Holt looked past Skip's shoulder at the door of the restaurant. Skip turned in his chair and followed Holt's line of sight.

"What?" Skip asked. "Have you come up with some newly discovered evidence?"

"No, but reviewing the old evidence has me asking questions. Ralph doesn't know I'm looking into it—"

"And you don't want him to find out because Greg Stevens is giving him a bunch of money for the campaign."

"Right. Why did you jump so fast to Stevens?"

"Because if you're looking into an alternate theory for the cause of Meredith's death, Stevens would be the first person I'd pull up on the viewfinder. On the practical side, he's the person who benefited the most from Meredith's untimely demise. He may have been the old man's son-in-law, but he had no real say in the way Meredith ran his empire. He'd even been demoted."

"Demoted?"

"Yeah. Meredith hired Stevens because he was a CPA, but he wasn't even the top financial adviser on the payroll. He reported to a man named Cantor. Then Stevens starts dating Valerie and ends up marrying her. Cantor retires and Stevens takes his place. This all happened before I came to town, but about a year before his death, Meredith jerks the rug out from under Stevens and hires a guy named Boatwright and puts him in charge. It was a hot item of business gossip."

"Why did he do that?"

"Most people chalked it up to Meredith's being a jerk, which is a plausible explanation. He had the reputation of changing his mind as quickly as the humidity shoots up or down during the summer."

"Did you ever meet him?"

"Nothing beyond a handshake at a public function. He didn't like Ralph, and that carried over to everyone who worked in the office." Skip paused. "But if we stop hypothesizing and realize we're talking about real people, I can't imagine Greg Stevens having anything to do with Meredith's death. I don't doubt he was thrilled to have the old man out of his life, but killing Meredith or hiring somebody to do it seems far-fetched. Stevens is a mousy accountant. I don't think he has a sinister dark side. And even if he did, convincing the sheriff's department and Ralph to cover it up is a crazy theory."

Hearing Skip describe so openly what Holt had been secretly mulling over made sense.

"You're probably right," he said. "But I'd still like to ask McDermott a few questions."

Holt told him what happened earlier in the day at the printer. Skip shrugged. "Ralph will forget about McDermott, then bring it up out of the blue when you least expect it next week or next month. The stuff in his brain isn't well organized, but it isn't lost, either."

"I know."

Skip's face grew serious.

"And he is your boss. Holt, going rogue as an assistant DA is not how things are done."

"You think I should tell him?"

"Yes, and get his okay to interview McDermott. The idea that Ralph is part of a criminal cover-up isn't believable. His greatest fear is that he will lose his job, and he knows there aren't any district attorneys prosecuting cases from inside a jail cell. Ralph isn't a risk taker. He may plead out cases to pad his statistics, but he wouldn't take a bribe or tell a lie that might send him to prison."

Holt couldn't disagree with any aspect of Skip's assessment of Ralph. He wasn't as sure about Greg Stevens. Skip pointed to the display case for the pastries.

"I'll get one of those éclairs if you do," he said.

"That would cancel out the benefits of the salad."

"You'll burn up one of those éclairs in ten minutes on the basketball court."

"You convinced me."

"Man, I'm good." Skip smiled. "And fast. Oh, and tell Angelina that not only is she gorgeous, but she's an awesome matchmaker. I'd be honored to go out to dinner with Brittany so long as Angelina is along to chaperone."

"That means I'll be there, too."

"A necessary evil. Maybe you can pick up the tab."

"You know what I make a year."

"And that's what I'll tell my clients this afternoon when I hit them up for more gift cards."

—

Holt parked next to Jim Montgomery's car. Only Ralph had a reserved space, and he parked closer to the front door than someone with a handicap sticker. Inside, Holt was on his way into his office when Belinda called out to him.

"Holt!"

He went over to the administrator's desk.

"Come closer," she said.

Holt leaned over.

"Do you want to hear some good news?" she asked in a soft voice.

"Yes."

"The county budget committee is going to recommend the full supplement Ralph wants to add to your base salary."

"Really?" Holt raised his eyebrows. "I'd heard there was going to be a budget shortfall for the coming fiscal year."

"The county got a big shot in their bank account from an unexpected source. It's a designated gift."

"A gift?"

"From the Meredith Trust. Most of the money is allocated for education and health care, but there was a slice for law enforcement. A piece of that is going to you."

Holt was about to go on Greg Stevens's payroll. "That's amazing," he managed. "How much is Stevens giving?"

"Ralph didn't tell me," Belinda replied, pointing to a stack of notes. "But he asked me to type up his notes from the meeting, and I figured out what happened. I'm sure they'll make a huge announcement in the newspaper. Act surprised and grateful when Ralph tells you. He'll take the credit for pulling it off."

Holt went into his office. Greg Stevens wasn't fitting into the mold of a cold, calculating killer.

Unless, of course, generosity was his way of dealing with guilt.

—

When her shift ended at 3:00 p.m., Trish didn't go home. Instead, she phoned Sue Ann. On the way to her friend's apartment, she stopped at a local ice-cream shop and ordered three scoops of double chocolate chunk in an extra-large cup. The ice cream was getting soft by the time Trish walked up the steps and rang the doorbell. As soon as Sue Ann opened the door, Candace scrambled past her mother's legs and onto the landing. Holding the cup of ice cream in one hand, Trish managed to corral the toddler with the other.

"She's worse than a puppy that wants to bolt out the door as soon as it's cracked open," Sue Ann said.

"I've got something that will convince her to go back inside."

Trish lowered the cup of ice cream so Candace could see it. The little girl squealed, stuck her index finger in it, and popped it into her mouth.

"No!" Sue Ann yelled. "You don't know where that finger has been!"

Trish held the cup of ice cream higher and led Candace back into the house.

"Put that in the fridge while I wash her hands," Sue Ann said. "She's going to get messy eating it, but at least it will be a sanitary mess."

Trish went into the kitchen and opened the freezer door. The refrigerator was well stocked with identical frozen pizzas.

"Does Mark love pizza?" she called out.

Sue Ann returned with Candace in tow. "What did you say? I couldn't hear over the running water."

"What's with all the pizzas in the freezer?"

"Most of the time Mark would rather have a pizza than a home-cooked meal. My mother gives me a hard time about it, but I told her it's a blessing that he's easy to please. Especially with—" Sue Ann stopped.

"What?" Trish looked at her wide-eyed.

Sue Ann gave her a sheepish grin. "Another baby on the way. It was a total accident, but now that it's happened I'm happy. Mark is excited, too. I hope he stays positive if it's another girl. He really wants a boy."

"Congratulations!" Trish gave Sue Ann a big hug.

Candace pulled on her mother's shirt. "Ice dream," the little girl said.

Sue Ann put Candace in her booster seat with a towel wrapped around her so only her right hand was free. Sue Ann then secured the towel with a clothes pin and put another towel beneath the little girl's chair.

"Okay, I think we're ready for ice dream."

Trish took out her phone and snapped a picture. "I want before-and-after shots."

Sue Ann put a small portion of the ice cream in a plastic bowl for

Candace and a larger amount for her and Trish. Candace looked at the three bowls and yelled in protest. Sue Ann gave the child a tiny bit more.

"If you get mad, I'm going to take all of it away from you," she warned.

Trish watched the little girl's face as she processed the seriousness of the threat. Without saying anything else, Candace picked up her spoon and deposited most of a messy bite into her mouth. Sue Ann ate a spoonful and closed her eyes.

"How did you know this was what I needed more than anything else in the world this afternoon?" she asked.

"Because that's what you've wanted more than anything else in the world every afternoon since we were in elementary school."

"I do love chocolate."

"That's double chocolate," Trish corrected.

They ate in silence for a few moments. Candace seemed to enjoy the chance to play with her ice cream as much as eating it. Eventually she laid her spoon on the table and, just as she did when greeting Trish at the door, began sticking her finger into the ice cream and transferring it to her mouth.

"Speaking of love," Sue Ann said, "what's the status of your love life? Any progress with Holt?"

"That's gotten more complicated."

"Complicated sounds interesting." Sue Ann perked up.

Trish told Sue Ann about dinner with Keith and his excitement about the property on Cockburn Road.

"I wish Mark had new-house fever," Sue Ann sighed, then quickly added, "Sorry. I shouldn't be thinking about myself while you're telling me about you."

"That's okay. You need a bigger nest for more baby chicks."

Sue Ann scraped the bottom of her bowl with a spoon. "You

know, I understand why you're questioning your interest in Holt, but the way you talk about Keith sounds more like shopping for a new car than falling in love with a man."

Sue Ann's comment stuck like a barb of truth in Trish's heart. She quickly ate a last bite of ice cream to ease the sting. Chocolate wasn't her favorite. She liked French vanilla.

Trish reached for her phone and took a photo of Candace, who looked like she'd rubbed her face with brown goo.

"I don't know," Trish said. "Sometimes my dreams about the future are as messy as Candace when she's finished eating her ice dream."

19

Holt apprehensively waited for Ralph to come by his office. At 4:30 p.m. he received a text message from the DA, who'd left without Holt knowing it:

At Quail Ridge. Just birdied number 9. Have good news for you. What time will you be at the office in the morning?

Holt knew that Ralph preferred early meetings even if neither of them needed to be in court.

8:00 a.m. Okay? Congrats on the birdie.

Yes.

The ninth hole on the Quail Ridge golf course was a short par four that yielded a lot of birdies so golfers would be in a good mood when taking a midround break in the clubhouse. For Ralph, any birdie involved a healthy dose of fortuitous ball striking.

With Ralph on the golf course, Holt decided asking for forgiveness was better than waiting for permission. He called the phone number for Tony McDermott. A woman answered. According to the database, McDermott hadn't remarried.

"Tony McDermott, please," Holt said.

"Daddy!" the woman called out. "Telephone!"

Holt checked his info sheet. McDermott had two daughters, both of whom were in their thirties.

"McDermott here," said a male voice that still had a police-beat sound to it.

"This is Holt Douglas. I'm an assistant district attorney in Ashley County, and I'd like to ask you a few questions about a case you investigated when you were with the sheriff's department a few years ago."

"Douglas?"

"Yes. I came to town after you left."

"How do I know you're really with the DA's office?"

It wasn't a question Holt had anticipated. "Uh, what sort of proof do you need?"

"Just a second," McDermott said. "Something I can verify that's not on the county website I just pulled up."

"Do you see my picture?" Holt asked.

"Tall guy with curly brown hair. How old are you?"

"Twenty-eight." Holt racked his brain for a credible piece of additional information. "How about this? For years the busiest defense lawyer in this circuit has been Dirk Rangel. When he's talking to Judge Lomax he likes to hold out his hand like he's posing for a Michelangelo statue."

McDermott laughed. "I haven't thought about Rangel since I left Paxton. He can be an arrogant jerk, especially when he has something to work with on a case."

"He recently beat me on a motion to suppress in a drug case,"

Holt replied. "It stung, but I had a big evidentiary problem caused by the detective who made the arrest."

"Who was that?"

Holt immediately regretted bringing up the Morton case because it would require him to criticize a law enforcement officer, but he knew he had to answer. McDermott didn't seem like the type who would accept a diversion.

"Butch Clovis."

Holt could hear McDermott grunt. "I'm not surprised. What's on your mind?"

"Rex Meredith's death."

The phone was silent for a moment.

"Go ahead," McDermott said.

"I obtained a copy of the file at the sheriff's office. It contains a report from Clovis concluding that Meredith committed suicide. You're listed as the other detective who worked the case, but there isn't a report from you. Did you prepare one?"

"Yes."

"Where is it?"

"Here with me."

Holt stopped breathing for a second. "Could I ask you a few questions about it?"

"Yeah. I'll be right back."

While McDermott was away from the phone, Holt chided himself for not being better prepared for the call. He quickly jotted down several more questions.

"I'm back," McDermott said.

Holt glanced down at his legal pad. "Why wasn't your report in the sheriff's department file?"

"Because they didn't want a minority opinion. Clovis and Sheriff Blackstone told me to shred it, but I didn't. Their primary concern was that my report might get out to the press and cause a stink. I wasn't interested in that. I just wanted to do my job."

"Did Ralph Granger know about your report?"

"I can't say. We never discussed it. He worked directly with Blackstone on that case. Clovis knew I had questions, but he and Blackstone were against me so I let it go. Did you listen to the 911 call from Meredith's son-in-law?"

"No, all I had was a transcript, but it didn't read like he was upset."

"That's what my notes say, too. I wanted to spend some time with Stevens and probe from different angles to see if his story held up under pressure, but I wasn't given the chance to do it."

"What would you have asked him?"

"About the timeline of events on the evening of Meredith's death. Who, what, when, where questions with Stevens, his wife, who was Meredith's stepdaughter, and the caretaker who lived on the property."

"The caretaker was there the night of Meredith's death?"

"Yeah, the guy with the speech impediment. I didn't get a chance to interview him, either. Clovis talked to him and told me he didn't have anything to add. It was the same with the stepdaughter. According to Clovis, they all came into the room about the same time and found Meredith lying on the floor. He'd been shot at close range in the chest. However, I never got a clear answer as to how each person came to be in the house and then ended up together when the body was found."

"Is there a summary of what Clovis claims the caretaker said?"

"Nothing except that he confirmed Stevens's story. Of course, what bothered me the most were the questions about the gun."

"I don't know anything about that."

"I thought Clovis included it in his report, but maybe he didn't. The fingerprints on the weapon were a mess, which made me think more than one person in the study may have handled it. Greg

Stevens told Clovis that Meredith was still alive when they found him, and he took the gun from the old man's hand so he couldn't get off another shot."

"He didn't shoot himself in the heart?"

"Close to it, but no. It tore up his chest enough that he didn't make it to the hospital."

"What about the fingerprints?"

"In addition to Stevens messing with the gun, the medics got there and disturbed everything while trying to keep Meredith alive. Before I got shut down by Blackstone, I got a fingerprint card from Greg Stevens and one from Meredith's corpse at the hospital morgue and then supervised the dusting of the gun myself."

"Were there any identifiable prints?"

"None that we could lift. Everything was smudged and partial and there were gaps, as if someone tried to wipe the gun clean and did a sloppy job. One thing particularly stuck out. The trigger was completely spotless, nothing on it. Nobody claimed Meredith was wearing gloves when he shot himself. You wouldn't expect to find a full print on the trigger, but it should have something. I would have dug into that if I'd been given the chance. The other issue related to the shot fired prior to the one that hit Meredith in the chest."

Holt sat bolt upright in his chair. "That wasn't in Clovis's report."

"Yeah, I've seen better investigations of the theft of a carton of cigarettes at a convenience store. Anyway, there was a hole in a painting on the wall in the room where they found the body."

"Where was the painting hanging?"

"Did you see the diagram of the room with the location of the body?"

"Yes."

"The painting was across the room. There were two entrances to the study: one from the foyer, another from a hallway that led to the kitchen. The bullet hit the painting in the upper-right corner, pierced the wall, and ended up in the foyer. I found the remains of the slug."

"Where is the bullet now?"

"If they haven't thrown it away, it should be in storage at the sheriff's department, but I'm not sure it can reveal anything."

"What was your explanation for the gunshot?"

"The most obvious conclusion was that Meredith shot at something or someone. It could have been an accidental discharge of the weapon prior to the bullet he put in his chest. Or it may have been something else."

"Did any of the people in the house hear two shots?"

"Mr. and Mrs. Stevens and the caretaker admitted hearing one shot. They all came running into the study and found Meredith on the floor. I found that very strange."

"Why?"

"Think about it. If you're a rich person, and there's a gunshot in the house, the first thing you consider is a break-in, isn't it? Have you met Greg Stevens?"

"Yes."

"Does he seem like the kind of guy itching to wrestle a thief to the floor and make a citizen's arrest? And would most husbands bring their wives along to see what's going on if a gun has been fired? Wouldn't the first call have been to 911 to get the police on the scene as soon as possible? That's some of the stuff I wanted to explore. Most fabricated stories aren't detailed enough to stand up under prolonged questioning. Eventually, the person who's lying trips up in a small way that turns into a bigger discrepancy. I've been around long enough to know that all investigations are not created equal, but the way this one was rammed through bugged me then, and it bothers me now."

Listening to McDermott strengthened Holt's resolve to continue to dig until he uncovered the truth. "What do you believe happened?"

"I don't know and hate to assume anything until it's proven."

McDermott covered the phone receiver with his hand and said something Holt couldn't hear.

"Who's working with you?" McDermott asked when he returned to the call.

"Uh, a low-level contact at the sheriff's department is feeding me a little bit of information on the side."

"I get it," McDermott said. "You're going lone ranger on this one, trying to make a name for yourself as a hotshot prosecutor who goes up against the local power structure."

"Not really. The DA's file ended up on my desk by mistake a couple of weeks ago, and I immediately saw how little was done. A man's death deserves more than what I read on a few sheets of paper, so I decided to do a little digging on my own. You've told me a lot more than I knew before."

"Are you going to tell Ralph Granger about our conversation?"

"If it's okay with you."

McDermott gave a short laugh. "I never really fit in down there, and nobody can do anything to me now. I don't care what you say to Granger. He's a political animal, not a professional prosecutor."

It was a crisp, biting, and accurate summary. Holt couldn't disagree. He looked down at his notes. There were no more questions, but he knew he'd have a bunch after he digested what the former detective had told him.

"Can I call you back if I need to?"

"Yeah, but I work by the hour now. If you need an expert witness, it won't be a freebie. This conversation was on the house. The next one won't be."

"Would you send me a copy of your report?"

McDermott was silent for a moment. "Only if you promise to keep it confidential until you go public with this thing. And that means an indictment. Otherwise it stays buried. I don't want to get sued for slander."

Holt's hands suddenly felt clammy. Until his conversation with McDermott, there had been an academic quality to the investigation. Now it was beginning to feel real.

"Agreed. I don't want it coming to the office. One of the staff might open it."

Holt gave McDermott his home address.

"Could you send it overnight?" Holt asked.

"Yeah, if you reimburse the cost."

"Sure."

"And let me know what happens with your investigation," the former detective said, "even if you drop it."

"Will do."

After work, Holt took Henry out for a walk in the direction of Magnolia Avenue. It was a pleasant evening. He let Henry stop to explore smells that caught the attention of the dog's sensitive nose. When they reached the Meredith mansion, Holt saw an expensive car parked in the driveway. Standing beside the car and talking to the caretaker was Valerie Stevens. The Meredith heiress was wearing a yellow summer dress. Prancing around at her feet was a rambunctious Chihuahua. Holt stopped as if admiring the house. Valerie and the caretaker didn't notice him. As Holt watched, Valerie handed an envelope to the caretaker, who touched the bill of his cap in a sign of respect. Holt continued down the street. When he reached the corner, he turned around and retraced his steps. As he approached the Meredith house, a figure was coming toward him on the sidewalk.

It was Valerie Stevens.

The Chihuahua was on a slender leash. Holt heard a growl rumble up in Henry's throat. As they came closer together, Holt pulled back on Henry's leash until the dog was rubbing against Holt's leg. When they were about ten feet from each other, Valerie made eye contact with Holt and smiled.

"That's a handsome Jack Russell," she said. "I bet he loves going for walks."

"Yes, there's no limit to his energy," Holt said as he stopped.

Valerie picked up her wiggling Chihuahua in her arms. Then, to Holt's horror, she leaned over and stretched out her hand toward Henry's mouth.

"No!" Holt called out.

But it was too late. Valerie Stevens was already stroking Henry under the chin. The dog closed his eyes and seemed to purr.

"That's incredible," Holt said. "Henry usually bites first and asks questions later."

"He told me it would be okay when I looked in his eyes," Valerie said as she stood up. "I'm Valerie Stevens."

Holt introduced himself. Valerie eyed him for a moment.

"The charity auction," she said. "You were there."

"Yes, and I saw your husband the other day at the office. He was meeting with Ralph Granger."

"Why was he there?"

Holt hadn't considered the possibility that Stevens's wife might not know about his political activities. But then, people with a lot of money didn't have the time to keep track of every dollar.

"He's on Ralph Granger's reelection committee. I hope Mr. Stevens won't get in trouble at home for me telling you."

"No," Valerie said and dismissed his concern with a wave of her hand. "He does a lot I don't know about."

The Chihuahua yelped sharply.

"What's your dog's name?" Holt asked.

"Peps." She stroked the tiny dog's head. "I've had Chihuahuas for years and years. Tell me about Henry."

"He's my first dog since I left home. I rented a house on Montgomery Street with a big fenced-in backyard just so I could get a dog."

"I like your priorities." Valerie smiled again. "Is Henry friendlier with dogs than he is with people?"

"Not really. Let me introduce them and see how it goes."

Holt picked up Henry and held him close enough to Peps that the two dogs could touch noses. Peps trembled with a mixture of excitement and fear. Henry, perhaps after satisfying himself that Peps wasn't a new form of squirrel, seemed disinterested.

"I think it will be okay," Holt said. "But I'll keep a tight rein on Henry."

Valerie lowered Peps to the ground, and the Chihuahua showed unmistakable signs of submission. Henry majestically accepted the little dog's homage. Valerie laughed.

"It seems Henry likes both the owner and the dog," Holt said.

"Most dogs can sense a friend when they meet one. I'm around a lot of them. At least once a week I go to the rescue facility on Nelson Street."

Holt had passed by the building, which was much nicer than expected for a town the size of Paxton. He guessed Valerie Stevens had a lot to do with that.

"We can't save every animal," Valerie continued, "but matching the right one with a loving family is very satisfying."

"I prosecuted a cruelty to animal case last year," Holt said. "The dogs ended up at that shelter."

"Yes," Valerie responded sadly. "I remember but didn't know you were involved. There were four dogs. We only placed one of them, a six-month-old puppy. The others were older and so traumatized we couldn't socialize them enough to release them. They had to be put down."

"The man involved went to jail."

"For six months with two years on probation." Valerie looked into Holt's eyes. "Thanks for making sure he was punished. A lot of people wouldn't think mistreating dogs is worth taking seriously."

"That's my job," Holt replied. "To prosecute the guilty."

20

Trish left Sue Ann's apartment in time to pick up supper for Marge. Once a month her mother liked to eat fish from a carryout place that sold deep-fried salt-and-pepper catfish fillets. It wasn't healthy, but it was a holdover from the days when Trish's father brought home dinner so Marge wouldn't have to cook. He loved catfish more than steak. Trish also ordered coleslaw and green beans. Hopefully she could convince her mother to drink water instead of sweet tea with the meal. When Trish entered the house, the TV was off and her mother was napping in the recliner in the living room. She stirred when Trish shut the front door.

"Sorry I woke you," Trish said.

"I need to get up," Marge said, yawning. "If I sleep too much during the day, it makes it harder to fall asleep at night."

"I have catfish." Trish held up two Styrofoam containers.

"Yummy. I made tea this afternoon. It's in the fridge. Did they give you any tartar sauce?"

"Yes."

Marge liked to spice up her tartar sauce with a generous dash of red pepper flakes. Trish nibbled a piece of catfish. It was thin and crispy, not overly greasy. Her conversation with Sue Ann was still on her mind.

"Mama, what do you think about Keith?"

"Shouldn't you be the one to answer that question?"

"Yes, but I don't know what my heart is saying to me."

"Then that's your answer. Your heart will tell you when it has an opinion. Until that happens, you can't make it talk. I like Keith a lot. Nothing about him worries me"—Marge paused—"except that he stays on the road so much. That would be tough on a marriage, especially once babies come along."

Trish was feeling sorry for herself, but her mother's comment about children made her chuckle.

"What's funny?"

"Keith Pierce and babies in the same sentence. He's focused on a house, not a family."

"A house is where babies live. Have you asked him about children?"

"No!" Trish replied emphatically. "I don't want to give him the wrong idea."

"That's part of your problem," Marge replied evenly. "You're afraid to ask the questions your heart needs to know to make up its mind. You're a smart woman. You could ask him about kids without his realizing it."

"How?"

"Talk to him about one of your friends like Sue Ann who has a child and see what he says."

"Oh, I meant to tell you. I stopped by Sue Ann's apartment on the way home from work. She's pregnant."

"That makes it even easier. Mention Sue Ann's news to Keith. If he shakes his head and says how hard that must be on Mark, you'll know what he thinks, at least for now. Your daddy was scared of having children. But after he met you, he changed his mind."

Trish glanced up at a photo Marge kept on the side of the refrigerator. In the picture Trish was wearing her high school basketball uniform and standing beside her father, who was beaming with pride. She wished he could step out of the picture and tell her what he thought about Keith.

Marge continued, "You know, it may be important to know Keith's perspective on children, but what matters most is whether he loves you."

After supper Trish skipped *Jeopardy.* Retreating to her bedroom, she turned on her computer. Her mind wasn't on Keith; it was on Holt. Using the fresh information Belinda had given her, Trish resumed her journey into the assistant DA's past. She read more articles in the neighborhood newspaper about Holt's sports career, then researched lacrosse so she could learn about the game and its rules. As originally played by Native Americans, there could be up to a thousand men on each side. It sounded more like war than a game.

She found an article in Holt's neighborhood newspaper about a funeral for a young man named Kenneth Morgan who'd died in an automobile accident. Also in the car was an eighteen-year-old named Holton Douglas. Trish stopped and looked up from the screen.

That was it.

Kenneth Morgan's death was the source of Holt's tears at the sub shop. Trish did a quick calculation. The accident happened not long before Holt graduated from high school. Trish would have been finishing the ninth grade. She looked for other news reports about the fatal accident and found one in the *Atlanta Journal-Constitution.* According to that article, Holt was injured but treated at a local hospital and released. Trish knew being released from the hospital didn't mean Holt was fine.

The deep sadness Holt experienced at the tragic death of his friend was of course different from the grief she felt for her father, but Trish recognized that the pain resulting from the premature passing of a young person, before life had had a chance to flourish, was particularly sharp. Compassion for Holt rose up in Trish's heart. She reached for a tissue and wiped her eyes.

The way Holt reacted revealed how raw he remained. Trish's sorrow had appeared with many faces. She tried to cope with grief, not resist or deny it. The desire to help Holt do the same caused a fresh tear to flow down her cheek.

Trish read each article several times before finally pushing her chair away from the computer. She wasn't any closer to knowing what her heart had to say about Keith or Holt. But she knew Holt needed the kind of touch only Jesus could give him, possibly through her.

—

The next day Holt called the sheriff's department to thank Trish for sending over the packet of information about Greg Stevens, Butch Clovis, and Vincent Calhoun. As he waited on hold, he debated how much, if any, of his conversation with Tony McDermott to share with her.

"This is Trish Carmichael," the deputy said in a perky voice.

"Hey, it's Holt."

"Oh," Trish replied, her tone of voice becoming serious. "How are you?"

"Okay for a Tuesday," Holt replied, slightly puzzled. "Thanks for tipping me off about Vincent Calhoun. It's not specifically relevant to Rex Meredith's death, but it's evidence of Stevens's manipulating Clovis and the sheriff's department for personal means."

"That's what I thought. Have you found out anything else?"

Holt hesitated, then decided not to hold anything back. "Yes. I called Tony McDermott yesterday. I wasn't sure he would talk to me, but he had plenty to say. He's sending me a copy of his file. I'd rather go over that with you in person. What's your schedule this week?"

"During the day?"

"Yes."

Trish was silent for a moment. "I'm working first shift. I don't think we should discuss this when I'm on duty since I don't have the sheriff's permission to—"

"I totally understand," Holt interrupted. "How about Thursday around three thirty?"

"Okay," Trish said slowly.

"What would be a good place to meet?"

"The library? They have those little rooms nobody uses next to the circulation desk."

"No," Holt replied. "I think the courthouse would be a better option. That way, if anyone sees us together, they will assume we're talking about your cases."

"Yeah, that makes sense."

"Meet me in the main courtroom around three thirty."

Holt hung up the phone and pushed the Meredith matter out of his mind. He spent most of the rest of the day working on an appellate brief in a drug-trafficking case. Daring Holt to take the case to trial, Dirk Rangel had turned down a generous plea offer. Holt knew there were holes in the state's evidence, but the jury conveniently filled them in, and it would be hard for Rangel to convince the Georgia Court of Appeals to overturn the jury's guilty verdict. Late in the afternoon, Kathy buzzed his phone.

"You've been in hiding most of the day," she said. "Are you working on the Sanford brief?"

"Yes. I should have the first draft finished and dictated by noon tomorrow."

"Don't get carried away. Every brief doesn't have to meet the maximum page limit."

"I'm getting it to you early. Be grateful for that."

"Sally says there's a man named Burkdale out front who wants to see you."

It was an unfamiliar name.

"What does he want?"

"He wouldn't say except that he has information about a pending investigation. When Sally asked him which one, he refused to tell her."

Holt rolled his eyes. "Okay, he may be a nut, but I need to take a break for a few minutes. I'll talk to him."

It wasn't unusual for someone to come by the district attorney's office and insist they had vital information about a crime. Usually, their facts weren't facts and the opinions they offered were less helpful than throwing darts at a sheet of possibilities. But every so often a nugget of gold turned up. Holt hoped he'd be able to tell quickly which category Mr. Burkdale fell into.

Unlike a private law firm, the reception area for the DA's office wasn't filled with antique furniture and plush rugs. Sally sat behind a scratched wooden desk. The room contained eight orange plastic chairs and a banged-up coffee table covered with out-of-date magazines. Adjacent to the reception area was a small room for private conferences. A small, balding man wearing an ill-fitting suit was sitting on the edge of one of the chairs.

"Mr. Burkdale?" Holt said when he entered. "I'm Holt Douglas. You wanted to see me?"

"Can we talk privately?"

"In here." Holt motioned to the conference room and then led the way. Burkdale followed.

Holt closed the door but remained standing. If this needed to be a thirty-second meeting, he didn't want Burkdale to get too comfortable.

"What did you want to talk to me about?" Holt asked.

"I know you spoke with Tony McDermott yesterday," he said.

Holt's eyes opened wider. "I'm listening."

He sat down. They faced each other across the table. Burkdale's nose twitched as he spoke.

"Detective McDermott, uh, I know he's retired, but that's still what I call him, told me you were reopening the investigation into Rex Meredith's death and suggested I come see you. I wasn't sure I wanted to, but the more I thought about it, I knew it was the right thing to do."

Holt was curious to hear what Burkdale had to say but also miffed at McDermott. He'd made Holt promise to keep everything they discussed quiet until an indictment was issued. Apparently the same rule didn't apply to the former detective's lips.

"Reopening the investigation may be an overstatement, but go ahead," Holt said.

"I worked for Mr. Meredith for ten years. My job was to keep up with rent payments and maintenance costs on his residential and commercial property. I don't know how long you've been in Paxton, but he owned a lot of buildings in the downtown area and leased thousands of acres of farmland." Burkdale paused and glanced over his shoulder at the closed door. "I was at Mr. Meredith's house the night he died."

"McDermott told me Greg and Valerie Stevens and Sonny the caretaker were the only people there."

"I stopped by earlier in the evening. Mr. Meredith called and told me to come over so I could deliver my monthly report. When I got there, Claudine Davis, his housekeeper, was pulling out of the driveway. Mr. Meredith took me through the kitchen on the way to his study. There were dirty dishes on the table, and the kitchen hadn't been straightened up. It struck me as odd that Claudine left before doing her job, and I asked Mr. Meredith about it. He said Valerie had an emergency at her house and needed Claudine to come immediately."

"What kind of emergency?"

"I don't know."

"Go on."

"Mr. Meredith was in a good mood and offered me a drink and a cigar, which caught me off guard since we rarely socialized. I turned down the cigar, but we each drank a whiskey while he looked over my report. He told me what a good job I was doing and how loyal I'd been to him. Then he said he wanted to tell me something he hadn't told anyone else. Mr. Boatwright was leaving the company for a new job in Atlanta, and even though Greg Stevens was Mr. Meredith's son-in-law, Stevens was going to be fired."

"Someone else told me Stevens's job duties had already been scaled back. Is that true?"

"Yes, but Boatwright delegated a lot of work to him anyway. I think Boatwright didn't want to be here in the first place and considered it a temporary position until he could find something else."

"Who was going to get Boatwright's job?"

Burkdale blinked his eyes. "I was. Mr. Meredith promised we would meet in a few days and go over the details of my new position. He was going to double my salary. After we finished our drinks, we shook hands on it."

Holt wasn't convinced of the truthfulness of Burkdale's story. It was plausible on its face but needed verification.

"Did Mr. Meredith give you anything in writing confirming his plans—a memo or anything like that?"

"No, that was going to be worked out at a later meeting. But there was nothing about the way Mr. Meredith acted that gave any indication he was suicidal or about to end his life. He was planning for the future. And that's what I told Detective McDermott."

"Do you think Greg Stevens knew Mr. Meredith was about to fire him?"

"He had to."

"Why?"

"Because of what happened."

"What do you mean?"

"Isn't it obvious?"

Holt realized the conclusion Burkdale wanted him to make. "You believe Stevens had something to do with Meredith's death?"

Burkdale glanced over his shoulder at the door again. "If I knew for certain, I'd say so. But there's plenty of circumstantial evidence against Mr. Stevens."

"Such as?"

"Claudine getting called away so she wouldn't be in the house, and the way Stevens has run Meredith Enterprises since Mr. Meredith died."

"Have you talked to Claudine about the emergency at the Stevens house?"

"Yes. I pulled her aside at the funeral home. She told me it looked like Mr. and Mrs. Stevens had gotten into a huge fight because a lot of stuff was broken and scattered all over the main floor of the house."

"Where's Claudine now?"

"She died about a year ago."

"Did McDermott interview her?"

"I don't know. I'm not sure I told him about her. It was something I thought about later."

"Does she have family in the area?"

"A daughter, but I can't remember her name."

Holt tapped the table with his pen. He'd not taken any notes.

"What is the problem with the way Stevens operates Meredith Enterprises?" he asked.

"I have my sources," Burkdale responded cryptically.

Holt decided not to press the point at an initial meeting. "What happened to your job after Meredith's death?" he asked.

"I worked for a couple of months and then Mr. Stevens fired me."

"Did he give you a reason?"

"That it was a consolidation move."

"Did you tell him about your conversation with his father-in-law?"

"No." Burkdale paused. "I was afraid to."

"Is there anybody else who worked for Mr. Meredith who can verify his plan to fire Stevens and promote you?"

"Other than Mr. Stevens?"

"Yes."

Burkdale shook his head. "Not that I know of. Mr. Meredith hired and fired a lot of people over the years. He did what he wanted to do without asking anybody's opinion."

Holt studied Burkdale again. It was hard to put his finger on the reason why the bookkeeper seemed off.

"Anything else you want to tell me?"

"Please don't let Mr. Stevens know I've talked to you. After he fired me, I couldn't get a regular job and had to open my own business. I do the books for a dry-cleaning shop, a couple of insurance agencies, and a few restaurants. If Mr. Stevens wanted to hurt what little business I have, he could put me under."

"We'll both keep this conversation between us, agreed?"

"Yes."

"What is the best way for me to get in touch with you if I have a question later?"

Burkdale reached inside his coat and took out a business card. When he did, Holt caught a glimpse of dark metal in a leather holster. Burkdale was carrying a gun.

"That's it for today," Holt said as he quickly took the card and stood up. "Thanks for stopping by."

Sally was sorting papers at her desk. Holt stayed beside her and watched Burkdale until the front door of the office closed behind him.

21

Holt went directly to see Belinda. The administrator was on the phone and raised a finger to her lips as he approached.

"I understand," she said to the caller on the phone. "But even though Mr. Granger is the district attorney, he can't handle every case in the office. Mr. Douglas is a very competent attorney with plenty of trial experience."

Belinda listened for a few more seconds. She looked at Holt and rolled her eyes.

"Mr. Douglas may look younger than your grandson, but I can assure you that he'll do everything he can to make sure the defendant receives the punishment he deserves. I'll let him know you called. Make sure you're in the courtroom thirty minutes early on Monday morning."

Belinda hung up the phone.

"What was that about?" Holt asked.

"A misdemeanor shoplifting case that's on the arraignment calendar next week. That was the owner of the store. When she found out the case had been assigned to you, she got upset because Ralph isn't personally taking care of it. She reminded me that she gave his campaign twenty-five dollars the last time he ran for reelection."

"I agree with her," Holt responded. "Ralph should definitely be lead prosecutor on that one. Who's representing the defendant?"

"Clare Dixon was appointed to the case last week."

"Another reason Ralph should handle it. After what happened in the Callaway case, Clare is going to be gunning for me with both barrels blazing."

Belinda chuckled. "Overruled. But I don't want you to be blindsided. The store owner wants the defendant sent to a prison where he'll have to bust rocks for ten or fifteen years."

"How old is the defendant?"

Belinda flipped open a folder on her desk. "Do you want to guess?"

"Eighteen and a half," Holt replied. "Barely old enough for the case to get kicked up to superior court."

"You're off," Belinda said, doing some quick mental calculations, "by forty-six years."

"The defendant is sixty-four?"

"And a half," Belinda added.

"What did he steal? Pain medication for his arthritis?"

Belinda glanced down again. "No, a six-pack of beer, a bag of corn chips, and some bean dip. He couldn't post bond and has been in jail ever since his arrest last month."

"Sounds like a house party that didn't happen. Give me the file so I can call Clare. It's costing the taxpayers a lot to keep him locked up."

"Judge Lomax will know this guy. He's had a bunch of petty stuff in his past."

"Okay, but I came by to see you about somebody else." Holt lowered his voice. "I just had a conversation in the conference room with a man named Burkdale. Do you know him?"

"Yeah, Cecil Burkdale. He's a bookkeeper, but he used to be a hit man for Rex Meredith."

"A hit man?" Holt raised his eyebrows.

"Not literally, of course. But Burkdale was the guy who'd kick people out of their houses and put them on the street if they missed a payment. I know because he wouldn't give one of my nephews who lost his job a little extra time to catch up the rent. It really ticked me off, so I agreed to loan my nephew the money. Burkdale wouldn't accept my payment until I also paid a bunch of late fees and a crazy attorney's fee for a form letter sent by a lawyer at the Spratt firm."

"He didn't seem so hard-nosed to me."

"He was. Burkdale is a little man who got some power and went crazy with it. When Greg Stevens took over Meredith Enterprises, one of the first things he did was fire him. Nobody felt sorry for Burkdale."

"I didn't expect you to know so much."

Belinda tapped her head. "The Bible says to forgive, but that doesn't mean I have to forget. What did he want with you?"

"To talk to me about a closed file. When he gave me his business card, I saw he was carrying a gun in a shoulder holster."

"I'm sure he has a concealed weapon permit from his days of working for Mr. Meredith. But if he ever pulled a gun on someone, I'd put my money on the other guy jerking it out of his hand and pistol-whipping the little weasel with it."

Holt had rarely heard Belinda speak so negatively about someone. He went to his office and pulled open the bottom drawer. The brief glimpse of Burkdale's weapon had raised a question in his mind. Holt checked, and there was nothing in Butch Clovis's report about ownership of the gun in Rex Meredith's hand at the time of his death.

—

Wednesday afternoon, Keith came over to Trish's house about an hour before it was time to leave for church. He had his laptop computer in his hand.

"I've done a lot more with the house plans since we visited the property on Sunday," he said as she led the way to the kitchen table. "Where's your mom?"

"Resting," Trish said.

In reality, Marge had vacated the front part of the house so Trish and Keith could be alone.

"Is she okay?"

"Yes, she's going to church later. Would you like something to drink?"

"Water would be great."

Trish poured him a glass of ice water. Keith took a big drink.

"This water is delicious," he said. "You're on a well here, aren't you?"

"Yes."

"Well water can be so much better than city water."

"Yeah, I like the taste," Trish said. "But it's not fun when the line to the house freezes in the winter. And the calcium levels are so high the towels come out of the wash terribly scratchy. Mama and I have talked about installing a whole-house water-softening unit, but they're expensive and require a lot of upkeep."

Trish couldn't believe she was talking to Keith about water treatment issues, but he seemed vitally interested.

"What about washing your hair?" Keith asked.

Trish raised her eyebrows. "That's kind of personal, but I use more shampoo than recommended on the bottle and extra conditioner," Trish said and then burst out laughing.

"What is it?" Keith asked.

"I don't know," Trish said, trying to rein in her giggles. "It's just so scientific sitting here and talking to you about how to cope with well water."

"It is a big deal," Keith replied. "We're on city water at my parents' house, but the property on Cockburn Road will require a well. I need to learn all I can from people who know about them."

"What did Mr. Eakins say about his well?" Trish asked with a straight face, then started laughing again.

"The water table is high in that area, which isn't surprising given the creek nearby. They didn't have to drill very deep before they hit a good vein."

"I guess not," Trish said. "And your ability to try to have a conversation with me while I'm laughing like a child being tickled is amazing. I'll try to get a grip so I can listen."

Keith grinned. "I like hearing you laugh. If talking about drilling a well makes it happen, I'm not going to change the subject."

"That's sweet. But I think I'm under control now. Did Mr. Eakins say how many gallons an hour his well produces?"

No sooner had the words come out of her mouth than Trish exploded again with laughter. Giving way to her impulse, she sat back in her chair and laughed and laughed until there was nothing left. Keith waited patiently. Trish picked up a napkin and wiped her eyes.

"You know how something that isn't funny can seem funny?" she asked when she'd regained a measure of control.

"Yeah, and I think this is one of those times."

Trish nodded. "Let's move on to the house plans. Maybe I can look at those and give you some legitimate feedback."

Keith turned on his computer. While they waited for it to boot up, he took another drink of water. Trish watched. She knew if Keith said something about how good the water tasted she would lose it again. Thankfully, he remained silent. She scooted her chair closer to his. The wallpaper photo on Keith's laptop appeared. It was a candid picture someone had taken of the two of them talking at the Sunday school Christmas party. Trish was wearing one of her favorite outfits.

"Who took that picture?" Trish asked in surprise at the photo and Keith's use of it on his computer. "I haven't seen it before."

"Jerry Dunn. Remember, he was running around with the new camera he bought as a present for himself."

"Can you send it to me?"

"Yes, and there are a few others, too."

While they waited for the house plan program to load, Trish wondered if Keith had been greeted by her face every time he turned on his computer for the past six months.

"This is how the program works," Keith said. "You put in parameters for square footage, number of bedrooms, bathrooms, et cetera. Then it gives options that can be manipulated until you come up with something you like. I've developed plans for several different-size houses that exclude a basement since I know that won't be possible on this land. The program doesn't just spit out a floor plan with dimensions. There's a 3-D feature that lets you walk through the house as it would actually look. Would you like to see what I built last week when I was in Alabama?"

"Sure."

While Trish watched, Keith opened a folder. In a few seconds the floor plan for a house popped up. Keith moved his cursor to the combination living room and den.

"This is a big open room that would face the creek, not the road. I don't know if you noticed the other day, but there's a line of trees along the creek that would pop with color in the fall. Beyond that is a pasture with a nice herd of Angus cattle. The large windows in this room face north, so there wouldn't be a lot of direct sun to cause it to overheat."

Trish's eyes wandered to the kitchen, which was laid out galley-style and looked a little too narrow.

"Now look at it in 3-D," Keith said.

He hit a button and the drawing came alive as if a camera were moving through the house. There was even fake furniture in place to give it a lived-in look.

"I like that sofa," Trish said.

"Me too. That's why I picked it."

"You decorated the house?"

"Yeah, I've stored an inventory of furniture, and the program selects from that when furnishing the house."

"Go to the kitchen," Trish said.

As Keith moved the cursor, the camera traveled through a dining area and into the kitchen.

"Doesn't that seem too narrow?" Trish asked.

"The walkway is three feet across." Keith leaned closer to the computer screen. "But it can be expanded without changing anything except the laundry room and the garage. Let's add two feet and see what you think."

Trish watched the kitchen widen by one-third. "That makes a lot of difference," she said.

"And adds seventy-seven hundred dollars," Keith said, directing her attention to a bar at the bottom of the screen that projected construction costs.

"But there's room for two people to be in there at once without running over each other."

"I like that thought," Keith said with a smile.

—

Keith rode to church with Trish and Marge. On the way home, they took a slight detour and drove past the property on Cockburn Road. The sun was setting and the trees along the creek cast long, spindly shadows on the rows of soybeans. After seeing the house plans,

Trish's level of interest was higher. She pulled onto the shoulder of the road.

"Are you worried the property might sell before you decide what to do?" Marge asked Keith.

"No," Keith responded. "After we came over on Sunday, I signed an option that gives me the right to purchase it anytime I want within the next six months. It's been on the market for a couple of years without any takers, and the seller was happy to work out a deal. I even negotiated a reduction of $750 an acre."

Trish listened slightly wide-eyed. "This is going to happen, isn't it?" she asked.

"It's what I want. Not many people go from living at home to home ownership without an intermediate step or two." He paused. "And the thought that I could drink my own well water sends me over the moon."

Trish smiled. "That's not going to work now. The time has passed."

"The time for what has passed?" Marge asked.

"For me to be silly," Trish replied. "I'm going to have to start pretending I'm an adult even if I don't always act like it."

—

Holt finished the last page of Tony McDermott's report. There wasn't much new in the packet from the former detective beyond a brief reference to Cecil Burkdale that included the bookkeeper's phone number and a note from McDermott to follow up with a second interview. There was no mention of Claudine, the housekeeper, which increased Holt's doubt about Burkdale's description of the events on the night of Rex Meredith's death.

Holt spent most of the morning making final corrections to his brief in the Sanford case. He felt good about his chances. Generally, the court of appeals didn't disturb a jury's verdict in a criminal trial, but no judge was completely predictable. He'd already seen cases in which a ruling at trial that didn't seem crucial at the time turned out to be so when examined in the academic air of the appellate court.

For lunch he picked up a salad for himself, another for Angelina, and took the food to the salon. Brittany greeted him with a half-eaten apple in her hand. She put her fingers over her mouth as she swallowed. Angelina and Holt were scheduled for a double date with Brittany and Skip on Saturday night.

"I think there's a piece of peel stuck in my teeth," Brittany said from behind her hand.

"Don't touch it. Skip Patrick thinks girls with stray bits of food in their mouths are super attractive."

"Gross." Brittany rubbed the front of her teeth with a tissue, then ran her tongue over them. "I think I got it."

Holt leaned over the counter as she flashed a bright smile. "Blinding white," he said. "And tell me, because Skip and I both want to know. How did you get to be so totally gorgeous?"

"Quit." Brittany blushed.

"Whoa, I didn't know I could make you blush with a compliment. That is going to be my new game—make Brittany blush in ten seconds or less."

"Don't, or I'll tell Angelina something terrible about you."

"What?"

"I'll make it up."

"Where is she? I'm the delivery boy for her lunch."

"Finishing up with a customer. Go to the kitchen, and I'll let her know you're here."

Holt headed toward the kitchen.

"Holt," Brittany called after him, "thanks for setting this up with Skip. I know it may not lead anywhere, but my social life has been stuck in neutral for a while—actually, a long while—and it will be fun to do something, especially with you and Angelina."

"We're looking forward to it."

"Just promise me that you and Skip won't go off in a corner and talk about law stuff."

"Only if you and Angelina promise not to talk about new shades of nail polish."

Holt went into the kitchen. He knew not to wait for Angelina and started eating his salad. After a couple of bites, Angelina appeared in the doorway. Her countenance was a dark cloud.

"Starving?" she asked curtly, raising her eyebrows.

Holt swallowed his bite. "I would have waited," he said, "but I didn't know how long you'd be."

Angelina sat down across from him at the little round table. Holt could tell she was ticked off. His first instinct was to ask why, but he knew that might make her madder because he didn't know in advance why she was upset. There was nothing to do but wait until the storm clouds revealed the source of their rain. He ate another bite and watched her as she vigorously stirred the dressing into her salad.

"I can tell when you're preoccupied," Angelina said, "and if you're hiding something from me."

It was an obscure clue, but it was all Holt had to work with. The first thing that popped into his head was the Meredith investigation. Angelina stabbed her salad with vicious intensity.

"Eaten any good sandwiches lately?" she asked in a clipped tone of voice.

"Uh, I fixed a roast beef and Swiss cheese on rye for supper last night," he said. "But what made it good was a farm-grown tomato I bought at that little stand beside the gas station on Eastway Drive."

"Yeah." Angelina nodded. "Eastway Drive. You're getting hot."

Mystified, Holt ignored his food. Angelina glared at him.

"The blond deputy sheriff," she spit out. "The one we met at the steak house the other night. I knew in my bones she was interested in you when you introduced me to her, but I tried to ignore my instincts."

"Trish Carmichael?"

"Yes. Am I supposed to be surprised that you remember her name?" Angelina shook her head angrily. "You ran out of here the other day after giving me a long kiss so you could meet her for dinner at the sandwich shop on Eastway Drive."

"That was business."

"That's not the way it looked to my customer who came in this morning and asked if you and I were still dating. Unlike today, when you couldn't wait for me before stuffing your face, she said you ignored your food and stared deep into Deputy Carmichael's face with tears in your eyes."

"Oh—" Holt started, then stopped. He wasn't sure where to begin or end.

"Give it to me straight, Holt," Angelina said, her lower lip quivering. "What's going on and when were you going to tell me?"

"Nothing is going on between me and Trish Carmichael," Holt said, trying to keep his voice calm. "She's been helping me with an investigation into a cold case, and we needed to talk about it away from the sheriff's department."

"And this case makes you cry?"

"No"—Holt paused—"that was something else I've never mentioned to you."

As soon as the words were out of his mouth, Holt desperately wanted to call them back. "Not that I wouldn't tell you," he quickly added.

But it was too late. Angelina slammed shut the top of her salad container and stormed out of the kitchen.

"Angelina, wait!" Holt called after her.

She didn't slow down but held up her hand to keep him from

saying anything else. When she reached the door, she paused for a second and glared at him. Her face was red.

"Don't call, text, or come by," she said in a trembling voice. "I mean it."

And with that, she was gone.

22

Stunned, Holt remained in the kitchen. He and Angelina had argued before. They'd had misunderstandings. But this had a deeper feel to it. He tried to think what he should or could do to make it right. Options from flowers to a handwritten note to use of an intermediary such as Skip crossed his mind.

But nothing felt right.

Pushing his chair away from the little table, he dropped the uneaten remains of his lunch into the trash can beside the refrigerator. Angelina would need time to cool off before he'd have any hope of reconciliation.

Holt cautiously opened the kitchen door and glanced down the hallway. There was no one in sight. All he had to do was run the gauntlet past Brittany. He eased down the hall. He could see that the receptionist was on the phone, so he picked up his pace and briskly walked past her workstation.

"That was a quick lunch," Brittany called out after him in a cheerful voice. "See you Saturday."

With his back to her, Holt raised his hand in the air in farewell as he continued out the front door. Numb, he drove back to work and retreated to his office. Hunkered down behind his desk, he tried to convince himself this was a temporary problem. Eventually Angelina would give him a chance to explain himself. When that happened, he'd tell her about Calico's death and how his memories were triggered by the tragedy in Trish Carmichael's family, which had nothing to do with any romantic feelings toward the female deputy. One key would be timing. Another would be place. A neutral setting would be best. It couldn't look like a date.

And it couldn't be the sandwich shop on Eastway Drive.

There wasn't time for Holt to mope and feel sorry for himself. He had work to do. He listened to his voice-mail messages. The second one sent him back into the black hole he'd crawled out of. It was from Skip.

"Hey, buddy. Do you want to strategize a little bit about Saturday night? My cleaning lady is coming tomorrow to straighten up my place, so we could come back here for a drink or two after dinner. I sure hope she can find what's causing the foul smell around here. I think it's a pair of socks you left after we went for a run a few weeks ago. Did you stick them someplace as a joke? Anyway, call me before the end of the day. Oh, and maybe Angelina can find out what Brittany likes to do. I'd just as soon chill and talk as put together something organized. But if they want to do something else, let me know. You know how I hate card games, except Texas Hold'em poker."

Holt deleted the voice mail. He wasn't ready to call Skip and unpack the disaster with Angelina. He listened to the rest of his messages. Several required immediate action on cases, so he returned the calls. The process of talking with people about matters unrelated to his romantic woes nudged him back into his work groove. One message was from Butch Clovis about a bad-check case on the trial calendar in a couple of weeks. Holt called the detective.

"I've lined up someone from the bank who can testify that the account had been closed for six months," Clovis said. "And there are eyewitnesses from both of the stores where the defendant passed off the checks. They knew him from previous transactions at the stores."

"The defense lawyer claims the defendant's brother wrote the checks without his client's permission," Holt replied.

"If he did, the defendant is the one who negotiated them to the tune of almost twenty-five hundred dollars."

"Okay, e-mail the witnesses' contact information to Belinda so she can prepare subpoenas. Copy me so I can talk to them myself before our trial date."

"Sure."

Holt paused for a second. "Do you know a guy named Cecil Burkdale?"

"Yeah, he used to work for Rex Meredith. Is he in trouble?"

"Not yet. Would you believe him?"

"It depends. He runs a little bookkeeping business out of his house. I wouldn't put it past him to cross the line if he thought he could get away with it. Is there something you want me to check out?"

"No thanks."

After the call ended, Holt wondered why he'd brought up Burkdale to Clovis. There was no good reason to do it. The detective certainly wasn't going to be an ally in the hunt for truth related to Rex Meredith's death. Holt shook his head. His blowup with Angelina had made his judgment fuzzy.

Holt worked until shortly before the time he needed to leave for his meeting with Trish Carmichael at the courthouse. He considered canceling the appointment with the deputy. In the bigger scheme of things, ending her involvement in the Meredith matter would be smart, both personally and professionally. He picked up the phone, called the sheriff's office, and asked to speak with her.

"She's off duty," the dispatcher said. "Would you like to leave a message with me or on her voice mail?"

"No thanks."

The expanding Meredith folder in his hand, Holt left the office. It was a short walk across the parking lot to the courthouse. Whatever he had to tell Trish, it would happen face-to-face.

—

Trish sat on a bench at the rear of the main courtroom, which was as empty and quiet as a church sanctuary on Monday morning. She looked up. There were flecks of paint beginning to loosen their grip at the creases where the elaborate crown molding met the ceiling.

All day she'd been praying for Holt Douglas. In her braver moments, she saw herself telling him she knew the details of his high school friend's death and was ready to offer sympathy and help. A passage she'd pondered many times from 2 Corinthians kept rolling through her mind: *Praise be to the God and Father of our Lord Jesus Christ, the Father of compassion and the God of all comfort, who comforts us in all our troubles, so that we can comfort those in any trouble with the comfort we ourselves receive from God.* Time didn't heal all wounds. Unlike physical scabs, emotional hurts were outside the body's capacity to restore. They needed the supernatural balm of Gilead. And the verses in 2 Corinthians revealed that God wanted his people to join him in the healing business. If he'd let her, Trish could comfort Holt with the measure of comfort she'd received.

The tears in Holt's eyes at the sandwich shop were signs of a grief that had no hope attached to its sorrow. His friend died, but God spared Holt for a reason, and Trish wanted to tell him that being thankful for the gift of life wouldn't dishonor his friend's memory. Rather, Holt's existence was a flower growing out of dark soil. It should blossom with appreciation. And a godly gratitude would bring Holt a step closer to the Lord Jesus, whose love and forgiveness were the only remedy for the past and a sure foundation for the future.

Trish sighed. All her thoughts hadn't been filled with triumphant faith.

In one imaginary scenario, Holt looked at her with disdain and told her to mind her own business. In another, he immediately started cross-examining her to discover why she wanted to dig up his past. In a third, he told her he'd called out to God for help and, hearing nothing, concluded there was no one there to answer. The back door to the courtroom opened, and Trish turned sideways. It was Holt.

"Sorry I'm late," he said.

"That's okay," she said. "It's been good for me to sit here for a few moments and be quiet. One of my favorite Bible verses is 'Be still and know that I am God.'"

Holt gave her a puzzled look.

"Do you ever get quiet and pray?" Trish continued, trying to sound confident.

"No, but I'm sure I should," Holt replied. "Let's go to the jury room and talk."

With each step, the place where Trish had been when she prayed for Holt seemed further and further away. The jury room contained a long rectangular wooden table surrounded by simple chairs. In the corner was an old-fashioned coatrack. On one wall was a chalkboard that gave the room a schoolhouse feel. Written on the chalkboard was the figure "$2,500" and, beside it, "nothing for pain and suffering."

"I bet a plaintiff's lawyer was upset when that verdict was announced in court," Holt grunted.

Holt sat at the end of the table, and Trish slid into a chair to his left. She wasn't yet willing to completely let go of her desire that they talk about something other than Rex Meredith's death.

"How's your day been?" she asked.

Holt turned to her with a look of shock that hit her like a cup of cold water to the face. "What?" he asked.

"Um, I just asked about your day. I didn't mean to pry into anything that's going on at the DA's office or your personal life."

Holt pressed his lips together tightly before he spoke. "Well, a little over three hours ago my girlfriend kicked me out of her life and her salon because she heard from one of her customers that I was cheating on her."

Trish grew pale. Holt leaned toward her.

"And guess who Angelina believes I was seeing on the side?"

"I don't know," Trish responded in a shaky voice.

Holt raised his hand and pointed his finger at her nose.

"Me?" Trish asked, trying hard to swallow.

"Yes. This is all based on our meeting the other day at the sandwich shop on Eastway when you told me about your family, and I brought up the death of my friend. Angelina's customer didn't hear anything we said but interpreted from the emotion on our faces that we were sharing intimate secrets with each other." Holt paused. "Which I guess was true but not in the way she believed. Then when Angelina met you the other night at the steak restaurant, she had some crazy woman's intuition thing that you had a crush on me, and I was hiding my true feelings about you from her. Other than that, it's been a great day."

Stunned, Trish could barely breathe. Holt sat back in his chair and studied her for a moment.

"I had no intention of telling you about this," he said, "but when you asked about my day, it spilled out. Maybe you need to know in case you hear something about it from someone else. I'd hate for you to be blindsided like I was."

"Thanks," Trish said weakly.

"Is the guy you were with at the steak house your boyfriend?"

"Kind of," Trish said. "He goes to my church."

"You should say something to him. Any hint of gossip gets blown around this town like a piece of paper in a tornado."

"Thanks for letting me know," Trish said numbly.

Holt touched the folder on the table. "And after what's happened, I'm not sure it's a good idea for us to have any contact with each other except in your court cases. I appreciate your willingness to help me investigate Rex Meredith's death, but if I'm going to have any chance of getting back together with Angelina, I can't risk another layer of misunderstanding."

Trish's heart was beating so hard she knew Holt had to hear it. If he asked her whether there was any truth to Angelina's intuition about her feelings toward him, Trish would crawl under the table to escape.

"Of course," she said quickly. "And I'm very sorry this misunderstanding happened."

As soon as the words were out of her mouth, Trish knew they weren't true. They should have been true, but in her heart she knew they weren't. And that made her feel even worse.

"I wondered if it would do any good for you to call Angelina," Holt said, "or maybe go by and talk to her."

Trish wanted to scream out, "No!" Talking on the phone with Angelina would be dangerous. Meeting her face-to-face would be a disaster. Even without the benefit of female intuition, Angelina would see through Trish in an instant.

"I guess not." Holt shook his head. "That's not how this is going to get fixed. It's my problem, not yours."

Trish nodded, which was the second lie she'd communicated in less than a minute. Holt reached for the folder on the table.

"So, there's no point in going over the information Tony

McDermott sent or telling you about an odd conversation I had with a man named Cecil Burkdale."

Trish didn't say anything.

Holt tapped the top of the table with his finger. "Don't we have a case or two on Judge Lomax's calendar toward the end of next week?"

"Yes."

"Okay. We're done here. I'll see you then," Holt said.

As they left the jury room, Trish lagged behind. When they reached the courtroom, she waited until Holt left and then sat down on the bench where she'd waited for him and hid her face in her hands.

23

Trish left the courthouse and drove to Sue Ann's apartment. She climbed the stairs and rang the doorbell. The next sound she heard was a loud bang from a collision against the lower half of the door, followed by a wailing cry. Trish winced. It was too late to turn and leave. When the door opened, Sue Ann had Candace in her arms. The little girl's head was buried against her mother's shoulder.

"Sorry, that was my fault," Trish said. "I should have called to see if it was a good time to stop by."

Sue Ann stroked the back of Candace's head. "And I would have said yes, until the last ten seconds. Come in. Maybe you can distract her."

The apartment was a wreck. Toys and dolls were scattered everywhere. Adults' and children's clothes were strewn about the room. Dishes were piled up in the sink. Trish reached out for Candace, who turned her head toward her. The little girl's eyes were red, and there was a puffy spot on her forehead.

"Hey, baby," Trish said. "Would you like Aunt Tish to read a book to you?"

Candace sniffled and nodded. Trish took her from Sue Ann, who let out a big yawn.

"She had an earache, and I was up most of the night," Sue Ann said. "Her ear is better, but it's made her irritable. And my energy level is on empty. Making a second baby is a lot of work."

Trish hoisted Candace higher up on her hip. The little girl was getting heavier by the day.

"Then I want you to lie down for a few minutes while I distract Candace."

"No." Sue Ann shook her head. "I can't let you—"

"See this badge?" Trish pointed to the gold-colored shield pinned to her uniform. "That means you have to do what I say, or I'll arrest you and put you in a jail cell where you'll have nothing to do but sleep."

"Sounds wonderful." Sue Ann smiled.

"Go." Trish pointed toward the master bedroom. "Now."

Sue Ann obeyed. The fact that she'd not asked why Trish stopped by unannounced was proof of her extreme fatigue. Trish made space for herself and Candace on the couch. Four books later, Candace's head nodded forward and her eyes closed. Trish gently laid her on the couch and covered her with a thin blanket, then tiptoed down the hall and peeked in on Sue Ann, who was passed out. Trish closed the master bedroom door and returned to the living room.

With quiet efficiency, she went to work. She determined which clothes were clean and needed to be folded. The dirty clothes went into the washer. She then picked up Candace's toys and returned them to the little girl's bedroom. Candace and Sue Ann slept through it all. Trish softly sang to herself. Next, she tackled the kitchen. The dishes in the dishwasher were clean, so she carefully unloaded it, put in the dirty dishes, and started the wash cycle. There was a pound of ground beef in the refrigerator, and Trish found the ingredients for spaghetti in the cabinet. Within thirty minutes, the meat was simmering on the stove while Trish cut up fresh mushrooms and diced tomatoes to add at the last minute. As she stirred the meat, she wished she'd stopped by the store for salad fixings and a loaf of French bread. After she turned the heat down on the meat sauce, she mopped the kitchen floor. She was returning the mop to the narrow broom closet when Sue Ann came into the kitchen.

"What are you doing?" Sue Ann exclaimed.

Trish put her finger to her lips and pointed at Candace. "I hope it was okay to let her take a nap."

Sue Ann peeked into the tidy living room and then gave Trish a long hug.

"You're an angel," she said when she released her. "I needed this so much today, and suddenly you showed up on my doorstep."

"I needed it more than you did," Trish replied. "I'd better get going. Mark should be here soon."

The two women walked to the front door.

"Wait," Sue Ann said. "Why did you stop by? You didn't know what kind of day I was having."

"But I knew what kind of day I was having, and I needed to be with someone who loves me even when I don't love myself."

Sue Ann pointed to the couch where Candace was sleeping and then to her own heart. "There are two of those people here. Are you sure you don't want to stay and talk?"

"Not now." Trish shook her head. "Just being here has been therapy."

Sue Ann gave Trish another hug. "Come back anytime you want to take care of Candace, let me take a nap, clean up the apartment, and fix dinner."

—

Holt returned to his office. It was probably a mistake mentioning his personal problems to Trish Carmichael, but he was frustrated. He plopped down in his chair and glanced at an empty picture frame he'd reserved for an engagement photo. It was destined to remain blank, perhaps forever. There was a knock on his door.

"Come in," he said.

It was Ralph Granger. The Meredith case was still on top of the desk.

"Busy?" Ralph asked.

"I'm finishing up the brief to the court of appeals in the Sanford case," Holt replied. "It should go out tomorrow."

Ralph sat down in one of the two chairs on the opposite side of Holt's desk. "How does it look?"

"Solid. And thanks again for going to bat for me with the county commissioners. A fifteen percent raise is more than generous."

Ralph didn't move. Holt waited. The DA looked up at the ceiling and moved his head to the side as if popping his neck. Holt put his hand on the Meredith information but realized he couldn't move it out of sight without being noticed.

"I understand Cecil Burkdale came by to see you," Ralph said.

"Yes," Holt said, licking his lips.

"What did he want?"

There was no way to avoid a response. "To talk to me about Rex Meredith."

"And?"

Holt swallowed. If he'd been on the witness stand, everyone in the courtroom would know he hadn't yet told the truth, the whole truth, and nothing but the truth. He tried to sound as casual as possible.

"He mentioned a conversation they had the night Meredith died. According to Burkdale, Mr. Meredith promised him a promotion and discussed plans for future business activities. In Burkdale's mind, Meredith didn't seem like a man contemplating suicide. I listened to what he had to say, but I had serious doubts about his credibility."

"I would, too," Ralph replied, looking directly into Holt's face. "He lost his job when Greg Stevens assumed control of Meredith Enterprises. I'm not surprised Burkdale is still stewing about that, but why would he want to talk to you now? This is old news."

Ralph Granger wasn't a great trial lawyer. Tony McDermott was right about that. However, the DA's suspicious nature was enough to generate an unending series of questions until his paranoia was satisfied. Holt made a quick decision that stonewalling through silence was his best strategy. After a few moments passed, Ralph shifted in his seat and stood up.

"I know crazy people come by here all the time with hot tips, but I don't want you to neglect your caseload to chase rabbits."

"I'm too busy to do that."

Ralph pressed his lips together and nodded slowly. "Good."

"Thanks," Holt replied, hoping to signal an end to the conversation.

The strategy worked, and Ralph continued toward the door. Holt let out a sigh of relief when he was gone. However, something in his boss's demeanor made him suspect it was the DA, not Holt, who was withholding information. Holt tried to put his finger on what it might be but couldn't. Then he smiled. Some of Ralph's pervasive paranoia had rubbed off on him. Like the DA, Holt was becoming suspicious when there was no reason to be.

Shortly before leaving the office, Holt called Skip to break the news about Angelina. At first Skip thought he was joking. When he realized Holt was serious, his mood changed.

"I thought you and Angelina were set for life," Skip said. "Don't you think the chances are good that you'll get back together after she cools off?"

"I hope so, but winning back a woman's trust when she thinks you've cheated on her is one of the toughest things to do on the planet."

"Yeah, every time I decided to get back into circulation, I ended any existing relationship first."

Holt cringed. He remembered a girl he'd dated for over a year in college. He knew they didn't have a future, but instead of telling her directly, he went out a couple of times with another girl. The first girl found out, and they had a messy public meltdown in the student activity center. Maybe what happened today with Angelina was delayed justice.

"Are you still going out with Brittany on Saturday night?" he asked.

"Yeah, I mean, I have to. If I didn't, Angelina would be mad at both of us."

"Yeah, that's true."

"But don't worry, I've got your back. I know Brittany will want to talk about it, which will give me a chance to put in a good word for you. Tell me again. How do you want me to explain your need for alone time with the blond deputy?"

"It wasn't alone time. She was helping me with the Meredith investigation, but you can't tell Brittany that."

"Did you ever come clean with Ralph?"

"No."

Skip was silent for a moment. "Holt, as a prosecutor you know how hard it is to maintain a lie."

"I'm not lying," Holt protested.

"Right. But you sound like some of the guys I sent to prison, especially the ones who claimed they never saw the drugs in plain view on the kitchen table."

"I'll be careful."

"You'd better be. Ralph's tolerance for risk taking is a negative number, and having you snooping around town asking questions about a high-profile death like that, even if it's been years ago, is a recipe for a huge public relations snafu. If a reporter finds out that Greg Stevens is the object of an investigation by the DA's office, the whole thing will blow up in less than a second, and you'll be in the middle of the explosion."

Holt had a sinking feeling in the pit of his stomach. "Call me after the date," he said, changing the subject.

"What if it's late?"

"If you're smart, you won't keep Brittany out all night."

"Okay, Dad. And I'll make sure I fill up the car with gas and park it in the garage."

24

When Saturday night arrived, Holt tried to keep his mind off the canceled double date by watching one of his favorite movies, *A Few Good Men.* He'd seen the film so many times that he'd almost memorized the climactic cross-examination of Jack Nicholson's character, a decorated Marine Corps colonel, by Tom Cruise, a young navy defense lawyer trying to emerge from his famous father's shadow. Nicholson was lecturing Cruise about the dangers facing those on the wall of America's first line of defense when Holt's cell phone vibrated. It was Skip.

"What are you doing?" Skip asked as soon as Holt answered.

"What do you think I'm doing," Holt replied in a grumpy voice. "I'm sitting here watching *A Few Good Men* and feeling sorry for myself. How was your date with Brittany?"

"It's still going on."

"Where is she?"

"In the ladies' room. We're at the coffee shop on Prince Avenue. Brittany didn't want to go to my place after dinner."

"I told you she was smart."

"She's an awesome girl, much better than I expected. But I called to let you know that when I picked her up, she came out carrying a big cardboard box. Inside were pictures of you and Angelina and some of the stuff you've given her. There's also a fragile-looking plant I know will die within twenty minutes of entering my house."

Holt immediately knew what Skip was talking about. "It's a tropical bird of paradise. It's not yet mature so it hasn't bloomed. We saw a big one in a hotel lobby in Atlanta a little over a year ago. Angelina loved it so much I bought one for her. I'm not sure what I'll do with it."

"Well, I'm not assuming the risk if it croaks before you get it."

"Don't worry about it. Did Brittany say anything about me and Angelina?"

"Yeah." Skip was silent for a second. "Gotta go. Here comes Brittany."

The phone call ended, leaving Holt hanging. He sighed, rewound a short section of the movie, and pressed the Play button. Nicholson's character glowered at Cruise and shouted, *"You can't handle the truth!"*

Yes, the truth could be hard to handle.

—

The following day, Holt woke up to the sound of Henry whining in the kitchen and scratching at the door. The dog didn't know the difference between Sunday morning and a weekday. Rubbing his eyes, Holt rolled out of bed and took Henry outside. When they returned to the house, Holt poured fresh food into Henry's dish and went back to bed. After tossing and turning for a few minutes, he gave up on going back to sleep.

Holt brewed a cup of coffee and turned on his computer to read the morning news. Thankfully, there were no fresh catastrophes in the world. He thought about shooting some baskets but couldn't because of Sunday morning church services. Holt turned off his computer and sat still for a moment. Then, getting up, he went into the bathroom to shave and shower. He was going to church, not to shoot baskets, but to attend a service.

Going to church, except for a wedding, funeral, or Christmas Eve service, had never been a significant part of Holt's life. He wasn't sure what men wore to Bishop Pennington's church, but he knew it was safer to err on the side of being overdressed than to be underdressed. He put on a dark blue suit he often wore to court. Not wanting to arrive too early for the 11:00 a.m. service, he left the house at 10:56.

In small towns like Paxton, Sunday morning hours remained the most segregated of the week; however, Holt saw a white couple with two small children enter the church as he drove up. Everyone seemed to be dressed in their Sunday best. Holt parked at the far corner of the parking lot near one of the basketball goals and positioned his car so there was no chance it could be blocked in.

The sound of singing greeted Holt before he entered the sanctuary. In the narthex, he found himself surrounded by people in gold-and-red robes singing at the top of their voices and lifting their hands in the air. It reminded Holt of Mardi Gras, but without the booze. He felt a hand on his back. Turning around, he came face-to-face with a large young black man wearing a gray suit, a carnation in his lapel. Giving Holt a big smile, he extended his hand. A brass tag on the man's jacket was engraved with the name "Brendan West."

"Good morning!" he said in a loud voice. "Welcome to the house of the Lord! Let the choir go down the aisle, and then you can have a seat wherever you like."

"I'm Holt Douglas, a friend of the bishop."

"We're glad you came. I'm sure he'll spot you."

Holt didn't doubt that. Every member of the choir except one had a dark face. They moved down the aisle singing and swaying, a big contrast to most of the church services Holt had attended. The bass singers were at the end of the line. Holt followed the deep voices into the sanctuary.

The sanctuary had a steeply sloped ceiling and deep-red carpeting. Narrow windows with opaque white glass lined the walls. The congregation was standing and worshipping along with the choir. It was an enthusiastic song about God, who meets the needs of his people. There was an open seat near the aisle in the third pew from the rear, and Holt slipped into it. To his right was a family of four. The father had his eyes closed and held his hands in the air as he sang. Bishop Alexander stood on a raised platform clapping his hands. He caught Holt's eye and wagged a finger at him. Holt wasn't sure exactly what that meant.

The choir made its way into the choir loft, but instead of sitting down, they launched into another song. The words to this one were projected onto a screen suspended from the ceiling at the front of the church and included multiple names for God, each describing an aspect of his character and nature. All of it was new to Holt, who was able to sing the chorus the third time it cycled around, in a voice barely audible to his own ears. The song finished, and Holt prepared to sit down, but the choir didn't stop. Holt had suspected the church service would be different, but not how much so. He gave up counting the number of songs the congregation sang, but it had to be at least six or seven, some fast, others slow, before there was a lull and Bishop Pennington took his place behind the pulpit.

Leaning in close to the microphone, he spoke in a soft voice that sharply contrasted with the previous exuberance of the meeting. "Does anybody have anything better to do than worship the Lord?"

"No!" the congregation thundered.

Bishop Pennington turned to the choir director, who was on his feet playing a synthesizer, and waved his hand. The choir began another song. Holt glanced around. A face or two looked familiar. He didn't see Jamal, the young basketball player from the pickup game. At the end of the second additional song, Holt looked down at his watch. It was 11:55. The service wasn't going to end at noon.

When the music stopped, the ushers, all wearing gray suits and sporting carnations in their lapels, took up an offering. While the men passed brass plates, a group of four women stepped out of the choir loft and sang. Holt was amazed at the talent of the quartet. They sounded professional. As the ushers took the offering plates to the front of the sanctuary, a man who was assisting Bishop Pennington took his place behind the pulpit.

"Who has a hallelujah offering this morning?" the man called out.

Within seconds, the man next to Holt was on his way down the aisle. Others followed, holding cash or checks in the air. Holt didn't know what to make of it, but the people seemed happy to give. The bishop touched one young woman on the arm and kept her at the front.

"Alecia has a word of testimony this morning," the bishop said.

Holt recognized Alecia. She was an assistant in the county clerk's office. They'd never had a lengthy conversation, but he'd given her papers to file many times.

"Praise God," she began. "Some of you know about my cousin Cornelia, who lives in Macon. Two months ago she had a lumpectomy and was diagnosed with breast cancer. People all over have been praying for the Lord to touch her. Before the doctors were going to put her under for surgery, they checked her again, and the cancer was gone." Alecia raised her right hand in the air. "The surgery has been canceled. They're going to keep checking her every six months, and we're going to keep praying."

The young woman left the platform. It was certainly good news, but Holt wasn't sure what to make of such a specific claim of answered prayer. Alecia had always impressed him as an efficient young woman with common sense. Holt wished he could see the medical reports and read the doctors' explanation for the canceled surgery.

Next, the man sitting on the platform with Bishop Pennington stepped to the microphone and prayed for the bishop's message. When the man said "Amen," Holt checked his watch. It was 12:30 p.m. His stomach growled. Bishop Pennington opened a large Bible on the pulpit in front of him.

"My text today is 1 John 1:5–10."

Holt heard pages rustling around him. The bishop began to read:

> This then is the message which we have heard of him, and declare unto you, that God is light, and in him is no darkness at all. If we say that we have fellowship with him, and walk in darkness, we lie, and do not the truth: But if we walk in the light, as he is in the light, we have fellowship one with another, and the blood of Jesus Christ his Son cleanseth us from all sin. If we say that we have no sin, we deceive ourselves, and the truth is not in us. If we confess our sins, he is faithful and just to forgive us our sins, and to cleanse us from all unrighteousness. If we say that we have not sinned, we make him a liar, and his word is not in us.

After the first few words, Bishop Pennington didn't look down at the page in front of him, and Holt realized the old man had memorized the passage. At one point the bishop captured Holt's eye. Mercifully, he released him after a couple of seconds.

When he finished quoting the Scripture, the bishop said, "I'm going to preach this passage from the back to the front. All of us—young and old, rich and poor, male and female, church member and visitor—will find ourselves in this sermon. I've lived all week with these words, and I bring this message as a thirsty man who has found water for my soul and refreshment for my spirit."

The bishop launched into his exposition. While the minister spoke Holt barely moved a muscle. It was as good as or better than any speech Holt had heard in a courtroom. The bishop had mastered the oratorical art of parallel sentence structure and skillful alliteration that caused his sentences to repeatedly find their mark. The words *light*, *darkness*, *liar*, *truth*, *sin*, *fellowship*, *confess*, and *forgive* echoed across the sanctuary.

Bishop Pennington wasn't in a hurry, and several times when Holt thought there was nothing more the minister could squeeze from a phrase or thought, the preacher opened another window of insight. Then, suddenly, the bishop stopped. The congregation, which at times had been vocal in its response to the sermon, was silent.

"This passage shows the way to the Lord," the bishop said. "If anyone wants to follow that path, let him come."

Within seconds, several people were walking down the aisle. Holt watched them go. Part of him wanted to join them, but he stayed put. The man sitting next to Holt touched him on the arm.

"Do you want to go forward for prayer?"

"No, I'm a visitor."

"You stopped being a visitor the minute you arrived," the man said with a smile. "Oh, I think the bishop wants to talk to you."

Holt looked to the front and saw Bishop Pennington motioning for him to come forward. To refuse would be rude, so Holt made his way down the aisle. The bishop shook his hand and gave him a quick pat on the back.

Holt was acutely aware of the people around him who were praying.

"You're a fantastic speaker," he said to the bishop. "You'd have made a great lawyer. A lot of what you said made sense."

"And?" The bishop raised his eyebrows.

"That's it."

"You were convinced," the minister said with a slow nod of his head, "but not convicted."

"What do you mean?"

"I convinced the jury of your mind but didn't get a conviction from your will. The jury is going to have to keep deliberating. Let's pray."

Holt closed his eyes, and the older man asked God to speak to Holt's heart and bless him in more ways than Holt knew existed. But the thing that touched Holt the most was the obvious affection the bishop had for him as a person.

"Thank you," Holt said when the bishop finished. "I didn't really want to come up here, but I'm glad I did."

"Me too."

"What should I do now?" Holt asked, not entirely sure he wanted to hear the answer.

The bishop paused. "Do you own a Bible?"

"No."

"I suggest you buy one and read it."

25

As soon as she saw Keith in Sunday school, Trish felt guilty and relieved—guilty about her secret feelings for Holt and relieved Keith couldn't read her mind and discover what had been lurking there during the past few weeks. The obvious pleasure Keith took in doing something as simple as sharing a Bible with her during the class helped her relax. They took their relationship to the next level that day and sat together in church, with Marge on the other side of Trish.

Brother Carpenter's sermon was about Moses and the Israelites building the tabernacle in the wilderness, with particular emphasis on the liberal giving by the people of God that preceded actual construction.

"Most of that wealth was given to them by the Egyptians when the Israelites left Egypt," Keith whispered to her at one point. "I mean, they still had to let go of it, but it wasn't like they'd saved for years and years."

"Hush," Trish responded. "They didn't get paid for years and years, either."

As if on cue, Brother Carpenter said, "I can't prove this from the

Bible, but I believe when the children of Israel came out of bondage in Egypt, the riches they brought with them equaled the wages they were owed." Trish elbowed Keith in the side and saw him smile out of the corner of her eye.

"I believe this congregation is made up of true Israelites," Brother Carpenter said as he came to the climax of his sermon. "Give as God has blessed you, and the resources will pour in so fast that the deacons will have to order you to stop! Won't that be a testimony to the glory of God?"

After the service, Trish, Keith, and Marge lingered in the pew.

"Trish showed me the house plans you attached to an e-mail," Marge said to Keith. "It's amazing what you can do on the computer."

"Did you like the house?" Keith asked.

"Yes. It really fits the lay of the land."

"It's important to me that you like it."

Marge beamed. "I printed out a copy to keep on the kitchen table so Trish and I can talk about it while we eat," she added.

"Can I take you out to lunch?" Keith asked Trish.

"I have to go into work. It's one of the few Sundays they schedule me on second shift."

"How about you?" Keith turned to Marge.

Trish caught a sudden surge of red in her mother's cheeks.

"That's sweet," she replied. "But I'll pass."

"Then I look forward to seeing both of you later this week."

As Trish was loading the wheelchair into the van, she patted Marge on the shoulder. "I thought you were going to pass out when Keith invited you out for lunch."

"It was a shock. How did I handle it?"

"You clamped down like I do when something surprises me. Maybe you should have gone with him."

Trish started the van and backed out of the parking space. A mile down the road from the church, Marge spoke. "What would we talk about?" she asked.

"Who?"

"Keith and I."

Trish glanced at her mother and smiled. "You and Keith share the same favorite subject."

Marge paused. "Is Keith a big Braves fan?"

Trish laughed. "No, Mama. Me."

"You're joking," Marge replied with a sniff, "but you're right. That boy is crazy about you."

"And all he had to do to win you over was ask you to lunch."

—

Sunday afternoons at the sheriff's department were quiet with only a skeleton staff on duty. Trish hoped to locate one of her more slippery defendants who might be enjoying a day of rest.

She logged on to her computer and pulled a case file involving a father who'd abandoned a longtime girlfriend and their three children. He'd denied paternity during an earlier round of legal sparring, and when DNA testing established with 99.99 percent accuracy that he was the father of all three children, he took off. Recently, the mother received a tip that the father was living in a rural part of the Florida panhandle, and Trish wanted to check it out. Before doing so, she called the phone number for the mother.

"Ms. Peters, this is Trish Carmichael at the sheriff's department. I wanted to call and—"

"Are you working today?" the woman interrupted.

"Yes, ma'am. And I thought it might be a good time to see if Ricky is still in north Florida."

"Well, I can tell you for sure that he's not in Florida. My baby sister called half an hour ago and said she saw his truck parked at the house where his girlfriend's parents live."

"Did your sister see him?"

"No, but it was his truck."

Trish twirled the phone cord around her finger. "What's the address?"

Trish wrote the street name and house number down on a notepad beside her computer. It was fifteen miles outside Paxton in a very rural part of the county. Why did the men in her caseload always hunker down in out-of-the-way places?

"We're short-staffed on Sunday," she said. "I'd hate to pull in a male deputy, drive all the way out there, and find out Rick isn't at the house. Could you make sure he's really there?"

"I already tried. His cousin ain't answering her phone, and I didn't want to leave a message that someone else might pick up and listen to."

Trish debated what to do. "Okay, I'm going to check it out myself and verify that it's Ricky's truck."

"He may have Florida plates on it by now. He knows the law is looking for him."

"That won't make any difference. I can access a national database."

"Do what?"

"Find out if it's Ricky's truck, whether the license plate was issued by Georgia or Florida."

"Be careful. He's not too bad when he's sober, but if he's drinking, he's meaner than a coyote."

"I know. You showed me the pictures of you and your older boy."

Recalling the bruised faces in the photos strengthened Trish's resolve. She hung up and contacted one of the two patrol cars on the road. Nick Watkins was on duty, and she told him where she was going and what she wanted to do.

"I have a subpoena to serve on a man who lives about five miles from there," Nick said. "If the truck checks out, let me know, and I'll be there as quick as I can."

"Are you by yourself?" Trish asked.

"Yeah, my partner called in sick, so I'm doing civil court duty on my own."

Before leaving, Trish made sure the dispatcher knew where she would be. Both the unmarked cars were checked out for the weekend, so Trish drove her personal vehicle.

Her route out of town took her past the Paxton Apostolic Church. She slowed for a stop sign at the corner in front of the church as Holt and Bishop Alexander Pennington came out the front door.

Trish's mouth dropped open, and on reflex she honked the horn. Holt jerked his head in her direction. She limply waved, and he motioned for her to turn into the parking lot. She pulled up next to the two men and lowered her window.

"Hey," Holt said. "Do you know Bishop Pennington?"

"Everybody who grows up in Paxton knows the bishop."

"Patricia Carmichael," the bishop responded, putting his hand on the window frame. "I met your father several times. He was a good man who loved the Lord."

"Yes, he did," Trish said as she prepared to take her foot off the brake and leave.

"Are you on duty?" Holt asked.

"Yeah, I'm on my way to check on a suspect who may have slipped into town for a few days."

"Has an arrest warrant been issued?"

"Yes, and he's been on the run in Florida for months. I thought I was going to have to request extradition. If he's here, it will save a lot of time and effort."

"Is a deputy meeting you there?"

"Nick Watkins is on standby if I spot the defendant."

"Would you like me to ride with you?"

Trish felt her face flush. "I thought you didn't want to be seen with me. I mean, not that you're mad at me—"

"Go," the bishop said to Holt. "You need to tell someone what the Lord is doing in your soul."

"I think I have to obey the bishop," Holt said with a smile.

"Okay, get in."

Holt shook the bishop's hand and walked around the back of the car. The bishop leaned close to Trish.

"Have you been praying for Holt?" he asked in a soft voice.

Trish nodded. "Yes."

"Is that why you honked your horn when you saw him coming out of the church?"

"I was shocked."

Holt opened the passenger door of the car and got in.

"This is a good woman," the bishop announced in a louder voice. "The grace that was on her father rests on her."

After telling the bishop good-bye, Trish drove slowly across the parking lot. They skirted the edge of the basketball court.

"Tell me, why did you offer to come with me?" she asked.

"That's where I play ball," Holt said, ignoring her question. "Sometimes the bishop comes out, and we talk."

Trish turned onto West Avenue. "Are you going to answer me?" she asked.

Holt shrugged. "I'm not sure I can, except that after being in church it seemed like the right thing to do."

"How long have you been going there?"

"About four hours," Holt replied. "They weren't in a hurry to end the meeting."

Trish smiled. Holt was much calmer than he'd been during their last meeting in the jury room at the courthouse. They passed the city limits and she accelerated.

"Tell me about the service."

As Holt talked, Trish thought about her time of prayer for him at the rear of the courtroom. There was no doubt God was moving in the assistant DA's life. It might not be taking the exact form she'd requested, but that didn't matter. Jesus was weaving a fabric of grace tailor-made for Holt. When he described Bishop Pennington praying for him at the church altar, Trish couldn't keep a huge grin from creasing her face. Holt stopped and stared at her.

"Have you been praying for me, too?" he asked.

Trish nodded. "And I bet Bishop Pennington has been praying for you ever since you met him. People would line up from here to the courthouse for a chance to be on his prayer list. All you had to do was show up on the basketball court."

"He likes my dog, too." Holt told her what the bishop said about the distinction between being convinced and being convicted.

"Does that make sense to you?" he asked.

"I think so. It's the difference between knowing the truth in your head and believing it in your heart."

"The last thing the bishop said was that I needed to start reading the Bible."

"Look in the rear seat. That's an extra one you can have."

"Thanks, but I can get my own."

"Of course you can, but I'd love to give it to you."

Holt reached into the backseat and picked up the book. He turned it over in his hands. "It's weird, but I really want to get into this," he said.

Holt's statement took Trish back to the hunger she'd experienced when her eyes first opened to the fact that the Bible was not just words on a page but a spiritual book to nourish her soul. "That makes total sense," she said.

They turned onto the road where Ricky's girlfriend lived. There were no zoning regulations in the rural areas of Ashley County. They passed a dilapidated farmhouse next door to a brand-new two-story brick home with a white concrete driveway that looped through a carefully manicured yard. A quarter mile farther down the road, Trish slowed the car.

"It should be coming up," she said.

Trish saw a mailbox precariously tilted to one side. Lines of paint ran down from where the house number had been hand-painted on the side of the box.

"That's it," she said. "The ex-wife says the defendant's truck should be parked beside the house. It's a dark blue Ford."

They passed the house, but Trish didn't see a truck.

"There it is," Holt said. "It's in a barn behind the house."

Trish made a U-turn. When she did, she could barely see the glint of dark blue paint through the trees.

"How did you spot it?" she asked.

"It was moving a few seconds ago. Stop and let's see who gets out."

Trish pulled onto the shoulder of the road. Holt craned his neck to the left.

"Go forward a few feet," he said. "Someone opened the driver's-side door, but I don't have a clear view. Do you have a description of the defendant?"

Trish had left that part of the file on her desk.

"He's a white male in his thirties."

"I need to get a closer look." Holt opened the car door.

"Don't get out," Trish said.

"We're on the road right-of-way, and if we can't see him, he can't see us."

Holt eased around to the front of the car. Crouching down near the bumper, he stared at the area behind the house. After less than a minute, he got back in the car.

"A woman was driving. She's walking across the yard toward the house. I didn't see anyone else. Do you know anything about the girlfriend?"

"Nothing except her name and that her parents live here."

"Do you want to call the deputy? He could knock on the door and ask if the defendant is there."

Trish paused. "I could do that, but I don't want him to waste his time."

At that moment, the front door of the house opened, and a man in his mid- to late thirties stepped onto the narrow porch.

In his hands was a shotgun.

26

Get outta here!" Holt yelled.

Trish started the engine and jerked the shifter into drive. The car lurched forward, but instead of running onto the pavement, it hit a dip in the shoulder and veered to the left. In a couple of seconds, the car was facing downward into a ditch. Trish looked up and saw the man leave the porch and start walking toward them.

"Reverse!" Holt said.

Biting her lower lip, Trish moved the shifter and stepped on the gas. The tires spun as the car slowly moved backward. She saw the man with the gun stop and raise it to his shoulder.

"Put your head down!" Holt yelled.

Trish obeyed a second before she heard the blast of a gunshot. She waited for the sound of glass shattering, but nothing happened. Holt had leaned over in her direction, and their heads were close together.

"Don't move!" he commanded.

He leaned over and reached for the door handle.

"What are you going to do?" Trish asked in alarm.

Holt didn't answer. He opened the car door and got out. Trish thought about lifting her head to see what was happening, but fear and obedience to Holt's orders kept her frozen in place. She strained to hear. There was nothing. Grabbing her purse from the seat, she took out her cell phone and called Nick. Her voice shook.

"Nick, it's Trish Carmichael. I'm stuck in a ditch in front of the house on Gilpin Road. A man just came out with a shotgun and fired at the car."

"Are you inside the car?"

"Yes, but Holt Douglas got out to confront him."

"The DA?"

"Yes."

"Stay where you are. I'm on my way."

Trish stayed bent over with her head against the console. At any moment she expected Ricky to appear at the window and point a gun at her. Her heart was beating as rapidly as if she'd run up several flights of stairs. She closed her eyes and tried to pray.

Finally, she heard the sound of a siren in the distance. It came closer and closer. She saw a blue light flashing and heard a door open. For each second that passed without another shot being fired, Trish's hope that a tragedy could be averted increased. There was a loud knock on the driver's-side car window. She jumped.

It was Nick. He motioned for Trish to sit up. She rubbed the back of her neck and looked out the windshield. Holt and the man who'd come out of the house were standing beside each other in the front yard. There was no sign of the gun. Nick opened the car door.

"You can get out," he said.

"Where's the shotgun?" she asked.

"On the ground."

Trish slipped from her seat behind the wheel.

"Come on," Nick said.

"We're going to talk to him?"

"Yes, he has information for you about the defendant."

Trish followed the deputy into the ditch and across the yard. Holt, his tie loosened, was standing beside the man who had fired the shotgun. As she approached, Trish could see the gun lying in the grass not far from the man's feet.

"Trish," Holt said when she came closer, "this is Granville Jenkins. His sister is the one who's dating your suspect."

The man squinted his eyes at Trish, then spit on the ground. "He ain't here," Jenkins said. "He left out about three hours ago."

"Is that his truck behind the house?"

"Yep, he took my sister's car and left that piece of junk for her. I wasn't here when she gave him the keys." Jenkins motioned toward the shotgun. "But if I had been, he would have left with some extra lead in his britches. My folks won't speak up, but when I found out Ricky was here, I ran right over. But I was too late."

"Is your sister inside the house?" Trish asked.

"Yeah, but she ain't going to talk to you. He's got her snowed under so deep she can't see the truth. Anyways, I was telling Mr. Douglas here that I'm sorry I popped off that shot. I wasn't aiming at the car. If'n I had been, I would have hit it from this close. They's been some teenagers who've been cutting holes in my old man's fence and letting the cattle out. Their car is the same color as yours, and I wanted to give them a good scare."

"You scared me," Trish answered. "Do you know where Ricky was going?"

"Nope," the man said and motioned toward the house. "Ain't no one in there telling me nothing. They know what I think about him."

Trish glanced at the house as Jenkins spoke and thought she saw a woman's face peeking out through one of the windows. The face quickly disappeared.

"If I had a chance to talk to your sister or parents, maybe I could convince them to cooperate. Once they hear how Ricky abandoned his family, they might be willing to help me bring him to justice."

Jenkins smiled a crooked smile that revealed several missing teeth. "That's a right smart little speech, but it won't work." He turned to Holt. "Do you need any help getting out of that ditch? I could hook a chain up to the bumper and pull it out with our tractor."

"That would be great," Holt said before Trish could reply.

"All right," Jenkins said. "I'll be gittin' it."

They watched as Jenkins walked across the yard toward the old barn.

"Why did you agree to let him hook his tractor to my car?" Trish asked. "He might tear something up."

Holt looked at Nick. "Do you think Jenkins knows what he's doing?"

"Yeah," the deputy said. "There's less likelihood he'll hurt your car pulling it out than if I tried to back it up. I'm not even sure that would work. Your tires have already dug down in the dirt."

"Okay," Trish said reluctantly.

"And this is a goodwill gesture that might bear fruit in the future," Holt added. "Once Jenkins sees you trust him with your car, he may be willing to pass along information to you down the road. He could become your inside source for information about Ricky."

"I already have one of those. That's why we're here."

"And two are better than one," Holt said.

Trish glanced at Holt, who obviously didn't know he'd quoted a well-known Bible verse.

"Do you want to try to talk to the sister and the parents?" Nick asked. "I can knock on the door if you like."

Trish hesitated for a moment. "No, Jenkins is probably right. There's no use doing that now. If the girlfriend had half a brain cell, she wouldn't be hanging around Ricky in the first place."

"Eventually he'll show his true colors," Holt said. "When that happens, someone in the family will call you."

Jenkins rumbled around the side of the house aboard a large red tractor. He drove through the ditch and then attached a thick chain to Trish's car. Holt sat in the driver's seat of the car and turned the steering wheel as the tractor slowly pulled the car onto the road. Trish scrambled across the ditch.

"Do you want me to drive?" Holt asked. "I thought you might still be a little shaken up."

"Yes, that would be nice."

Holt turned onto a two-lane highway. Trish glanced over at him. Even though she was the one wearing a uniform, he'd been the one who acted like a law enforcement officer.

"Why did you get out of the car back there?" she asked. "You didn't know what was going to happen."

"Having someone point a shotgun at your head is a rush," Holt replied with a grin. "Not having the person pull the trigger is positively euphoric."

"That may be true, but you didn't answer my question."

"If something bad was going to happen to one of us, I wanted it to be me, not you," he said matter-of-factly.

It wasn't a totally shocking answer, but the raw self-sacrifice in Holt's words took Trish's breath away. She stared out the window at the passing landscape for a few moments.

"It was a very brave thing to do. My feet were glued to the floorboard."

"There's no shame in that, and I told you to keep your head down and stay put." Holt paused. "I've always thought if I ever got another chance to save someone's life, I was going to do it. I knew this might be it."

Trish was quiet for a few moments. "Did you make that decision after your high school friend died in the car wreck?"

Holt didn't respond.

"But that wasn't your fault," Trish continued. "You were a passenger. It would be different if you'd been drinking and ended up driving the car."

Trish saw Holt's hands visibly tighten their grip on the steering wheel. From out of nowhere the possibility that Holt was the one driving the car suddenly flashed across her mind. She tried to dismiss it but couldn't. His hands seemed to tighten more.

"You weren't driving the car when your friend died, were you?" she asked, trying to keep her voice steady.

"Why would you ask that?"

"Were you?" she persisted.

Holt, his jaw set, kept his gaze straight ahead. Suddenly, Trish felt nauseous. Holt slowed down and pulled into the empty parking lot of a country store that was closed on Sunday. He stared at the steering wheel for a moment. Trish barely breathed.

"I was a confused teenager who'd been in a terrible wreck," Holt said without looking in her eyes. "I can't change the past."

"For whom? You? And now you're an assistant district attorney who's taken an oath to uphold the law."

"I do my job, and I do it well."

Trish shook her head. "Drinking and driving killed my father and put my mother in a wheelchair. Whatever you did at the Jenkins place a few minutes ago isn't going to take away your guilt. The only cure for that is the truth."

Holt turned to her, his face lined with tension. "Look, I did what I thought was best for my friend. Calico, that was his nickname, was totally drunk. I'd been drinking, too, but I believed I could get us home. We should have called his parents and dealt with the consequences, but we were immature kids who thought nothing bad could happen to us. On the way home one of the car's front tires slipped off the shoulder, and the car flipped over. It was a convertible and neither of us was wearing a seat belt. Calico was ejected and his head hit a tree, killing him instantly. I was banged up with some cracked ribs. At the hospital, a state patrol officer asked me who was driving. I was scared and I lied."

"Have you ever admitted this—" Trish started, then stopped.

"No one else knows," Holt replied. "Not my parents, not Angelina, no one. And I don't see why that should change. It can't bring Calico back, and if I went to his parents now, it would only dredge up all the pain of the past. It's like picking a scab that should be left alone."

Holt closed his eyes for a second before continuing. "And now you know the truth. You're a deputy sheriff and you've heard my confession, but I hope you can understand why I've kept my silence."

Trish studied Holt for a moment. She couldn't promise to keep her mouth shut. A crime was a crime, no matter who committed it or when it happened. She wasn't sure about the statute of limitations for vehicular homicide, and Holt certainly wasn't the person to ask about it. However, what bothered her the most was his attitude. He seemed self-serving, not repentant.

"Let's get back to the church," Trish said flatly.

They rode in silence.

"I'll see you later," Holt said when he got out of the car.

Trish didn't respond. As she watched Holt walk away toward his vehicle, she knew one thing for certain. Holt Douglas was a moral twin to the teenager who had killed her father and paralyzed her mother.

Holt sat in his car and looked in the rearview mirror. As soon as Trish's car was out of sight, he rested his head against the steering wheel and began to cry. At first, he wasn't exactly sure why, but as the tears continued, he knew it was grief over Calico's death and regret about what had happened that summer night. He'd shed a tear or two at the hospital on the night of the accident and when he'd heard Trish's story at the sandwich shop, but the energy needed to keep his dark secret had dammed the river of sorrow.

And he felt ashamed. It was bad enough that he'd lied as a scared eighteen-year-old, but he'd maintained his deception long after maturity should have caused him to rethink what he'd done and try to make it right. He was a coward.

Starting the car, he glanced down at the fuel gauge. The vehicle had a full tank of gas. Perhaps it would be better for everyone if he left the church parking lot, drove as far as he could, filled up the tank again, and kept going until he reached a place where no one knew him and he could begin an invisible, anonymous life.

He left the parking lot. At the first intersection, he turned toward home. He could try to escape, but it wouldn't do any good. A change in geography wouldn't alter who he was. His past was woven into the fabric of his present.

That had just been proved beyond a reasonable doubt.

27

After the wave of intense emotion subsided, Holt wasn't sure what to do. In the process of telling Trish the truth about Calico, he'd forgotten her gift of the Bible and hadn't thought to retrieve it when he got out of her car. Holt drove to a local discount retailer.

Going to the book section, he found multiple options for Bibles. He was holding one in his hand when a voice interrupted him.

"I like that translation," a man said.

Holt turned and faced an older man with a full head of white hair standing behind him.

"And the study notes are good," the man continued. "There's even a section in the back where you can look up topics you're interested in and read about them."

"I'm sure that's helpful," Holt said, embarrassed that his private search had attracted public attention.

The man continued to look at Holt, who felt as vulnerable as a witness about to be impeached. He flipped to the end of the book, glanced down, and saw the word *confess*, followed by multiple references and a brief text.

"Yeah, this is probably the one I need," he said. "Thanks."

The man smiled as Holt moved away. On his way to the cash register, Holt grabbed a package of dog treats for Henry.

—

Trish didn't look in her rearview mirror as she drove away from the church parking lot. How could she ever have considered entrusting her heart to a man like Holt Douglas? She never wanted to see him again.

Her anger grew and grew. Holt's arrogance in daily prosecuting people for crimes not nearly as severe as what he'd done infuriated her. By the time she reached the sheriff's office, she was about to explode. She stomped inside the building and plopped down in her cubicle.

Trish desperately needed to talk to someone and let off steam. But she couldn't phone Sue Ann and say, "Oh, you'll never guess the latest news about Holt Douglas. We spent the afternoon together, and he told me he's guilty of a vehicular homicide that he's covered up for ten years. And this is the real shocker: He has the remorse of a rock. It's all water over the dam to him or something like that. I'm sure he expects me to keep it a secret so he won't get embarrassed or lose his law license or go to jail or who knows what else since I'm only a lowly deputy, and he's a big-shot lawyer."

Her mother wasn't an option, either. It would be double cruelty to force Marge to revisit her own devastating loss. And Keith. Daydreaming with him about building a house on Cockburn Road didn't make him an intimate confidant about something like this. Trish ground her teeth. She'd never slapped a boy or man in her life, but if Holt appeared in front of her at that moment, she knew she would slap him as hard as she could. And it would be for his own good. Someone needed to knock some sense into him.

Trish went to the break room for a drink of water. She stood by the sink and drank a full glass in a few gulps. In addition to quenching her thirst, Trish hoped the water would cleanse her from the defilement she felt caused by the revelation of Holt's past. She returned to her cubicle.

Still agitated, she forced herself to write an account of her attempt to locate and arrest Ricky. In writing the report she had to mention Holt, which caused the rage inside to flare up again. Even his brave action in leaving the car to confront the shotgun-wielding Jenkins now seemed like a self-exalting attempt at false penance.

Trish stopped in the middle of writing the report and put her head in her hands. Holt was making her miserable without being in the room.

"Deputy Carmichael," a male voice interrupted her. "Are you okay?"

Trish looked up. It was Butch Clovis.

"Uh, yes, sir."

"When you get a break, I need to see you in my office."

"I can come now—"

"No, make it about thirty minutes. I just wanted to make sure you were on duty."

The thought of meeting with Clovis doubled Trish's level of stress. She struggled to complete the report. When she did, she printed out a hard copy and saved one on the computer.

Butch Clovis, as the senior detective in the department, had an office directly next to Sheriff Blackstone's. The detective's door was closed, and Trish knocked.

"Come in!" the detective barked.

Trish opened the door and peeked inside. "Is this a good time?" she asked. "Do I need to get a file?"

"No, have a seat."

In the years she'd been with the sheriff's office, Trish had only been in group meetings with Clovis. They'd never had a private meeting in his office.

"Tell me about earlier this afternoon," Clovis said. "I heard the radio traffic between Deputy Watkins and the dispatcher."

"That's the report I was working on when you came by my cubicle." Trish started to get up from her chair. "I'll get it."

"No," Clovis said and held out his hand to stop her. "I want to hear directly from you. Why was Holt Douglas there?"

"I saw him coming out of Bishop Pennington's church on my way to the location, and he volunteered to come with me. I was in my personal vehicle and thought it might be a good idea. I didn't realize it was going to turn into a dangerous situation."

"Isn't that always a possibility?"

"Yes," Trish admitted. "It is."

"Douglas may be an assistant district attorney, but that doesn't authorize you to have him on the scene of a possible arrest. That decision needs to be made by one of the detectives or the sheriff."

Even after the recent drink of water, Trish's mouth felt dry. "Yes, sir. I'm sorry. I can assure you it won't happen again."

"Do you realize you could be terminated over this?"

Trish tried to swallow but couldn't. "I do now," she said. "But I won't make the same mistake again. It was a spur-of-the-moment decision."

"Is that what you want me to tell the sheriff? That it was a spur-of-the-moment decision?"

"I don't know," Trish said, unable to keep the desperation from creeping into her voice.

The possibility of having to tell her mother that she'd been fired flashed through her mind.

"What can I do to keep that from happening?" she continued, her voice trembling.

Clovis leaned back in his chair. "Before I answer, I have another question for you. What is the extent of your interaction with Douglas? Be complete and don't leave out anything."

Trish quickly tried to calm down and organize her thoughts. "Well, for the past two years he's been the liaison for my files with the district attorney's office. At least once or twice a month I'm in court with him. If one of my defendants is arrested, he usually prosecutes the case."

Clovis nodded. "Is that all?"

Trish tried to remember anything else. "The other day I asked him to give a man I knew in high school a break on the traffic ticket. It was a speeding charge, and I shouldn't have stuck my nose into it, but—"

"Other than the speeding ticket for an old boyfriend, is there anything else?"

"He wasn't a boyfriend," Trish corrected. "He was on the football team, and I played basketball."

Clovis continued to stare at Trish. As she grew more and more anxious, her ability to think diminished by the same degree. She struggled through a few more sentences. Finally, there was nothing left in her brain, and she simply shook her head.

"That's all I can come up with."

"That's too bad." Clovis tapped a folder that was lying on the corner of his desk. "Why did you pull the investigative file about Rex Meredith's death for Douglas? Who authorized that?"

Trish felt her face flush. "No one. He asked me to do it so I did."

"Why did he want it?"

Any loyalty Trish had to Holt was lying on the asphalt of the country store parking lot on the road into Paxton. She certainly wasn't going to try to protect him if it might jeopardize her own job. She took a deep breath and told Clovis everything she could remember about Holt's interest in Rex Meredith's death. The only thing she left out was his suspicion about Clovis himself. She couldn't think of a way to bring that up without sounding like she agreed with Holt's theory. Clovis listened without asking questions or taking notes. The fact that he didn't interrupt made Trish uneasy. If it was a technique the detective used to get people who felt guilty to say more than they intended, it worked. She kept jabbering after she really didn't have anything else to add and was repeating herself.

"Last week we agreed that I wouldn't help him anymore," she said. "We haven't talked about it since. His investigation didn't come up this afternoon when we were in the car together."

"Why did you stop helping him?"

The question caught Trish completely off guard. She hesitated.

"Are you refusing to tell me?" Clovis asked, a menacing tone creeping into his voice.

"No, no," Trish replied. "There was a misunderstanding with Holt's girlfriend. She thought he was romantically interested in me and broke off their relationship. Holt said we shouldn't be seen together in public while he tried to patch things up with her."

"Hmm," Clovis grunted. "That's not good."

"You think Holt and Angelina ought to get back together?" Trish asked, mystified.

"Don't be ridiculous." Clovis looked directly at her. "You're going to be my eyes and ears and report back to me what Douglas does next. If you're not helping him with his investigation, that won't be possible."

"Why do you want to know what he's—"

"Has Ralph Granger authorized Douglas to reopen an investigation?" Clovis interrupted.

"No, and I'm not sure I can convince him now to tell me what he's found out."

"You'd better figure out a way to make it happen. It's going to take more than chasing down a few deadbeat dads for you to justify your continued employment here. Is that clear?"

Trish had to blink back tears. She managed to nod her head.

"Yes, sir."

"And I don't want to have to ask you for updates. I expect you to let me know. Immediately."

"Yes, sir."

"That's all." Clovis dismissed her with a wave of his hand.

28

The sun dipped behind the trees as Holt sat on his back deck with an open Bible in his lap. It was mosquito season in Paxton, and a purple bug light on a pole about twenty-five feet away zapped an intruder every few seconds. Henry lay contentedly at Holt's feet.

Holt read the first few chapters of Genesis and immediately picked up on blame-shifting as an ancient strategy to avoid the consequences of wrongful conduct. He wasn't surprised that Adam's attempt to transfer responsibility for his sin to Eve was doomed to failure as surely as the same tactic would fall flat in front of Judge Lomax in the Paxton Superior Court.

Holt then used the concordance in the back of the book to find passages about confession. He quickly saw the link between confession and repentance, a term he thought he understood before realizing his definition was closer to regret. Biblical repentance was similar to voluntary restitution, which explained why Trish Carmichael had hammered him over the head with the idea that he had to do something about his lie. A criminal defendant who came forward with a plan to pay back stolen money could, in some situations, receive a lesser sentence. The same seemed to apply to matters of faith, although Bishop Pennington had emphasized in his sermon that God's forgiveness was a gift.

Nothing Holt read showed him what form repentance should take in his circumstance. Every scenario he played out in his mind ended up hurting the people connected with him or Calico. He didn't walk into a courtroom unprepared, and on a personal matter this important Holt wasn't going to act without a clear sense of what he wanted to accomplish. On the quiet deck in the fading light, he closed his eyes and offered a simple, silent prayer for guidance.

—

Trish was scheduled to work first shift the following day, so after six hours of restless sleep, she stood in front of her bathroom mirror and adjusted the dark brown tie that was part of her uniform. Going into the kitchen, she poured an extra-large glass of orange juice. She toasted half a blueberry bagel and spread cream cheese on top of it.

Deeply upset about her conversation with Holt and still reeling from her encounter with Butch Clovis, Trish wasn't hungry, but she knew if she didn't eat, a headache loomed in her future. So she dutifully chewed the bagel as she sat at the kitchen table. The first streaks of morning light filtered through the curtains into the kitchen. Marge emerged with a yawn from her bedroom.

"Sorry I didn't wait up for you," she said. "The baseball game was over earlier than normal, and I barely kept my eyes open for the postgame show."

"That's okay. I went straight to bed."

"Did you have a good evening at work?" Marge asked as she held the empty coffeepot under the faucet.

"Let me do that for you," Trish said, stepping forward. "Why don't you watch the morning news on TV?"

Trish handed her mother the TV remote. As soon as the picture and sound came up, Trish knew she'd be able to avoid her mother's questions. Being confined to the house and a wheelchair only increased Marge's interest in the outside world. Before the accident, Marge worked for a local florist and rarely slowed down to watch TV news. Now it was a regular part of her life.

"The coffee will be ready in less than a minute," Trish said as she watched the black liquid drip into the clear glass pot. "Do you want me to stay and fix your first cup?"

"No," Marge said without taking her eyes off the screen. "But I look forward to seeing you this afternoon. Maybe after you take a nap we can go out to dinner. I'm craving a steak."

Trish thought about the new steak restaurant. It was pricey, but she and Marge were normally so frugal that it might be fun to splurge on a Monday night, and it would distract Trish from her recent troubles.

"How about the new place Keith took me to the other night?"

Marge turned toward her. "No, the café on Main Street is fine for me."

"Their steaks are as thin as a piece of cardboard and have about as much flavor. I'm already getting excited about both of us dressing up and going out someplace nice. It will be fun, and I'm going to pay for it."

"No," Marge started. "It's a waste of—"

"Bye, Mama," Trish said, cutting her off. "See you later. Your blue-and-yellow dress would be a good choice. Think about it as an early birthday dinner."

"My birthday isn't until September."

"Neither is mine. That's why I said 'early.'"

Trish knew Marge's resistance was token opposition to satisfy her conscience. She would love a chance to get out of the house for a special time together.

Monday morning at the sheriff's office was one of the busiest times of the week. Crimes that occurred during the weekend had to be processed and funneled into the criminal justice pipeline. Most offenses were petty, but today the office was buzzing about a man from Alabama who was arrested late Saturday night and charged with kidnapping and aggravated assault. The facts of the case made Trish shudder. On her way to her cubicle, she looked up and saw Butch Clovis approaching from the opposite direction. There was no place to hide.

"Good morning," she said as she hurried by him.

"Just a minute," the detective said.

Trish froze and slowly turned around. "Yes, sir."

"I've thought some more about our conversation yesterday," Clovis said in a low voice. "You realize it was off the record, don't you?"

"Uh, yes, sir."

Clovis eyed her closely. "Do you believe Douglas is on to something in his investigation? The way you spoke about it gave me the impression you believe his theory about Greg Stevens."

Trish swallowed. One of the things that had kept her tossing and turning in the night was concern about that very issue. Clovis stepped closer. Trish was already up against the wall and couldn't move.

"He's a smart lawyer," she managed. "And persuasive."

"Meredith's death was thoroughly investigated," Clovis replied emphatically. "As the first detective on the scene, I interviewed potential witnesses, analyzed every piece of evidence, and ran down all possible theories, including Greg Stevens as his father-in-law's murderer. There was only one logical conclusion—Rex Meredith committed suicide. Tony McDermott came in late to the investigation and started asking questions I'd already answered. His nose got bent out of shape when the sheriff told him to move on to other cases that needed his attention. Now he's retired up in the mountains with nothing better to do than stir up trouble here. I don't know what's motivating Douglas. Maybe he has his eye on Ralph Granger's job. Whatever his reason, it would be terribly wrong to drag Mr. Stevens through the mud of public opinion with false accusations. He and his wife do a lot for this town that no one knows about and should be treated with respect."

"They're giving money to the building fund at my church even though they aren't members," Trish offered.

"I didn't know about that, but it proves my point."

"Yes, sir."

Clovis fixed his gaze on Trish. "I want you to contact Douglas by the end of your shift and get back in the loop. I want real-time data."

"Today?" Trish asked, suddenly feeling even more trapped. "What am I supposed to say to him?"

"That you want to continue helping with the investigation."

"But the situation with his girlfriend—"

"Is something you as a woman should be able to handle. She runs the beauty salon in that blue house on Broadmore Street, doesn't she?"

"Yes."

"Talk to her, if that's what it takes. Convince her you aren't interested in Douglas."

Trish's mouth dropped open.

"Detective Clovis!" a female voice called out on the interoffice intercom. "Someone from the crime lab in Atlanta is on the phone for you."

Clovis kept his attention fixed on Trish. "Get back to me. No excuses."

It was 7:15 a.m. when Trish sat down in her cubicle, but she felt like she'd already worked an eight-hour shift. She turned on her computer and checked her to-do list. The first five items were cases she needed to prepare for court on Thursday. She mentally added *Convince Holt Douglas to tell me about the Meredith/Stevens investigation* to the top of the list.

If she could stall for time, Trish would see Holt in court on Thursday, but it would be in the midst of the controlled chaos of managing a court calendar, and there wouldn't be a good chance to talk. Trish's eyes returned to her list. She could ask Holt to meet with her in private to discuss an upcoming case on the calendar; however, the cases in her queue were as ordinary as a bushel of turnips. They presented no legal questions that couldn't be solved in a matter of seconds. And even if she manufactured an excuse to arrange a meeting, there was no guarantee Holt would change his mind about letting her help with the investigation.

Toward noon Trish scooted her chair away from her computer and peeked down the hallway toward Sheriff Blackstone's office. The sheriff and Butch Clovis were talking near the sheriff's door. Trish jerked her head back into her cubicle before they saw her. Half the day was gone, and she'd not come up with a plan. Against her will, she was being forced to consider talking to Angelina Peabody. She looked up the phone number for the salon and, after staring at it for several seconds, punched in the number. While the phone rang, she tried to decide what to say.

"All About You Salon and Spa," a chirpy female voice answered. "How may I help you?"

"Uh, I'd like to schedule an appointment with Angelina Peabody."

"Certainly. Cut, color, or both?"

"Just a trim and style. I know it's short notice, but I'd really like to see her today." Trish had a sudden inspiration. "I'm taking my mother out for a special dinner tonight. She's in a wheelchair, so this is a big event."

"We appreciate you calling, but that's not possible. Angelina doesn't have any openings for new clients until next Tuesday. Let me check our other stylists and see if there's someone who can work you in. Your name please?"

"Uh, that's okay. Thanks."

Stymied, Trish hung up the phone. She took a mirror from her purse and checked her hair. She really did need a trim. As she lowered the mirror, something shiny caught her eye.

It was her badge.

29

Holt spent the morning in front of Judge Lomax. The court calendar was primarily arraignments and the entry of guilty pleas. The high point was the first appearance in court of the man arrested over the weekend and charged with kidnapping and aggravated assault. A high-priced lawyer from Atlanta appeared on the man's behalf and tried to convince the judge to lower the man's bond to $250,000. After the lawyer finished his presentation, Holt stood to respond.

"Your Honor, the state respectfully shows the court that the current bond of one million dollars—"

"Is perhaps too low," the judge interrupted. "The defendant poses a significant flight risk on these serious charges. Do you have a motion to increase the bond?"

"Objection!" The defense lawyer was immediately on his feet. "We've not been notified of any motion to modify my client's bond."

"The fact that you requested the matter be placed on this morning's calendar demonstrates to the court's satisfaction that you are prepared to address the issue," the judge replied. "Mr. Douglas?"

"The state asks that the bond be increased to five million dollars."

"Any evidence in response?" The judge turned to the defense lawyer.

The lawyer, who was huddling with his client, faced the judge. "Such an exorbitant increase is an abuse of the court's discretion," he said, his face turning red. "Mr. Perez has no prior criminal record."

"And is charged with kidnapping the children of an alleged co-conspirator in a multinational drug operation and holding them hostage in a house in Ashley County to ensure the coconspirator's cooperation. You presented evidence that Mr. Perez is a citizen of Venezuela. The court takes judicial notice that Venezuela does not have an extradition treaty with the United States. The state's motion is granted."

The drama associated with the Perez case sent a surge of adrenaline through Holt. It took a few not-guilty pleas in misdemeanor cases to calm him down. As the calendar call came to an end, he checked the gallery to see who remained. There were a handful of people sitting together, and a solitary older man with close-cut gray hair seated on the back bench. When Holt turned around, the man raised his hand slightly in greeting. Puzzled, Holt did the same.

Judge Lomax left immediately upon completion of the final case for the day. The only other people remaining in the courtroom were the court reporter and a lawyer huddled on the opposite side of the room with a client and his family.

"Mr. Douglas?"

Holt turned around. It was the man who'd been sitting in the rear of the courtroom.

"Yes, I'm Holt Douglas."

The man extended a beefy hand. "I'm Tony McDermott. Do you have time to talk?"

Holt quickly glanced around. "Uh, sure. I was going to grab lunch. Would you like to join me?"

"Yeah, what's the name of that barbecue restaurant off Main Street?"

"Jake's Smokehouse."

"Right." McDermott smiled. "I was thinking about that place during the drive down from the mountains this morning."

Holt checked his watch. "I need to return these files to the office. Can you meet me there in ten minutes?"

"See you then."

Holt watched the former detective leave the courtroom. McDermott was a large man whose broad shoulders hinted at what must have been, at one time, a very intimidating physique.

When Holt arrived at the restaurant, there was no sign of McDermott. Several groups were waiting to be seated, but as soon as Holt came in and held up two fingers, HC escorted him to a table against the wall.

"I appreciate the VIP treatment, but I don't want to make those other folks mad," Holt said.

"Jake says, 'They'll forget the wait when they get their plates,'" HC replied with a smile. "And you're a VIP to us."

"I'm meeting a guy who should be here in a couple of minutes."

"I'll fetch your tea and take your order when he gets here."

There was a menu on the table. Holt didn't need to look at it. He'd memorized it long ago, but he picked it up to pass the time. After verifying that the price of Brunswick stew and a pulled-pork plate hadn't changed, he checked his watch. It was a short drive from the courthouse to the restaurant. The only reason for delay would be the need to park farther down the street than normal. HC returned. The crowd waiting to be seated was growing larger.

"It looks like the man I was supposed to meet is late," Holt said apologetically, "so I'll go ahead and order."

"Burnt ends with—" HC started.

"No, a bowl of Brunswick stew with corn bread. I'm not as hungry as usual."

"Spicy or mild?"

"Spicy."

While he waited for his food, Holt sipped tea and tried to guess why McDermott drove all the way to Paxton to meet with him in person instead of calling on the phone. In Holt's mind there could be only one reason—significant information about Rex Meredith's death.

HC returned with a steaming bowl of stew. Jake's version of the Southern goulash contained both smoked chicken and pork in a tomato base, along with corn, diced tomatoes, onions, and baby lima beans. Holt tore off a piece of corn bread and dropped it into the stew to soak up some of the red broth. He then used his spoon to retrieve the bread. The stew had just the right amount of hot-sauce kick. Holt loved the stew, but he wanted to talk to Tony McDermott.

—

Trish touched the gun in her holster as she walked up the steps of the salon. Her heart was pounding. She knew what she was about to do could get her fired—and she knew if she didn't do it she could get fired. She paused for a few seconds on the front porch, shrugged her shoulders, and adjusted her posture to what she hoped was an authoritative stance. Channeling her inner Butch Clovis, she opened the door and stepped inside.

"Good afternoon," said a smiling young woman with blond hair. "I'm Brittany. How may I help you?"

Keeping a stern expression on her face, Trish touched her badge. "I'm Deputy Patricia Carmichael. I need to speak with Ms. Angelina Peabody."

A woman who was sitting to the side reading a magazine looked up at Trish, and her mouth dropped open. The smile on Brittany's face evaporated.

"She's with a customer who's getting a color—"

"I need to speak with her immediately," Trish interrupted. "I don't care if she's in the middle of a perm."

Trish felt foolish for throwing in the extra comment about interrupting a permanent, but Brittany didn't smile. Instead, her eyes widened.

"Okay. I'll go upstairs and tell her you're here."

After Brittany left, Trish continued to stand with her legs spread wide in front of the receptionist's desk. She could feel the customer staring at her but didn't turn around. Trish wished she were wearing sunglasses to hide her eyes, but it would have made it hard to see inside the building. Two sets of legs descended the stairs. Angelina came down in front of the receptionist. She had a worried look on her face.

"What's wrong?" the owner of the salon said.

"I need to speak to you privately," Trish said.

"Is it about Holt?" Angelina asked, her level of anxiety obviously rising. "Is he okay?"

Trish suddenly realized Holt's former girlfriend was worried that something horrible had happened to him and the sheriff's office had sent Trish to deliver the bad news.

"He's fine," she said, her voice softer. "Where can we talk?"

"In the kitchen," Angelina said.

Trish followed her down a short hallway. With each step Trish felt more and more remorse for using her badge to strong-arm her way into the salon and interrupting Angelina's busy schedule. They went into the kitchen. Angelina faced Trish.

"Am I in some kind of trouble?" Angelina asked.

"No, and I'm sorry to pull you away from a customer," Trish began. "But this is about Holt. I know you're upset with him because we met at the sub shop on Eastway Drive to discuss a case we're working on together, but there's nothing going on with us other than business. I didn't want to be the cause of friction between you, so I came over here to remove any misunderstanding."

"Holt and I are finished," Angelina replied flatly.

Trish took a deep breath. "I realize you're upset with him, but I wish you'd give him a second chance."

"Aren't you interested in him?"

"No," Trish answered with confidence, now that she knew the true circumstances surrounding Calico's death.

Angelina pressed her lips together tightly for a moment before she spoke. "Look, it's nice of you to come over to let me know there's nothing between you and Holt, but if it's okay, I really need to get back to my customer. Right now she's part light brown and part brunette."

Trish was standing between Angelina and the door. She didn't move.

"Would you at least contact Holt and let him know it's okay with you if I help him with the case? I can't tell you what it's about, but he ended my involvement because he didn't want to upset you."

"I'm not sure he'll take my advice about something like—"

"But could you try?" Trish tried to keep the desperation from her voice. "Coming from you, I think it would make a huge difference."

Angelina gave her a puzzled look. "I'll consider it, but here's another plan. Why don't you tell him we talked, and I said I don't care what he does. He can work with you on all of his cases if he wants to."

"I guess I could do that," Trish said hesitantly.

"Are we finished?"

"Yes."

Trish stepped to the side. Angelina gave her a dubious look and led the way out of the kitchen. As Angelina went upstairs, Trish paused in the receptionist area. Both Brittany and the woman waiting for her appointment were staring at her.

"Everything is fine here," Trish said to the customer. "There are no problems. I'm sure it's a great place, and you can recommend it to your friends."

Neither of the women said anything.

"Bye," Trish said to Brittany. "Thanks for your help."

—

During the drive back to the sheriff's department, Trish felt more foolish by the second. As she walked toward the building, Butch Clovis and a large older man who looked vaguely familiar approached her.

"Deputy Carmichael!" Clovis called out. "Come over here."

Trish reluctantly changed direction to intersect with the detective.

"Yes, sir," she said when she reached the two men.

"Do you remember Tony McDermott?" Clovis asked. "He was one of our detectives a few years ago."

"Yes."

Trish shook the detective's hand.

"Your father works for the farm equipment dealership, doesn't he?" McDermott asked. "He sold me a yard tractor. Great piece of equipment. I'm still using it."

"Her father was killed by a drunk driver," Clovis said. "It happened shortly after you left the department."

"I'm sorry to hear that," McDermott said.

"Thanks," Trish said. "It still hurts."

Trish was trying to recall exactly what Holt had told her about McDermott's interest in Rex Meredith's death. All she could remember was that they'd talked on the phone and McDermott was going to send Holt information that wasn't in the sheriff's department file.

"The driver is still in prison," Clovis said. "And I hope the parole board keeps him there until he serves every day of his sentence."

Clovis had never mentioned the case to Trish, and his concern seemed fake. He put his hand on McDermott's shoulder.

"Tony and I were going over the old case I mentioned to you yesterday. He had a few questions that I was able to clear up for him about the investigation and the reasons behind my report."

"Yes." McDermott nodded. "It's easy to jump to a wrong conclusion when you don't have all the facts."

"I'm sure it is," Trish said.

"And I'm on my way back to the mountains," McDermott said, turning to Clovis. "And my grandsons will have a blast on that Jet Ski."

"It'll be on the truck to Lake Burton by the end of the week. I appreciate you taking it off my hands."

"At that price, how could I refuse? Nice to see you again, Deputy Carmichael. Sorry again about your loss."

The two men continued across the parking lot. Trish heard them laugh. McDermott's obvious change of opinion about the Rex Meredith case was troubling. It was one thing for Clovis to browbeat her into believing Holt's theory was wrong. Convincing McDermott, a seasoned detective no longer employed by the sheriff's department, would have been much harder to do. Trish wondered what Clovis showed him. Or if a discounted price on a used Jet Ski was part of the argument.

—

Holt finished his solitary lunch, returned to the office, and checked his voice mail to see if McDermott had called. He hadn't.

Midafternoon, the phone on his desk buzzed, and he picked it up.

"Deputy Carmichael is on line five," Sally said.

Getting chewed out again by Trish wasn't on his calendar, but he couldn't totally ignore her as long as he remained her liaison with the DA's office.

"Hello," he said.

No one spoke. Holt waited a second.

"Are you there?" he asked.

"Yes, I was waiting for someone to move past my desk before I said anything."

"What's going on?"

"I know you said you didn't want my help in the Meredith investigation, but I can't get it out of my mind."

"Okay," Holt said slowly.

"Did Angelina call you?"

"No. Why?"

"I went by the salon to clear the air about why we met at the sandwich shop."

"You did what?" Holt blurted out.

"Calm down. I'm trying to help you."

Holt listened with increasing anxiety as Trish told him what she'd done.

"Once I explained everything, Angelina was very nice," Trish concluded. "She doesn't mind if we work together."

"You told her about the Meredith investigation?"

"No, I'm not stupid. I just said our time together at the sub shop had to do with a case. I didn't even tell her it was an old one."

There was an odd note in Trish Carmichael's tone of voice.

"You sound stressed," Holt said. "Are you okay?"

"I'm fine."

"Are you still mad at me?"

"Yeah, but that doesn't keep me from wanting to help you do the right thing."

"I'm not even sure what's next. Tony McDermott turned up in court this morning and wanted to go to lunch with me. Then he didn't show."

"I know where he was and what he was doing."

Holt leaned forward in his chair. "Tell me."

"Are you letting me back into the investigation?"

"Yeah, yeah. Go ahead."

"I ran into McDermott and Clovis in the parking lot at the sheriff's office when I came back from the salon."

"Did you talk to them?"

"Just for a minute. McDermott remembered me from his days with the sheriff's department. He and Clovis acted like best friends." Trish stopped.

Holt tapped the top of his desk with a pen as he thought for a moment before he spoke. "McDermott must have bumped into Clovis outside the courthouse and told him he'd talked to me about Rex Meredith's death, which caused Clovis to launch into damage-control mode. That means Clovis knows—"

Holt stopped. Trish didn't say anything.

"Does Clovis know you've helped me?" he asked.

Trish didn't respond.

"Does he?"

"Yes, but—"

Holt pressed his teeth together tightly for a second. "And he's ordered you to find out what I'm doing so you can report back to him."

The phone line went dead.

30

Holt immediately redialed the sheriff's office and asked to speak to Trish.

"May I ask who's calling?" the woman on the switchboard responded.

Holt considered giving a false name but didn't.

"Hold, please," the woman said.

Holt was furious with Clovis. It was unconscionable for the detective to bully and intimidate Trish.

"This is Trish Carmichael—"

"Trish, look, I'm sorry—"

"I'm not available, but please leave me a message at the beep. I'll return your call as soon as possible."

Holt waited for the beep. "What Clovis is doing to you isn't right! If he's threatened your job over this, he deserves all the trouble that's coming his way." Holt was about to end the message with a plea that she get in touch with him when he had another idea. "But I'm willing to work with you to make it look like you're pumping me for information so you won't get into trouble. Even though Clovis is in the wrong, I feel responsible for dragging you into this mess."

The time allotted for a message ended. Holt considered calling back to add more but figured he'd said enough. Trish would have to decide what she wanted to do.

He buzzed Sally and told her to let him know if Trish called. He then left a message at Tony McDermott's house, asking him to return the call when he got home and including his cell phone number. It would take the former detective several hours to get to Lake Burton. There wasn't much else Holt could do. Returning to the files from the morning calendar, he forced himself to plow through them. Between each case, he kept hoping Sally would interrupt him with a message that Trish was on the line. No call came.

When Holt arrived home from work, there was an unfamiliar pickup truck parked on the street in front of his house. Getting out of his car, he saw two men in their thirties wearing faded jeans and dirty T-shirts covered with splotches of paint.

"What are you doing here?" Holt called out.

"Is this your house?" one of the men responded.

"Yeah, and I want to know—"

"Do you own a little brown-and-white dog?"

Holt suddenly realized the men had come from the direction of the backyard. There was no way Henry would allow strangers into his private domain without putting up a ferocious fight.

"Yes." Holt started walking rapidly toward the men. "Where is he?"

"Lying on the deck," the larger of the two men said. "We were doing some remodeling on the house next door, heard the commotion, and came running over. We saw the whole thing."

"It went on for at least half an hour before he killed it," the second man said. "They was all balled up in a knot, and we couldn't do nuthin' to help. He's a tough little booger."

The second man stepped to the side. Draped over the fence was a thick snake at least four feet long. The snake's body was gashed in multiple places, the most severe a few inches below its head, which was flopped over to one side.

"It's the biggest copperhead I've ever seen," the first man said. "It must have crawled into the yard from that drainage ditch running behind your property. I reckon your dog jumped on it and—"

Holt didn't hear anything else as he broke into a run through the gate and around the corner of the house. Henry was lying on his side on the wooden deck. The dog's eyes followed Holt's movements, but his head didn't budge. Holt knelt down, and Henry's tail gave the faintest quiver. The left side of the dog's face was swollen, and his eye was drooping closed. There were several raised wounds on his body. Holt gently touched Henry's head and moved his hand to the dog's throat, where he felt a slight gurgling. Henry was having trouble breathing. Holt scooped him up in his arms.

"I'm sorry we couldn't help him," the first man said when Holt stepped through the gate. "As soon as he killed the snake, he dragged himself up to the porch."

"I'm taking him to the vet," Holt said.

"What about the snake?" the second man asked as they walked with Holt toward his car.

"I don't care," Holt responded over his shoulder.

"We took pictures and a video on a cell phone," the second man called after him. "We'll be workin' next door for a couple more days if you want to see them. That snake must have popped him at least five or six times, but it just seemed to make him madder."

Holt didn't answer as he opened the passenger door of the car and gently laid Henry in the seat. The dog was now completely immobile, his eyes glassy. Holt ran around to the driver's side.

"I hope he makes it," the first man said. "I've never seen anything like it. After he killed the snake, he gnawed it for a little bit to prove he'd won."

Holt slammed the car into reverse and backed down his driveway. On the way he called the veterinarian's office to let them know he was coming.

"Are you sure it was a copperhead?" asked the woman who answered the phone.

"That's what the workers who saw the fight told me."

"Did you see the snake?"

"Yes. It had light and dark brown splotches on its body, and the top of its head was the color of a penny."

"How long will it take you to get here?"

"Less than five minutes."

"I'll let Dr. Wade know."

Holt glanced down at Henry. There were flecks of foam at the corners of the dog's mouth. A traffic light turned red, and Holt had to stop. There were cars passing through the intersection, so running the light wasn't an option. Holt tapped the steering wheel with his fingers in frustration. The light turned green, and he stepped on the gas. The veterinarian's office was on the opposite side of town, and the increase in traffic caused by the end of the workday slowed Holt down more than he'd anticipated. He had trouble keeping his eyes on the road. He was more concerned that Henry's chest continued to rise and fall. A car in front of him unexpectedly slowed to make a turn. Holt stomped on the brake and grabbed Henry to keep him from being tossed onto the floorboard.

Holt zipped into the parking lot for the vet. When he picked up Henry, the dog felt stiffer than when he put him in the car. Holt rushed into the building.

"Mr. Douglas?" asked one of two women behind the desk.

"Yes."

"Follow me. Dr. Wade knows you're coming."

They went into an examination room, and Holt placed Henry on the table. The dog moaned slightly. Holt could see several fang marks, including one on the left side of the dog's face. Holt's stomach was in a knot, and he lifted up a silent prayer for help. The door of the room opened and the veterinarian came in. Henry didn't respond.

The vet quickly inspected the bite marks. "He got him in the back and neck," he said.

"Is that why his eye is droopy?"

"Yes. How long has it been since he was bitten?"

"I'm not sure. He killed the snake before I got home from work. Two construction workers saw the fight and said it lasted about half an hour."

"All right, I'll administer the antivenin. Let's hope Henry lives to fight another day."

"You think he'll be okay?"

"We won't know until we see how he responds to the medicine, but it's usually effective. You'll need to leave him here so we can monitor him through the night."

Holt gently stroked the back of Henry's head. Not a muscle twitched as the vet inserted the needle.

"Okay, now we wait and see," the vet said.

"I'll hang out in the waiting room—" Holt began.

"No," Dr. Wade said. "We're closing in a few minutes, and it will be awhile before we know if this will work. Do we have your cell phone number on his chart?"

"Yes."

"The tech on duty knows what to look for, and I'll swing by to check on him before I go to bed."

"Thanks."

With one last look at Henry, whose eyes no longer made the effort to follow his movements, Holt left the veterinarian's office with a heavy heart.

After hanging up on Holt, Trish fought back tears of frustration. She'd never been so completely backed into a corner in her life.

It was an hour and a half until the end of her shift—a long time to avoid Butch Clovis. Trish hadn't seen or heard from the detective since their encounter in the parking lot.

Trish listened to Holt's voice-mail message three times. She shook her head at his arrogance in thinking he could finesse Clovis into believing she was helping Holt voluntarily. Trish knew in her gut that at some point Holt's strategy would require her to lie. And although she didn't consider herself perfect, everything in her resisted deceit. Unlike Holt, who'd embraced a massive deception for over a decade.

Trish tried to concentrate on her other work. About thirty minutes before the end of her shift, Marge called.

"What time are you going to get home?" her mother asked.

"Uh, I'm not sure. I may run some errands. I'm beat."

"Don't be too late, and save a little bit of energy. I'm excited about our dinner."

In the midst of all the commotion of the day, Trish had completely forgotten her promise to take her mother to the new steak house.

"Oh, I'll be home in plenty of time to get ready."

"I hope so. I've hardly eaten all day."

Except for a quick snack at the desk, Trish hadn't eaten, either. But her abstinence from food wasn't preparation for a big meal; it was a by-product of extreme anxiety.

"See you soon," she said in what she hoped was a cheerful voice.

As the clock crept toward the end of her shift, Trish's hope that she could avoid Clovis began to increase. Normally she wasn't a procrastinator, and she knew she'd have to talk to him eventually, but she didn't want to do so now, not yet. She needed time to pray and ask God to get her out of this mess. She logged out of her work program and turned off her computer. Keeping her head low, she made her way past the other cubicles toward the exit. When she reached the door, she paused and looked at the parking lot. The sheriff and the detectives had reserved spots not far from the entrance. Clovis's space was empty.

With a sigh of relief, Trish began walking rapidly toward her car at the far end of the lot. She started the engine and backed out of her parking space. When she did, she heard a horn honk and quickly applied the brake. An unmarked car sped past her rear bumper.

Butch Clovis was behind the wheel.

With a resigned sigh, Trish put her vehicle in drive and rolled forward into the parking space she'd vacated. There was no use trying to flee. That would only cause the detective to follow her, turn on his blue light, and pull her over. Trish bowed her head slightly as she waited for Clovis to return. After a few seconds she looked in the rearview mirror. There was no sign of Clovis's car. She looked out the passenger window and saw the detective walking rapidly up the sidewalk to the sheriff's department entrance. As hard as it was for her to believe it, he didn't seem intent on tracking her down for interrogation. Trish eased out of the parking spot.

31

Holt's drive home from the vet's office was much slower. Several of his neighbors were clustered around his fence looking at the dead snake. Included in the group was Bishop Pennington.

"I'm sorry about Henry," the minister said. "I was driving by and saw the commotion. How is he?"

"It's serious. Do you have time to come inside?"

"Yes, I was coming by to see you anyway. But if it's not a good time—"

"No, I don't want to be alone while I wait for the call from the vet. I believe Henry's going to make it, but TV isn't going to do the job of distracting me."

Holt held the front door open for the bishop.

"I've spent many a night at the hospital with family members waiting on news from a doctor about a loved one. Waiting on a vet to call will be a new experience."

They went into the kitchen. The room was full of reminders of Henry: food dish, water bowl, two chew toys, a half-eaten dog biscuit, a ragged blanket. Holt took a couple of bottles of water from the refrigerator and gave one to the bishop.

"I bought a Bible," Holt said.

"Have you been reading it?"

Holt sat down at the kitchen table. "You don't have to cross-examine me," he said with a slight smile.

"Sorry. Too many Bibles end up gathering dust. It's a pet peeve of mine. You wouldn't have gotten one if you didn't intend on opening the cover."

Holt told him what he'd read while sitting on the deck. The bishop listened until he finished.

"How did what you read speak to you?"

"What do you mean?"

"To your life. Something's troubling you, Holt," the bishop said, scratching his chin. "I can't put my finger on it, but I know it's in there."

Holt took a sip of water. "Your sermon about confession and repentance pulled back the curtain on events from my past I've kept hidden for a long time." Holt paused. "And I wish I'd waited until now to tell Trish about it."

Holt told Bishop Pennington about Calico. It was different from when he'd talked with Trish. The minister didn't express emotion or reveal shock. Instead, the older man's eyes seemed to draw the anguish from Holt's soul. Holt held nothing back. He laid out every motive, each lie, all deception. Both water bottles were empty when he finished.

"There was a lot I did wrong that night. One bad choice led to a second, and a third. But it all boiled down to the fact that my best friend was dead, and I lied to protect myself."

"Have you ever asked God to forgive you?" the bishop asked.

"Not really. I always thought the forgiveness I needed would have to come from Calico's family. And I can't get my head around what that would look like."

"My suggestion is you start with God and work out from there."

Holt sat with his hands resting on the table. "Do you mean right now?" he asked.

"It's already been ten years. Can you think of a good reason to wait any longer?"

"No, except it feels awkward to talk to someone I can't see."

"It's more important that he sees you than that you see him," the bishop said and smiled. "He already knows everything you've done, even the parts you've forgotten to tell me. Confessing your sins to God is like a boy who does something wrong while his parents are watching. When the boy admits what he did, the confession isn't shocking news to the parents, but his admission of guilt opens the door for them to forgive him."

"That makes sense."

"And when a person receives forgiveness from the Lord, it sets him free to do what he needs to do on earth."

Even if the end of his journey was obscured by the mists of the future, Holt could believe the bishop was right about the needs of the present.

"I'll do it," he said resolutely.

"Not yet," the bishop replied. "Your problem is bigger than one lie, no matter how serious or far-reaching its consequences."

"I don't understand," Holt said, a puzzled look on his face. "I thought this was what you wanted me to do."

The bishop leaned forward. "When you prosecute a case, how often are you confident that you've uncovered all the crimes the defendant ever committed?"

"Never."

"But the unknown offenses are still crimes, aren't they?"

"Sure."

"Have you committed other sins?"

"Oh." Holt paused. "Do I have to make a giant list?"

"It wouldn't hurt to mention specific things that come to mind, but the plea bargain Jesus offers is a blanket deal. He took the punishment for all your sins on the cross, once and for all, no matter the charges against you. Your part is to accept the offer. And if you take the deal, you'll find out what freedom really looks like."

"What kind of freedom?"

"Freedom from the dominion of sin because Jesus is in charge of your life."

Holt felt a sudden tightness in his throat. He wasn't sure if it was a good feeling or bad. The bishop smiled.

"I like what I see on your face," he said.

"What's that?"

"The realization that if you do this, everything is going to change."

Holt trusted the bishop and believed what he was saying was true. But it wasn't the logic of the bishop's analogy that persuaded Holt. Something deeper than his mind was influencing his response. He put his hand on his chest.

"What is it that I'm feeling right now?" he asked.

"My best guess would be the Holy Spirit speaking to your heart."

"It hurts, but in a good way."

The bishop lifted his hands in the air. "God is great. Now's the time. Are you ready?"

"Yes," Holt said. "I am."

—

That night a kitchen table became a fiery altar. Through the cleansing flames of God's forgiveness, Holt took his first steps into a new life. Bishop Pennington prayed. Holt followed. His words were halting at first but grew in strength.

"And what God has forgiven is forgiven indeed. In Jesus' name, amen," the bishop said.

When Holt opened his eyes, the light overhead burned brighter; the air in the kitchen seemed clearer.

His cell phone, which was lying on the table, vibrated. It was the veterinarian's office. Holt quickly picked it up.

"How's Henry?" he asked.

"He's taken a bad turn," Dr. Wade replied. "You should come immediately if you want to see him."

Holt was shocked. Despite the vet's cautionary words, he'd been confident the antidote would do its job.

"Do you want me to come with you?" Bishop Pennington asked when Holt delivered the bad news.

"No, but thanks for offering."

32

The festive atmosphere at home was a stark contrast to the somber pall at work. Marge was dressed and ready to go when Trish walked through the front door. Due to her paralysis it took her longer to do simple tasks, and it was clear she'd not wanted to delay the dinner date with her daughter. Seeing her mother's smiling face brought Trish to the verge of tears. She hurried to her bedroom. It took her a few extra minutes in the shower to compose herself and try to wash off some of the burdens of the day. She then put on a dress she knew her mother liked.

"I was hoping you would wear that," Marge said when Trish appeared. "It really goes great with your hair."

"Do you think I need a trim?" Trish asked.

"Soon," Marge replied. "I know you feel loyal to Cindy, but she's really my beautician, not yours. Grace Butler told me her daughter loves the new salon that's on Broadmore Street."

"That's not the place for me," Trish replied quickly. "I hear there's a long waiting list to get an appointment."

Trish loaded her mother and the wheelchair into the van. Marge had a backlog of conversation that didn't require Trish to talk as they traveled across town to the restaurant.

"Oh, Keith's mother stopped by the house this morning and gave us some summer squash from their garden," Marge said. "I thanked her, but make sure you let Keith know, too."

Trish drove past the sheriff's office and the courthouse. "He'll appreciate it more if we make him a casserole," she said.

"I was hoping you'd say that. You've been so quiet about the two of you, I thought maybe something was wrong."

"He was called out of town unexpectedly, and I've been busy at work."

"When does he get back?"

Keith had sent her a text message with his schedule, but Trish couldn't remember the details, and her phone was in her purse on the floorboard at her mother's feet.

"Um, I'm not sure, but I think toward the end of the week."

"Would you like to invite him over for supper? We could cook the casserole then. I know you'd probably rather go out, just the two of you, but—"

"No, that would be great. I know he'd like to see you, too. I'll try to call him later this evening."

"Okay." Marge nodded and smiled.

Giving her mother an opportunity for a simple pleasure like entertaining via a home-cooked meal was an easy thing to do. Trish glanced at her mother's thin legs, which had atrophied from lack of use. Before the accident Marge could stand on her feet all day making floral arrangements and run errands on the way home. Now she was practically a hermit.

"Have you played any interesting chess games recently?" Marge asked.

Trish shook her head. "No, but it would probably be good for me, even if it was only a few speed games."

"Your daddy was so proud of you."

Tears rushed to Trish's eyes. She desperately fought against an uncontrolled release of her emotions. She parked in a handicapped spot directly in front of the entrance.

"There are a lot of cars here for this early on a weekday evening," she said, trying to keep her voice steady. "That looks like Sue Ann's van."

"I've seen several like hers around town. Since it's such a nice place, they probably have a big staff."

Trish wiped her eyes with a tissue before she got out of the van. She couldn't let anything spoil the evening for her mother.

Surprisingly, the restaurant wasn't crowded, and a hostess led them to a table with plenty of room for Marge to maneuver. After placing their drink order, Trish took her mother down the salad line. She tried to anticipate what Marge wanted.

"I was about ninety percent right on your salad selections," Trish said as she rolled her mother back to their table. "But you surprised me with the macaroni salad and the scoop of red pepper hummus. I didn't know you liked humus."

"I'm not sure I do, but I wanted to try it."

Trish returned to the salad bar and hurriedly prepared a plate for herself. When she returned to the table, Marge wasn't there. Trish stepped around the corner to the hostess's station.

"Where's my mother?" she asked.

"Oh, she wanted to see our banquet room. I'll take you to her."

Puzzled, Trish followed the hostess to the back of the restaurant. The woman opened a pair of double doors and stepped aside. The room was filled with about twenty-five people. At the front of the crowd was Marge, who had a huge smile on her face. Alongside her were Keith, Sue Ann, Mark, and Candace. The group included a smattering of friends from church, former high school classmates, and two women from the sheriff's office. Across the back wall was a large birthday banner.

"Happy birthday!" everyone yelled at once.

Trish's mouth dropped open. "What?" she asked. "It's not my birthday."

"Or mine," Marge said. "But when you asked me to come here and joked about an early birthday party, I decided to put one together for you."

Keith stepped forward and hugged her. His embrace was quickly followed by others from Sue Ann, Candace, and everyone else in the room. Tears streamed down Trish's cheeks. Everyone assumed they flowed from joy. She knew they were also mixed with release from pent-up stress.

Dinner was served banquet-style at two long tables with a choice of a small rib eye steak or roasted chicken, and à la carte vegetables. Trish sat between her mother and Keith. Sue Ann and her family were across the table.

"How did you pull this off on such short notice?" Trish asked her mother in a low voice as conversations swirled around them.

"I had plenty of help."

"And who's paying for it? I've never had such a fancy party."

"That's not the concern of the birthday girl, but different people chipped in," her mother replied cryptically. "All you need to know is that everybody here loves you. Enjoy yourself."

After the meal was over, Candace led the group in singing "Happy Birthday." Keith brought Trish a piece of cake with a pink heart on it. When he balanced a piece on a fork and offered to put it in her mouth, a voice called out.

"Save that for the wedding!"

Trish quickly looked around with a sheepish grin on her face. She took the fork from Keith's hand and ate the cake.

"This is really nice," she said to him as she licked a piece of icing from her fork. "How did you manage to be here?"

"When Marge called this morning, I was able to flip some of my meetings to next week. There's no way I would miss this." He leaned over and whispered in her ear, "I have a present, but I don't want to give it to you until everyone else is gone."

"I'll need to take my mother—"

"Thelma's going to take her home," Keith replied, referring to an older woman who'd taught Trish for several years in Sunday school.

Sue Ann presented Trish with a giant card signed by everyone, and Candace gave her a small plate with an outline of the little girl's hands on it. Above the hands was printed Candace's name along with the date. Beneath the hands was a Bible verse:

My times are in your hands.—Psalm 31:15.

"We've been working on this for a couple of weeks," Sue Ann explained. "And when your mama called about tonight, I couldn't think of a better time to give it to you."

"That is so sweet," Trish said, giving Candace a hug. "I pray it will always be true for you, too."

Candace scampered off to her father, leaving Trish beside Sue Ann.

"I know you've had to wait for a lot of things," Sue Ann said. "Everything will work out in the end."

"I hope so," Trish sighed.

The party began to break up.

"Keith says Thelma is going to drive our van and take you home," Trish said to her mother.

"That's right. She rode with Keith."

"He has a gift for me," Trish continued in a whisper. "Do you know what it is?"

"What do you want it to be?"

Trish clenched her hands together nervously, then glanced at the ring finger on her left hand.

"I'm not ready for a ring. I mean, we're still in the early stages of our relationship. Or maybe at the beginning of the middle stages. Anyway, it would be terribly embarrassing if he pulled out a box—"

Marge reached over and put her index finger on Trish's lips. "I don't know what he wants to give you, but I wish you could have heard how excited he was when I called him. He dropped everything and drove back to town by noon. Since then he's been running around like a crazy man."

Trish sighed and handed the car keys to her mother. "Tell Thelma to take you straight home. I don't want you looking for another place to party."

—

Holt drove as fast as he dared to the veterinarian's office. This time there weren't many cars on the roads, and the traffic lights didn't slow him down. He whipped the car into the lot. The front door was locked, but he could see a light on in the back of the office. Holt knocked loudly and waited. In a few moments, Dr. Wade appeared and let him inside.

"Sorry I called," the vet began. "If I'd known—"

"He's gone?" Holt cried out. "I drove as fast as I could!"

"No, no. He's made a turn for the better. Come see for yourself."

Holt followed the vet to a holding area where animals were kept for the night. A young male worker was cleaning out an empty cage. Henry was lying on his side in a small cage. When Holt entered the room, the dog gave a faint woof.

"See," Dr. Wade said. "The antivenin kicked in and jerked him back from the brink in a hurry. I'm very glad you brought him in when you did."

Holt stepped over and rubbed the short fur on top of the dog's nose. Henry's tongue came out and licked Holt's hand.

"Wow," Holt said.

"He's a fighter," Dr. Wade said.

"Yeah"—Holt nodded—"that's all he knows to do."

Holt called Bishop Pennington and gave him the good news.

"That's great," the minister said. "I can't wait to see him chasing a ball across the basketball court. I'll head on home and talk to you later. Should I lock the door behind me?"

"Yes," Holt said. "And thanks for everything."

Holt stayed by Henry's cage until his pet drifted into a fitful sleep. Each twitch of the dog's body was a sign of encouragement. Holt believed Henry dreamed about chasing squirrels, and if the dog could stalk squirrels in his sleep, hopefully he'd be able to do it soon while awake.

—

Driving home from the vet's office, Holt passed the Meredith mansion. Its lights continued to shine even though no one was home. The investigation was at a dead end, and Holt wasn't sure he had the energy or willpower to revive it. McDermott had abandoned him, and Butch Clovis was on to him. He didn't trust Cecil Burkdale, and Trish Carmichael was useless as a resource.

Then Holt thought about Henry and the snake. The little dog was created to fight, and once engaged, he never gave up.

And Henry battled the snake alone.

33

Keith and Trish began cleaning up the banquet room.

"What do you want to do with the leftover cake?" Keith asked.

"I could take it to work. It wouldn't last half an hour in the kitchen. People at the sheriff's department will eat stale bread so long as it's free."

"I'd like to take a piece to my mom," Keith said.

"Take more than a piece," Trish said as she sliced off a thick slab and put it on a large paper plate.

"And I guess you'll want the balloon."

"I wish I'd given it to Candace, but I can take it to her tomorrow. She'd love tying it to the end of her big-girl bed."

They carried the cake and balloon to Keith's car and then returned to the banquet room.

"I'll be back in a minute," Keith said. "I need to see the manager."

Trish sat alone in the empty room. She did a quick calculation of how much it would cost to feed twenty-five people at a place this nice. It was easily more than she made in two weeks at the sheriff's department. Keith returned with a smile on his face. It said a lot about a man if he could swipe his credit card for hundreds of dollars at a restaurant and still look happy.

"How did you like the party?" he asked.

"It was a complete surprise, and I loved it," Trish said. "Thanks for all you did to make it happen. Mama had a great time, too. She was bubbling over with excitement coming here, and I couldn't figure out why. We've never kept secrets from each other."

"Marge is a great lady."

"Yes, she is."

"There's one other thing," Keith said, clearing his throat. "Your present."

"How did you have time—"

"Oh, this is like Candace's plate. I've been working on it for a while."

He reached into his pocket and took out a small square box wrapped in gold foil. All the blood drained out of Trish's face, and she knew if she tried to stand she might pass out.

"Keith, you shouldn't—" she began.

"Don't say anything until you open it," he said as he handed the box to her.

It was scarily light. Trish turned it over in her fingers. Keith moved closer until he was standing directly beside her. He put his hand on her shoulder.

"You can shake it if you want to," he said. "It's not breakable."

Trish didn't want to shake it. She didn't want to open it. The only thing she wanted to do was give it back to Keith so he could return it to his pocket. She glanced at the door to the banquet room.

"Nobody's going to disturb us," Keith said, following her gaze. "I told the manager we needed a few minutes of privacy."

Trish took a deep breath. She was going to have to face the box. She picked at the edge of the wrapping paper until a tiny corner came loose. She gently tore it away from the box. A narrow strip peeled away.

"If it took you this long to open your gifts on Christmas morning when you were a little girl, I bet you didn't finish until March," Keith said.

"No," Trish said and managed a brave smile, "but as an only child I received way too much."

She tore off the rest of the gold foil. It suddenly felt odd that she, not Keith, was opening the box. If he wanted to get down on his knee and ask her to marry him, he needed to have the ring in his hand to do so.

"Do you want to open it?" she asked, looking up into his face.

"No," Keith responded with a puzzled expression. "Why would I want to do that?"

Trish pulled up on the lid of the box and saw the glint of gold and diamonds. She put her hand to her mouth.

"Is that what I think it is?" she exclaimed.

"The most powerful piece on the board."

Trish took out a golden chess queen with a row of tiny diamonds for a crown. Attached to the pendant was a delicate gold chain.

"This is so unique!" she said with a mixture of joy and relief. "Where in the world did you find it?"

"On the Internet, but I went to the store in Atlanta to see it for myself. It looked bigger in the sales photo, but I hope that's okay—"

"No, it's perfect."

Trish put the necklace around her neck. The pendant hung down exactly as she liked.

"How did you know the length of the chain?"

"I guessed."

Trish fingered the pendant again. "It's exquisite. I love it."

"A queen for a princess." Keith smiled.

Trish looked up into Keith's eyes and saw affection and tenderness she didn't know could live in the heart of a man.

—

Holt phoned the veterinarian's office as soon as he woke up in the morning. The answering service took the call and told him he'd have to call back at 7:30 a.m. to get a status report on Henry. Holt wasn't worried. If something bad had happened in the middle of the night, the tech on duty would have let him know.

Instead of going directly to the office, he swung by the vet's office. He recognized one of the women on duty from the night before.

"Your dog is drinking water and growled at me when I slipped the bowl into his cage," she said before Holt could ask a question. "But he's still unsteady on his feet."

"May I see him?"

The woman picked up the phone. In a few seconds another woman came out and led Holt to the holding area. Henry was lying on his side, but he wagged his tail when Holt approached.

"Still fighting?" Holt asked as he opened the door of the cage to stroke the dog.

Henry twitched his nose as his tail continued to thump against the floor of the cage. The woman who'd greeted Holt in the reception area opened the door and called out.

"Mrs. Stevens is here to pick up Peps," she said.

"She's early," the female tech replied roughly.

"And doesn't want to wait."

"Okay, okay. I'll get him ready."

Holt watched as a worker took the white Chihuahua from the cage on the opposite side of the room. A card on the cage identified the dog as belonging to "Mrs. Valerie Stevens."

"What was wrong with Peps?" Holt asked as the tech put a bright red collar around the dog's neck. "He looks healthy enough."

"Nothing, he's a regular overnight customer. Mrs. Stevens doesn't trust anyone to take care of him when she's out of town. That dog means the world to her."

Holt gave Henry a final pat on the head and shut the door of the cage.

"Did Dr. Wade mention how long Henry will have to stay?"

"No, but it will probably be a couple of days. If you want him to call you, let them know at the front desk."

"I'll do that. Be careful with Henry. Once he's back to normal, he has a tendency to bite first and ask questions later."

"I'll keep that in mind, but I rarely have a problem, especially when I've taken care of a sick animal for a few days."

Holt went to the waiting area. Valerie Stevens was standing in front of a magazine rack. She was wearing casual clothes with the touch of extra tailoring that set them apart from items off a sales rack.

"Hello," he said. "I saw you the other day in front of—"

"Henry's owner," Valerie interrupted with a bright smile. "Is he okay?"

"Barely. Yesterday he killed the largest copperhead I've ever seen. It bit him several times and it was touch and go for a while last night, but he's going to make it."

"I'm terrified of snakes." Valerie's eyes widened. "How big was it?"

Holt extended his arms out from his sides. "About this long and as thick as my wrist. I wasn't at home, but two construction workers saw the fight and said Henry and the snake were in a death struggle for at least half an hour."

The tech brought out Peps, who yelped when he saw Valerie and began to wiggle. The worker put the dog in Valerie's arms. She held him up so he could quickly lick her chin before nestling down in her arms.

"He has to give me a kiss," she said, "or he'll pester me until he does."

"You're all set, Mrs. Stevens," the woman behind the desk called out.

Valerie turned to Holt. "I hope Henry gets better soon."

"I'm sure he'll be chasing squirrels before I know it."

Holt watched Valerie Stevens leave the vet's office. As she did, he wondered what the shy dog-lover really knew about her stepfather's death.

—

Trish didn't put the chess queen in her jewelry box. Instead, she draped the chain over a knob on the case so she could continue to admire it. The look in Keith's eyes when he gave it to her revealed what he thought about her. She needed to be honest with herself about her feelings.

As soon as she figured out what they were.

Trish turned off the lamp on her nightstand. The faint light from the moon caused the pendant to glisten. She lay on her back and stared at the ceiling. Keith had changed a lot since high school. If she wanted to relate to who he was now, she had to throw away the paradigms of previous perceptions. She might not have a tingly feeling of excitement when she was with him, but they shared a common faith and were able to communicate about life. Trish turned on her side so she could see the pendant once more before falling asleep.

When she awoke in the morning, her first thought wasn't about the surprise birthday party or the chess queen pendant. Today she'd have to face Butch Clovis. She went to the kitchen for her glass of orange juice. Marge was awake and oblivious to Trish's burden.

"Wasn't that a grand party?" Marge asked. "And the pendant Keith bought you is stunning."

"Yes, but you don't ever have to do something like that again."

"Are you kidding? I had as much fun as you did."

"I'll totally focus on your birthday in September—" Trish began.

"And if you make me the center of attention at a big gathering, I'll be miserable and want to crawl back in my shell. Secondhand glory suits me a lot better." Marge paused. "Oh, did you talk to Keith about coming over for squash casserole later this week?"

"Yes, he said Friday would be the best day for him. He's going bass fishing on Saturday with some of his buddies. What else do you want to feed him?"

"I'll call his mom and find out some of his favorites."

"I'm not sure it's smart to compete with his mom's cooking."

"Yeah, I never could make banana pudding like your grandma."

Trish left Marge happily planning dinner. During the drive to work, she alternated between praying for help and worrying about what might happen if God didn't come to her aid. There was no sign of Clovis when she arrived at the sheriff's office, and she slipped into her cubicle. Midmorning, the detective stood beside her desk.

"I didn't hear back from you yesterday," Clovis growled. "Did you talk to Holt Douglas?"

Without a plan, Trish fell back on the simple, unadorned truth.

"Yes, sir, and I told him I'd like to help with his investigation. He guessed that you wanted me to do it, and I hung up on him."

"How did my name come up?"

"He was supposed to have lunch with Detective McDermott. When I mentioned that I saw the two of you in the parking lot, he guessed what you'd asked me to do."

Clovis swore. Trish flinched, not at the language, but at the intent behind it. Negative emotions raced across the detective's face. Trish was in water so deep she had no hope of survival if Clovis wanted to drown her. She cast off any remaining caution.

"Do you think the sheriff should talk to Ralph Granger?" she asked.

"That thought crossed my mind," the detective replied in a voice that was slightly less harsh. "The danger is that this could become a bigger problem in trying to control it than if I let it run its course and die on its own. There's nothing for Douglas to find."

"What about showing him the information you shared with Detective McDermott?"

Clovis eyed Trish suspiciously. "What information?"

"I don't know. I've not seen anything except the folder that was in the closed files."

"Keep it that way," Clovis said. "No more snooping around or asking questions."

"Yes, sir. What about Holt? Do you want me to call him back?"

"Not until I tell you to," the detective said.

Clovis turned and left. Trish realized she'd been holding her breath since her last question. She began to breathe normally.

And offered up a prayer of thanks.

34

Holt began getting ready for a calendar call. He'd reviewed the list of cases the previous day and, on the surface, it appeared to be a routine morning. However, that didn't guarantee the absence of drama. Jim stuck his head through the opening to Holt's office.

"I'll take care of the calendar," the senior assistant DA said. "I'm going to try some misdemeanor cases later in the week and need to confirm the days and times with the judge and defense counsel."

"I can do everything except—"

"Thanks, but I've got it covered. Since you don't have to go to court, you may want to talk to Ralph."

Jim disappeared before Holt could ask him why their boss wanted to see him.

Holt stepped down the hallway to Ralph Granger's office. The DA was talking on the phone and motioned for Holt to come in and sit down.

"No, Carl," Ralph said to the man on the other end of the call. "I'll be there, but I can't promise the case will be resolved at that time. These things depend a lot on the judge, and if he—"

The caller obviously interrupted Ralph, who rolled his eyes at Holt as he listened.

"I realize how many folks in Triplett County listen to you. They're my best supporters, too. But don't quote me on that. I don't want anyone in Ashley County to get bent out of shape about my loyalty to my roots."

Ralph listened again. "I can't go to the judge directly. That would be an ex parte communication—"

The caller interrupted again. Holt could see Ralph's face beginning to turn red.

"I'm not talking down to you," the DA said when he had a chance to speak again. "It's a legal term that means I can't go to the judge in private about a case when there's a lawyer representing the defendant. But I promise you that I will put on a full-court press with the defense lawyer and try to get this thing put to bed before your family reunion in July."

Ralph paused. "Yes, I wouldn't miss it for anything. Are you going to cook a whole hog?"

Holt could see the DA begin to relax.

"Okay, I'll report back to you pronto. Thanks for the call."

Ralph hung up the phone and looked across the table at Holt. "Do you want my job?" he asked.

Even though Ralph asked the question on the heels of a stressful conversation with a politically powerful constituent, Holt knew not to treat the DA's words lightly.

"Never," he said. "I don't have any political ambitions. I enjoy what I'm doing and want to keep doing it under your regime. Who was that on the phone?"

"Carl Ligon. He's related to more people in Triplett County than anyone else. Somebody burglarized a business owned by one of his first cousins, and Carl wants speedy justice. The defendant is only nineteen years old and stole a computer that didn't work. They caught him with blood on his arm that matched blood in a sample they took from a broken window. It's the boy's third burglary offense, and he's looking at the recidivist statute if we don't work out a plea."

"Does Carl want the defendant locked up for the rest of his life?"

"He doesn't know that's a possibility, so I think I can sell him on anything the defense lawyer convinces his client to accept. There's no doubt the kid is looking at serious jail time. Judge Lomax will see to that."

Holt nodded. Most outsiders didn't realize how much of a prosecutor's energy was devoted to managing expectations. The recidivist statute, which mandated long jail sentences for repeat felons, was a big, big stick.

"Yeah, let me know if you need me to work on it," Holt said. "Jim said you wanted to see me."

"Close the door."

When Holt retook his seat, Ralph stared out the window to the right of his desk for a moment before turning toward him.

"I'm shutting down your secret investigation into Rex Meredith's death, effective immediately," the DA said.

Holt swallowed.

"Did you really think you could get away with something like that?" Ralph continued.

"I was trying to figure out—"

"No," Ralph said, cutting him off with a chop of his hand. "The sheriff called and gloated about the lack of control I exercise over my staff. I had to act like I knew what you were doing and had a tight rein on you. But, Holt, if word of this leaked out, there would be a bunch of false accusations flying through the newspaper. Just like that call with Carl Ligon, all pigeons eventually come to roost on my doorstep, not yours."

The DA was right, and Holt knew it. But the image in his mind wasn't of a pigeon; it was of a snake.

"You're right," he said. "I understand."

Ralph put his fingers together beneath his chin and eyed Holt for a moment. "You may not have political ambitions, but you know how to give a political answer. Agreeing with my assessment of the situation isn't the same as promising to pull the plug on this. That's what I'm asking you to do." Ralph paused. "No, that's what I'm telling you to do."

"Yes, sir."

"Yes, sir, what?"

Holt took a breath and exhaled. He was hemmed in without any options as surely as the boy who broke the window and stole the computer.

"I'll shut it down immediately."

"Where's your file? I looked in the cabinet where it should have been, and it wasn't there."

"In my office. I never formally reopened it."

"Bring it to me."

Ralph continued to keep his eyes on Holt, who shifted in his chair.

"Yes, sir."

"And you realize how lenient I'm being with you about this, don't you?"

"Yes, sir."

"It could have resulted in serious consequences for your career."

Holt swallowed. "I know. I'm sorry."

The phone on Ralph's desk buzzed, and he picked it up. "I'll take it," he said, then spoke to Holt: "Close the door on your way out. I need to keep this conversation private. Get me that file."

Holt returned to his office. He was frustrated, angry, and

embarrassed. Ralph had backed him into a corner and treated him like a kid summoned to the school principal's office. He grabbed the folder from the bottom drawer of his desk but paused in front of the copy machine. He'd promised to shut down the investigation, but he'd not committed to the destruction of everything he'd collected. Making sure Ralph's door was still shut, he put the transcript of the 911 call in the document feeder and prepared to press the Print button.

Then he stopped.

He put the papers back in the folder. He was beaten. Ralph hadn't left him any wiggle room. The investigation was dead and draped over a chain-link fence.

Holt had thought he was Henry. It turned out he was the snake.

35

Trish had sent written summaries of her cases to Holt the previous afternoon but received no reply. Making sure her khaki shirt was neatly tucked into her dark brown pants, she walked into the courtroom. The pendant Keith gave her was concealed beneath her shirt, and she touched it through the cloth to remind herself of how she felt when he gave it to her.

The courtroom was filling up with people. Trish spotted a woman named Maddie Dorman sitting beside a man who looked vaguely familiar. Sitting behind the prosecution table, she opened the woman's file. Stapled to the right-hand side of the folder was a mug shot of the woman's ex-husband. The man was clearly intoxicated in the photo, and there were traces of blood on his shirt from the fight that had caused his arrest, but it was the same guy. There was usually only one reason why a man like that would be sitting with his wife in the courtroom. He'd convinced her to ask the judge to give him additional time to catch up on past-due child support. Trish checked the arrearage. Based on the amount of support given by the government to the couple's three children, it would take a lot more than a few words from his ex-wife to keep the defendant out of jail.

"Trish," a male voice said.

It was Holt. He'd entered the courtroom through a side door while she was studying the file.

"The Meredith investigation is shut down. I was going to call and let you know, but I didn't think you'd talk to me. Ralph found out about it and made it clear he doesn't want a hint of what we did becoming public, especially to the newspaper."

Trish didn't like Holt's use of the words "what we did."

"Butch Clovis may already know it's closed," Holt continued, "but in case he doesn't, you can tell him. Hopefully, that will get him off your back. I'm sorry for all the hassle this has caused you, and I hope we can cooperate as well on your cases in the future as we have in the past. You do a great job."

"Thanks."

Apologies and compliments were nice, but they didn't change the truth. Judge Lomax entered and everyone stood. Trish watched Holt orchestrate the calendar. He didn't act like a horrible person hiding a terrible lie.

When the case involving Maddie Dorman and her ex-husband was called, both of them came forward. Trish joined Holt in front of the judge. Often, she testified standing in place to save time. Holt swore her in and asked her to summarize the seriously delinquent status of unpaid child support for the couple's three children.

"Judge, I'd like to say something," Ms. Dorman said when Trish finished.

"Put her on the stand," Judge Lomax said.

The woman took the witness stand, and Holt administered the oath.

"Before he asks me anything, I want to speak," Ms. Dorman said, turning in the chair so she could see the judge.

"Ma'am, I have a full calendar," the judge replied. "I'm not going to listen to long speeches that won't have an impact on what I have to decide. Go ahead, but I'll stop you if you get out of line."

"Yes, sir. Mickey is behind on support, and I know the state has paid out a bunch of money so me and the kids don't starve and so we have a roof over our heads. But he's gotten his life turned around. He's stopped drinking, and we've been to church together every Sunday for the past month. He's living with his mama and started a new job two weeks ago. He gave me half of his first paycheck."

"Judge," Holt interrupted. "Child support payments have to be made through the clerk of court. Deputy Carmichael, is there any record of payment by the defendant in the past month?"

"No, and we'd ask the court to hold the defendant in contempt until such time as he—"

"The state has no objection to continuing this matter for ninety days," Holt interrupted.

Trish's mouth dropped open. She turned to Holt. "He's had two years to do what he should—"

"Deputy Carmichael," the judge said. "If you want to discuss this with Mr. Douglas, please don't take up the court's time doing so. I'll put the case at the end of the calendar so the two of you can agree on the state's position."

Red-faced, Trish returned to her seat behind the prosecution table. Mickey and his ex-wife walked past her. Trish was sure she detected the hint of a smirk on the defendant's face. Using jailhouse religion to reduce a sentence was one of the oldest ploys in the history of criminal proceedings. Granted, Mickey hadn't yet gone to jail. He simply adopted the tactic to avoid being locked up in the first place. Trish fumed while Holt handled several matters in which she had no interest. At 10:30 a.m., Judge Lomax tapped his gavel on the small square block of wood on the bench before him.

"The court will be in recess for fifteen minutes. If you've received a subpoena, you are not excused and should be back in your seat when court resumes."

People began moving around. Holt had his back to Trish. She leaned against the railing that separated the gallery from the area where the lawyers sat.

"Well?" she asked, clearing her throat. "Are we going to agree on the state's position?"

Holt continued to keep his back to her for a few irritating seconds before turning around. He had a slightly sheepish look on his face.

"When Ms. Dorman explained what happened to her husband, the thought crossed my mind that maybe he's really had a change of heart."

"He had two years to repent," Trish responded.

"Sometimes it takes longer than that."

Trish eyed Holt for a moment. "And there's more to it than words. Ask Bishop Pennington. Most of the time, genuine repentance involves action."

"And that's exactly why I'm going to give Mickey Dorman ninety days to prove he's legit. If he's not, he's going to have a free place to stay behind bars for a while." Holt leaned a bit closer to her. "Is it really so much extra work for you to verify that he makes his payments to the clerk's office? If you don't have time to do it, I can assign it to someone in my office. They'll do it without giving me any pushback."

Holt's condescending tone was infuriating.

"I'll do my job," Trish responded crisply. "And unless you need me to stand beside you while you tell the judge what you're going to do, I'm going to go back to the sheriff's department."

"You're not under subpoena, so you're free to leave."

Holt turned around. Steaming, Trish marched up the aisle to the rear of the courtroom.

—

Holt was miffed that Trish had barely acknowledged his attempt at an apology and reconciliation. For a while he would have to be on guard around her. He didn't want his unspoken frustration to pop out in an inappropriate comment.

Judge Lomax returned and accepted Holt's recommendation regarding Mickey Dorman. Holt then asked the defendant and his ex-wife to remain in the courtroom. Shortly before noon he called them over to the prosecutor's table.

"Do you know what's going to happen if you don't follow through with your child support obligations, including extra payment to start reducing the amount you're behind?" Holt asked Mickey.

"I'll get locked up."

"And you know you have to make the payments through the clerk of court's office, not directly to your ex-wife?"

"Yeah, I done that before."

"About three or four times and then stopped," Holt reminded him.

"It's goin' to be different this time." The defendant glanced sideways at Maddie.

"Deputy Carmichael is going to monitor it and let me know. Don't mess this up."

"Yeah."

Holt had doubts as he watched the couple walk away. His greatest fear was that Mickey would see his three months of grace as an opportunity to skip town and abandon his family. Fathers behind in child support weren't considered high-priority fugitives. Most of the time, they were caught through tips like the one that sent Holt and Trish to the Jenkins house. Holt didn't want another face-to-face encounter with the wrong end of a shotgun.

Toward the end of the day, he got a call from Dr. Wade.

"Come get your beast," the veterinarian said. "If he's well enough to snap at my staff, he's healthy enough to go back to protecting your property."

"He was weak and whiny when I saw him yesterday."

"That's not the dog who woke up this morning and spent an hour or so gnawing the bars of his cage. He couldn't bite his way through the metal, but a flesh-and-blood finger would be a different story. Although he's definitely on the mend, it will be weeks before he's back to normal. You have a fenced-in backyard, don't you?"

"Yes."

"That's where he needs to be, and let's hope the brother or sister of the snake he killed doesn't come looking for revenge."

—

Holt swiped his credit card to pay the bill. Treatment for multiple snake bites was twice a monthly car payment. Henry tried to lick Holt's face as his master carried him to the car.

"You'll never be like Peps," Holt said, "and you can show your gratitude by staying out of fights that could kill you and put me into bankruptcy."

Henry sat up in the seat and looked out the window. When they reached the house, he slowly hopped out of the car and walked to the backyard fence. The dog sniffed up and down the fence, stopping at the place where the construction workers had draped the dead copperhead over the metal chain links. Holt knelt beside him. There was a deep rumbling in Henry's throat.

"Yes, you killed the snake," Holt said quietly. "And if it was still here I bet you'd drag it onto the deck and gnaw on it some more."

Holt stood up and opened the gate. Still moving gingerly, Henry went into the backyard. A squirrel scampered across the grass, but the dog showed no interest in it. Dr. Wade was right. It was going to take awhile for Henry's killer instinct to recover.

Trish returned to the sheriff's department and vigorously pounded the letters on her keyboard as she prepared a memo for the file. By the time she finished, she'd calmed down. One thing that helped was recognizing that her frustration was directed more at Holt than at Mickey Dorman. Trish, too, hoped Mickey had changed for the better. If he had, it would make her job easier and mean his children had food on the table and clothes on their bodies. And unlike Holt, Trish hadn't recently come to believe in God's ability to transform a bad person into a good person.

Butch Clovis stopped by her cubicle.

"I understand you were in court this morning," the detective said.

"Yes. And I talked briefly with Holt Douglas. Did you know Ralph Granger ordered him to drop the investigation into Mr. Meredith's death?"

"No." Clovis shook his head. "And don't talk so loudly. What exactly did Douglas say?"

Trish lowered her voice. "Mr. Granger doesn't want the newspaper to get wind of the existence of an investigation and told Holt to leave it alone. That's about it."

She didn't include Holt's apology.

"Are you sure there wasn't anything else?" the detective asked.

"No. He was running the calendar call by himself so there wasn't much time to talk."

"Okay. What are you going to do if you catch wind of Douglas ignoring Granger's orders and snooping around town?"

"Tell you about it immediately?"

"That's right."

After Clovis left, Trish went to the restroom and washed her hands. Regardless of the tone and substance of the conversation, the detective made her feel unclean.

As soon as her shift ended, she called Sue Ann to see if she could stop by on her way home from work.

"I guess so," Sue Ann replied.

"If you're busy I can make it another—"

"Don't be silly," Sue Ann quickly added. "What do you think I'm doing? Lying on a Swedish massage table getting a hot stone treatment?"

"Didn't you get one of those on your honeymoon?"

"No, but I read about it yesterday in a magazine. The only massage in my future is when I lie on the floor and let Candy pretend I'm an alligator while she walks on my back."

"Is she awake?"

"No, still down for her nap. It's a perfect time for you to visit. Don't knock. I'll unlock the door for you."

In a few minutes, Trish carefully opened the front door of the apartment and went inside. Sue Ann was sitting in the living room with her feet propped up on an ottoman.

"My energy level is way down," Sue Ann said. "My body is beginning to focus more and more on manufacturing this new baby."

"Any morning sickness? I know that was bad when you were pregnant with Candace."

Sue Ann stuck her finger in her mouth and nodded. "Mark is leaving for work fifteen minutes earlier than usual so he won't have to listen to me gag."

"That's terrible."

"No, he can't do anything to help me, and I don't want him to carry an image of his wife leaning over a toilet with him all day. By the time he gets home in the evening, I'm ready for pizza and tacos with chocolate syrup and ice cream."

Trish smiled. "You're my hero."

"And I'm riding on your romantic coattails. What did Keith give you at the party? I know he had something special because I saw him slip a little gold box into his pocket. It wasn't a ring, because that was the first thing I checked when you walked through the door."

"I'm not ready for that," Trish said, "but he gave me this."

She slipped out the pendant and leaned closer so Sue Ann could see it.

"Do you like it?" Sue Ann asked.

"Of course. He didn't get me something generic. He put a lot of thought into it."

"I know, but I wanted to make sure you realized it, too."

Trish eyed the pendant again, then slipped it beneath her shirt.

"So, does this mean Holt Douglas has been dumped on the ash heap of lost-love history?" Sue Ann asked.

"Buried and covered over without a trace."

"I had questions about him all along," Sue Ann said. "I wanted to support you, but I wasn't sure the reality matched the fantasy you'd created in your mind."

"Your intuition was one hundred percent accurate. I wish you'd told me."

"Would it have done any good?"

"Probably not," Trish admitted. "Now my focus is on seeing where the relationship with Keith is headed."

"Tell me more about that dream home he's building for you. He's sounding more and more romantic by the hour."

Trish hesitated. She glanced around the apartment.

"Don't let where we're sitting right now stop you," Sue Ann said. "Remember, we're good enough friends that I would be happy for you to have a beautiful home even if I have to wait."

"Okay," Trish said somewhat reluctantly. "The first thing I told him was that he needed to expand the kitchen . . ."

36

Saturday morning Henry remained lethargic. He slowly walked out onto the deck when Holt opened the door but didn't navigate the steps to go down into the yard. Instead, he was content to spend his time watching his world without interacting with it. Sitting on the deck and drinking a cup of coffee, Holt decided on a plan of action.

He went back inside the house and put on a T-shirt, jogging shorts, and running shoes, then loaded Henry into the car. The dog wasn't up for a run, or even a slow jog, but there was a place Holt could take him that might stimulate the dog without taxing his strength.

In the middle of the most affluent section of Paxton was a neighborhood park that included a rose garden, a playground made from treated redwood, and a series of short walking trails beneath large shade trees. Normally, Holt wouldn't consider taking Henry to the park because the dog wanted to run, not walk. But like a retirement home resident recovering from hip surgery, Henry's exposure to the outdoors needed to be parceled out in small bits. Holt parked in a shaded spot beneath a large sugar maple tree.

Henry sniffed the air and wiggled his body. He didn't pull on the leash but waited for Holt. They walked toward a rose garden planted around a sundial. The sun wasn't high enough in the sky to cast a shadow, but Henry located an interesting smell at the base of the sundial, and Holt waited while the dog sniffed around the area. There was the sound of footsteps on the pea gravel walkway, and Holt turned around.

It was Angelina.

"What are you doing here?" he blurted out.

"I needed a quiet place to walk and think before going to the salon," Angelina replied. "Is there anything wrong with that?"

"No, it was a stupid question."

"I didn't think smart lawyers asked stupid questions."

"This one does."

Holt waited for Angelina to move on, but she stayed put. Henry inched forward stiffly and sniffed her foot.

"He's moving slow this morning," Angelina observed.

"He has five or six good reasons."

"What happened to him?"

Holt told Angelina about Henry and the copperhead. Angelina's eyes got bigger and bigger, which made Holt's heart ache. He stretched the story out as long as he could.

"I'm glad he's okay," she said when Holt finished. "How are you doing?"

"Right now, I'm feeling very sorry that I hurt you."

"Is that an apology?"

Holt thought about the difference between repentance and regret. "Not a good one," he replied. "But I'd like to do it better."

Angelina glanced down at the path for a moment. "Did you know the blond deputy came by the salon and talked to me?"

"Not until after she did it."

"It was very strange. She flashed her badge to Brittany and forced me to leave a customer. Then she claimed there was nothing between the two of you and wanted me to talk you into letting her continue to work on some kind of case. When she showed up, I thought something horrible had happened to you, and they'd sent someone from the sheriff's office to tell me."

Holt winced. "I'm sorry—"

"No," Angelina interrupted. "It showed me that I still cared. And after meeting the deputy, I knew she wasn't your type."

"You're my type," Holt said.

"How sure are you about that?"

"Enough that I hope you'll give me a chance to prove it."

Angelina smiled slightly.

"Is that a yes?" Holt asked.

"Maybe. Although the fact that I followed you all the way over here from your house should tell you something."

"You did?"

Angelina nodded. "I was coming to see you and saw you pull out of your driveway."

They sat on a bench and talked until it was time for Angelina to leave for work.

—

Sunday morning Holt returned to Bishop Pennington's church. Knowing what to expect helped him enjoy the service. As soon as the minister finished the sermon, Holt slipped out and returned home. There was an unfamiliar car with its hood raised parked in front of his house. Holt slowed down. The driver turned and Holt saw his face.

It was Cecil Burkdale.

Holt pulled into his driveway. Getting out, he walked over to Burkdale's vehicle, an older car with multiple dents and faded paint on the trunk. Burkdale lowered the window as Holt approached.

"Do you want me to call a wrecker?" Holt asked.

"No, there's nothing wrong with my car. I didn't want anyone who drove by to think I was waiting for you."

"Why are you here?"

"We need to talk."

"I've shut down my investigation into Mr. Meredith's death," Holt interrupted. "It's over. There's nothing for us to talk about."

"Yes, there is," Burkdale replied, looking into his rearview mirror. "And unless you want someone else to die, you need to listen to me."

Holt leaned closer to the vehicle. When he did, he saw a pistol lying on the seat beside Burkdale.

"Why do you have a gun in your car?"

"I have a permit. Are you going to talk to me or not?"

Holt hesitated. Seventy-five percent of his mind wanted to send Burkdale on his way. The other twenty-five percent lobbied for the chance to evaluate the strange man's story one last time. As with politics, the majority doesn't always rule.

"Okay, but I have a sick dog and can't waste an afternoon listening to you vent about losing your job with Meredith Enterprises."

"Meet me in fifteen minutes at the farm equipment store on the Madison Highway. I'll be parked behind one of the big combines."

"Why there?"

"It's closed on Sunday, but it's not unusual for people to stop by and check out the machinery without a salesman on hand to hassle them. Are you coming?"

"I guess so."

"Lower the hood? I don't want to get out."

Feeling like that quarter of his mind had convinced the rest of him to go temporarily insane, Holt walked around to the front of Burkdale's vehicle. The engine was dirty; the battery posts corroded. If Burkdale didn't start taking care of his car, he wouldn't have to pretend to be disabled on the side of the road. Holt shut the hood with a thud. Burkdale started the engine and took off, coming dangerously close to Holt's feet. Holt jumped back and stared at the rapidly disappearing car.

When Holt looked into the backyard, there was no sign of Henry on the deck. Holt quickly scanned the open grassy area and didn't see the dog. His concern for Henry immediately took precedence over Burkdale's wild claim that someone's life was in danger.

"Henry!" Holt called out. "Henry!"

A few seconds later, a faint woof came from the rear of the yard. In a couple of seconds, Henry emerged from the thick bushes along the back fence line. He shook himself and trotted over to Holt, who squatted down to pat the dog. A quick inspection revealed nothing out of the ordinary.

"Don't be going into the bushes looking for trouble," Holt scolded the dog. "You don't know what might be in there."

As soon as the words were out of Holt's mouth, he knew that was exactly what he was about to do.

—

Trish and Keith sat next to each other in Sunday school and the church service that followed. Now, in the eyes of the whole congregation, they were officially a couple, a fact that Trish was becoming more and more comfortable with.

They'd spent Friday evening together at Trish's house. After supper, Marge pretended to be tired and went to her bedroom so they could be alone. Trish chuckled as her mother shut the door.

"She's not going to sleep," Trish said. "She'll often stay up and watch a baseball game until after midnight, even if it goes to extra innings. I promise she'll listen to the game on the radio in her bedroom."

"Should we leave so she can see it on TV?" Keith asked.

"No, it's fun for her to make a small sacrifice for someone else's happiness."

"That's neat," Keith said and then looked at Trish. "Does being with me make you happy?"

Trish could finally give him an answer without a tortured inner debate.

"Yes, it does."

Keith stayed for several hours. Much of that time he asked Trish questions. She didn't mind talking about herself but wondered why he kept directing the conversation back to her. Finally, she asked him.

"Why do you want to talk about me all the time?"

"Why wouldn't I?"

Trish felt herself blush. "Well, I want to talk about you for a while."

It was the first time Trish had intentionally stepped into Keith's world. She already knew a lot about his family, but as he talked, more and more came out, especially about his relationship with his father. Jack Pierce rarely came to church. Like Keith, he traveled in his job. Everybody said they were alike in many ways.

"Yeah, last month my father rented an apartment in Cartersville," Keith said.

"Why would he do that?"

"His company made a big sale to a carpet company, and he'll be in charge of installing the equipment. It will take about a year to finish, and he didn't want to run back and forth all the time."

Trish felt sad for Bonita Pierce, who was such a cheerful woman. Keith's little sister was attending college in South Carolina, so with Keith on the road, it meant his mother would be alone most of the time.

"I'll probably stop by and see him when I'm in the area," Keith said.

"Won't he come home on the weekends?"

"No, for the first month it's a seven-day-a-week commitment."

Keith seemed momentarily lost in his own thoughts.

"Hey," he said, shaking his head, "would you and your mother like to drive over to the Wayfarer for dinner after church?"

"I'll ask her, but I'm sure she'll say yes."

—

Sunday afternoon they stopped at Trish's house to drop off Keith's car before traveling together to the restaurant. Keith sat in the passenger seat with Marge behind him. Trish glanced in the rearview mirror. Her mother had a contented look on her face.

"Do you wish we were going to the new steak house?" Marge asked as they neared the turnoff for the new restaurant.

"No, one birthday party a year is enough for me," Trish said.

"Yeah, that biological clock is ticking," Keith added.

Trish gave him a startled look, but Keith was looking out the window.

The Wayfarer was a popular place for families to eat after church on Sunday, and the parking lot was full.

"There may be a wait," Keith said. "Is that okay?"

"Most of the county got here ahead of us," Trish replied, turning toward her mother, "but I don't mind, if it's all right with you."

"We're here now," Marge replied. "Let's stay."

The teenage hostess's prediction of a twenty-minute delay turned out to be optimistic. Keith constantly checked his watch, and as soon as twenty minutes passed, he began checking with the hostess. After the fifth time he talked to the girl, Trish spoke to him.

"There's nothing she can do about it," she said. "Why don't you leave her alone?"

"Nothing upsets me more than someone who doesn't do what they've promised to do," he said irritably. "If I'm supposed to meet with a prospect on a sales call at two o'clock, I don't show up at two thirty."

Trish looked at her mother. "Am I always on time?"

"I'm not talking about you," Keith cut in. "I'll be fine once we're seated."

Less than a minute later, the hostess tentatively approached. "Your table is ready, sir," she said to Keith. "Please follow me."

"How often does someone call you 'sir'?" Trish asked Keith.

He didn't respond. Trish maneuvered Marge's wheelchair around the tables.

Lunch was a dreary affair. Trish and her mother made attempts to jump-start the conversation, but Keith didn't seem willing to participate. After they finished the main meal, Marge saw a woman she knew at another table and rolled her chair over to see her.

"Why are you in such a bad mood?" Trish asked Keith. "I thought you wanted to come here. You knew it would be crowded for Sunday dinner."

"It's not the restaurant or the meal," he said, sighing. "My mom got a call from my father this morning before I left the house for church. He's going to divorce her. The move to Cartersville I told you about on Friday night was a setup."

Divorce was common in most places but not in Trish's world.

"Keith, I'm so sorry."

"Yeah, it's shaken me up. My mom is a total wreck."

"So it wasn't a headache that kept her home from church."

"Partly, but mostly it's a broken heart."

It was silent in the van as they drove away from the restaurant. Trish could tell that her mother was puzzled by the lack of conversation, but an explanation would have to wait until they got home.

"How do you think the dealership is doing?" Marge asked as they approached the business where Trish's father had worked for so many years. "Clayton always thought the place would shut down if he wasn't there to tend to it."

The farm equipment business came into view on the right-hand side of the road. There was a row of shiny tractors and multiple implements lined up in front of the main building. A car they were following stopped and waited for oncoming traffic to clear so the driver could make a turn.

"Business looks good if Mr. Henderson can sell all the stuff he's brought in on his floor plan," Keith said. "The carrying charges can eat up—"

"That's Holt Douglas's car behind that combine," Trish interrupted. "What's he doing there?"

While they watched, Holt got out of his car and approached a short bald man who was leaning against a beat-up reddish vehicle.

"He's talking to Cecil Burkdale," Keith said.

"What do you know about him?" Trish asked.

"He's been trying to convince Gerald Pickett to hire him to keep the books for the auto parts store. Gerald was talking to me about him the other day. Burkdale runs an accounting business out of his house. Gerald felt sorry for him, but I told him that's no reason to hire someone for something as important as keeping track of the store's finances."

Trish only half listened to Keith. She was wondering what Holt Douglas was up to.

37

Holt pulled into the parking area for the equipment dealer. Lowell Henderson was a political supporter of Ralph Granger, and it felt doubly wrong to disobey Ralph's orders on property owned by one of his bigger contributors. Also, it didn't seem particularly private. The road in front of the business was a busy connector between Paxton and the historic town of Madison to the east. Holt pulled behind a combine, stopped next to Burkdale's car, and got out. The bookkeeper was leaning against the driver's-side door of his vehicle.

"We'll sit in your car," Burkdale said. "I never know if mine is clean or not."

Holt resisted the urge to point out that no one would accuse Burkdale of maintaining a neat vehicle. Then Holt realized the bookkeeper wasn't talking about physical cleanliness.

"You mean, you think it may be bugged?"

Burkdale put a finger to his lips and gave Holt a conspiratorial look. The gesture finished the job of convincing Holt that the bookkeeper was a suspicious bundle of confused humanity. They sat in Holt's car.

"Turn on the engine and the air-conditioning," Burkdale said.

"Do you think my car is bugged?" Holt asked.

"It could be," Burkdale said, "but it's also getting hot outside."

Once the cool air was blowing in their faces, Burkdale seemed to relax. He closed his eyes for a moment.

"Don't go to sleep," Holt said.

Burkdale opened his eyes and gave Holt a forlorn look.

"I'm under so much stress I think I'm having a nervous breakdown."

"Then maybe you should be talking to a doctor, not me."

"You could be right," Burkdale said, not seeming to notice the sarcasm in Holt's voice.

Holt pressed his lips together.

"I know you may not believe me," Burkdale continued, "but that doesn't mean I'm not telling the truth. I didn't want to contact you again because it puts me in greater danger, but I couldn't live with myself if something bad happens and I didn't try to stop it."

"I'm listening."

"Are you recording this conversation?" Burkdale asked.

"No! And it's about to end if you don't tell me why you want to talk to me!"

"Calm down," Burkdale said.

Holt forced himself to remain quiet for a moment. "Go ahead," he said.

Burkdale shifted in his seat. "When I worked for Meredith Enterprises, I had backdoor access to the company's computer network. Mr. Meredith wanted me to double-check financial information and confirm employee loyalty. It was one of the checks and balances he put in place to make sure no one was stealing from him or communicating information that might be harmful to his business. No one else knew about my clearance. After he died and I was fired by Mr. Stevens, I didn't want to have anything to do with Meredith Enterprises. But about a year later, I decided to see if I could still access the company's computer system. It was a triple-coded entry point, but when I typed in the passwords, I was back in."

"That was illegal."

"And I could have siphoned off money without anyone knowing it, but I didn't." Burkdale gave Holt a hurt look. "I was a loyal ex-employee who still cared about the company."

Holt didn't respond.

"I also wanted to see if my name ever came up. Knowing what Mr. Stevens did to his father-in-law, I was concerned about my own safety. There were critical comments about me in internal memos"—Burkdale paused—"but I guess you don't need to hear about that."

"Not unless it's relevant to why you wanted to meet with me today."

"Anyway, Mr. Stevens knows I came to see you at the DA's office. It turned up in a memo to him from the corporate security firm that has a contract with the company. When I saw that, I started checking your name and found out they'd been watching you for several weeks. At that point—"

"Wait a minute," Holt said, holding up his hand. "You claim Greg Stevens hired people to follow me around and see who I was talking to?"

"Of course he did. He had to. He knows about your phone call to Tony McDermott and that a female deputy sheriff named Carmichael is feeding you inside information."

At the mention of Trish Carmichael, Holt sat up straighter. This was the first tidbit of confirmed data that made Burkdale's wild allegations seem legitimate.

"You saw Trish Carmichael's name in a report."

"Yes. One that was marked for 'Greg Stevens Only.'"

"Do you have copies of these memos and reports?"

"Yes."

"I need to see them."

"No. If I give you hard copies of the memos, you could prosecute me."

Holt felt like he'd suddenly slipped into Burkdale's delusional world.

"Then why talk to me?"

"Because I believe you'll try to do something about Stevens."

"Your testimony by itself isn't enough for me to go after him for anything serious. I need corroboration."

"Who said anything about Mr. Stevens? It's Valerie I'm worried about."

It felt like Burkdale had grabbed Holt's head and given it a spin. "You've lost me," he said.

"When I went back further in the archives, I discovered that Mr. Stevens started tracking you several weeks before I came to see you. His security people noted your contact with Valerie based on their surveillance of her."

"Greg Stevens is spying on his wife?"

"Of course he is. He has to."

"Why?"

Burkdale gave Holt an incredulous look. "Because she knows how her stepfather really died. A secret this bad won't stay hidden forever. Valerie is a good woman. Her conscience has to be driving her crazy."

Holt was stunned. "And you believe Greg Stevens is afraid his wife might tell me the truth?"

"And he might be prosecuted for murder. That means Valerie is in danger."

It was a good thing Holt knew the way back to his house. His eyes were on the road and his hands gripped the steering wheel, but his mind was trying to process the information Cecil Burkdale had dumped on him. According to the bookkeeper, the security firm retained by Meredith Enterprises hired former law enforcement and military police personnel. Nothing in the computer records indicated that the firm had complicity in any illegal activity Stevens might be planning. They assumed Stevens was a rich, jealous husband keeping tabs on his wife and anyone else who might be a threat.

Burkdale steadfastly stuck by his refusal to show Holt hard copies of the information he'd gleaned from the Meredith Enterprises computer server. That left Holt swimming in the waters of unproved conspiracy.

As he slowed to turn into the driveway for his house, Holt glanced in the rearview mirror. There was a dark blue sedan a hundred yards behind him. He waited until the car continued past his house. The windows on the vehicle weren't heavily tinted, and a man in his forties was driving. He didn't look in Holt's direction. Of course, if the driver was a trained investigator, he wouldn't do anything to indicate his true intentions. Holt could feel anxiety rising up from his gut. Cecil Burkdale was worse than Ralph Granger. A few months of living like this and Holt would be ready for a psychiatrist's couch.

Inside, Holt filled Henry's food bowl. The dog's appetite was returning, and with it, his strength. Holt ate an energy bar and then changed into his workout clothes. Exercise cleared his mind, which was something he very much needed right now.

Henry stayed close to his side as they walked to the car. Holt glanced around as he opened the passenger door. The blue sedan wasn't in sight. It was a quiet Sunday afternoon in the neighborhood. He drove the few blocks to the church.

When he saw the basketball court, Henry jumped out of the car and trotted over to the free throw line. Holt bounced the ball and took a shot that went in. As the ball hit the pavement, Henry ran over and rolled it back to Holt.

Thirty minutes later, Holt put his hands on his knees to catch his breath. Henry was lying down in the shade of a large oak tree. Holt took a long drink from a bottle of water, then poured some into his hand for Henry to lap up. Bishop Pennington's car entered the lot, and the minister came over to them after parking his car.

"How's Henry?" he asked.

"Not bad for a patient who was near death in the hospital a few days ago."

"I wish everyone I prayed for recovered as well as he has," the bishop said, leaning over to pat Henry's head. "And it was good seeing you in church this morning. What did you think about the sermon?"

"It's what the sermon thinks about me."

"I like that. But you left so fast I wondered if you preferred the pigpen."

"Not after the way you described it," Holt said. "I've never considered myself a prodigal son, but after listening to you, I guess there's some of him in all of us."

"And a Father waiting with open arms to welcome us home."

"No matter what we've done, according to you."

"Yes." The bishop smiled. "I never know how far my words make it once they leave my mouth."

"They made it to the pew where I was sitting." Holt bounced the basketball a few times. "What are you doing here so late in the afternoon?"

"I have a pastoral counseling session in about fifteen minutes with someone who's not a member of the church."

"You counsel people who aren't members?"

"Yes. There are plenty of sheep in God's fold whose names aren't on the church roll."

"Like me?"

"Especially you," the bishop said with a grin.

After giving Henry a final pat, the minister went inside the church. Holt returned to the free throw line and stayed there until he'd made ten shots in a row. Then he gathered up Henry and put him in the car. As he left, Holt didn't notice a car that entered the parking lot or the person who got out.

It was Valerie Stevens.

—

Trish knew why Holt was meeting with Cecil Burkdale. There was only one explanation. Her dilemma was what it meant to her.

"Do you want to come inside?" Marge asked Keith when they reached the house. "You could take a nap on the sofa in the living room. A big meal means a Sunday afternoon snooze for me."

"No, thanks," Keith said, glancing at Trish. "I need to get home and spend time with my mother."

"Wait here while I help Mama get into the house," Trish said.

After she helped navigate her mother's wheelchair through the narrow front door, Trish returned to the driveway where Keith was leaning against his car.

"I'm so sorry about your folks," she said. "You really shouldn't have taken the time to take us out to dinner."

Keith shrugged. "Life goes on. And my mother insisted. She'd do anything to make things work out for you and me."

"That's sweet of her."

Keith was quiet for a moment. "Everybody says I'm just like my dad. So when he does something like this, it makes me wonder—"

"Don't go there," Trish interrupted. "If there's one thing I've realized about you over the past couple of months, it's that you've changed.

You're not the jock who sat at the back of physics class and thought making paper airplanes was a substitute for learning about matter, motion, energy, and force."

"You remember that stuff?"

"There are tons of stray bits of information filed away in parts of my brain I rarely visit. But that's not my point. And we're talking about you, not me. I'm not going to stand here and listen to you doubt yourself because your father is making some bad choices. I believe in you and respect you a bunch."

"Thanks."

Trish took a deep breath. "And I appreciate your patience with me. Often the way I work through things doesn't make sense, even to me."

"You're hard to read," Keith said.

Trish suddenly realized how the way she treated Keith must have made him feel like a knight trapped on the chessboard with no place to move.

"I'm sorry," she said. "Trust has been tough for me, especially since my daddy died. When your world is turned upside down, like yours was a few hours ago, it's hard to handle. But I want to be here for you, no matter what happens between your folks."

"Will you promise not to say anything to Marge? The news will get out within a day or two anyway, but I'd rather my mother tell her in person."

"Sure."

Keith pushed the button on his key that unlocked the car door. Trish wanted to give him a hug but held back.

"Let's keep in close touch this week," she said instead.

"Okay."

Trish's heart started pounding. "Keith," she said. "Look at me."

As soon as Keith turned around, Trish threw her arms around his neck and kissed him firmly on the lips.

"There," she said when their lips parted. "Is that easy to understand?"

Keith's eyes were big. "Yes."

"And here's another one to make sure there's no question about it."

Trish kissed him even longer. There was a tenderness and strength in Keith's response that melted her heart.

"Okay," she said when they parted. "Remember that when you have doubts about what kind of man you are."

"That won't be a problem." Keith smiled. "And it's way better than talking to you about the quality of well water."

Trish laughed and pushed him away. He leaned over and kissed her again.

Trish waved as he backed out of the driveway. She was beginning to believe Keith was the right man for her.

And she wanted to be the right woman for him.

Inside the house, Marge was rinsing a bowl in the sink before putting it in the dishwasher.

"Keith and I had a good talk before he left," Trish said when she came into the kitchen.

"It didn't look like talking to me."

"Mama! Were you spying on us?"

"It wasn't like you were hiding. Anyone driving past the house could have seen you. The hard part was rolling my wheelchair fast enough to the sink after he left so I could pretend to be loading the dishwasher."

38

After taking a shower, Holt called Angelina and asked if she would like to go to dinner.

"Yes," she said.

"Great. How about Camille's? It shouldn't be very crowded on a Sunday evening and—"

"No, I'm in the mood for a sandwich. We could meet at the sub shop on Eastway Drive."

"Are you serious?"

"Yes. If I still want to be with you after going there, I think our relationship has turned the corner."

Holt wasn't sure about Angelina's logic, but he wasn't about to argue with her wishes.

Thirty minutes later, he held the door open for her at the sub shop. They went up to the counter. A young man with a thin fuzz of beard on his chin stood in front of trays of deli items.

"Go ahead," Angelina said to Holt. "I'm not sure what I want."

"Smoked turkey with provolone on whole wheat, toasted, with light mayo, tomato, a few pickles, lettuce, and seasoning mix on top," Holt said.

"Is that what you ordered when you came here with the blond deputy?" Angelina asked.

"Uh, I think so."

"What did she get?"

"The same," Holt replied, opting not to lie. "We made it a jumbo. That way it was cheaper."

Angelina faced the young sandwich artist. "I'll have rare roast beef, cheddar, tomato, lettuce, and the balsamic vinegar sauce."

"Toasted?" the young man asked.

"Sure."

The young man prepared the sandwiches and handed them across the counter. Holt paid.

"Where did you sit?" Angelina asked.

"Over there," Holt said and pointed to a table near the back wall. "I didn't want to be too close to a rowdy kid who was in here with his parents."

Angelina took off for the table. A puzzled Holt followed.

"Here?" Angelina asked, touching one of the chairs.

"Yes, Trish sat there, and I sat here."

"That's what I want," Angelina replied.

They sat across from each other.

"Then she prayed a blessing for the food," Holt said.

"I'm not up to doing that."

"I am," Holt said.

"Really?" Angelina asked in surprise. "When did you start praying?"

"I've gone to Bishop Pennington's church the past two Sundays. I'm a beginner, so don't put me under a microscope."

Holt bowed his head. "Thank you, God, for this food, and that Angelina has forgiven me. Amen."

Angelina chuckled. "So that's one of the new ways you're going to manipulate me. If I say you're not forgiven, it makes me look like I'm disobeying God."

"You would be," Holt said as he took the first bite of his sandwich.

Angelina shook her head. They ate in silence for a few minutes. Angelina took a sip of water.

"Do you know the reason I wanted to come here?" she asked.

"It wasn't for roast beef and cheddar?"

"No." She leaned forward. "What did Trish Carmichael say to you that made you cry?"

Holt placed his half-eaten sandwich on the tray in front of him.

"Five years ago her father was killed and her mother paralyzed in an accident involving a drunk teenage driver. What she said about her family brought up things I've kept hidden for a long time."

And with that brief introduction, Holt told Angelina about Calico. Unlike Trish, who'd viewed everything through the lens of her own tragedy, and Bishop Pennington, whose goal was to bring Holt to the Lord, Angelina listened as a person who simply cared for Holt. At one point he had to stop for a moment as his emotions bubbled to the surface.

"I feel like such a kid," he said.

"You were," Angelina said with compassion in her eyes. "A scared, drunk, eighteen-year-old kid."

Holt finished the account of his conversation with Officer Merriwether and the pain of Calico's funeral.

"Now you know," he said, taking a deep breath and exhaling. "And I'm not going to try to manipulate or control how you respond."

Angelina reached across the table and took his hand in hers. "Here's my response," she said, squeezing his hand. "I believe if you had to make the same choice today, you'd do the right thing. What matters to me is who you are now, not what you did then."

Holt didn't speak. Instead, he raised Angelina's hand to his lips and kissed it.

—

Trish arrived at the sheriff's office shortly before 7:00 a.m. on Monday and stopped at the dispatch desk. She knew the first item on her to-do list.

"What is Detective Clovis's schedule today?" she asked the officer on duty.

The woman turned to her computer screen. "He and the sheriff have a meeting at the board of commissioners' office first thing this morning, but he should be in later."

"Please let me know when he gets here. I need to talk to him as soon as possible."

Trish resolutely went to her cubicle and began working. Five new cases had landed on her desk, and she was busy opening files when her phone buzzed.

"Holt Douglas from the DA's office wants to talk to you."

Trish hesitated. She didn't want to talk to Holt, but two of her new cases were going to require his immediate assistance. "Okay."

"Thanks for taking my call," Holt said when she answered. "I was preparing the order for the judge to sign in the Dorman case, and I'm not sure I have a current address for the defendant."

"Just a minute. I'll check."

Trish pulled up the information on the screen and gave it to him. She tapped her finger against the top of her desk.

"Did you mean what you said in court on Thursday about shutting down the Rex Meredith investigation?"

"Yeah, that's what Ralph told me to do."

"Then why would you meet with Cecil Burkdale?" she asked. "I saw you talking to him yesterday afternoon at Henderson's Farm Equipment where my father used to work."

"That was a strange deal," Holt answered without hesitation.

"Burkdale was parked in front of my house when I got home from church and wanted to meet with me."

"You went to church again?"

"Yes. And I intend on going next Sunday, too. Anyway, Burkdale wouldn't talk to me at my house but insisted we go to the dealership. I'm not sure if he's crazy or not." Holt paused. "Are you going to tell Butch Clovis about this? Burkdale is a strange man with weird theories, but I don't want him getting hassled by Clovis."

Trapped by her curiosity, Trish knew Holt was right about the detective's possible reaction. She scrambled to come up with a response.

"Not if your investigation is still shut down. That's all he cares about."

"I have the same questions I did when you and I were working on this together," Holt replied, "but I'm not going to disobey an order from Ralph without a compelling reason to do so. Anyway, Burkdale is mentally fragile. A visit from Clovis might send him to the psych ward of the hospital."

Trish hated it when Holt made her sound like a coconspirator. But she didn't want to trigger a nervous breakdown.

"Okay. I won't say anything to Detective Clovis."

"Thanks. And let's hope Mickey Dorman pays his child support."

—

When Trish mentioned Cecil Burkdale, Holt's heart had started racing as fast as it did right before a jury announced the verdict in a felony case. It was a good thing the conversation took place over the phone, because his face wouldn't have appeared as calm and matter-of-fact as he hoped his voice sounded. He'd not lied to Trish. If true, Burkdale's accusations would be a compelling reason to disregard Ralph's command to shut down the investigation into Mr. Meredith's death. More important, they would provide ample justification to open another one into the threat to Valerie Stevens.

Holt wasn't sure Trish would keep her mouth shut. And if Cecil Burkdale was right about the level of sophistication employed by the security firm retained by Greg Stevens, several people might already know about Holt's trip to the farm equipment dealership.

He spent part of the morning researching the security firm mentioned by Burkdale. Everything the bookkeeper said checked out. It was a bona fide business with a good reputation. Like similar outfits, it promised to be professional and discreet. Shortly before noon, the receptionist buzzed him.

"Mr. Bernard S. Patrick is on the phone for you."

Holt accepted the call. "Skip?" he asked.

"I've dropped that. It worked fine when I was eight years old, but it doesn't fit my current station in life."

"What's happened?"

"I'll buy your lunch and tell you. Meet me at Camille's in ten minutes. This news can't be shared over baked beans and burnt ends."

The phone went dead. Holt was puzzled. Skip had always considered barbecue the height of culinary experience.

Holt arrived at the boutique eatery before Skip. While he waited, he admired a glass-enclosed case filled with pastries that would each take a five-mile run to burn off. He was calculating a workout regimen that would justify a freshly baked éclair when Skip sauntered through the front door.

"Get one to go if you want to," Skip said when he saw what Holt was doing. "Make that two."

"Maybe I can resist the temptation if I eat lunch," Holt said.

"That's on me, so don't hold back," Skip replied.

Holt ordered soup and half a sandwich. Skip opted for a salad with salmon.

"Please double the salmon on that," he said to the young woman behind the counter. "I want a piece of meat in every bite."

They sat down at a peach-colored wrought-iron table.

"What in the world is going on with you?" Holt asked. "You're acting like you won the lottery."

"Better," Skip replied. "At the end of the month I'm going to be an equity partner at the law firm."

"Congratulations. You weren't expecting that to happen for at least another couple of years."

"I know," Skip said as he leaned in closer. "And it gets better. This part is totally confidential. Mr. Spratt is going to retire and phase out of the practice. A big portion of his work is going to flow down to me. He'll receive business credit on the billings for a while, but eventually it will completely shift to me. You wouldn't believe the quality of his clientele. If I do a good job and keep the clients happy, I'll be set for the rest of my career."

The income earned by partners in a lucrative small-town practice could rival that of all but the top lawyers in big-city law firms and involve far fewer hassles. Holt could understand why Skip was pumped up.

"You timed it right," Holt said admiringly.

"And I want to make this work for you. I'm going to need an associate sooner rather than later, and there's no one I'd rather work with than you. I'm enjoying office practice more than I thought, so that will open up as much litigation as you want to do. I know Mr. Ayers and Mr. Goldfarb have had their eyes on you. They told me Judge Lomax holds you in high regard."

"Really?"

"Yeah, the judge talks to the senior members of the bar. All my info is secondhand, but your name has come up around the office."

Skip's invitation wasn't a total shock to Holt. He'd mulled over the possibility that they might join forces in the future. But standing as a barrier was his commitment to fulfill Calico's ideal to be a prosecutor. It had now become Holt's dream, too.

"I don't know," he said. "Ralph just went to bat for me with the county commissioners and obtained approval for a salary supplement."

"Which is nothing compared to what you'll pull down jumping into private practice. And you won't be limited to straight hourly work. Mr. Ayers is getting tired of handling contingency work, and when those cases hit, the hourly rate assigned to the amount collected is insane. I'll make sure your employment agreement provides for bonuses if you pass certain performance goals. That will be a cinch if you do well in the contingency part of the practice."

"You've really thought this through."

"Of course I have. And we'll have a blast being in the same office. Don't tell me you're having fun now. Jim is constantly wrapped up in AA, and Ralph runs around in perpetual fear of losing an election."

"AA has been good for Jim."

"I know." Skip rolled his eyes. "And he should be proud of those sobriety chips. It's amazing that he can stick with Ralph and not go back to drinking."

Skip pointed his finger at Holt's chest. "Society needs good prosecutors," he continued, "but you've paid your debt, and it's time to move on."

"You know nothing about my debt," Holt mumbled.

Skip didn't ask a follow-up question. Instead, he speared a piece of salmon and held it up in front of him.

"If you join me, you'll be able to afford trips to pull live salmon from the crisp, cold waters of an Alaskan river."

39

Holt cast a wary eye toward Ralph's office. If Greg Stevens knew about Holt's meeting with Cecil Burkdale, then the next logical step would be to inform Ralph. Toward the end of the day, Holt was on the phone with an Atlanta lawyer who represented the defendant in a drug possession case. Ralph appeared in the doorway and heard the end of the conversation.

"Have you made a plea offer in that case?" Ralph asked. "You have a real problem with probable cause for the search of the defendant's mobile home. There was enough for an auto search, but it looks shaky for a residence."

"It wasn't a mobile home. It was an RV, or really a homemade rig the defendant built out of plywood and dropped into the bed of his pickup truck. The expectation of privacy wouldn't be as strong for that as a mobile home or fixed dwelling. It's an interesting issue that might end up in the court of appeals—"

"Answer my question."

"No, I was still softening him up with stories about how conservative Ashley County juries can be," Holt said defensively.

"You have to get to a jury first. Call him back and see if his client will plea to two years to serve followed by five on probation."

It had been awhile since Ralph had micromanaged one of Holt's cases. His abrupt instruction rankled.

"Can I wait until the end of the week? The case isn't on the upcoming trial calendar."

"Yeah."

Ralph glanced over his shoulder, then stepped over and closed the door. "Have you heard the news?" the DA asked.

Holt licked his lips and hoped it didn't have anything to do with something he'd done.

"No."

"The Coosawattee Club in all three counties is going to back Lynnwood Nolte for DA. I mean, they won't do it at the meetings; however, the word has gone out. The Triplett County chapter has a new president, and he's listened to a load of garbage about me from the president here in Paxton. Citizens has never been as strong as Coosawattee, so this could have a huge impact."

Holt tried to hide his relief. "What about Judge Lomax?" he asked. "He's big in Coosawattee. He could put a stop to it."

"I had the same thought, but he's taking a hands-off stance that some people will interpret as opposition to me." Ralph lowered his voice. "But you can help."

"You want me to talk to Judge Lomax?" Holt asked incredulously.

"No, I want you to get with Skip Patrick. He's going to become a partner at the Spratt firm by the end of the month. Mr. Spratt will never back me, but Skip could try to convince the firm to stay on the sidelines since they'll have to work with the winner."

"Mr. Spratt was one of Nolte's biggest backers during the last election. As a new partner, Skip won't carry that kind of influence."

"It's not based on Skip. Meredith Enterprises is one of the firm's biggest clients. What do you think is more important to Spratt, money or politics?"

Holt's eyes widened. "Would Greg Stevens really pull his business from the Spratt firm over a district attorney's race?"

As soon as the words were out of his mouth, Holt wanted to pull them back. Ralph's job was the center of his life, and Holt had just minimized its importance. He hurriedly continued, "I mean, I don't want to communicate a threat to Skip that Stevens won't back up."

"He'll back it up. Will you talk to Skip?"

There was only one answer Holt could give. "Yes," he said. "Oh, and how did you find out Skip is going to become a partner?"

"Craig Stevens told me."

"It's Greg," Holt corrected him.

Ralph slapped his hands together. "I've got to forget about the guy named Craig Stevens from my high school class. He's going to cause me a huge embarrassment."

Holt found it hard to put the blame on Ralph's high school classmate. After the DA left, Holt thought of a question he wished he'd asked: Had Greg Stevens suggested that Holt be the one to approach Skip Patrick?

If so, why?

After talking to Holt, Trish wanted to avoid Butch Clovis. The dispatcher notified Trish when the detective returned from the meeting at the county commissioner's office.

"Did you tell him I wanted to talk to him?"

"No, he zipped by. He should be in his office by now."

"There's no need for you to say anything to him."

"Okay," the woman answered. "I'm not sure what you'd expect me to say since I don't know what you wanted to tell him."

"You're right," Trish answered crisply. "Thanks."

She hung up the phone and rubbed her temples with the tips of her fingers. Holt had been the cause of more than one tension headache.

Taking a short break from work, she sent a text message to Keith asking him how he and his mother were doing. He responded immediately:

More bad news. We'll talk later.

Trish knew that probably meant Jack Pierce had another woman in his life. Trish had no tolerance for marital infidelity. She stared at the message on her phone while she thought about Keith and his family.

"Deputy Carmichael, if it's not an inconvenience, and you can take a break from texting, I'd like to see you in my office for a few minutes."

It was Sheriff Blackstone.

"Yes, sir," she said, quickly closing out the screen.

Trying to stay calm, she followed the sheriff down the hallway. Sheriff Blackstone was a large, overweight man with a thin ring of dark hair encircling his bald head. He had a big voice, a ready smile, and the firm handshake of a veteran politician. Seated in his office was Butch Clovis. The sheriff stepped behind his desk and then stared at Trish for a moment.

"Go ahead and have a seat," he said, motioning to a chair beside Clovis.

Trish sat on the edge of the chair. In the pit of her stomach she knew the next few moments might end her employment with the sheriff's department.

"Tell me what you know about Holt Douglas," the sheriff said.

"I talked to Detective Clovis about him the other—"

"I want to hear for myself," the sheriff interrupted.

Trish felt her throat close up. "He's the assistant DA who handles most of the delinquent child support cases that are turned over for criminal prosecution. He grew up north of Atlanta, and I think he has an older sister. He played basketball in high school, and lacrosse. He had a girlfriend, Angelina Peabody, who owns the All About You Salon on Broadmore Street, but they broke up. Recently, he started attending Bishop Pennington's church. It's not far from where he lives. He has a little dog. Detective Clovis knows about his interest in Mr. Meredith's death—"

"We'll get to that in a minute," the sheriff said, again cutting her off. "What does Douglas think about Ralph Granger?"

Trish tried to remember any comments, either positive or negative, about the DA.

"Nothing that I can recall except that he thinks Mr. Granger sometimes works out plea arrangements that are too lenient."

"We agree on that," Clovis grunted.

"Do you think he supports Granger for reelection?" the sheriff asked.

"I don't know."

"Has he ever talked to you about a man named Cecil Burkdale?"

"Yes, sir," Trish said, licking her lips. "Burkdale spoke to Holt about his investigation into the cause of Rex Meredith's death."

"What did Burkdale tell him?"

"I don't know specifically, but Holt said Burkdale had some crazy theories about what happened."

"That's the word Douglas used?"

"Yes, and he doubted Burkdale's credibility. Last week he told me Mr. Granger told him to stop looking into the Meredith situation. The case had been closed years ago and wasn't going to be reopened."

The last statement wasn't exactly the way Holt put it, but it was what came out of Trish's mouth. She started to correct herself. The sheriff spoke first.

"That's true. I want to know if Douglas says anything to you about the DA race. It's going to heat up hotter than a sidewalk in July."

"We don't talk about politics. Do you want me to ask him directly?"

The sheriff looked at Clovis, who shook his head. "She couldn't pull it off," the detective said.

"Well, if it comes up, keep your ears open," the sheriff said. "There are people who want insider information from a DA's office employee about what's really going on over there."

"Yes, sir."

"And keep this conversation confidential," Clovis added. "Will you do that?"

"Yes, sir."

"Back to work," the sheriff said, dismissing her.

As she returned to her cubicle, Trish was thankful that Detective Clovis considered her incompetent as a political spy. The less the sheriff and the detective wanted her to do, the better.

—

When Trish arrived home at the end of the day, her mother was sitting quietly in the living room with the lights off and without the TV on.

"Are you okay?" Trish asked.

"No, Bonita Pierce came by to see me. I know why Keith was out of sorts yesterday."

Trish sat down on the couch near her mother's chair. "He wanted her to tell you, not me. I haven't talked to him today, but he sent me a text saying there's more bad news."

"It's Bonita's health. She has a heart condition and is going to need either stents or bypass surgery. And two months ago Jack dropped his family health coverage at work, so she doesn't have any insurance to pay for the treatment."

"Why would he do that?" Trish asked in shock.

"Bonita doesn't know. She went to see Brother Carpenter at the church. He thinks Jack may have another woman."

"Yeah, that's what I thought." Trish sighed.

"Jack cleaned out their bank account and won't tell her where he put the money. It wasn't more than a few thousand dollars, but Bonita doesn't have money for groceries. I gave her two hundred dollars before she left."

"She needs a good lawyer."

"Who would you recommend?"

Trish thought for a moment. "Probably Clare Dixon. She's not as expensive as someone from one of the larger firms and knows what she's doing."

"Would you call her for Bonita and find out if she's interested in helping?"

"Yes."

"One good thing happened," Marge said. "When Brother Carpenter found out about the health insurance problem, he called Mr. Stevens. He's going to help with the doctor bills."

"Greg Stevens is going to pay for a heart surgery?" Trish asked in shock.

"Bonita wasn't exactly sure how it's going to be handled. It has something to do with Mr. Stevens being on the board of directors for the hospital, which has to provide a certain amount of free treatment every year. I guess Mr. Stevens can decide who gets it."

"Wow," Trish responded. "That's amazing."

"Yes." Marge ran her fingers through her hair. "And I think you should change your mind about Mr. and Mrs. Stevens helping with the building fund at church. Their hearts are in the right place. Are you willing to consider you might be wrong?"

"Yeah." Trish nodded. "Recently, I've been wrong about a lot of things."

—

There was a parking spot open on the street in front of the salon. Holt wanted to tell Angelina about his conversation with Skip and ask her opinion. Looking at himself in the rearview mirror, he adjusted his tie, then got out and climbed the front steps. He'd not seen Brittany since the blowup over Trish Carmichael and wasn't sure how she'd treat him. The receptionist was on the phone when he came through the door. After a few seconds, she hung up.

"May I help you?" she asked with a flat expression on her face.

"Come on," Holt said. "Don't do that to me. I've suffered enough."

"From what my pregnant friends tell me, no man has ever suffered enough. But after what happened the other day, I can't believe you would leave Angelina for that psycho blond deputy."

"You're right."

"She practically waved a gun in my face demanding to see Angelina," Brittany said with a flourish of her hand. "But I guess that's the kind of woman who's attracted to a job in law enforcement. It didn't make me feel safer about who's protecting us from the bad guys."

"She's under a lot of stress. Where's the boss?"

"Already gone for the day. She and Caroline went to the nursing home on Cambridge Avenue for round two with the blue-haired ladies."

"Oh, I didn't know."

"Yeah, you've been out of the loop for a few days."

Holt stepped closer and leaned on the counter in front of the receptionist. "What's the latest with you and Skip?"

Brittany picked up a vase of fresh-cut flowers on the corner of her desk. "Skip sent these with a sweet note."

"Nice. On the way over here I thought about buying flowers for Angelina."

"Where are they?" Brittany craned her head to look past Holt. "In your car?"

"At the florist's. It's the thought that counts."

"Yeah, if you believe that, you should try another thought."

"I'd better get going," Holt said. "Perhaps we can reschedule that double date."

"Maybe, but this time Skip will have to ask me himself. No go-betweens."

"I'll take that as a yes."

Holt had a smile on his face as he walked down the steps toward his car. At least part of his life was getting back to normal.

40

Henry stood at the bottom of a tree barking at a gray squirrel that angrily chattered from a limb a few feet above the dog's head. When he saw Holt, the dog ran a few steps before slowing to a trot. Holt grabbed an old tennis ball and tossed it across the yard. Henry ran after it at normal speed and returned it two times. On the third throw, the dog ran to retrieve the ball, but when he brought it back to Holt's feet, he dropped it and collapsed on the ground. Holt leaned down and scratched the dog's stomach.

"Sorry, boy," he said. "I didn't mean to wear you out, but I wanted to check how you're doing."

After feeding Henry and giving him fresh water, Holt left the house for a run. He kept up a fast pace for ten minutes to elevate his heart rate, then slowed to a tempo he was capable of maintaining for a long distance. As he approached the Meredith house, he saw a familiar car pulling into the driveway.

It was Bishop Pennington.

Holt slowed and stopped behind the minister's car. He could see the bishop looking in the rearview mirror. Holt put his hands on his hips as he caught his breath. Bishop Pennington got out and came over to him.

"What brings you over here?" Holt asked.

"Sonny called. I had trouble understanding exactly what he needed, but it was clear he wanted to see me as soon as possible."

The caretaker came around the corner of the house. He was wearing overalls and a ragged cap on top of his head. He mopped his face with a red kerchief. He nodded to the bishop but eyed Holt suspiciously.

"Be that who what?" he asked.

"This is Holt Douglas, a friend of mine," the bishop replied. "He's an attorney who works at the district attorney's office. He attends the church."

Sonny looked more closely at Holt. The caretaker then thumped his forehead and shook his head sadly.

"What's wrong, Sonny?" the bishop asked.

Sonny reached into the top pocket of his overalls. He took out a small pad and a pencil that had been ground down close to the eraser. He scribbled something on the pad and handed it to the bishop.

"The doctor says there's something wrong with your head?" the bishop asked. "Is it serious?"

Sonny drew his hand across his throat. It was such an abrupt, harsh gesture that it caught Holt off guard.

"I'm sorry," Holt blurted out.

Sonny looked at him. "Bad be that."

The bishop stepped forward and put his hand on Sonny's shoulder. "Do you want to tell me more about it?"

Sonny nodded and pointed to the big house.

"Well, I'd better be on my way," Holt said.

Sonny reached out and touched Holt on the arm. He shook his head. "Agree be more."

"You want us to pray for you?" the bishop asked.

"Be that."

"He's referring to the verse in the Bible that says if two or more agree about something in prayer, it will be done," the bishop said.

Sonny grunted in agreement.

"I'm hot and sweaty," Holt protested. "I shouldn't—"

"Do you think he cares about that?"

"And I don't know much about praying."

"You know enough to say 'amen' when we finish."

Sonny pulled a green kerchief from a pocket in his overalls and tossed it to Holt, then turned and started walking toward the house.

"Are you sure about this?" Holt asked the bishop.

"Trust Sonny. If he's comfortable with you, then it's an honor that he's asked you to be a part of this."

Holt inspected the kerchief. It seemed clean, so he used it to wipe the sweat from his face.

Sonny led them around to the back of the big house. There was a large key ring attached to one of the loops on his overalls. He unhooked the ring and inserted a key into the lock. Opening the door, a beep sounded, and the caretaker entered a code, disarming the security system.

They were in the kitchen. It was neat and tidy. There was no sign of food on the counters. A small round table held a vase of fresh flowers in the middle. Sonny led the way through a swinging door to the left and across a hallway. Holt and the bishop followed into another room. Holt immediately knew where they were.

It was the study where Rex Meredith died.

Built-in bookcases filled with gilt-edged volumes lined two walls. There was a slightly frayed antique rug on the floor. Several oil paintings of landscapes hung on the walls. The largest painting in the room was a portrait of Rex Meredith hanging over a fireplace with a brass grate. In the painting, Meredith appeared to be about sixty years old. He was wearing an open-collared shirt and sitting in the study. Lying on the floor beside him was an Irish setter.

Two leather wing chairs were positioned on opposite sides of a small table upon which a Tiffany lamp sat. Holt could easily imagine Rex Meredith and Cecil Burkdale sitting and talking in the chairs. To the right of the wing chairs was a leather sofa with a low table in front of it. A smaller leather chair was placed beside the sofa. Holt glanced at the wall across from the wing chairs. In the dimly lit room it was impossible to tell if the bullet hole mentioned by Tony McDermott was still there. Sonny turned on a brass lamp next to the sofa. He sat down on the sofa and motioned for the bishop to join him. Holt sat in the single chair.

The caretaker took out his pad and began to write. Holt and the bishop waited as Sonny scribbled on the piece of paper. He flipped to a fresh sheet and kept writing. Finally, he ripped off three sheets and handed them to the bishop, who silently read them.

"Yes, we can do that."

"What's on the paper?" Holt asked.

"He wants to ask God to forgive him. He's listing his sins. The doctor has told him he has an inoperable brain tumor and is going to die."

Sonny slipped from his seat on the sofa and knelt like a child about to say his bedtime prayers. The bishop got on his knees and put his arm around Sonny's shoulders. With his other hand he spread the sheets of paper on the sofa in front of them. Holt stayed in his seat.

And listened.

Bishop Pennington gently touched each scribbled line on the sheets of paper and spoke softly into Sonny's left ear. Holt was close enough to hear some of the words—a mix of questions to which Sonny nodded in agreement and pronouncements of forgiveness by the bishop. Holt knew he was witnessing the culmination of a lifetime of kindness and mutual respect between friends.

A grandfather clock twice chimed quarter hours before the two older men arose from their knees and embraced. There was a look of peace in Sonny's eyes. Holt knew how he felt.

Sonny wrote something on his pad and handed it to the bishop.

"He does," the bishop said, glancing at Holt.

"What?" Holt asked.

"He wants to know if you send criminals to jail."

"Yes," Holt confirmed, facing Sonny. "If someone commits a crime, it's my job to make sure they are punished under the law."

"Yes that do." The caretaker gestured toward the portrait over the fireplace and then pointed to his chest as if holding a gun in his hand.

Holt's mouth went dry. Sonny started rapidly scribbling on the pad. Holt turned to the bishop.

"I've been investigating Rex Meredith's death," he said.

Sonny looked up and nodded his head. He handed a sheet of paper to the bishop.

"He knows what happened," the bishop said, his eyes opening wider. "And it's bothered him a lot."

Sonny put down his pad and walked over to the bookcase. Reaching up, he pulled down a book bound in dark green leather. The caretaker stuck his hand into the empty space behind the book and took out something Holt couldn't see. He then handed it to Holt. It was a small cassette.

"What is this?" Holt asked.

Sonny pointed to the corner of the room behind them. Holt turned around.

And saw a small security camera positioned on a metal bracket.

41

Is this from the night Mr. Meredith died?" Holt asked.

"Be it."

Holt turned to the bishop. "Please remember this," he said. "You may need to testify about it in court someday."

"I'm not sure—" the bishop started, then stopped.

"Is there a place where we can watch this?" Holt asked Sonny.

Sonny got up, and they followed him from the room. They reentered the hallway that separated the study from the kitchen, but instead of turning right, they went left to a closet at the end of the hall. Inside, on a broad shelf, was the control center for the home's security system. A small video monitor rested on a large rectangular metal box with blinking lights on the front. The box was configured as a carousel so tapes would cycle through the system. Positioned around the equipment were bottles of cleaning supplies.

"This is an ancient system," Holt said.

Sonny nodded and held up fingers for 1974. He pressed a button on the front of the small box beside the monitor. Nothing happened. He then banged his fist sharply against the right corner of the box.

A green light flickered on. Sonny opened the front of the device and inserted the tape. He turned on the monitor and pressed the Play button. All three men squeezed close together in the confined space.

A grainy screen greeted them. It was an image of the study without anyone present. Sonny pressed a button to fast-forward the tape. They waited. Holt kept expecting him to stop the tape, but he didn't. Finally, Sonny hit the Play button. It still showed an empty study. They watched it for almost a minute. Nothing changed.

"Are you sure—" Holt asked.

As soon as the words were out of his mouth, a body lying on the floor almost magically appeared. An unidentified man knelt beside it. The face of the person on the floor was hidden by one of the wing chairs, and the man kneeling on the floor had his back to the camera. There was a whiskey bottle on a small table beside the prone figure. Then the man kneeling on the floor moved slightly to the side. He was positioning a gun in the right hand of the man on the floor. The kneeling man raised his head so his profile came into view.

It was Greg Stevens.

Stevens stood up. There was a handkerchief on the floor beside the gun. Stevens stepped back and looked down at the figure on the floor. It was impossible to read his expression, but his actions were deliberate. He knelt down again, and what he did was hidden from the camera's eye. He then stood and backed away, as if inspecting his work. The camera captured his face. Stevens glanced at his right hand and rubbed it against the side of his pants.

"There's blood on his hand," Holt said.

Neither Sonny nor the bishop responded. Stevens backed out of the frame and disappeared. They continued to stare at the image of the body lying on the floor. Holt couldn't pick up on any discernible movement.

"Did you see that?" the bishop said.

"What?" Holt asked.

"His hand moved or twitched."

Holt leaned in closer. Sure enough, the position of the gun in the hand had changed.

"Is that all?" Holt asked.

Sonny shook his head and pointed at the monitor. Stevens came back into the frame and moved the wing chair slightly. The face of the man on the floor came into view. It was Rex Meredith.

Seeing Meredith's face wasn't a shock, but it brought the video to a new level of stark reality. Stevens left and returned again. He was wearing a different pair of pants and stood with his arms folded across his chest. The tape ended.

Sonny leaned forward and turned off the machine.

Holt turned to the bishop, who once again had his arm around Sonny's shoulders. The questions Holt wanted to ask stuck in his throat. The minister needed to do his job first. Sonny began to sob, his back heaving.

Bishop Pennington led Sonny down the hallway and guided him into the kitchen. Holt didn't follow. Instead, he returned to the study and walked around the room. He stopped at the place on the floor where Rex Meredith died, then knelt where Greg Stevens placed the gun in his father-in-law's hand and glanced up at the camera.

Several minutes passed before Sonny and Bishop Pennington returned to the study. When they did, Sonny rubbed his eyes and looked at Holt.

"Tape that gone," he said. "Stevens mister be—"

"Write, Sonny," the bishop interrupted.

Sonny took out his pad and began to scribble. He flipped over another page and continued. Holt tried to imagine what it would be like when the caretaker took the witness stand. The judge would have to accommodate Sonny's disability and the need to laboriously write out his answers. It would be at least a full day or two of testimony. A savvy defense lawyer, whom Greg Stevens would doubtlessly hire, might try to wear the caretaker down until he slipped up and wrote something that could be turned against him. Holt's jaw set. Nothing could erase or confuse the images recorded on the surveillance tape. Sonny tore out the sheets and handed them to Holt, who quickly read them.

"Greg Stevens ran another set of images on a surveillance tape that the police took?" he asked incredulously.

Sonny nodded his head.

"How did you get this tape?"

Sonny left the study. Holt and the bishop followed. The caretaker led them back to the closet that contained the surveillance equipment. He wrote again, then handed the sheet of paper to Holt, who read it and asked, "The tape we watched filmed a minute or two when the system turned on for the evening. When it ran out of tape, the carousel dropped a fresh one into the unit. Right?"

"Be that." Sonny nodded.

"Where's that tape?"

Sonny wrote again and handed the sheet to Holt, who handed it to the bishop.

"Greg Stevens destroyed it," the bishop said.

Holt held up the tape they'd watched. "Why did you think to check this one?" he asked Sonny.

Sonny looked at Bishop Pennington.

"He told me in the kitchen that he couldn't sleep the night Mr. Meredith died and came in to check the tapes. He knew the system was set to come on at 9:00 p.m. and wondered if it showed anything. He didn't want to see Mr. Meredith kill himself but couldn't keep from looking."

"How do you know Greg Stevens changed the tape?"

Sonny took out his pad and wrote for several moments before handing a sheet to Holt.

"Unless it was turned on manually, the surveillance system automatically started at 9:00 p.m. every evening?" Holt asked.

Sonny nodded and wrote again. This time he handed the sheet to the bishop, who read it out loud: "'Mr. Rex be lying on the floor with the gun in his hand, and Mr. Greg, he coming in like he help him. The sheriff men take that tape.'"

Holt looked at the bishop. "There's no mention of a videotape in either the DA's file or the information I reviewed at the sheriff's office."

Bishop Pennington shook his head sadly.

"Where were you when Mr. Meredith was shot?" Holt asked Sonny.

Sonny turned and led them through the kitchen and outside. He pointed to the small cottage where he lived. He held up his hand like a gun firing, then touched his ear.

"You heard the gunshot and came over?"

"No that be."

"Why not?"

Sonny began to write.

"You thought it was a truck backfiring?" Holt asked.

Sonny nodded. He wrote again and handed the sheet of paper to Holt, who raised his eyebrows.

"Valerie Stevens came to get you?"

"Yes."

Sonny made signs of tears running down his cheeks.

"She was crying?"

Sonny, his own eyes sad, nodded. Holt held up the tape.

"Why didn't you give this tape to the sheriff's department?"

"She be that," Sonny replied immediately.

Before Holt could ask another question, Bishop Pennington spoke. "Sonny didn't want to do anything that would hurt Valerie. He knew if Greg went to prison it would destroy her life, too. He explained that to me when we were in the kitchen. He's known Valerie since before her mother married Rex. To him she's the little girl who asked him to peel an apple for her. He knew it was wrong not to speak up, but all he could think about was what it would do to her."

The forlorn look on Sonny's face confirmed the truth of the bishop's words.

"Does Valerie or Greg Stevens know about the tape you showed us?" Holt asked Sonny.

"No be that."

"Are you willing to tell the truth now in court?"

The caretaker hesitated and looked at the bishop. Holt held his breath.

"Yes be that."

"We went over that in the kitchen," the bishop said. "As much as he doesn't want Valerie to be hurt, he knows he has to tell the truth while there's still time to do so."

Holt left the house with the tape and the notes written by Sonny in his hand. As he closed the door, Holt could see the bishop and Sonny sitting together in the kitchen. The old friends had their heads together; their eyes were closed. Holt jogged slowly down the driveway, then picked up the pace when he reached the sidewalk.

—

Trish was relieved. The pressure of the Meredith matter had been forcibly taken from her by Sheriff Blackstone and Detective Clovis. Beyond tracking down deadbeat dads, she wasn't cut out for anything more exciting than deciding if it made sense to castle her king in the cyberspace chess world. During her lunch break, she left the sheriff's office and took her laptop computer with her to a local coffee shop with a Wi-Fi connection. She ordered a fruit smoothie and logged on to the speed chess website. The name of a familiar foe, Six Move Charlie, popped up, and he invited her to play.

"Where have you been?" Charlie typed in the chat box for the game. "Did the Unbeatable Wonder get beaten and have to retool her game?"

"No, just busy at work," she typed back.

Charlie made the opening move, which Trish immediately countered. After five moves, Trish suspected what her opponent's strategy might be. Charlie had memorized several opening gambits designed to bring a game to a rapid conclusion. After his next move, Trish was certain what he hoped to do.

"A Stonewall Attack isn't going to work," she typed in the chat box.

"That's not what I'm doing," Charlie responded.

Trish then typed in his next two moves. Charlie didn't respond.

"Are you a mind reader?" he asked.

"No, law enforcement."

"You're a cop?"

"Yes."

"Where?"

"Not saying."

"I've always thought you were a woman," Charlie replied. "Sorry about that."

Trish smiled. There was no point in correcting Charlie's mistake.

"Are you saying I play chess like a girl?" she typed.

"No, no. You're really good. Can you track my location on your computer?"

"Don't log off for two more minutes, and I'll have you. Charlie isn't your real name, is it?"

"I resign," her opponent immediately replied.

Charlie's name disappeared from the list of players in the room. Maybe Charlie had more problems than trotting out a well-known opening to a chess game and expecting Trish to fall for it. She took a sip of her smoothie and closed the top of her computer.

"Hey, Trish."

It was Holt Douglas. He had a large coffee in his hand.

"Am I interrupting anything important?" he asked.

"No, I was playing speed chess, but the game is over."

"I didn't know you played chess. I never graduated from checkers."

"It was something I liked to do with my father," Trish answered, standing up. "Holt, I'm not interested in having a casual conversation with you. Let's keep everything professional."

Holt stepped to the side. "Certainly," he said. "See you on Thursday."

Trish felt her face flush. She almost tripped over the leg of her chair as she made her way out of the coffee shop. She didn't look back as the glass door closed behind her.

—

Nestled in her cubicle, Trish fumed. It was easier engaging in anonymous chess battles than navigating live human interaction. Holt Douglas had perfected the ability to push the wrong buttons when it came to her. Still on her lunch break, she decided to see if there was any more dirt to dig up on the assistant DA. Typing in his name, she retraced the steps that had led her to newspaper accounts of the car wreck in which his friend died. She couldn't believe how sorry she'd felt for him the first time she read the story and how wrong she'd been. Now that she knew what really happened, Holt's lies made her angry. The smug expression on his face would evaporate if people knew the truth about his past.

She reread Kenneth Morgan's obituary and then checked out his parents. They were still living at the same address listed in the death notice. It would take Trish less than a minute to obtain their home and cell phone numbers. They deserved to know that it wasn't the alcohol in their son's blood that killed him.

"Who is Kenneth Morgan?" a male voice behind her asked.

She swiveled in her chair. It was Butch Clovis.

"Nothing. I'm still on my lunch break."

Clovis leaned in closer. There was a tab opened on the top of Trish's task bar that read "Holton Douglas."

"And what is his connection with Holt Douglas?"

42

Butch Clovis held the recorder so close to Trish's mouth that she would have touched it with her tongue if she licked her lips. Sheriff Blackstone sat to her right in the interrogation room.

"Is there anything else you can add to your statement?" the detective asked.

"That's all I remember," Trish said.

Clovis picked up a computer printout of one of the newspaper accounts of Kenneth Morgan's death.

"Are you sure Holt Douglas is unaware you've conducted an independent investigation into his involvement in the death of Kenneth Morgan?"

"I've never mentioned it to him. Like I said, I found the articles and read the obituary before Holt told me he was the one driving the car."

"Did he tell you how much he'd had to drink that night?"

"No."

Clovis looked at the sheriff. "We could subpoena the hospital records. I'm sure they ran a blood test."

"Finish the statement," the sheriff said.

Clovis leaned in close to Trish. His breath made her feel nauseous. All through the interview process, the detective had alternated between invading her personal space and backing off for a few questions.

"Is everything you've told us today the truth under penalty of perjury?"

"Yes, sir," Trish sighed. "If I made a mistake it wasn't on purpose."

"What part of what you've told us may have been a mistake?"

"Shut it down, Butch," the sheriff said before Trish could answer. "We can always bring her back in for a supplemental interview."

When she heard the sheriff's words, Trish couldn't hold back the tears. The thought of being subjected again to the humiliation and stress of the interrogation room was more than she could bear. She now understood why defendants confessed to crimes they hadn't committed just to stop the ordeal.

"Do you want me to resign?" she asked, her voice trembling.

"No," Sheriff Blackstone said. "I believe you're telling the truth. Your mistake was not bringing this information to my attention immediately."

"I'm sorry."

"Stay in here until you calm down," the sheriff continued.

"What are you going to do about what I've told you?"

"What happens to Douglas is not your concern, Deputy Carmichael," the sheriff said.

"Will I have to testify against him?"

"That will be decided later."

A fresh wave of tears rolled from Trish's eyes and down her cheeks. She didn't like Holt. He was a deceitful hypocrite with blood on his hands. But to have to face him across a courtroom would be agony.

"Stay in here as long as you like," the sheriff said. "Then clock out early. I doubt we'd get any productive work from you for the rest of your shift."

The two men left Trish alone. She grabbed another tissue from a box in the center of the table and blew her nose.

—

Holt walked out of the video lab in Atlanta with five DVD copies of the surveillance tape from the Meredith residence. He wasn't sure why he'd asked the technician to dub five copies, but it seemed prudent to have extras. He was going to keep one at his house, another in his desk at the office, and maybe give one to Skip for safekeeping. He wasn't sure what to do with the other two. The original tape would go into an evidence locker at the DA's office. He would put it in a sealed envelope and ask Belinda to log it in as *State v. John Doe*, an unidentified defendant.

During the drive from Atlanta to Paxton, Holt mulled over his next steps. At the top of his list would be obtaining a statement from Sonny. After that things became murky. At some point Holt would have to show the video to Ralph, but he didn't know whether to do it now or after he'd built a better case. The DA would freak out, but what would happen on the other side of that was a guessing game.

There was no use contacting the sheriff's department. Butch Clovis himself might be subject to criminal charges in covering up Meredith's murder. Trish Carmichael was no longer an ally. And Sheriff Blackstone had never impressed Holt as a fearless enforcer of the law.

Contacting the local newspaper was a step Holt had never thought he'd consider to promote justice. If he leaked the video, media from all over the region would descend on Paxton in a feeding frenzy. However, once the information became public knowledge, Holt would lose a measure of control. And no newspaper editor had the authority to indict Greg Stevens for murder.

Holt saw a state patrol officer parked on the shoulder of the highway and slowed down a few miles an hour. One person deserved to know what Holt had found. That's where he'd start. He placed the call.

"Who is this?" Cecil Burkdale said when he answered.

"Holt Douglas. I'm on my way back from Atlanta, and I need to see you."

"Who's in the car with you?"

"No one. Why?"

"I heard someone else talking."

"That's the radio. I'll turn it down." Holt lowered the volume. "Is that better?"

Burkdale was silent for a moment. "Yes. That's what I was hearing. What do you want to show me?"

"Something I can't talk about on the phone."

"Of course, I understand," Burkdale replied. "Where do you want to meet? It can't be at your house."

"Or yours," Holt answered. "All I need is a laptop to show you what I have. How about the courthouse? We can use the jury room."

"No way. Let's meet in the parking lot for the supermarket on Jackson Street. It's a busy place. We can sit in your car. I'm one hundred percent sure mine has been compromised."

Holt checked the time. "I'll see you there in forty-five minutes."

"Park in the southeast corner of the lot. There's a buffer of trees that provides privacy."

"I wouldn't have it any other way."

Holt ended the call. Burkdale was a mess, but the bookkeeper had stumbled onto the truth. Holt stopped at his house to check on Henry and drop off one copy of the DVD. He wrote "Video—Night of Rex Meredith's Death" on a slipcover and put the DVD in plain view on the nightstand beside his bed. If something happened to him, he didn't want what he'd uncovered to be buried.

Jackson Street was close to the veterinarian's office in an area that also contained a mix of cheap rental properties and light-manufacturing facilities. The supermarket occupied a 1950s building and sold groceries and general merchandise. It was the only place in town where someone could buy milk, cigarettes, beer, duct tape, lottery tickets, and an air filter for a 1979 Plymouth. There was no sign of Burkdale's car when Holt pulled into the parking lot. He drove to the southeast corner of the parking lot and backed into a space.

After ten minutes of watching a diverse assortment of humanity enter and leave the store, Holt was ready to give up on Burkdale. Then Burkdale's beat-up car turned into the parking lot. Holt could see Burkdale looking to both sides and then glancing over his shoulder. As he came closer, the bookkeeper avoided eye contact with Holt until he pulled into an empty space beside him. Burkdale opened the passenger door of Holt's car and spread an aluminum sunscreen across the windshield. Holt watched in silence.

"The aluminum has reflective qualities," Burkdale said. "It's not effective against something inside the vehicle, but it will disrupt anyone trying to listen via a radio-frequency device."

"Where's your gun?" Holt asked.

"In the car. Do I need it?"

"No."

Holt turned on his laptop. "What about someone eavesdropping on my wireless Internet connection? Are you worried about that?" he asked.

"Will you connect to the network in the store or through your service provider?"

"I didn't know they had Wi-Fi in the supermarket."

"They have everything in there."

"It doesn't matter," Holt said. "What I want to show you doesn't require a connection. It's on this DVD."

Holt inserted the disc into the computer and positioned the screen so Burkdale could see it.

"What is it?" Burkdale asked.

"Surveillance footage from the Meredith home the night Mr. Meredith died."

"Am I on it?" Burkdale asked with alarm in his eyes.

"Would that be a problem?" Holt asked.

"Powerful people twist things!"

Burkdale reached over, pressed the Eject button, grabbed the DVD, and bent it slightly between his fingers.

"I have four other copies," Holt said calmly. "If you have something you need to tell me, now would be the time to do it."

"What do you mean?"

"About Mr. Meredith's death."

"Are you accusing me of killing him?"

"No," Holt said in a level voice. "But the way you act would make anyone suspicious."

Burkdale reached for the door handle but then froze. Every fiber in Holt's body was on alert. Burkdale slowly turned his head toward Holt.

"I want to see the DVD," he said.

"Are you sure?"

"Yes, I have to know what I'm facing."

Holt didn't try to unravel Burkdale's response. The bookkeeper handed the disc to him, and Holt reloaded it. He positioned the laptop so Burkdale had a clear view and pressed the Play button. As the images flashed on the screen, Holt focused on Burkdale, who leaned over, his attention glued to the computer. Several times he blinked his eyes in rapid succession but didn't say anything. When the screen went to black, he sat back in his seat.

"I can't believe it," he said.

"Why not?"

Burkdale sniffled. Holt wasn't sure if he was about to cry or simply needed to blow his nose.

"There were plenty of times during the years since Mr. Meredith's death that I thought I was crazy. I mean, in my heart I knew Stevens had a hand in it, but to finally see it . . ."

Burkdale looked Holt in the eyes with obvious gratitude on his face.

"What can you add to the evidence?" Holt asked. "I don't want to seek an indictment until I have as much proof, both direct and circumstantial, as I can pull together. All you've told me so far is that Stevens spies on people, including his wife."

"And about the meeting I had with Mr. Meredith the night he died."

"Yes. Are you willing to sign an affidavit about your conversation and impressions of Mr. Meredith's mental state?"

"Who will see the affidavit?"

"Eventually anybody in the world who's interested. You will certainly have to testify in court."

Burkdale spoke slowly. "If Mr. Stevens isn't convicted, what would happen to me?"

"It's hard to say." Holt shrugged. "You'll have to make that decision without knowing the consequences. And I also want total access to anything on your computer that might be helpful."

Burkdale hesitated. He glanced out the window. Holt waited.

"You've got it."

"Do you want me to prepare an affidavit based on what you told me or do you want to write a draft yourself?"

"You know how to put it in legal language. But don't send it to me as an e-mail attachment. Call and we'll meet again to go over it."

"That won't be necessary," Holt replied.

"Why not?"

"Because we're going to do it right now."

Holt opened the word processing program on his computer.

"All affidavits begin the same," he said. "'Before the undersigned officer duly authorized to administer oaths, appeared Cecil Burkdale, who, being duly sworn, states the following on personal knowledge, information, and belief.'"

For the next forty-five minutes they hammered out Burkdale's affidavit. It was slow going at first, but Burkdale's reluctance lessened, and Holt composed the final paragraphs fairly quickly.

"I wish I had a printer and a notary public," Holt said when he saved the document. "Can we get together tomorrow to make it official?"

"They have print and notary services in the supermarket," Burkdale said.

"Are you sure?"

"Yes."

Holt transferred the affidavit to a flash drive. "Let's go," he said.

"You first," Burkdale responded. "I'll follow three minutes later."

"Whatever works for you," Holt said. "I'll print it out."

Holt didn't want to leave Burkdale alone in his car, but there wasn't an alternative. He removed the keys from the ignition and went inside the store. A heavily tattooed young woman sat on a stool behind one of two cash registers. He held up the flash drive.

"Against the back wall on the left," she said before he could ask a question. "It only takes debit cards."

Sure enough, there was an old desktop computer sitting beside a pinball machine. A sign indicated the cost for Internet and Skype usage, but the computer was also linked to a printer. Holt slid in his card and logged on. The printer was spitting out the affidavit when Burkdale entered the store. Holt logged out and went back to the cashier.

"This is an affidavit, and we need—"

"I'm a notary public. It's twenty dollars per document."

It was more than authorized by the law, but Holt wasn't going to quibble. He took a twenty-dollar bill from his pocket and laid it on the counter.

"Are you the affiant?" the woman asked Burkdale.

"Yes."

"Show me your driver's license."

Burkdale hesitated. Another customer came up to the register to check out.

"Do you want me to do this or not?" the woman asked.

Burkdale got out his wallet and held up his license without letting it go. The woman didn't look at it close enough to read it.

"Sign and drive," she said.

"She didn't swear me in." Burkdale looked at Holt.

"Is this thing true?" she asked.

"Uh, yes," Burkdale answered.

The woman handed Burkdale a cheap ballpoint pen. He signed the affidavit, and she scribbled her name and affixed a seal. Holt picked up the document from the counter.

"Thanks," Holt said to the woman.

"No problem, Mr. Douglas."

Burkdale started to say something, but Holt grabbed his arm and led him out of the store.

"How do you know her?" Burkdale demanded as soon as they were in the parking lot.

"I don't. Either she's had friends or relatives in criminal court, or I've prosecuted someone who robbed the store."

"You don't remember?"

"No. Most victims aren't as rich as Rex Meredith. And few defendants are as cunning as Greg Stevens."

43

After leaving the sheriff's department, Trish drove around for half an hour, then wandered aimlessly through a clothing store until her normal time to leave for home. She didn't want to arrive early and face questions from her mother. Trish was worried that her red and puffy eyes would reveal more than she wanted to say. She checked her face in the rearview mirror of her car before going into the house. Except for an impossible-to-conceal sadness, she appeared okay.

"I'm home!" she called out in a cheery voice as soon as she opened the door.

"Hey!" her mother responded from the living room. "I'm in here."

Trish went into the kitchen and spoke through the open space between the two rooms. "I'm going to eat a snack and take a nap," she said. "It was a stressful day at work."

Marge, who was sitting in a special recliner in the living room, turned so she could see her.

"Can we talk for a few minutes?" she asked. "It's been a lonely day. I've not had a single phone call."

Trish drank half a glass of milk and nibbled on an oatmeal-and-raisin cookie. She then stepped into the living room but kept her distance from her mother.

"What do you want to talk about?"

"Would you sit down?"

"I've been sitting all day."

Marge made a sound that could only be interpreted as exasperation. "Okay, stand if you want to," she said. "Is there anything you can tell me about your day that won't violate the rules?"

Trish's lower lip trembled, and she sat down on a love seat across from Marge. She held up her right index finger and thumb so that they almost touched.

"I'm this close to getting fired," she said.

Marge pushed herself up straighter in the recliner with her hands and arms and shifted her weight so she was looking directly at Trish.

"I've thought something was wrong for several weeks," she said. "You've tried to hide it, but your face hasn't been very cooperative. If you don't tell me, I don't know how to pray for you."

Trish sighed. "It has to do with Holt Douglas, the assistant district attorney."

Marge listened as Trish unburdened her heart, including her fantasy crush on Holt and discovery of his secret past. The only thing she left out was their cooperation in the Rex Meredith investigation. She described it simply as "a cold case investigation that went very bad."

"Why didn't you say anything to me about this?" Marge asked.

"I didn't want to upset you by reopening what happened to Daddy and you."

"Do you think a day passes that I don't think about what happened? It's with me every morning when I have to lift my legs out of bed with my arms." Marge touched her heart. "But the pain in here is worse than the paralysis in my legs. The only way I make it is with a daily infusion of God's grace."

"I need some of that myself. One of the detectives saw me reading about Holt and his dead friend on my computer and dragged me into an interrogation room where he and the sheriff grilled me and made me record a statement."

"Why would they do that?"

"I guess so they can prosecute Holt for driving drunk and killing someone or use it to force him to undermine Ralph Granger. There's a bunch of politics involved."

"And you feel sorry for him?"

"No," Trish said emphatically. "He deserves to go to jail. But the situation has put me in a terrible light with the sheriff and placed my job in jeopardy. Talking to you helps me see what I have to do. I have to treat Holt Douglas like he's one of the deadbeat dads on my docket. Some of them haven't paid child support in years and years, but when I catch them there is a day of reckoning. It's going to be the same for him. Even though what happened to me today was excruciating, it was necessary."

Holt had to move fast. The US Army had developed shock-and-awe tactics for reasons that applied equally well to a criminal case. Overwhelming Greg Stevens quickly would increase the chance of ultimate success. Even the best defense lawyers struggled when they had to fight from behind and off balance.

After leaving Cecil Burkdale, Holt avoided the office. Instead, he drove to the church to see Bishop Pennington. The minister wasn't in his office, but Holt found him in the sanctuary walking through the pews.

"What are you doing?" Holt asked.

"Combining physical and spiritual exercise," the bishop replied, stopping at the end of a row. "It takes me ten to fifteen minutes to walk through all the pews and around the inside of the sanctuary. I'm praying for God's presence to be here and touch every person who walks through these doors. It doesn't get my heart rate up, but it's good for my heart. You ought to consider praying in the courtroom before a trial or for Paxton when you're out running—"

Holt didn't want to get drawn into a religious conversation.

"I'm not sure how that would work," he interrupted. "I'm going to prepare a draft affidavit for Sonny based on the video and the notes he wrote. If I need your help, can I call you?"

"Yes. When will the sheriff's department get involved?"

"That's complicated. At this point I'm handling the investigation on my own."

The bishop raised his eyebrows in question.

"Don't ask," Holt interjected. "Trust me."

—

Holt drove to the office so he could prepare Sonny's affidavit. In his jacket pocket was the DVD to put in the evidence locker. He stopped by Belinda's desk.

"I need an evidence envelope for this," he said, holding up the disc.

She opened a drawer in her desk and took out a small brown envelope. "What is it?" she asked.

"A surveillance video in a John Doe case."

"Drug charge?"

"No, it's not even an open file, but I'd like to assign a number to keep track of it."

Belinda swiveled in her chair so she faced her computer screen.

In a few seconds she jotted down a case number on the envelope and handed it to Holt.

"Do you want me to lock it up for you?"

"Not yet." Holt paused. "Hey, would you be available later this afternoon to notarize an affidavit for a witness? We need to go to his house."

"Sure, unless Ralph chains me to my desk on a project for him."

"It would only take a few minutes. I'm going to make sure the witness agrees before giving you a call."

"Where will you be?"

"Not far."

Holt took the DVD to his office, closed the door, watched it again, and took notes to include in Sonny's sworn statement. Even though he'd watched the video several times, the images hadn't lost their calculated, coldhearted impact. He was typing the opening paragraphs of the affidavit when Sally buzzed his phone.

"Detective Clovis is on line four," she said.

"Did he mention a case?"

"No, but he said it was important."

"I'm in the middle of something more important. Connect him to my voice mail."

An hour later, Holt put the finishing touches on the affidavit. When he printed it out and reviewed it, he found a couple of errors that needed to be corrected. He did so, then grabbed the evidence envelope so he could drop it off with Belinda, but she wasn't at her desk. Jim was taking a file from a nearby cabinet.

"Do you know where Belinda is?" he asked the other assistant DA.

"She had to make a delivery for Ralph but should be back in half an hour."

"I can't wait. I'll call her."

Holt left with the DVD and the affidavit in his briefcase. On his way out of the building, he ran into Ralph.

"Where are you off to in such a hurry?" the DA asked.

Holt hadn't realized how fast he was walking. "I'm late for a meeting with a witness."

"Which case?"

"Can we talk about it later?" Holt responded as he continued past the DA. "It will take a few minutes to lay it out with the detail you deserve."

Ralph said something else, but Holt didn't hear it. Nothing the DA could have said would have stopped Holt anyway. He drove through two orange lights on his way to the Meredith house. Holt was both nervous and excited.

Unlike the depictions of prosecutors on TV and in novels, an assistant DA rarely became involved in the nuts-and-bolts investigation of cases. Detectives and police officers prepared the cases with advice from lawyers limited to technical legal issues. For a prosecutor to build a case from the ground up without significant law enforcement help was extremely rare. It was a major adrenaline rush. Holt went around the back of the house to Sonny's cottage. Before he reached the door, the caretaker came out to meet him. He was dressed in blue jeans and a dingy white shirt. He wasn't wearing a cap, and his head was covered with wispy white hair.

"Is it okay for me to go over your affidavit with you now?" Holt asked.

"Be that." Sonny nodded briskly and started walking toward the main house. "Me call that him bishop."

"You called Bishop Pennington?"

"Be that."

They entered through the kitchen door.

"We can sit at the table in here," Holt suggested.

Ignoring him, Sonny continued through the kitchen and across the hallway to the study door. Puzzled, Holt followed.

"Why do you want to meet in here?" he asked.

Sonny pointed at the massive portrait of Rex Meredith on the wall. Holt wasn't sure exactly what Sonny meant.

"You want to do this in a place where Mr. Meredith can see you?"

Sonny nodded and then pointed at the spot on the floor where Rex Meredith's body fell. It was bizarre, but Holt wasn't going to quibble about the venue. All he wanted was for Sonny to read and approve the statement so he could call Belinda and get her over to the house to notarize it. Once that happened, Holt would be ready to lay out the case for Ralph. They sat close to each other in the two leather wing chairs with a small end table between them. The thought crossed Holt's mind that they were probably sitting where Rex Meredith and Cecil Burkdale sat on the night Meredith died. He involuntarily shivered.

"Here's the affidavit," Holt said, opening his briefcase and handing the paperwork to Sonny. "There are some big words at the beginning, but after that I tried to make it sound like you. The notes you gave me the other day helped a lot."

Sonny squinted at the papers for a few seconds, then laid them down and pointed to his eyes.

"My glasses be," he said, pointing with his finger toward the rear wall of the study and his cottage beyond.

"Okay. Do you want me to wait here?"

Sonny left the room. A bell beeped when the caretaker left the house. Holt remained on the edge of the chair. It didn't seem right to lean back and relax against the supple leather. He took out his cell phone and called Bishop Pennington. The bishop didn't answer, and Holt left a message that he and Sonny were going over the affidavit. The bell beeped again, and seconds later Sonny returned to the room. The caretaker put a pair of cheap reading glasses on his nose and picked up the affidavit. Holt handed him a pen.

"If you see something that's incorrect or isn't the truth, mark it. I want this to be completely accurate."

Sonny grunted and started reading. It was slow going. Several times he made marks on a page. The beep for the door sounded again.

"That's Bishop Pennington," Holt said.

Sonny kept reading. Holt stood up to go to the kitchen and let the bishop know where they were. Before he reached the study door, it opened.

And Greg Stevens came into the room.

44

Stevens was wearing a dark suit and red tie. He locked eyes with Holt as soon as he stepped into the room.

"What are you doing here?" he asked.

"Talking with Sonny," Holt replied.

"No one talks to Sonny."

Stevens quickly surveyed the room. His eyes stopped at the affidavit in Sonny's hands.

"What's going on in here? Give me those papers," he demanded.

Sonny, his eyes wide, held out the affidavit, but before Stevens could take it, Holt snatched the sheets from the caretaker's hands and dropped them into the open briefcase. He stood and faced Stevens.

"That information belongs to me, not you."

"What information?"

Before Holt answered, Sonny pointed at the portrait over the mantel. "Be that him."

Holt started to push past Stevens and leave. However, concern for Sonny held him back.

"What does this have to do with Mr. Meredith?" Stevens asked Holt.

"When the time is right, you'll find out," Holt responded, trying to sound confident and in charge.

Sonny grunted and made the motion with his fingers of a gun going off. Stevens's eyes got bigger.

"No!" he yelled at Sonny. "What did you tell him?"

Holt quickly placed himself between the caretaker and Stevens. He held up his hands with his palms out.

"It's over. I know how Mr. Meredith died."

Greg Stevens's face was bright red. He clenched his hands together into fists. Holt braced himself. He was younger, bigger, and stronger, but he hadn't been in a physical fight since ninth grade. He kept his eyes on Stevens as he spoke.

"There are multiple copies of the surveillance tape from the night of Mr. Meredith's death, and there's nothing you can do about it."

"What tape?"

"The real tape, not the phony one you staged and gave to Detective Clovis. And Sonny is prepared to verify it."

As quickly as Stevens's face became red, it now turned pale. He looked at Sonny and then Holt, who touched his briefcase.

"Sonny's testimony and the surveillance video are going to send you to prison for the murder of Rex Meredith."

"Me?" Stevens blurted out in shock. "That's impossible!"

Holt's indignation rose to the surface. "Mr. Stevens, you may hire the best lawyers money can buy, but facts don't lie, and whether it's one year, two years, or longer, you will be held responsible for what you've done."

Stevens's eyes darted about the room like a cornered animal. Holt wasn't sure if he was looking for something to pick up and use as a weapon or seeking a way to escape. Finally, his shoulders slumped, and he collapsed on the small leather couch. He put his face in his hands and didn't move for several seconds. Raising his head, he looked at Holt with surrender in his eyes.

"I want to see a copy of the tape," he said.

Holt hesitated. The only question in his mind was whether there was an advantage to withholding the information until later or showing it now. Stevens would eventually watch the DVD while sitting in a paneled conference room with his lawyers. When that happened, Holt would be stuck in his cheap office in Paxton. Holt wanted to see Stevens's initial reaction to the images. He reached into the briefcase and took out the envelope.

"Okay."

Holt watched Stevens as he turned on the TV and powered up the old DVD player beneath it. The former accountant remained in his place on the couch. Sonny scratched the top of his head and shifted nervously in his chair. Holt inserted the DVD and waited for it to load. Never in his life had time passed so slowly. Finally, he pressed the Play button, then moved to the side so he could watch Stevens's reactions. The copy had been edited so it contained only a few seconds of the empty study.

When Rex Meredith's body appeared, Holt saw Stevens's jaw muscles tighten. His eyes remained glued to the screen, and he began rubbing his hands together as if washing them. When he saw himself leaning over to place the gun in Rex Meredith's hand, Stevens nodded his head as if reliving the moment. He showed no sign of emotion. As soon as Meredith's face became visible, Stevens looked away.

"Is that it?" he asked.

Holt was incredulous. "Believe me, Mr. Stevens," he replied, "it's more than enough. Did you record another tape and give it to Detective Clovis?"

"Yes," Stevens said as his shoulders slumped forward.

"What's on the tape you gave Clovis?"

"I come into the room and discover the body. The EMTs arrived a few minutes later. I'd called 911 immediately after the replacement video started recording."

It was a huge admission, the first step to a full-blown confession. Holt decided to lay another foundation stone, albeit a cracked one.

"I've also obtained an affidavit from Cecil Burkdale," he said. "He says that on the evening of Mr. Meredith's death, he and your father-in-law met in this room, and Meredith told Burkdale you were going to be removed from your position at Meredith Enterprises."

"That's true."

Holt glanced at Sonny. The caretaker was hearing everything. As soon as possible Holt would depose Sonny to preserve his testimony in case he died before Stevens went to trial.

Stevens spoke: "Rex came over to our house a few hours before that and told me I was going to be fired. My wife began crying. Rex had been drinking, and when Valerie got emotional it made him furious. He started throwing and breaking things."

"Is that why he later sent Claudine over to clean up?"

"Yes."

"Burkdale thought you and your wife had a fight."

"No." Stevens shook his head. "I love Valerie more than my own life."

It was a startling statement from a cold-blooded murderer. Stevens seemed vulnerable, and Holt decided to exploit it.

"Do you want to tell me everything else that happened?" he asked in a soft voice.

Stevens didn't respond. Holt waited. Stevens took out his phone and stared at it and then closed his eyes. He held up his phone so Holt could see a photo of Valerie in a yellow-and-red sundress standing on a white beach with her hair blowing in a breeze.

"That's my favorite picture of Valerie. Did you know she's the most sensitive, courageous person in the whole world?"

Confused, Holt didn't know what to say. Greg Stevens was following an invisible path. He glanced again at the photo on his phone.

"I shot Mr. Meredith," he said in a monotone voice.

Holt paused to let the impact of the words sink in. He'd done it. He'd broken the case. It was his greatest moment of honoring Calico's dream.

"Is that what you need to know?"

"Yes, but I want details, from the time Mr. Meredith came to your house until—"

"No," Stevens interrupted. "I've told you all that's necessary. I don't want to relive that night ever again. It's tormented my dreams for years. Maybe now I can find peace."

"Will you sign a statement admitting what you've told me?"

"Yes. Write up a confession, and I'll sign it."

Holt hurriedly wrote down a statement in which Greg Stevens admitted to the murder of Rex Meredith. He added a few sentences that eliminated self-defense or any other basis for a justifiable killing. When he went over the language, Stevens didn't argue or change a word. Holt couldn't believe it. Stevens's will was broken as totally as a scared juvenile arrested on a shoplifting charge. He signed the confession. Sonny and Holt witnessed the signature. Holt put the confession in his briefcase and snapped it shut.

"How long do I have before I'm arrested?" Stevens asked in a flat tone of voice. "I want to say good-bye to Valerie."

"A warrant will be issued within a couple of hours."

"I'll be at home. Call me, and I'll come to the jail. I don't want to be led from the house in handcuffs."

"Okay. And you know there's no point in trying to flee—"

"If I was going to run, Mr. Douglas, I would have left as soon as I saw the surveillance video. Deep down, I always knew this day would come. I just didn't know when and how."

Holt waited until Stevens was gone before leaving the house. He gave his cell phone number to Sonny. Holt could tell that the caretaker was still in shock.

"Valerie," Sonny said in a slightly garbled manner, then stopped and touched his heart.

"You love Valerie?"

Sonny nodded and pointed to the portrait of Rex Meredith.

"You've shown your loyalty and love to both of them for many years," Holt said. "What happened tonight won't change that. But now your conscience is clear."

—

Holt drove away from the Meredith house. There was a lot to do. The first step would be to provide Ralph Granger the details he'd promised. Holt glanced down at his briefcase on the seat beside him and thought about the confession it contained. Murder suspects were a peculiar breed. Some were conscienceless brutes. But others, like Stevens, were seemingly mild-mannered, nonviolent people who, for a twisted reason or a moment of uncontrolled passion, committed the ultimate crime.

Holt pulled into the parking lot of the DA's office and got out of the car. He wished he had more time to prepare his presentation for Ralph, but that wasn't possible. He doubted Stevens would flee; however, the same unpredictability that had caused him to become a murderer might convince him to do something else irrational. Holt walked rapidly through the front door of the DA's office. Standing in the reception area were Butch Clovis and Nick Watkins.

"Stop right there," Clovis said as soon as he saw Holt. "Don't take another step."

45

"You've been fired and have to leave the premises immediately," Clovis said.

"That's crazy!" Holt protested as he moved forward. "I want to talk to Ralph Granger."

Clovis held out his hand. "Mr. Granger is the one who asked me to come over and make sure you don't attempt to return to your former office. I left you a voice mail to set up a meeting, but you ignored it."

Belinda came into the reception area with a large cardboard box in her arms. Holt could tell she'd been crying.

"What's going on?" Holt asked her. "Is Ralph back there?"

"Here are the personal items from your office," Belinda said and sniffled. "There may be a few other odds and ends. I'll double-check and let you know."

Holt moved close as Belinda handed him the box. He spoke in a low voice. "Belinda, I don't know what's behind this, but do you remember the case I told you about before I left the office—"

Holt felt a hand on his shoulder. It was Nick. He pulled Holt backward.

"This way, Mr. Douglas."

Holt angrily shrugged off the deputy's hand. Belinda, her eyes downcast, retreated through the door into the office suite. Sally wasn't at her desk. They'd obviously cleared the area in anticipation of Holt's arrival.

"It's time for you to leave," Clovis said.

"You're going to regret this," Holt said to the detective.

"Move on before we arrest you for trespassing and disorderly conduct."

"A citizen has a right to be on county property," Holt shot back.

"And I'll be glad to take you to jail so you can trot out your defense in front of Judge Lomax."

Steaming, Holt moved toward the door. He didn't want to risk an arrest because then Clovis would inventory the contents of his briefcase at the jail. If he did, Greg Stevens's confession would end up in the sheriff's department shredder.

"Who's going to tell me why I got fired?" Holt asked as he pushed the box against the front door to open it.

"I'm sure you'll receive appropriate notification in the mail," Clovis replied. "In the meantime, Mr. Granger instructed me to inform you that any attempt by you to reenter the district attorney's office complex will not be tolerated."

Holt passed through the door and into the parking lot. Clovis and the deputy kept in step with him. Holt reached his car and pressed the button that unlocked the doors.

"Is there information related to any of your cases in that briefcase?" Clovis asked. "If so, it needs to remain here."

"No," Holt replied. "All paperwork for my open files is in the district attorney's office."

"Open the briefcase so I can inspect it," Clovis responded.

Holt threw the briefcase into the backseat of his car and closed the door. "Not without a search warrant."

Holt watched the jaw muscles of Clovis's face tighten. He knew the detective could open the car door, take the briefcase, and later claim Holt opened it voluntarily. Holt took out his phone, turned on the voice record function, and faced Nick.

"Officer Watkins, did you hear what I told Detective Clovis about the need for probable cause and a search warrant before searching my briefcase?"

"Get out of here," Clovis cut in. "You and your smart mouth."

Holt got in the car and locked the doors. He carefully backed out of the parking space and left the lot. His body was trembling. There were only two possible reasons why he'd been fired.

Greg Stevens or Trish Carmichael.

—

Trish was working the second shift and didn't notice when Butch Clovis left the sheriff's office with Nick Watkins. She was on the phone with the shotgun-toting Granville Jenkins.

"My mama says Ricky is going to be in town within the next couple of days to see my sister," Jenkins said.

"Why did your mother let you know? She knows you don't like him."

"It came up when I asked about getting some hay out of the barn behind their house. I need my sister to move the truck, and Mama said Ricky was going to come back in a couple of days to get it."

"I really appreciate the call. Is there any way you can let me know for sure when he's there? I can't waste another trip. I want to make it count."

"I'll do what I can, but if he sees me coming, Ricky ain't going to hang around. He knows I'd like nothing better than to fill his britches with a load of buckshot."

Trish didn't doubt the sincerity of Jenkins's intention. "Okay. Do what you can. Call the dispatcher if you spot him. They can get in touch with me 24/7."

Trish hung up the phone. She'd finished updating two other cases when her line buzzed, and she pressed the intercom button.

"Holt Douglas is on the phone for you."

Trish's stomach immediately twisted in a knot. "Ask him which case it's about."

She held the phone and waited. She had no obligation to speak to Holt except on official business. The dispatcher came back on the line.

"He says a murder case."

"Okay," Trish sighed. "I'll take it."

She opened a new screen on her computer so she could take notes of the conversation in case Detective Clovis or the sheriff grilled her later about it, then pressed the blinking light on her phone.

"This is Trish Carmichael," she said.

"A little over an hour ago Greg Stevens confessed to killing his father-in-law," Holt said.

Trish's fingers, poised above the keyboard, didn't move.

"There's way more to it than I can go into," Holt continued, "but I need to know something else first. Do you have any idea why I've been fired from the district attorney's office?"

"You got fired?"

"Yes, and either Greg Stevens or you is responsible for it."

Trish swallowed. "It's probably me."

"What do you mean, 'probably'?" Holt asked, his voice louder.

Trish felt shaky. Her comparison of Holt to one of her deadbeat dads wasn't holding up in the face of reality.

"Sheriff Blackstone and Detective Clovis know about your involvement in the death of your friend. They took a recorded statement from me."

The phone was silent for a moment. Trish bit her lower lip.

"I hope betraying my trust satisfies the bitterness of your heart," Holt said in a steely tone of voice. "What I did years ago was wrong. But you're going to have to live with what you've done to me now."

The phone went dead.

—

Holt's anger had no outlet. On the brink of prosecuting the biggest case of his career, he'd been procedurally handcuffed and the key thrown away. Possible plans of attack raced through his mind so fast he couldn't slow them down enough to evaluate them. He considered everything from parking in Ralph Granger's driveway until the DA came out of his house to getting in touch with the *Atlanta Journal-Constitution* and offering a reporter an exclusive scoop about the cold-case murder of a small-town multimillionaire. In the end, he settled on a less dramatic step.

He called Bishop Pennington. Utilizing the bishop's influence in the community would be the most honorable way to handle Greg Stevens. Once word got out that Bishop Pennington had gone to the sheriff's department and DA's office, action against Stevens would have to be taken.

"It's Holt. Why didn't you come to the Meredith house?"

"I didn't know you were there until after you left. Then I had to deal with a pastoral emergency."

"I have something urgent to talk to you about. Can you come to my house?"

"I'll be there in five minutes."

Holt stood on his deck. It was a humid, stuffy night. He thought about Greg Stevens waiting for a call to come to the jail. Henry barked, signaling the bishop's arrival. Holt opened the front door, and the two men sat at the kitchen table.

"I'll begin with my meeting with Sonny," Holt said.

Holt moved quickly to the encounter with Greg Stevens and showed Bishop Pennington the signed confession. The bishop pressed his lips together tightly while he silently read it.

"Stevens's confession makes the case," Holt said, leaning back in the chair. "But when I returned to the DA's office, I was met by a detective who told me I'd been fired and escorted me off the premises. It turns out that Trish Carmichael told Sheriff Blackstone about my role in Calico's death. Ralph Granger didn't have the guts to come out and talk to me, but an assistant DA with a past like mine would be a huge political liability. Ralph wouldn't tolerate that long enough to listen to an explanation."

"I'm sorry," the bishop said.

"But right now my biggest concern isn't myself. It's what to do about Greg Stevens. You're an influential man in this town, and you're not afraid to do the right thing no matter the cost. Will you help me?"

The bishop put his hands together in front of him on the table, bowed his head, and closed his eyes for several seconds. When he raised his head, he looked at Holt.

"No, I can't."

"Why not?" Holt asked in surprise. "Justice demands it."

The bishop reached out and touched Greg Stevens's confession. "Because nothing written on this piece of paper is true."

Holt's mouth dropped open. He was stunned.

"How can you say that?" he managed. "How do you know that?"

"Trust me. This will never stand up in court."

"Tell me why."

"I can't do that, either." The bishop reluctantly shook his head. "What I know I learned in confidence."

Holt's mind was churning. "If a person tells you something about a crime, the clergy confidentiality rules don't apply," he said.

"I don't know there was a crime."

"Rex Meredith was murdered!" Holt raised his voice. "You saw the video!"

"The video doesn't show everything that happened that night."

"Burkdale?" Holt guessed. "You've been talking to Cecil Burkdale? There's a seductive quality to his paranoia—"

"I've not been meeting with Cecil Burkdale," the bishop replied, standing up. "And I'd better get going. My silence is only going to frustrate you. I'm terribly sorry about your job, and I'll be praying—"

"No!" Holt slammed his fist down on the table. "You cannot do this to me!"

The bishop stopped. Holt stared at him with a mixture of anger and desperation.

"Where can I make a private phone call?" the bishop asked.

"My spare bedroom," Holt replied immediately. "I'll stay in here."

While Holt waited, each click of the old-fashioned clock on the kitchen wall seemed like an eternity. He glanced down at Henry, who stretched his jaws wide in a big yawn. Finally, the bishop returned.

"Let's go," he said.

"Where?" Holt asked as he stood up.

"To the Meredith house."

"Who's going to be there?"

"Greg and Valerie Stevens."

46

Holt drove. Bishop Pennington sent a clear message that he didn't want to talk by staring out the window. When they arrived at the Meredith mansion, Holt saw Valerie's SUV in the driveway.

"You're sending me into this blind," Holt said as he pulled in behind her vehicle. "What's going on?"

"That's not for me to say," the bishop replied. "And don't ask me any more questions."

They got out of the car and walked around to the kitchen door. The bishop knocked, and in a few moments Sonny let them in. He looked even frailer to Holt than he had earlier. He didn't attempt to speak but led them to the study. Greg and Valerie Stevens were sitting close together on the small couch. Valerie's eyes were swollen and red. Greg Stevens's face was drawn. Holt and the bishop sat down in the wing chairs. Sonny took a seat directly beneath the portrait of Rex Meredith.

"Please don't make me talk," Valerie said in a trembling voice.

"There's nothing you have to say to me," the bishop replied softly. "But as I told both of you on the phone a few minutes ago, Holt has a right to the truth. What happens after that is in God's hands."

Greg Stevens looked at Holt. "Where do you want me to start?"

"All the bishop told me is that your confession is false. I need to know why you lied."

Stevens paused for a moment. "First, you need some background. Sonny can back me up that Rex had a wicked temper, especially when he'd been drinking."

Holt looked at the caretaker, who nodded his head.

"When he was drunk he could be physically abusive to Carrie, and before I came on the scene, to Valerie."

Holt saw Valerie's lower lip quiver.

"It didn't happen a lot, but when it did, it was bad. I'm not a doctor, but I've always suspected the cerebral blood clot that killed Carrie was related to what Rex did to her over the years."

"Bad that," Sonny interjected.

Valerie covered her face with her hands and started to stand up. Her husband held her down with his arm.

"Please," he said gently.

Valerie remained seated but kept her head lowered.

"He didn't punch her with his fists," Greg continued. "He'd push her against the wall, throw something at her, or knock her down. After he sobered up, he'd apologize and things would be somewhat normal for months."

It was the familiar story of a battered wife and falsely repentant husband that Holt had heard several times since becoming a prosecutor. Abuse didn't recognize economic boundaries.

"Rex and Carrie married when Valerie was twelve. Sometimes she'd get caught up in the fights, usually trying to protect her mother. She has a scar beneath her right eye caused by a piece of broken glass from a picture frame that shattered when Rex threw it at Carrie and Valerie got in the way."

Valerie raised her head, and Holt could see the faint outline of a scar that was only partially concealed by makeup.

"Rex took Valerie to the hospital and told the ER doctor she'd fallen in the bathroom. Because Rex was involved, nobody asked any questions."

"Were any reports of domestic violence filed with the sheriff's department?" Holt asked.

"Not by Carrie. I think Rex's second wife made some complaints, but in this county nothing was done."

Holt turned to Valerie. "Is everything he's saying true?"

"Yes," she said in a soft voice, "but it's only a tiny percentage of what we went through. Greg doesn't know most of it because I've never told him."

"Did your stepfather hurt you on the day of his death?" Holt asked.

Valerie turned to her husband. "You tell him."

"Yes, he did." Greg nodded grimly. "Like I said before, he came over drunk late in the afternoon and told us I was going to be fired. Valerie started crying and begged him not to do it. He knocked over a large cabinet and ripped down some curtains. Then he grabbed a heavy lamp and swung it at her head like a baseball bat. Valerie dodged the first blow, but he swung again and hit her in the side. I think she may have fractured a few ribs. I'd tried to reason with him, but at that point I grabbed him and forced him out of the house."

"Did you go to the doctor?" Holt asked Valerie.

"No. I put an ice pack on my ribs and took some medication I had at the house."

"An hour or so later, Rex called, apologized, and said he wanted to see us. I'd had enough. I didn't care if I never worked another day with Meredith Enterprises. However, Valerie wanted to try to patch things up, and we came over here."

Greg Stevens stopped and looked straight into Holt's eyes.

"I brought a gun with me. I wasn't going to accept a hollow apology.

In a warped way, he blamed other people for making him mad enough to react violently."

"I've heard that before," Holt said.

"And if Rex threatened Valerie again, I was going to stop it once and for all. The cycle of abuse in their family was going to end. When we got here, Rex had calmed down, and we came into the study to talk. He was sitting in the chair where you are now. He wanted to know how bad Valerie was hurt and told her again how sorry he was that he'd lost his temper. She was willing to listen to him, but I wasn't. I told Rex what I thought about him. That set him off again."

Stevens pointed to the small table between the two wing chairs. "Rex pulled open the drawer in that table, took out a pistol, and started waving it around. I told him to put it away. Instead, he fired a shot that hit a painting on the opposite wall. I wasn't going to take any chances, so I pulled out my gun. Valerie screamed. She grabbed Rex's gun, jerked it out of his hand, and shot him in the chest."

Valerie's head sank lower. Sonny's mouth dropped open in shock.

"Where were you when she fired the shot?" Holt asked softly.

"Standing over there," Greg said, pointing to a spot to the left of where Holt was sitting and toward the hallway door. "Valerie was in front of me. She dropped the gun, and I ran over to check on Rex. I suspected right away he wasn't going to make it and decided to make his death look like a suicide. I wiped her fingerprints from the gun and stuck it in Rex's hand. Then I remembered the security system. I told Valerie to take out the tape while I hid my gun in the kitchen. I then put in a new tape without realizing another one had recorded a portion of what happened before it flipped over in the carousel. I staged the tape I gave to Butch Clovis to support a finding of suicide."

Holt's mind was spinning. "Did Mr. Meredith point the gun at either you or Valerie?"

Greg hesitated. "If I tell you yes, she can plead self-defense, can't she?"

"Yes."

Greg reached over and took Valerie's hand. She looked up at him with tearstained cheeks, then faced Holt.

"Rex didn't point the gun at Greg or me," she said. "And if I'm going to be punished, I'll have to accept it. No matter how much he loves me, I can't let Greg try to take the blame for what I did."

Holt leaned back in the chair. He looked up at the portrait of Rex Meredith and then at Greg and Valerie Stevens sitting close together on the couch. He thought about himself; he thought about Calico.

"I don't know what verdict a jury would return if it heard your story," he said slowly. "They might decide you acted in self-defense; they might look at Mr. Meredith's history of abuse and conclude if he pulled out a gun and fired a shot he deserved to die; or they might find you guilty of manslaughter or murder and send you to prison for the rest of your life."

Valerie looked at Holt with a childlike fear.

"But I'm not here to judge you. And I don't have the power to charge you with any crime."

"What do you mean?" Greg Stevens asked. "You work at the DA's office."

"I was fired two hours ago."

Greg and Valerie couldn't hide their shock. Holt continued, "The important part for you is that I don't have an obligation to report you to the sheriff's department or inform Ralph Granger. As far as I'm concerned, what you've told me will stay within these walls."

Valerie's eyes grew bigger. Greg grabbed her hand.

"Thank you," she whispered.

"Why did you lose your job?" Greg asked.

"Something in my past didn't stay hidden."

—

Holt and Bishop Pennington walked outside. Even on this muggy night, Holt felt strangely refreshed. He turned to the bishop.

"Why do I feel better?" he asked.

"Because mercy triumphs over judgment."

"I assume that's someplace in the Bible."

"Correct. There are many facets to justice. You found a new one tonight."

47

Trish, a growing pile of used tissues in front of her, sat at the kitchen table with Marge and Keith.

"I'm sorry and ashamed," she said to Keith, wiping tears from her eyes. "I played you along while I was fantasizing about Holt Douglas. Then when I found out about his past, I spent way too much time hoping he would have to pay for his sins."

Keith looked down at the table and remained silent.

"What are you going to do next?" Marge asked.

"Crawl in a hole and not come out."

"It will be crowded with two of us in there," Marge said.

"That's just it," Trish said. "You're trapped in that chair, but you're more free on the inside than I am. If Daddy were alive and saw the way I've acted . . ."

Trish grabbed another tissue.

"He'd tell you to rise up and walk," Marge said, then leaned forward as much as she could. "Look at me."

Trish raised her tear-streaked face.

"Everyone who cares about you knows how stuck you've been since your daddy died. We've not been talking behind your back, but some unhealed sores can't be hidden. The beautiful thing is that the Lord has surrounded you with people who want to see you whole and would do anything in the world to help make it happen."

"I would," Keith interjected. "I'd do anything for you."

Keith's words sent another rivulet of tears streaming down Trish's face.

"Will you forgive me?" Trish sniffled.

Keith took a deep breath and looked directly in her face. "Yes."

Trish reached across the table and grabbed Keith's hand. He pulled her hand to his lips.

"Thank you," she said. "I'm sorry you have to see me like this—"

"No," he interrupted. "No matter what, you'll always be beautiful to me."

After Keith left, Trish returned to the living room where Marge was sitting in her chair with her eyes closed. Trish moved toward her bedroom.

"We're not finished yet," Marge said.

Trish stopped. "What else could there be?"

"Holt Douglas has given you a chance to take a big step toward your own healing."

"How?"

"Because if you can forgive him, it will help you forgive the boy who hit us. Trish, I love you, but what Holt said about the bitterness in your heart is true."

Trish leaned against the entranceway to the living room. "But, Mama—" she started to say.

There was an anguish in Marge's face that spoke louder than words.

"Okay," Trish said in surrender. "You're right. I've put that off for too long."

"Part of your healing will be asking Holt to forgive you. You can't take back what you've set in motion in his life, but you can tell him how sorry you are for doing it."

"It will be so embarrassing, and I'm not sure he'll even talk to me."

"That's all I'm going to say," Marge said. "Listen to your heart."

—

When Holt woke up, it took a couple of seconds for the events of the previous day to sink in. The sound of paws scratching the kitchen door that led out to the deck forced him out of bed. After he let Henry out, Holt slipped on a pair of jeans and brewed a pot of coffee. He was pouring the first cup when there was a loud knock on his door. He peeked through the living room window. It was Skip.

"I had to come by and see you on my way to work," Skip said. "I was totally shocked when I heard the news. I tried to call, but your phone was turned off."

"What did you hear? Ralph wouldn't talk to me, so I don't know how he spun it for the public."

"He issued a press release that went out to all the lawyers in the circuit late yesterday afternoon. Basically, he said you lied on your employment application about potential criminal conduct in your past. According to Ralph, the district attorney's office has a zero tolerance policy when it comes to the integrity of people enforcing the law in the Coosawattee Judicial Circuit."

"That's pretty much it. I can't blame him. If you're looking for a defamation of character case, I'm not a good prospect."

"What's he talking about?"

"Can you stay for a cup of coffee?"

"For you? Of course."

Holt told Skip the full story.

"It's been ten years," Skip said. "The statute of limitations has run out on the charge—"

"No, I lied to the state patrol officer who interviewed me at the hospital and told him my friend was driving."

"Ouch. That would toll the statute. However, I'm still not sure a vehicular homicide charge would stick. There wasn't a formal investigation, and by now the evidence—"

"You sound like my lawyer, but that's not the point, is it?"

"No, I guess not. At least Ralph doesn't have jurisdiction. Any prosecution would be up to the DA's office in your hometown since that's where the accident occurred. All Ralph can do is embarrass you, and you can bet there will be an article in the local paper this afternoon."

Holt winced. The public humiliation was just beginning.

"Oh, and Ralph put out the word that he's already working on a replacement—Sheriff Blackstone's nephew. It looks like our local DA and sheriff are burying the political hatchets."

"At least something good will come out of this for Ralph."

Skip took a sip of coffee. "It won't get him my vote. Have you talked to Angelina?"

"She knows about my past but not the job."

"How do you think she'll react?"

"I don't know."

"I hope it's better than Mr. Spratt. As soon as the e-mail from Ralph landed in his in-box, he came down to my office and ordered me not to discuss future employment at the firm with you."

It wasn't surprising news, but it nevertheless stung.

"Sure," Holt replied, trying not to sound hurt. "I appreciate you stopping by."

"Hey, we're solid. I did tons of stupid stuff growing up. Just nothing—" Skip stopped.

Holt finished the thought. "That ended up with your best friend dead."

48

After Skip left, Holt drank a second cup of coffee and then turned on his cell phone. Most of the voice-mail messages were sympathetic. Gossip travels with lightning speed in small towns, and the facts were garbled just as fast. A couple of people heard Holt had been arrested. The next to last message was from Tony McDermott.

"This is McDermott returning your call from the other day. Sorry I stood you up for lunch, but I ran into Butch Clovis outside the courthouse. As soon as he knew why I was in town, he came clean about the Meredith investigation. He showed me video surveillance footage from the residence that corroborated a suicide. They kept the video under wraps to avoid a media request under the state or federal Freedom of Information Act. Looks like you'll have to wait for another case to make your prosecutorial reputation."

McDermott was right, but for all the wrong reasons. A newspaper was more likely to file an FOIA request to uncover his past than anything about Rex Meredith's death. He called Angelina. She didn't answer. Her photo was the only one he wanted to see on his phone.

Midmorning, Holt was sitting on his deck when a call came in from an unexpected source—Trish Carmichael. He let the phone vibrate until the call went to voice mail, then listened to it.

"I didn't expect you to answer, and I understand why you don't want to hear from me. But please, I have to talk to you."

Holt had ridden the Trish Carmichael train to the end of the line, and instead of stopping at the station, it had careened over a cliff. He had no intention of talking to the deputy ever again.

A few minutes later Henry barked and ran over to the gate. Holt left the deck to see who'd driven up to the house. It was Angelina. She didn't say anything when she got out of her car and walked up to the gate. Holt rested his hands on the fence.

"Don't you have to be at the salon?" he asked as she approached.

"Holt," she said.

The tender, kind way she spoke his name communicated everything he needed to hear.

"What do you know?" he asked, just to be sure.

"Skip came by the salon and told me. He was really torn up. How are you?"

"Numb all over."

Angelina grabbed Holt's hands in hers, pulled him close over the top of the fence, and kissed him.

"Can you feel that?" she asked when their lips parted.

"Yeah. But I've lost my job, which means—"

"You haven't lost me. Holt, I'm not in love with a lawyer; I'm in love with a man."

Holt glanced down at the ground.

"Did you hear what I said?" Angelina insisted.

"Yes."

"Then open the gate so we can sit on your deck together."

—

Three days later, Holt returned to Paxton from Atlanta. He told his parents first. His mother was shocked; his father was more upset about Holt losing his job. Holt wasn't sure how the news would impact their relationship in the future. As bad as that was, he dreaded seeing Calico's parents more.

He arrived midafternoon, about the same time he and Calico often ended up at the Morgan house. The three of them sat in the den where Holt and Calico shot pool for pennies and played video games. Calico's mother cried buckets, which Holt understood. His father listened with his face set like flint. After Holt finished, their responses shocked him. Instead of being furious, they were relieved that Calico hadn't been directly responsible for his death. They talked quietly for over an hour, mostly reminiscing about Calico. At several points they all cried and laughed. They forgave Holt, which brought the greatest flow of tears.

"Talking to you today makes me feel closer to Kenny," Mrs. Morgan said, wiping her eyes.

"One last thing," Holt said. "Because I lied to the state trooper, I could still be prosecuted if you ask the local DA to do it. And if I'm indicted, the state bar would begin the process of taking away my law license. I wouldn't blame you if—"

Mr. Morgan put his hand on Holt's shoulder.

"Wrong as it was, I know you did what made sense to you and for Kenny at the time. We're not going to let anything bad happen to you now. But thank you for telling us the truth. We've all suffered enough."

"He was my best friend—" Holt began.

"Yes." Mrs. Morgan sniffled. "And he thought the world of you. We want you to succeed. Never look over your shoulder thinking we're judging you, because we're not."

"Calico is why I became a lawyer and a prosecutor. Before we left the party at the lake, he told me that's what he wanted to do. I've tried to honor his dream, but now—"

"You need to live your own life," Mr. Morgan cut in. "Just continue to make it count for good."

Shortly after taking his suitcase out of the car, Holt grabbed a basketball and attached a leash to Henry's collar. The dog danced about Holt's feet as they walked the few blocks to the church. Holt rolled a ball across the court, and the dog scampered after it. Thirty minutes later, Holt was taking a break from his workout when Bishop Pennington came out of the church.

"Thanks for taking care of Henry," Holt said.

"You're welcome. One morning I watched him stalk squirrels for an hour. He didn't get one, but he's on the mend."

"Yeah, I can see it, too."

Holt told the bishop about his trip to Atlanta. When he mentioned the words of Calico's father about making his life count for good, the bishop nodded.

"I know one way that can happen," he said. "I'd already been thinking about it, but I wasn't sure when you'd be ready."

"What is it? I don't have a lot on my schedule right now."

"I thought you could begin by telling your story to the youth group at the church. If a few young people listen to you and make a better choice in a similar circumstance, it would be invaluable. How about next Wednesday night at six thirty in the evening? I'll introduce you, and you can take it from there."

"Why so soon?"

"Fresh bread is always the best."

"Okay, and I'd like to bring Angelina to church with me on Sunday. She wants to hear you preach."

"Then I'll try to do my best," the bishop replied with a smile.

"Seeing the two of you sitting next to each other in a pew should get me fired up."

Holt looked up as a car turned into the parking lot. "Uh-oh," he said to the bishop. "Did you set this up?"

"Yes. I called when I saw you shooting baskets. Give it at least five minutes. Do you want me to stay?"

"No, I'll behave."

Holt took a long drink of water as Trish's car approached. She stopped near one of the goalposts and got out. She was wearing her uniform. Henry growled, and Holt picked him up.

"I'll put Henry back on his leash," Holt said as Trish approached.

"I usually get along with dogs," Trish replied. "Sometimes better than I do with people."

"I don't want to take any chances."

Holt snapped the leash on Henry's collar and secured it to the goalpost. Henry tugged once, then lay down. Holt and Trish stood facing each other at the free throw line. He cradled the ball in his arm and waited.

"You were right about the bitterness in my heart," she said. "And getting you fired didn't help with that. I know it's probably too early to ask, but is there any way you can forgive me for what I've done?"

After all Holt had been through during the past few days, he simply didn't have the energy or desire to hold on to an offense.

"You got it," he replied.

"I do?" Trish's eyes opened wider. "Are you sure?"

"Yes. I just got back from Atlanta. Calico's parents let me off the hook. How can I leave you hanging?"

Holt told her what they said.

"I wish I was more like that," Trish replied. "If I hadn't—"

"Then I wouldn't have gone to see them. I don't know how all this is going to end up, but the bishop believes good can come from it. I want that for you, too."

"I'm going to get a chance to make that happen this weekend. I'm taking my mother to the Jackson County CI to see the boy who hit their car." Trish paused. "I'm going to talk to him, too."

"When Calico's parents forgave me—" Holt stopped. "You'll just have to see for yourself."

"What about Greg Stevens?" Trish asked. "He needs to answer for his crime. Where is his confession?"

"It doesn't exist," Holt replied. "I was wrong about that, too."

Trish's eyes opened wider.

"And don't ask for details," Holt added. "Focus on the kids who aren't getting the support they deserve. That's a lot more important."

Holt took a shot that bounced off the front rim.

"Do you think you can do better?" he asked, tossing the ball to Trish.

She took a quick step back and launched a shot that rattled through the goal.

"Nice," Holt said. "If you ever want to challenge me to a game of horse, I'm available."

"Only if Angelina approves."

49

When Holt approached his house, there was a familiar-looking beat-up car parked in front with the hood up. It was Cecil Burkdale. Holt pulled into his driveway, then got out.

"Still having car trouble?"

"Where have you been?" Burkdale demanded. "I've been coming by every day since I saw the article in the newspaper. Stevens thinks he's destroyed you, but we'll turn the tables on him. All we have to do is—"

"Greg Stevens didn't kill Rex Meredith, and he's not a threat to Valerie," Holt interrupted.

"What? We sat in your car and watched the video."

"But we didn't see what happened before the tape started rolling."

"Tell me! I have a right to know!"

"I can't."

Burkdale eyed Holt suspiciously. "How did Stevens get to you? What is he paying you?"

"No comment."

Burkdale's face reddened. "I believed you were different," he spit out. "But I was wrong."

"No, I was wrong. And I strongly suggest you stop spying on Meredith Enterprises. Otherwise, you might end up in jail."

Burkdale got out of his car, slammed the hood shut, and drove off.

—

Holt spent the next few days repainting the inside of his house and building a ramp so Henry could run up to the top of his doghouse and survey his domain.

Late one afternoon, Holt was scrubbing his hands at the kitchen sink and thinking about the future. Angelina had offered to let him open a law office in one of the vacant rooms at the salon. At first Holt laughed at the suggestion, but now he was considering it. Rumors about his past would linger, but a few satisfied clients would help ease the transition. And if business was slow, he could always get a manicure. There was a knock at the door.

Henry yelped and took off for the foyer. Holt followed, rubbing his hands with a paper towel. It was Greg and Valerie Stevens. Valerie had Peps in her arms.

"Henry looks great," Valerie said as the Jack Russell sniffed her foot.

"He's making a comeback," Holt replied. "How are you doing?"

Valerie leaned over and scratched Henry's head. "I'm feeling thankful to you," she said.

"Can you come in for a minute?" Holt asked. "All I have to offer is a bottle of water."

"Sure," Greg replied. "And I have something for you."

From behind his back he pulled out a gorgeous bamboo fly-fishing rod and handed it to Holt.

"I can't—" Holt said.

"Yes, you can, and you will," Valerie cut in.

Holt took the rod in his hand and felt the lacquered ridges of the bamboo.

"Thanks. I'll finally have time to go fishing," he said, then paused. "Wait here, I have something for you."

He returned from the spare bedroom with the surveillance video and the DVD copies. He handed them to Greg.

"As far as I'm concerned, these no longer exist," Holt said.

Greg took them and glanced at Valerie. She handed Peps to Greg and took a tissue from her purse.

"Do you think Peps and Henry can play?" she asked after she touched the corner of her eye with the tissue.

"Let's hold them nose to nose and see," Holt suggested.

The two dogs sniffed, then Henry licked Peps.

"They can run around in the backyard," Holt suggested.

"Isn't that where Henry killed the snake?" Valerie asked anxiously.

"Yes, and I'm sure he'd love to show Peps where the fight took place. It's fenced in. We'll sit on the deck so we can keep an eye on them."

Holt brought out two more chairs, and they watched Henry prance around the yard with Peps trailing after him.

"Greg and I have been talking," Valerie said. "And, uh, we'd like to do more than give you a fishing pole."

"That's kind," Holt replied. "But you can see I don't live that extravagantly, and I can get by for a couple of months while I decide what to do next."

"What we have in mind is a bit more comprehensive than a rent check," Greg said. "A lot of companies smaller than Meredith Enterprises have in-house counsel. If you're interested, I'm sure we could come up with an acceptable job description and generous compensation."

"I don't have any experience in the corporate area, and you don't know why I was fired."

"Yes, I do," Greg answered.

"How?"

Greg smiled. "I have my sources. And it doesn't make any difference to us. I do realize you're a trial lawyer, and as a second option, I'd like to talk to the partners at Spratt, Ayers, and Goldfarb and see if they might have a position for you. Meredith Enterprises would become one of your clients."

"Mr. Spratt made it clear to Skip Patrick that any interest the firm had in me ended when I was fired by the DA's office."

"With the proper persuasion from me, I think the firm would reconsider."

"No, I wouldn't feel right getting a job like that."

"Then what about option one?" Valerie asked earnestly. "We really want to help you."

"You already have. The fact that you've come over here means a lot."

They watched the dogs scramble from beneath the bushes and shake off the dead leaves and twigs. Holt told Greg and Valerie about the possibility of opening his own office at Angelina's place.

"I think that's a great idea," Valerie said cheerfully. "Everybody in town would know about it because the women who come to the salon would spread the word."

"I hope no one expects legal advice while getting a pedicure."

Valerie laughed. It was a sound that made Holt feel good. Henry raced across the yard with Peps on his heels.

"And it would be great not having to worry about a snake from my past coming out of the bushes to bite me," Holt said. "Bishop Pennington told me the other day that from God's point of view, confessed sin is not only forgiven, it's forgotten."

Valerie reached over and took Greg's hand in hers, then looked at Holt. "And sometimes he uses people to bring that truth from heaven to earth."

Reading Group Guide

1. After the car accident at the beginning of the story, Holt tells the police officer that his friend Calico had been driving the vehicle. He rationalizes that, just because Calico's life is over, his own doesn't need to be. Have you ever hidden the truth to avoid getting in trouble? Did the truth end up coming out anyway? If so, what were the consequences?
2. Holt becomes an assistant district attorney and ultimately desires to become a federal prosecutor because that had been Calico's dream. Holt has good intentions to honor his friend's memory by making a difference in the world through his work. Describe a time when you pursued a noble goal as a way of easing your conscience about something wrong you had done.
3. Holt's job as an assistant DA is made easier when defendants confess to their crimes; then he simply has to calculate an appropriate punishment. Ironically, he struggles with great internal conflict because he refuses to confess the major crime

in his own past. Do you think confession is good for the soul? Does confession of wrongdoing come easily to you? Why or why not?

4. As a deputy sheriff, Trish sometimes works with Holt to prepare court cases. She admires him and hopes their working relationship will turn into something more. Even though Holt has a girlfriend, Trish holds on to her infatuation, despite the loving attention she receives from her good friend Keith. Have you ever overlooked a potentially great relationship because you were too focused on pursuing a different person? Have you neglected existing friendships in the quest to form new ones?
5. Trish likes to compete with anonymous players on a speed chess website when she needs a break from the pressure at work. What do you like to do when you feel stressed? How does this activity help you unwind?
6. Trish is bitter toward the drunk driver who caused the accident that killed her dad and paralyzed her mom. When she finds out Holt caused the accident that killed his best friend, her feelings for him shift drastically. When have you learned negative or scandalous information about a friend or loved one that made you view that person differently? How did your disappointment manifest itself in the way you treated this person?
7. Trish's mom, Marge, doesn't get out much since the accident that left her paralyzed. Yet at one point Trish tells her, "You're trapped in that chair, but you're more free on the inside than I am." Can you think of someone limited by physical disabilities who exhibits great freedom in Christ? What attitudes or traits can you borrow from this person?
8. At Trish's surprise birthday party, her friend Sue Ann's daughter, Candace, gives Trish a plate with the outline of her hands

and the verse "My times are in your hands" (Psalm 31:15). What does this verse mean to you?

9. Holt's scrappy dog, Henry, gets in a tussle with a copperhead snake. Henry almost dies from the encounter but eventually recovers. When have you stumbled across a "snake" in your life—an incident that caught you by surprise, punctured your peace, and left you barely hanging on? How did you fight back?
10. What was your opinion of Greg and Valerie Stevens at the beginning of the story? Did that opinion change by the time you reached the end of the book? If so, how? Have you ever made a judgment about someone, only to find out later that you had it all wrong?
11. When Holt feels the Holy Spirit speaking to his heart, he tells the bishop, "It hurts, but in a good way." Describe a time when the painful conviction of the Holy Spirit brought about emotional and spiritual healing in your life.
12. Before Holt could be forgiven, he had to admit his guilt; confession always comes before forgiveness. Bishop Pennington tells him, "When a person receives forgiveness from the Lord, it sets him free to do what he needs to do on earth." When have you found freedom through forgiveness? Describe a time when you forgave someone else, as well as a time when someone else forgave you.

Acknowledgments

Thanks to my editors, Ami McConnell, Natalie Hanemann, and Deborah Wiseman. It's an honor to invite you into the world of my stories. And to my wife, Kathy, who protects the time I need to live there.